OCTOBER
1970

A NOVEL

D0166623

OCTOBER 1970

A NOVEL

LOUIS HAMELIN

TRANSLATED BY
WAYNE GRADY

ARACHNIDE

© Éditions du Boréal Montréal, Canada, 2010
English translation copyright © 2013 by Wayne Grady

First published as *La constellation du lynx* in 2010 by Les Éditions du Boréal
First published in English in 2013 by House of Anansi Press Inc.

This edition published in 2013 by
House of Anansi Press Inc.
110 Spadina Avenue, Suite 801
Toronto, ON, M5V 2K4
Tel. 416-363-4343
Fax 416-363-1017
www.houseofanansi.com

Distributed in Canada by
HarperCollins Canada Ltd.
1995 Markham Road
Scarborough, ON, M1B 5M8
Toll free tel. 1-800-387-0117

House of Anansi Press is committed to protecting our natural environment.
As part of our efforts, the interior of this book is printed on paper that contains 100%
post-consumer recycled fibres, is acid-free, and is processed chlorine-free.

17 16 15 14 13   1 2 3 4 5

Library and Archives Canada Cataloguing in Publication

Hamelin, Louis, 1959–
[Constellation du Lynx. English]
October 1970 : a novel / Louis Hamelin ; translated by Wayne Grady.

Translation of: La constellation du Lynx.
Issued in print and electronic formats.
ISBN 978-1-77089-103-6 (pbk.).—ISBN 978-1-77089-410-5 (html)

I. Grady, Wayne, translator II. Title. II. Title: Constellation du Lynx. English.

PS8565.A487C6613 2013   C843'.54   C2013-903732-2
                                                 C2013-903733-0

Cover design: Marijke Friesen
Text design and typesetting: Marijke Friesen

Canada Council
for the Arts

Conseil des Arts
du Canada

ONTARIO ARTS COUNCIL
CONSEIL DES ARTS DE L'ONTARIO

*We acknowledge for their financial support of our publishing program
the Canada Council for the Arts, the Ontario Arts Council, and the Government of
Canada through the Canada Book Fund. We acknowledge the financial support of
the Government of Canada, through the National Translation Program for Book
Publishing, for our translation activities.*

Printed and bound in Canada

RECYCLÉ
Papier fait à partir
de matériaux recyclés
FSC® C103567

For Marie-Hélène

For them too history was a tale like any other too often heard.
JOYCE, *ULYSSES*

Agents continually infiltrate to work on other side and
discredit by excess of zeal; more accurately, agents rarely
know which side they are working on.
BURROUGHS, *THE LETTERS OF WILLIAM S. BURROUGHS,*
VOL. 1: 1945–1959

THE TERRORISTS

REBELLION CELL
Lancelot
Corbeau
Justin Francoeur
Élise Francoeur
François Langlais, alias Pierre Chevrier (le Chevreuil)
Nick Mansell

CHEVALIER CELL
Jean-Paul Lafleur
René Lafleur
Richard Godefroid
Benoit Desrosiers

FOREIGN DELEGATION
Francis Braffort (Paris)
Luc Goupil (London)
Raymond Brossard, alias Zadig (Algiers)
Daniel Prince, alias Madwar (Algiers)

THE LITERARIES

Chevalier Branlequeue, editor, poet, literature professor
Samuel Nihilo, literary journalist
Marie-Québec Brisebois, actress
Frédéric Falardeau, researcher

AND THE REST

General Jean-B. Bédard, commanding officer, Royal 22nd
Marie-France Bellechasse, student
Bobby, CATS (Combined Anti-Terrorist Squad) agent
Raoul Bonnard, cabaret performer
Maître Mario Brien, lawyer for the terrorists
Jacques "Coco" Cardinal, militant separatist
Madame Corps, Coco's ex-wife
Marcel Duquet, militant separatist
Mr. Grosleau, Crown prosecutor
Dick Kimball, Quiet American
Colonel Robert Lapierre, political adviser, grey eminence, etc.
Paul Lavoie, hostage
Claude Leclerc, police captain
Jean-Claude Marcel, MP from the back country, friend of Paul Lavoie
Miles "Machinegun" Martinek, detective-sergeant, emergency squad
    (Quebec Provincial Police)
Gilbert Massicotte, detective-lieutenant, CATS
Rénald Massicotte, Baby Barbecue chicken delivery man
Bernard Saint-Laurent, FLQ sympathizer
Giuseppe Scarpino, businessman
Luigi Temperio, businessman
John Travers, hostage
Albert Vézina, premier of Quebec

CHRONOLOGY

October 5, 1970: Kidnapping of John Travers, British trade commissioner, by the Quebec Liberation Front (FLQ).

October 10: Kidnapping of the Quebec government's Number Two.

October 15: Mobile forces of the Canadian Army intervene in Quebec.

October 16: Proclamation of the War Measures Act by the federal government of Canada; suspension of civil liberties; nearly 500 citizens detained without being charged...

October 17: Number Two's body found in the trunk of a car.

ONE

A QUESTION OF CHICKENS

L'AVENIR (QUEBEC), SUMMER 1975

MY NAME IS MARCEL DUQUET and I am going to die in about five minutes. The sky is blue, the sun is shining, the crows look like nuns' veils blown open by the wind, and I like the rumbling sound the tractor makes, the way it fills my ears as another row of hay falls before the harvester. I am forty-two years old, I have a round bald spot on the top of my head, which is so hot I feel like a prisoner who's been scalped by Indians and hung by my feet over a bed of coals until my brain starts boiling. The red scarf tied around my tonsure is brighter than the paint on the Massey-Ferguson; it must be a visible splash against the maples and the blue sky when I make the turn at the bottom of the field.

Now that I'm on the uphill run, I can see him walking toward me through the cut hay. It's Coco. And it's like my heart stops beating. Then it starts again: thoughts, the saliva in my mouth, the family of crows. In a way, I already know what he wants. I look around, nothing but the field bordered by the split-rail fence, the aspens and pines, the sugar bush, above them the thick blue arc of sky, the invisible river at the end of the land. And here, Coco Cardinal trudging across the field, face completely red, glistening with sweat, fat, hunched over, hands paddling the air, winded.

I get down from the tractor, leaving the motor running, and walk toward Cardinal, who has stopped a short distance from me. He's waiting until I reach him. Squinting into the sun, the light too harsh. As I close the distance, I wipe rivulets of burning sweat from my eyelids and forehead. I stop three feet from where he's standing. I swallow. I manage a smile.

"Hey, Coco. Been a while..."

He shrugs. He's sweating like a pig, his summer shirt completely unbuttoned and soaked under the armpits. His upper lip glistens, as though his lungs were trying to get out through his nose. His ant-red eyes want to unglue themselves from his face. Before he opens his mouth to speak, a black fist grips my insides.

"Well, if it ain't Marcel. They let you out of prison, eh? I hope they rammed a broomstick up your ass first."

He finds this funny. He giggles. I take another look around, the standing hay is stronger than I am. No one else in sight. My heart pounds in my chest but I hardly hear it. I can barely move. But, as I said, I manage to smile.

"I survived, as you see..."

He sneezes once, twice, again and again, his face twitching uncontrollably. Still doing coke, I see. As he sneezes he also seems to be thinking. I wonder if I should take advantage of it, get the jump on him, grab him by the throat and finish him off some way or other. But I let the opportunity pass.

"There's people say you talk too much. That since you got out you turned into a real chatterbox..."

I try to swallow; nothing. He spits on the ground.

"A goddamned stool pigeon!"

He's not using his normal voice. I try to gesture in protest, but my arm feels like it weighs a ton. With him it's the opposite: he moves his arm with the lightning speed of a cobra and suddenly there's a gun at the end of it. I feel the metal rim against my forehead, sucking everything out. My brain melts like a block of ice, useless, nothing else.

"And the other thing, you asshole, is that you stole my wife..."

I try to say no, but all I can do is shake my head, not so much because of the cold metal against my skin, although it's still there. Everything happening to me seems very far away, far from my head, which keeps falling, gently spreading out into the round darkness that pushes back at me harder and deeper, at the centre of my forehead, on my skin beaten by the sun. There's excitement in his heavy, menacing voice.

"On your knees, Duquet! Now! On your knees in front of me! I'm not gonna say it again..."

I let myself fall and it's like an act of deliverance, I start to say I'm sorry, I want to say it, my eyes raised through a valley of tears, to the muzzle that bores its hole into the silence, this blind full stop in the field, this pitch of forgotten light, of sun, earth, hot. The standing hay and the hay cut down by the reaper. Bewilderment.

The skull makes a cracking sound, like a coconut under the tractor's rear wheel, followed by a sickening squelch and the grinding of bones and other pulpy bits. Cardinal puts the engine back in neutral, his breath coming in great gasps, and, like an idiot, clutches his legs. A violent spasm has gripped them, thrown them into an interminable shaking fit. With every limb trembling, he forces his left foot down on the brake pedal.

When he's finished, he jumps to the ground and steps away from the tractor, turns back for a final look feeling almost calm, although his legs are as rubbery as they are after sex. Now he peers critically at the composition of his canvas. He closes his eyes, rubs the lids, opens them again, and takes another look.

He nods. Job well done. Takes a deep breath. Removes a plastic bag from his shirt pocket and, with a length of straw, knocks back a noisy snort of its contents. Then he turns his back on the scene and, for a moment, takes in the panorama of cultivated fields, woodlots, barns painted shades of red from strawberry to dried blood, the glinting silos that stretch from where he is standing to the horizon. Behind him, the tractor is still running. A final glance. There's no way he can hang around. He decides to get back to the side road via the neighbouring field by following a line of elms and hawthorns and wild apples that can't be seen from the main road. He reaches the cedar fence, climbs it, balances precariously on the knotty top rail, which is the colour of Appalachian granite sculpted by a century of weather, and remembers an expression, *rib fence*, what split-rail fences are called in the Baie-des-Chaleurs region. Maritime language.

And Coco loves boats.

VILLEBOIS, NORTH OF THE 49TH PARALLEL, WINTER 1951

THE CABIN IS MADE OF round logs chinked with dried sphagnum moss. Its dark grey walls stand out against the white snow, and the air around it is filled with the smell of woodsmoke, pine resin, and rancid animal fat. The chimney is a length of sheet metal, a plume of ethereal, grimy whiteness hanging from it.

Caribou antlers are nailed above the door. On the walls, beaver skins, fur side out, stretched in frames made of birch saplings. It's one of Godefroid's earliest memories.

The lake. The trapper's cabin.

This is country where dogs become wolves when they get loose.

Where barges come down the river midstream, furniture belonging to families from the old parishes lashed to their decks under tarpaulins. The Turgeon River's as wide as eight boulevards, broken up by rapids that can make a vessel shake like an old jalopy on a washboarded dirt road. Two hundred kilometres farther on it joins the Harricana, whose waters flow north to the sloped basin of Hudson Bay, where the last handful of land grants were given out, well north of the railway. Amid dark forests that exhaust the sky and sap the horizon.

It was country that had been seen only by the master fur traders, from their canoes as they passed through, and by the scattered tribes of the taiga nations who wandered there in search of the last of the beaver lodges. In the days of walking and paddling the Muskuchii hills, the vast swamps where the snow geese swim. No one would settle farther north than this.

Godefroid's father was a labourer, unemployed, a hired hand who'd filled out a questionnaire with the Ministry of Lands and Forests, received eight hundred bucks, a pat on the back, and a parcel of land in this burnt-out bushland somewhere north of Abitibi.

When did he crack? When did he turn into this silent, sullen, beaten man? It was his wife who saved the family by taking a job as a teacher in the village: seven hundred dollars a year, a roof over their heads, and twenty cords of firewood.

The dogs went crazy. Tied up in the snow in front of the trapper's cabin, they howled like banshees.

While Godefroid's mother taught a classroom full of lunkheads, his father went to visit the trapper in his cabin by the lake, taking a bottle of Seagram's with him, to listen to the old man's tricks of the trade. The X of sticks placed under the snare so the rabbit would leap into the noose. *When you shoot at roosting partridges, shoot the lowest one first so it doesn't scare off the others when it falls.*

This country where wolves run to the end of the forest and the dogs go crazy.

The trapper has to kick them out of the way to clear a path to the door for the father, his young son at his heels.

"What's wrong with the dogs today, Bill?"

Bill sniggers. His teeth are the colour of tobacco. He looks at the boy, then at the father, then at the boy again, then says:

"Come here. I'll show you something…"

Inside, steel traps hang by their chains from nails driven into the beams. A stretched otter hide, gleaming, sumptuous. The heavy smell of hanging meat, putrefying guts, sweat, damp, dirt, singed wool, wet fur, tobacco smoke, cold tea, and woodsmoke.

And piss. And something else, sweeter, more insidious, something men smell a mile away: fear.

Outside, the dogs go on barking themselves to death.

Slowly, the trapper turns to the back of the cabin. The two others, father and son, follow his gaze. As they passed through the door, they'd been aware of a warm, dark presence, and now they see the animal. Its sphinx-like face framed by sideburns worthy of a Dickensian banker, ears crowned with pointed tufts of fur. And its eyes, like two huge, amber lakes, swallowing them up.

The lynx sits on its haunches in the dark, a dog collar cinched around one paw and attached to a chain affixed to one of the cabin posts. Alert to any hint of movement, it fixes the three humans with an intense, devouring glare.

Mouth gaping, the father turns to the trapper, who keeps his eyes fixed on those of the big cat.

"You want him?" Bill asks after a moment has passed.

"Are you nuts?"

The woodsman reaches out, seizes a bottle of brandy from a plank that serves as a sideboard, removes the cork and takes a long swig. He offers the bottle to the father, who passes. Then he looks at the boy, grins at him, a stub-toothed rictus.

"It tastes like piss," he says.

The boy looks away without saying anything. He watches the lynx.

"He doesn't want to be my friend," says Bill.

"Who doesn't?" asks the father.

"Him," Bill replies, nodding at the lynx.

Another swig of brandy. Outside, the huskies bark, bark, bark themselves to death.

Still thirsty, the trapper takes another drink, then passes the bottle to Godefroid's father, who takes it without saying a word this time. Then Bill gets up and rummages in a trunk in the corner, traps, knives, everyday junk. He comes up with a pair of gloves, long protective gauntlets that go up to his elbows, made of some thick stuff, some kind of padded material, and he takes his time putting them on. They look like welder's gloves.

When he approaches the lynx, the animal shrinks to the floor and backs up without taking his eyes from the farthest corner. He reaches the end of his chain and curls into himself, ears flattened, eyes filled with murderous terror. Showing no fear, the man crouches before the animal. The entire cabin fills with a long, drawn-out hissing sound, backed by a deep, plaintive rumbling from the cat's chest. Its eyes widen, its face distorted by extraordinary tension as man and beast stare at each other without moving. Then the man moves quickly, grabbing the animal by the neck with both hands and lifting it slowly off the ground. The huge round paws, claws extended, scratch ineffectually at the man's gloves. He stands holding the lynx at arm's length, then tightens his grip on its throat. They hear a round of rumbling as two killers, united, execute a sort of dance together, a dance without movement. In the eternity that follows, in the cabin's half-light, the father and son watch mesmerized as the lynx's body goes from struggle to spasm, the fixed grimace, the evolution of death traced on its enigmatic face right up to the final tremor that rattles the animal's entire being.

His legs turn to rubber, the trapper falls to his knees, completely spent, and, after setting the animal down on the dirt floor, stretches out beside it. They hear his heavy breathing as he takes off his gloves and gently lifts an enormous paw, makes the fingers move under their fur, articulates the still-warm muscles as if the animal were a puppet, then, with an incredibly tender gesture, lets his hands stray for a moment into the long, silken fur.

SAM, AUTUMN 2000

THAT MORNING, AFTER FALLING BACK to sleep, Sam dreams of Marie-Québec. He was in the big house on Lake Kaganoma, deep in the forest fifty kilometres from Maldoror. They were on a white-sand beach somewhere, he could feel the pounding of the sea, and Marie-Québec walked in front of him, her back to him. She was moving away, not looking around but aware of his presence, moving away, her walk, almost formal, hardly swaying her hips, more from discretion than modesty, as though she were ashamed of her ass, which she was. As though her ass's fleshy abundance didn't exist in this world, which it did, and so she walked as though she wanted to tuck it between her legs, the way one tucks one's head between one's shoulders. That was how she went through life, too, the way she was passing through his dream, like a minor character who crosses a stage without realizing that she was playing a key role.

In the dream, Samuel was naked. Chevalier Branlequeue was in it, too, looking out to sea in a meditative pose, standing on one leg, like a hunter, with his other foot drawing the number four. He was holding a book up to the level of his eyes.

"Look," Marie-Québec said, "he's laying eggs."

What a stupid dream, he says to himself, opening his eyes.

When he goes to the window, the evergreen bush, tall black pines rooted in a thin layer of topsoil, and the pale, leafless birches are lightly powdered with an immaculate, fluffy blanket of snow that also covers the ground to a depth of some twenty centimetres, reflecting its violent white light into the room, which is welcome in October.

Sam Nihilo, who has registered forty clicks on the old odometer, is at the age when his dreams begin to look like emergency rooms. No girlfriend at the moment, and a writing career spinning its wheels. To keep his head above water he's had to get off his high horse and accept assignments handed to him by Big Guy Dumont, a man no one wants to know. Before starting Éditions _____, Dumont sold remaindered books in bars in Montreal's Latin Quarter, *step right up, ladies and gents*. Since then he has never stopped climbing; even now he'd climb anything that moved. He would have sold vacuum cleaners, but books were easier to lug around.

Around the large house, which is covered in brown CanExel siding, is a relatively unspoiled lake, a little more than a kilometre wide and something like a dozen long. Lake Kaganoma, about a hundred kilometres north of the imaginary line that divides civilized Canada from the rest of the country. The eastern shoreline has been broken up into hundred-metre lots that accommodate cabins and a few year-round residences. Across the lake, there's two hundred and fifty square kilometres of more or less virgin bush, the main function of which seems to be to catch the sun when it falls from the sky.

Once again Samuel has spent most of the night sweating blood in his study, and then remembers that he has a plane to catch today. Fortunately, security at the Maldoror airport is fairly slack. If worse came to worst, he could always run to the end of the runway and stick out his thumb.

He drags himself downstairs to the kitchen in jockeys and a T-shirt, where he fills a coffee carafe with cold water, dumps the water into the automatic coffee maker's reservoir, and then drops the carafe directly onto his foot. From there it bounces onto the ceramic-tile floor and explodes. As he wipes up the spill, he notices splotches of blood on the tiles.

He dabs the blood from his foot with an Enviro-Plus paper towel. Enviro-Plus paper towels employ sponge-pocket technology for maximum absorption, yet contain zero fibres from the planet's old-growth forests. The pale lips of the gash on his foot are in the vague shape of a cross. The wound is clean, deep, and precision-cut, with a sort of flap formed by a strip of skin and flesh that can be opened and closed at will. Sam sees it as an all-you-can-eat buffet for flesh-eating bacteria and their little microbial friends. He takes it to the shower, where he becomes engrossed in the contemplation of his feet, watching the pink water being flushed out by the flow. Then he washes the wound with soap, dries himself, and applies a gauze pad smeared with disinfectant cream. He affixes the bandage to his foot, which he has propped up on the toilet seat cover. Then he goes back to the kitchen — where he has a visitor ...

Paul Lavoie's ghost has pulled a chair up to the kitchen table. His left wrist and the thumb and palm of his right hand are roughly bandaged and stained with dried blood. The thin, blood-filled crease made by the wire around his neck is clearly visible. He sports a streak of grape jelly under each nostril, under both corners of his mouth, and in the folds of his ears. His face is blue.

The visitor lowers his head, rests his chin on his chest, half-closes his eyes. His hands are encrusted with blood. They rest on his thighs, palms up, as though he were offering his wrapped stigmata to the owner of the premises. His chest rises and falls slowly. He is sobbing silently. Sam goes about picking up the crumpled, blood-stained paper towels that he left strewn about the kitchen floor. He doesn't let his visitant bother him.

"It's the blood that brought you, isn't it?" he asks, looking at the paper towel in his hand. "You're like those corpses in the *Odyssey*, in the House of Hades. You look a bit peaked, wouldn't you say? But don't expect me to go out and slit the throat of a goat in order to give you your colour back..."

"You're leaving me..." murmurs the ghost.

"No, I'm not. I have to make a short trip to France. I have an Air Canada flight at ten o'clock, you-know-who is driving me to the airport. Sorry, but no one in my situation would turn his nose up at a ticket to Paris..."

"Yes, but the problem, you see, is that the longer you take writing your goddamned book, the longer I'm condemned to sitting around on my thumbs! Believe me, this is a lot worse than purgatory," the visitor adds in that whingeing voice of his, the one he always uses when he haunts the lake house.

"Oh? Why's that? No golf courses up here?"

Sam calmly considers the apparition, which reminds him of strawberry jam spread on burnt toast.

"Among other things," the phantom says politely.

"Sitting on your thumbs in your condition can't be all that comfortable," Nihilo observes.

"Let me go..."

"Then go, for Christ's sake, go!" he says angrily. "What are you waiting for? Me to get the rifle?"

When he looks again, the chair that the former Liberal minister was occupying has been taken by Noune, the cat he has had for the past two years. Noune is playing with a mouse, no, not a mouse, a shrew, a masked shrew. The cat is sitting back on its haunches, its teeth and claws bared, boxing at nothing, like a diminutive kangaroo. With a swipe of its right paw, which has the power of a slapshot by Guy Lafleur, Noune sends the thing spinning under the stove.

When the game resumes, Sam goes to the woodbox, selects a length of birch log, goes back, and, holding the log like a tomahawk, whacks away at the shrew's upper body. This necessitates another paper towel. *Those sponge pockets work miracles.* Then he reheats his coffee in the microwave. The thick, oily residue at the bottom of the cup makes him think of the Athabasca River tar sands as he goes back upstairs to pack his bags.

Sam drives a grey Toyota Corolla that rolled out of the factory in 1989, but it could just as easily have been a green Mazda Protegé or a red Colt as it takes him to the Maldoror airport, a distance of thirty or so kilometres, give or take. He's learned to leave himself twenty minutes for the trip to Maldo, the Hub of the Northwest.

The lake road runs north-south, along the ridge of an esker (a natural filter for potable water composed of several hundred metres of sand and gravel), more or less parallel with the lake's shoreline, which remains mostly hidden behind a thick stand of boreal forest. It winds its way through a series of undulations lined with black spruce, Scots pine, and sickly birch whose leaves, half-eaten by insect larvae, started turning red in the middle of August.

The snow that fell during the night makes the glare on the road almost painful. When the sun comes out between the clouds, which look like two chunks of lead threaded onto a fishing line, Nihilo can make out the bird tracks along the pristine roadside. Ahead of him, a vast cluster of Scots pines descends toward a peat bog. A bit farther along, the dirt road crosses a log bridge over the bog's drainage outlet. Spruce grouse forage in the tall grass on either side of the road, poking up with the regularity of cuckoos in Swiss clocks, and the car startles two or three of them, which then perch in some bare pines by the roadside. Sam keeps a .410-gauge shotgun in a pouch under the back window and has more than once got himself a free dinner with it, but he doesn't see himself trying to go through customs at Charles de Gaulle with a brace of grouse in his underwear.

He slows the car, rolls down his window, and keeps the vehicle moving at a walking pace. In the snow, he sees the large round paw prints of a lynx and follows them with his eyes to a point under a pine where a flurry of dark feathers are scattered in a circle. He smiles: the mark of a successful hunter. He looks briefly into the forest, into the thick underbrush, at the play of blue-tinted shadows between the spruce trunks, into clearings cauterized by the cold. Behind him, the slanted rays of the autumn sun beat down beneath the nearly black trees.

MADAME CORPS
AND THE SNOW

THE BEACH LOOKS LIKE a marble floor: fine white sand, well compacted, smooth. The tall concrete rectangles that overlook it form a kind of colony of giant vases around the circumference of the bay, the hotels, condos, and casinos give the impression of having been carved out of the same material. They have an incandescent glow, like the purest chalk bathed in light reflected off the sea.

The sea is nearly invisible, as if the horizon has pulled it toward itself like a carpet. The line of it can just be made out in the distance, under a fine golden fog. To get to it, Sam would have to walk across this porcelain Sahara, and he prefers not to. The beach is too white. Walking on it would only dirty it. He's happy admiring it from afar, from the height of a concrete promenade.

And Madame Corps couldn't look more French in her cream-coloured suit and charming red silk scarf.

Corps is her real name, too. A patronymic fairly common in France, where she — let's call her Ginette, and use her maiden name: Dufour — has remade her life. In Quebec, where her last name was Cardinal-Dufour, she'd been the legitimate wife of Jacques Cardinal, alias the Fat Cop, and the mother of his children. She was also the mistress of Marcel Duquet, the militant separatist, well known on the South Shore, who was condemned to eight years in prison for having aided and abetted the assassins of Minister Lavoie when they were fleeing the country in the fall of 1970.

Thirty years ago, as Madame Cardinal-Dufour, she enjoyed quite a reputation for being, shall we say, hot. A heroine of the sexual revolution. In fact, she more or less *was* the revolution, a kind of Odette de Crécy from Longueuil. Today she lives in France, in one of most exclusive coastal resort towns, in a chic condo she shares with Monsieur Albert Corps, chaser of sedate widows' petticoats, her chauvinistic husband.

Coffee on the terrace of the Sables-d'Olonne. Two cigarettes already stubbed out in an ashtray shaped like a Coquilles Saint-Jacques shell. Madame Corps buys packs of menthols and transfers the cigarettes into a gold-plated case. She uses a cigarette holder that looks like it might be made out of ivory. Small wrinkles radiate from her lips, which she soaks in barley water or something. It's still not polite to ask a woman her age, but Madame Dufour's offspring numbered four in 1970. Say she's somewhere between sixty and sixty-five and give her whatever hair colour you want.

From the terrace he could watch the passing parade: girls, sports cars, mothers pushing baby carriages, tourists dragging suitcases on wheels.

"You didn't cross the Atlantic just to see me." It's the first thing she's said to him.

Samuel smiles. "I don't have that kind of money," he says. "But in Quebec even a second-rate writer gets a lot of invitations. To sit on a jury for an obscure prize for short stories, for example, from anywhere in the French-speaking world, including those with tall, thin Africans. And if the jury meets in La Rochelle, the old slave port and supplier of fine French women for the colonies, not a hundred kilometres from here, then all the better!"

"You don't look like a writer," she says. "In France, writers look like writers. They dress like writers. I suppose you might be mistaken for a musician..."

"So I'm often told. But I'll have you know that I don't look like a regular at the Sables-d'Olonne, either. No smoking jacket. Which makes it hard for someone who's supposed to be here squandering the family fortune at the roulette table."

"That's because when you think casino, you think Françoise Sagan, when in reality casinos are full of a bunch of retired suburbanites from Baltimore on a group tour. I haven't read your books. I've never heard of you. How did you find me?"

"I found a Jacques Cardinal in the phone book, called the number, and talked to his son, who didn't want to know anything about anything. All he would tell me was that he'd burned all the bridges before his father croaked and that the last time he saw the old man he was snorting a line of coke. Then he let me squeeze your number out of him."

"That man spread a lot of bad around. Coco, I mean. What are you writing? A book about the Lavoie Affair?"

"I'm trying to."

"And...do you mind if I ask why?"

"I had a professor at university. He's dead now. He wanted to know what happened. He started a kind of...club. It would take too long to explain it to you. Anyway, it's your story I want to hear."

"Too late. No one's interested anymore."

"Like the song says, if there's only one left, let it be me."

"You're wasting your time."

"Maybe. But I'm not all that interested in making a living. Two or three more wasted hours won't make much difference..."

"What do you want to know?"

"Jacques Cardinal. A defrocked cop, formerly in the Montreal Police Force's morality squad, quietly let go after he was caught taking bribes from the mob, according to one version. In the 1960s he was mixed up in anything that involved the separatist movement and the patriot groups, from the Rassemblement pour l'indépendance nationale to the Parti Québécois, including the Front de Libération Populaire, the Phalange, the Comité Indépendance-Socialisme, the Intellectuels et ouvriers patriotes de Québec, and the FLQ. I'm wondering, Madame Corps, what was your husband living on during all that time?"

"Fraud."

"With a wife and four kids to look after? I'm just curious, is all."

"Before we go any further, let me tell you something, and it's really just to do you a favour: they kidnapped him, they hid him, and they killed him. That's all there is to know, that's the whole truth of the Lavoie Affair. Everything else is just smoke and mirrors, the wild imaginings of overworked brains. Are you a conspiracy theorist?"

"I'm more of a skeptic. Maybe, when it comes down to it, I'm a reluctant theorist. I hold on to my critical faculties. I believe in coincidences, but not in an accumulation of them."

"For example?"

"The fact that your former lover somehow managed to drive a tractor over his own head shortly after giving an interview to a journalist from *60 Minutes*. And also the routine checks. The cops are so visible in this story that it gets a bit hard to take. Like the time you went to the cabin in the sugar bush with Duquet to pick up the fugitives, do you remember that?"

"Vaguely."

"November 1970. The 'biggest manhunt in Canadian history'

was underway. And one fine day you get behind the wheel of a station wagon, Duquet follows you in a tow truck, you put the fugitives in the wagon, and then you pretend the car breaks down and Duquet gives you a tow. A cop stops you to see what's going on ... and he ends up giving you an escort! Without suspecting for a second, apparently, that the three most wanted men in the country are a few feet from him. If Duquet was trying to draw as much attention to himself as possible, he couldn't have come up with a better plan. Why the tow truck?"

"I seem to recall that it was snowing. A real dump. You're forgetting the snow, Samuel ..."

"No, Madame, I am not forgetting the snow. I never forget the snow. I'm coming to that."

"I've never liked it. Snow ..."

"Where I live, there's still snow under the spruce trees in July."

"And you like that? Really?"

"Snow?"

"Snow."

"Yes. I think so."

"Good. Well ... Can I buy you a drink?"

THE HUNT

HE OPENED HIS EYES. SHIVERING and grunting, he sat up to brush two centimetres of snow off his clothing. All around him, the sky was filled with wet snowflakes slowly falling to the ground.

"Okay, guys, time to get up . . ."

Godefroid rolled over and crawled through the fresh snow. Some ways off, a tractor was pulling a manure spreader across a ploughed field. Clods of manure were flying, filling the morning air with pungency and falling into furrows, where the early sunlight was just beginning to melt away the thin covering of snow that had accumulated during the night.

Jean-Paul's large, hairy head, bristling with twigs, emerged from the ditch where it ran under the fence. The sweet smell of manure and its hint of heat were borne to them by a cold wind, along with the tractor's staccato growl. René Lafleur joined them, scuttling on knees and elbows. His thick red fingers gripped the sawn-off 12-gauge shotgun, and snow clung to his military pea jacket like flour to a fillet of fish.

23

The three men were wide awake.

Crouching at the edge of the woods in their army-surplus jackets, they followed the tractor with their eyes as it moved away from them. The sky was low and grey, the air thick, and the coughing engine sent echoes ricocheting through the maples behind them. Jean-Paul beat his stiff arms together to keep warm.

They found the old sugar hut almost immediately. They'd spent hours searching for it the night before with only the failing light of a flashlight, its batteries almost dead. Their trampling through the thick layer of dead leaves, dry as cornflakes on the forest floor, had sounded like a rainstorm. They were somewhere near Orford, between Stukely South and Waterloo, at least a hundred kilometres east of Montreal. Accomplices had dropped them off on a side road at dusk. They'd lost the trail and, when they grew tired, they stopped at the edge of the field with their two boxes of food. There they huddled close together on the ground to conserve warmth like hunted animals, listening to a farm dog barking in the distance. Finally, shortly before dawn, they'd slept briefly, dreamlessly.

The cabin turned out to be less than fifty metres into the bush. Grey, dilapidated, peaceful under its sheet-metal chimney, it was covered by a thin coating of snow. The door sagged open on its hinges. When Gode forced his way inside, he gave out a loud, prolonged yelp, and a second later the others heard him call out.

"Guys! We've got company..."

The Lafleur brothers found him crouched in front of the old sap boiler, his box of provisions on the tamped-earth floor beside him. He had made the acquaintance of the cabin's occupant, an enormous, semi-somnolent porcupine, prickly and black, calmly curled up beside a mound of pale brown capsules: its own pile of scat. The harsh light coming through the open door caught the silvered tips of its quills. The intrusion of the three men elicited only a brief grunt of protest from the animal.

"Look at that! He lives in his own shit, just like a fat capitalist bastard."

They left the animal in peace and surveyed their new digs and its possibilities. The floorboards were rotten in places, some of the slats threatening to give way under their weight. Metal buckets once used to collect maple sap were rusting away in a corner. Those still in decent shape were arranged along the opposite wall. And covering everything, everywhere, was dust, sawdust, spiderwebs, and animal droppings.

René Lafleur took the lid off the stove, cleaned all the old leaves and cobwebs out of it, and was stuffing the firebox with dead sticks when Jean-Paul stopped him with a gesture.

"No fire."

Across the room, Gode had opened one of the boxes and was displaying its contents:

"Irish stew. Meatball stew. Oh, wow, canned spaghetti..."

"Has anyone seen a can opener anywhere?" asked René. He was taking an inventory of the second box. "Green Giant whole kernel canned corn ... Le Sieur number 3 green peas ... Del Monte sliced pineapples ... Hey! Weren't they the guys who kicked Arbenz out of Guatemala?"

"I can't believe they're making us eat our Chef Boyardee cold."

"Where's the can opener?"

"There is no can opener."

They ate sardines, Weston sliced bread, and Spam from cans that could be opened with little keys soldered to the lids. Later, in the attic of the cabin's half-rotted extension, they found an axe with a broken handle and used it to pierce the bottoms of some cans of preserves.

Early that afternoon they walked, sheltered by a fence row of trees and thorn shrubs studded with piles of rocks, then, bent double, followed a ditch to an abandoned barn, where they gathered armloads of old straw to take back to the cabin. The tractor was nowhere to be seen, and the road they had taken to get there the night before was deserted.

It had stopped snowing.

Back at the cabin, they tore up some of the floor planks and attacked the frozen ground with the axe, taking turns breaking up the hard brown earth and scooping it up with their hands. They carried the earth outside in the boxes they had used to transport their food. When the hole was deep enough, they spread the straw on the bottom of it, and it was there that they slept that night, and every night after.

The next day they resumed their work, using the axe as a pick to widen and deepen the hole. When the excavation was big enough, they went back to the barn to get more straw. They arranged two-by-fours over the hole and spread a thick mattress of straw on the bottom to finish it off. They slept fully dressed, as if they were corpses and the hole was their tomb, with a piece of panelling pulled into place above their heads, covering the opening like a door, or a lid.

The porcupine went out at dusk to dine on the tamaracks that grew in the area, and they heard it grunting and muttering to itself when it came back in the middle of the night to reclaim its sleeping quarters under the old sugar boiler. In the morning, they found it curled up in its usual spot close to its mound of scat, which had been augmented by a fresh contribution.

It started snowing again.

One moonless, foggy night when the smoke wouldn't be seen, they lit the fire. They devoured a slightly heated can of Cordon Bleu meatball stew and made tea by melting snow in one of the sap buckets. Smoke went everywhere but up the chimney, and soon the entire cabin was full of it. Coughing, they burned damp floorboards and green wood and had to huddle close to the old stove in order to feel the fire's warmth on their skin.

René found an antique in the attic: an old rocking chair, which he attempted to repair with sticks and a handful of rusty nails he painstakingly straightened with the back of the axe.

"When I'm done with it, it'll be as good as new."

"I think you're wasting your time. We aren't going to be hanging around here very long."

"Doesn't matter. We'll leave it here for someone else . . ."

And they sang songs by Félix Leclerc, Claude Gauthier, Pauline Julien. They sang Georges Brassens's "Song for the Man from Auvergne," four hunks of wood, four hunks of bread. They almost never mentioned Lavoie, the government minister. Or Ben, their comrade who'd been arrested and had gone a bit crazy, spilling his guts at the coroner's inquest. Rue Collins was behind them now. Time to think about the future, the coming winter. Find a house. Get some money. Hit a credit union in a small village somewhere. Make plans. Stay in their hole until spring.

Early one morning they heard three shots — sharp, incisive, fired in rapid succession. Then silence. René was already up, the 12-gauge levelled at the half-closed door. Gode poked his head through the gap in the floorboards, bits of straw clinging to his shaggy hair.

".30-.30. Deer."

When the weather was clear they didn't light a fire. They ate Spam and canned peaches in syrup. Lunched on Weston bread and Paris Pâté. Four hunks of wood, four hunks of bread.

After they'd heard the rifle shots, they jumped at the smallest sound. Eyed the edge of the clearing anxiously, spoke in low voices. Godefroid was small, a hundred and forty pounds, five-seven, blue eyes. René was bigger: wanted posters everywhere had him at a hundred and eighty pounds on a five-foot-ten frame, brown eyes and hair. They were the same age: twenty-three. Jean-Paul was four years older, built like a brick shithouse, weighing more than two hundred pounds and six feet tall in his stocking feet. The official photograph published in the newspapers and on television made him look like a serial killer. The first time he sat on the rocking chair after his brother repaired it, it collapsed under his weight, and he sat there, his arms and legs in the air, laughing as hard as the others.

One night they were awakened by what sounded like a police siren. Once they'd rubbed the sleep from their eyes, the only logical explanation they could come up with was that one of the ring-billed gulls they'd seen flying behind the manure spreader had been wounded and had somehow got into the cabin to hide.

René was the one to risk pushing back the panel and sticking his head up through the hole. A cry.

"There's two of them!"

In the feeble yellow beam of his flashlight, he saw what looked like an enormous ball of spikes electrified by a high-voltage current, vibrating and clicking, shooting out silvery flashes and emitting a series of continuous, piglike grunts.

"Well, guys, it looks like Drapeau has found himself a girlfriend."

Drapeau was the name they'd given the porcupine.

"Hey, René!"

"What?"

"How do they do it without skewering themselves?"

Gode was making his way through the bush, the 12-gauge in the crook of his arm. In his mind's eye he saw himself as a four- or five-year-old, walking behind his father through the immense forest that stretched all the way north to the huge bays of the frozen sea. The sudden detonation came like a holy revelation. Grouse lined up like bowling pins on the branches of the spruce trees.

Now he was following a barely discernable path, tense, his senses alert as his eyes swept the network of bare, grey branches around him. The relentless sky was the colour of steel. The snow was almost completely melted, a few patches here and there under the low conifer branches. Which meant he left few traces of his passing, so to hell with Jean-Paul and his security measures.

The only problem was the carpet of half-frozen dead leaves under his feet, which made as much noise as a mountain torrent if he wasn't careful. A squirrel running through it sounded like a herd of buffalo. He stopped, pointed his shotgun into the underbrush, safety off, heart pounding. Another good reason to keep his eyes peeled.

He came to the edge of the woods. A field opened up ahead of him. Caution told him he should stick to cover, but he preferred the little voice in his head that told him to keep going. There was a low stone wall dividing two fields further on, punctuated by patches of thorn bushes. As he got closer, he could see fruit on the branches — Saskatoon berries, some crabapples, even a few wild apple trees forming a narrow row along the fence.

He'd already strayed too far, but he knew that nothing would stop him from going to take a closer look.

He walked, reached a clump of Saskatoons first, passed them, and stopped by the apple tree. The flat brilliance of the fruit against the dull sky. The moment he reached out to pick an apple, there was an explosion. The next instant he was on the ground, not knowing what had happened or why.

The only visible result of his shotgun going off was a brief rain of broken twigs and an exploded apple, the core still swinging in his field of vision. At the same time, the air around him filled with grouse beating the air with their short wings, their darkly barred tails spread into fans, easily a dozen of them. They flew off in single file over the field, leaving him with his nerves shattered, his heart gripped by nostalgia, almost in tears.

He said nothing about it to the others.

The beam from an electric spotlight cut through the darkness and stopped on the cabin. Godefroid stood at the door with the shotgun. Blinded, he raised his open hand and shielded his eyes. The voice of a man came at him through the explosion of light.

"Hey, guys, don't shoot! It's us ..."

Bernard Saint-Laurent and another young man, their arms full of provisions, came toward the cabin, breathing heavily in the darkness. Behind them was a woman from one of the support groups. Brown hair, late thirties, almost old, compared to them. In his glasses, Saint-Laurent looked like an intellectual. He had a vaguely displeasing mug, with a kind of horse-like jaw that seemed to dislocate itself when he spoke. He was the liaison between the two cells. The other was thin and bearded. For a few moments all they could hear was the heavy sound of their footsteps on the frozen leaves.

Gode backed up to let the newcomers in and leaned the rifle against the cabin wall. Soon the space was filled with tense faces, their fantastical silhouettes projected against the brutally lit walls.

The Beard set down the cardboard box he'd been carrying. Drapeau, not pleased, hunched his back and with an impressive clatter of quills sought refuge in the darkest corner of the cabin.

"Have you tamed that thing?"

"It wasn't too hard."

Jean-Paul regarded the newcomers with a worried look.

"You were careful, I hope?"

Saint-Laurent spoke quickly before the other two could: "We took the back roads. No one followed us, we would've seen them..."

Jean-Paul seemed to think about it.

"We've brought you some newspapers," the Beard said, holding up a *Montréal-Matin*.

"Anything new?"

"Yeah. De Gaulle died..."

"Is this where you sleep?" the woman asked.

"Yes, ma'am. Curled up in the straw. The Lafleur boys are the bread, and I'm the baloney."

"I mean news about the others," said Jean-Paul.

Saint-Laurent assumed an air of importance, of being in the know.

"The guys have issued a new communiqué. With a picture of Travers sitting on a case of dynamite..."

"Bullshit."

"But guess what: the next communiqué is going to be addressed to U Thant and sent directly to the UN."

Gode gave an incredulous guffaw.

"Why not send it to the Pope?"

René aimed a thin stream of spit at the floor.

"What else?" asked Jean-Paul.

"We brought you a can opener."

"Have you guys considered my proposition?" asked Saint-Laurent.

They turned to face him. Jean-Paul stared at him intently for a moment.

"You can't stay here," Saint-Laurent said. "You'll freeze to death for one thing, and you've burned your bridges in Quebec. There's people waiting for you in the United States. I can get you across the border whenever you like ... There's people in New York and Algiers. Black Panthers. You could be in Algiers in no time."

"Before thinking about sending us to Algeria, you should have started by giving us better instructions on how to get here. We spent the first night between a woodlot and a fence, freezing our asses off."

"Everything's all set," Saint-Laurent went on as though Jean-Paul hadn't spoken. "I can get you across the border any time."

"You can tell our 'American friends,'" Jean-Paul cut in, "that there's no way we're leaving Quebec. This is where the struggle is, not in Algeria. We aren't going to abandon our friends. We aren't going to abandon the political prisoners."

"Our girlfriends are in prison ... You can tell them that," added René.

After making arrangements for another mission to top up supplies the following week, the visitors were about to leave, to slip back into the night, when Jean-Paul held the Beard back for a quiet word.

"I don't want to see him here again," he said. "And for fuck's sake, find us another place to hide out."

CHEVALIER BRANLEQUEUE
(1932–1999)

Where else in the world would you find churches almost the size of
cathedrals in villages with populations, including idiots and rubes
who rarely came in from the fields, that never exceeded 3,000 souls?

THAT WAS TYPICAL OF CHEVALIER'S style. Sam had come upon this
passage the previous night, while flipping through his annotated,
dog-eared copy of *Letters from a Chevalier in Good, Plain Joual*,
which had first been published by Top Flight Editions before being
reprinted by the prestigious BQ. It was classic Chevalier — vigorously
apostrophizing, facetiously pamphleteering — even from beyond
the grave he did his best to thumb his nose at authority, whether
political or ecclesiastic.

The man who had styled himself Chevalier Branlequeue was
born on the historic Chemin du Roy, the King's Road, a few steps

from the river that runs through Sainte-Anne-de-la-Pérade, and within sight of the marvellous neo-Gothic cathedral with its twin hundred-and-ten-foot steeples imitating those on Notre-Dame Basilica in Montreal. Branlequeue was still in his room in the palliative-care ward of Notre-Dame Hospital, barely a few minutes dead — brought down by lungs as thoroughly coated in tar, he said, as a provincial road at election time, as well as by a few other failed organs — when sundry representatives of Quebec's provincial government began talking through their hats about a state funeral.

They hadn't reckoned, however, on the old codger's last will and testament, which gave instructions for his funeral arrangements: his body was to be dropped through a hole in the ice with the Patriot flag as a shroud, while an academic lecture was being delivered from an ice-fishing hut from his native village, which was famous for its small fish. Chevalier wanted his remains to be wrapped in the national emblem, transported to their final resting place on a gun carriage, and delivered to the shrimp and the sharks. In a typical passage, the testator added: *For once they'll have the whole bull to eat, instead of just the liver* ... By "they," of course, he meant tomcod, or frostfish, which constitute the basis of the local economy in Sainte-Anne-de-la-Pérade and are traditionally baited with a piece of cow's liver.

The lawyer had suggested incineration. Afterward, the ashes could be spread anywhere, all over the Mouk-Mouk Islands, no problem. But Branlequeue had been adamant. His father was a lawyer and he himself was a Freudian guerrilla-fighter who expected to win. He had therefore prepared two wills: the official, specifying that the grisly remains be deposited in a quiet, out-of-the-way plot in the local cemetery; and the officious, apocryphal and drawn up in the hand of the principal player.

That opened the door to La Grosse Éléonore and the vultures in three-piece suits. The Catholic-politico machinery was set in recuperation mode, beginning with the under-secretary in charge of protocol in the Quebec government who, walking the tightrope between the undeniable importance of the man's work and the potential for controversy, slackened the already intentionally ambiguous formula for "state funerals but not really," which was then picked up by the literary editor and obituary columnist for the *Trois-Rivières Nouvelliste* — a man better known, as it happened, for his odes to the dead than for his literary criticism.

Good old human nature took over from there. From his observation point in the choir loft, had Samuel not seen, just a second before, the premier of what was still the province of Quebec advancing up the long centre aisle under the priceless pre-Conquest pascal chandelier and the famous sculpture in oak representing the mother-in-law of Christ, alone, with no first lady and without a bodyguard? And a few minutes earlier, had he not recognized the Minister of Culture, under his thick, carrot-coloured perm, dark as dye could make it, his face tinted a deep bronze with the aid of an extract of Guadeloupe sulphur, granting an interview to a television crew on the steps of the church?

Yes, he had.

In other words, without making too much of a fuss about it, the politicos had embraced the compromise so typical of them: the quasi state funeral. Cosily wrapped up in his own thoughts, Sam watched the ceremony roll beneath him like water under a bridge. He had made the trip from Montreal alone. In his grey Corolla or his new Protegé or his red Colt. The whole inner circle was there, assembled under his feet. He could take them all in without moving his head, contain them in a single thought. The body of the deceased was laid on a bier at the precise spot at which, subject to the same tidal forces, the great River of Literature and the remorseless Storm Surge of Politics met and joined before flowing into the eternal Sea of History. Poets and politicians, senior civil servants and novelists, critics, pillars of the law, protesters and theatre directors, university presidents, rockers, technocrats, pollsters, swashbuckling intellectuals, men who worked the fields and men who worked crowds: from ivory hunter to Ivory Tower. The nation's great mythmakers were gathered under Nihilo's astonished gaze.

It was the man himself, not his work, who was the centre of attention. Did the colleague who came to the microphone to honour his "master and friend" pass up the opportunity to regale the unjustly private assembly with extracts from his own semiological treatise, called *Branlequeue, or the Tail That Wagged the Dog*, completed during his recent sabbatical? Did he read from a chapter called "Elucubrations," "about the miracle of a work that exists forever in the future, since it is a unique text that has no end, is now and will forever remain unfinished, destined to find its ultimate achievement in our collective future, its only possible posterity."

Yes, he did.

"*Elucubrations* is an unclassifiable classic, a forever-unstamped passport to the Nobel Prize. The book of a single man who will only ever write a single book." And so the colleague, like so many others, erased the existence of the *Letters* to accommodate his own theory of the man.

The service went downhill from there, with authentic, touching, personal anecdotes in which the initiates, who formed a good four-fifths of the congregation, went on about the torrential drinking bouts that took place during interminable lunches at the Frères Jacques on rue Saint-Denis. Every one of them was delivered with broad winks in the direction of the well-roasted deceased lying in his box.

Next came his filthy rich publisher, who had plucked the author's little box of faded dreams from the cluttered chaos of a room in the apartment Branlequeue shared with his wife, Léonore, and their three children. One had to wonder how they got by after he had taken emphatic leave of the woman he had termed his "companion of the road." There followed a tribute from a revolutionary Trotsky-ite who had recently disclosed in the back seat of a limousine his bipolar difficulties. The Minister of Public Works and Paperwork evoked Branlequeue's valiant efforts, in the days leading up to the last sovereignty referendum, when the prematurely stooped author, brandishing a pilgrim's crook like the lance of a chevalier (a few po-lite titters from the audience, quickly smothered under one or two bouts of coughing), undertook a tour of the province's CEGEPs, not only those in the rural areas but also in Greater Montreal, in hopes of convincing the students of the advantages of political indepen-dence for a small nation as crucified by its differences as Quebec had been. By the time someone told Chevalier that the majority of CEGEP students were too young to vote (average age: seventeen), the referendum had already been lost.

"We came within a hair's breadth, I hasten to remind you all," the Minister of Paperwork continued in his bass vibrato, only partly justifying the lengthy series of daily meetings, the sum total of which had served only to mystify his driver. Moving on from evocation to invocation, the minister solemnly reaffirmed that there are never two without there being three, and that the next time we shall see what we shall see. "In sum, the people of Quebec owe a great debt of gratitude to Chevalier Branlequeue," concluded the minister, who obviously believed what he was saying about as sincerely as he be-lieved that Charles de Gaulle would be reincarnated and dancing the Brazilian samba.

Applause.

Several family members went to the podium to try to shore up as best they could the façade of their father's or husband's respect-ability.

Chevalier, get up, Sam begged from the depths of his reverie. *Push aside the lid of your coffin, raise your ruined lips in protest.*

He remembered the unofficial will with its codicil, specifying that Chevalier wanted "no religious music. But if someone could sing 'The Lament of the Mauricie' rather than mouth some celestial beatitude, they would make my soul very happy ..."

Suddenly there was a mild commotion. The novelist Jehan Bora, the terror of his generation, had slapped his wide-brimmed felt hat on his head and made his way from his seat, stepping on the toes of three or four people as he went, including those of the fair-weathermen who had come for the free coffee and cookies. Enormous and majestic, the neck of a bottle plainly sticking out of the pocket of his ample coat, he made his way up the side aisle, pausing at the door to the confessional to raise his hat only as much as was necessary to make sure his respects to the bier holding the corpse at the foot of the altar did not go unnoticed. Samuel knew him well enough to know that Bora had crushed those feet deliberately and had put his hat on for the sole purpose of paying tribute to the fallen Chevalier.

The loud snorts that bounced off the closed oak door of the confessional and rose upward to the loft had nothing to do with outrage. They were soon drowned out by the first measures of Handel's *Largo*, which played while the assembled faithful, roused from their stupor, went back to pretending that nothing at all ever happened.

Mistress of the hour at last, La Grosse Éléonore received her condolences in front of the church with ill-concealed impatience. Under a violet hat and her helmet of blue-white hair, a bland look and a mouth like a stingray, she struck the pose of a vestal virgin beset by virility. Although she'd been repeating to anyone who would listen her one and only criticism of the immortal work of her pitiful husband and even more pusillanimous head of the family — "Don't waste your time reading it ..." — on this day, she was cashing in on his fame and making her peace with posterity.

Samuel had no intention of giving her the satisfaction, not that she would notice. Now that she was rid of her husband, the Dogsbody, as Chevalier's students had dubbed her, had become the centre of attention of the young people he had liked to surround himself with.

The Patriot flag waved in the forecourt, whipped by a strong breeze blowing up from the river. It blew over the young militants wearing toques and *ceintures fléchés* who were carrying it, lacking only the pipe between their teeth and an ancient musket to complete their costumes. In the midst of it all, the Minister of Culture, his make-up visibly cracking in the cold, was giving another interview.

Nihilo had almost managed to slip away to the parking lot when a stern-looking man called his name from a distance and caught up with him. Athletic, in his forties, blond, forehead reaching all the way to the back of his head. Sam recognized Chevalier's long face, hooked nose, almost feminine chin, and receding hairline.

They shook hands. The man's name was on the tip of his tongue.

Chevalier had married Éléonore shortly after experiencing a traumatic homosexual incident in Copenhagen in 1950. That, at least, was how he'd explain the marriage after a third bottle of wine. He'd fled Copenhagen and its abundance of Good Samaritans, all wearing their hearts on their sleeves in the post-war clubs. He'd strayed into one one night, where the men all danced with one another (which had aroused more than his suspicions). He came back to Montreal to have a ruptured appendix attended to, thought himself to be dying, and married the nurse who had washed away his sins. His fear of being a fag gave them three children in short order. It was one of those offspring, the product not of love but of doubt, who stood before Nihilo now.

"Thanks for coming."

"It's ... nothing. You have ... uh, my sympathies."

"There's a small buffet ... later ... for ..."

"I'd like to, but I have to go."

"You know that my father had just retired when ..."

"Yes."

"But he stayed on, anyway, as a visiting professor. He still had his office. His papers are there waiting for him. No one has touched a thing. My mother asked me to find someone to straighten out his affairs, you know, go through them first before the evaluator from the National Library shows up. I found it ... interesting, let's say ... what you wrote about my father in *Statut particulier*."

"Ah. Yes."

"You know his work well. You're familiar with his research. I thought it might interest you."

"Yes."

The young Chevalier turned and, for a moment, watched the funeral cortège move off on foot toward the neighbouring cemetery. He smiled sadly.

"You aren't going to accompany the coffin to ..." he asked Sam.

"Into the hole with him?"

The son sighed with a kind of relief.

"Yes. There."

"In my own way, I suppose," said Sam.

And here I am, drifting away from the church, out on the frozen river covered with snow and ice-fishing huts as the death knell sounds in the wintry sky that drapes over the village like God's own cheesecloth.

I won't describe the "glacialated" (one of Chevalier's neologisms) village of Sainte-Anne-de-la-Pérade. If you called the municipal offices they'd no doubt mail you a pamphlet, even though there's almost certainly a web site. This old parish, surrounded by pastures and situated on the border between the northern wilderness and the river, is known as the "tommy cod fishing capital of the world" today, which is fine, Sainte-Anne being the only place in the world where the above-mentioned fish are fished, as far as I know. The village of huts (or the glacialated agglomeration) lasts for only six to eight weeks. Ahead of me, as though rising from the river's barely buttressed bed, less than a hundred metres wide at this point, lies a blossoming of white, yellow, red, slate, green, and blue cabins, each surmounted by a sheet-metal chimney spewing a thick plume of white smoke into the intensely blue sky. Roads have been ploughed on the ice between the huts, and vehicles are parked between mounds of snow. The village has been divided into "blocks," identifiable by the fact that the cabins in each block are all the same colour and belong to the same owner and provider.

I found myself standing in front of one of these fishing palaces, on the door: GASTON NOBERT, PURVEYOR. And I thought that's exactly what Chevalier Branlequeue never was for his family: a purveyor. After all his years of swimming against the tide, by the time the university reeled him back in, in the mid-1970s, on the strength of the overwhelming success of *Elucubrations* as much as for any degree he might have had, his children had already flown the familial coop and were spreading their wings somewhere else.

Not far from me, a tomcod suddenly flew out of an open window and landed on a pile of its fellows to be frozen alive on the ice. I walked over, bent down, and picked up the fish between my fingers. It was still wriggling. I looked at it closely, as though acting out a scene: Prince Hamlet with aquatic vertebrate instead of Yorick's skull. I don't know why, but I stuffed the fish into my coat pocket. I could feel it beating feebly against my side. It was still alive. I went back to the church, turned into the cemetery while the last cars were leaving the parking lot and driving off along the Chemin du Roy. Not so much as a cat at the graveside. The coffin had been lowered and was awaiting the gravediggers, who couldn't be far off, probably huddled around a Quebec heater in the shelter of a tool shed.

When I took the tomcod out of my pocket, it was no longer moving. I knew that Chevalier Branlequeue would approve of my little joke: a dead fish to bear the message *You're next*, like in the Mafia.

The little frostfish hardly made a sound when it hit the coffin lid. I walked back to the church. The bus rented by the Writers' Union had already left. Everyone was gone. Except for one old poet, sitting on the church steps, a brown paper bag with a bottle in it held tightly between his legs. He was singing "The Lament of the Mauricie."

RUE SAINT-DENIS

FROM THE WINDOW OF HIS office on the third floor of the Judith-Jasmin Building at the University of Quebec at Montréal (UQAM), Chevalier had enjoyed an unobstructed view of one of the densest concentrations of drinking spots in the city. On traditional English university campuses, usually self-contained enclaves in the verdant countryside, there would be a single pub, justly thought of as a scene of depravity, and that opened only at night. Students spent a few sordid hours in them relieving themselves of accumulated pressures, drinking themselves stupid, trying to pick up anything with a pulse, throwing up in toilets, falling asleep under a table for an hour or two, then getting up for a final hit on whoever looked fuckable and/or to get into a brawl, then go home to sleep it off.

Relatively speaking, with its urban campus in the Latin Quarter, UQAM was a modest, transatlantic imitation of the Sorbonne: barely a few strides separated the future bachelor of arts in the grip of a brilliant but boring course from a sidewalk café in which intellectually stimulating company sipped pints of beer. A perennial temptation, for students, as well as profs, which may explain why the two organs that had laid Professor Branlequeue low had been his liver and one of his kidneys. He had made a lot of demands on them, Samuel told himself, standing at the window looking down with disinterest at a drug dealer manning his post at the subway exit at the corner of de Maisonneuve and Saint-Denis.

He went back and sat down behind Branlequeue's desk. He took in, for a moment, the familiar disarray. At the foot of the paper Everest piled on it, or leaning against it, perched the professor's talismans. A wolf. A postcard from Percé. A hairy, eighteen-centimetre gorilla wearing green shorts with tri-coloured stripes and a pair of red boxing gloves. A key for who knew what. A card from a small hotel in Paris's Eighth District. A roadrunner feather. A chain of paperclips (32 mm, number 1) approximately fifteen feet long, folded into a pile, patiently assembled while a succession of students covering a large spectrum of intellectual possibilities sat across from him, droning away bravely about new theories concerning the Barthesian concept of textual bliss. And a chequebook with two rubber rectangles pasted to a piece of cardboard for a cover, a bit of bric-a-brac that Chevalier used to flog the same old chestnut every time the waiter at the Frère Jacques presented him with a bill: "Hold on, I've got my rubber cheques right here . . ."

On the back of a departmental directive announcing a new policy concerning student spelling mistakes, Chevalier had written, in his perky hand: *Zero taller ants.*

Energetic knocking on the door — he had left it half-open to conform with the spirit of ORAL, which Branlequeue had dubbed: Omni Regulations Anti-Libido — made him quickly look up.

Emma, who had seen the last of her forties, was wearing knee-high boots, breeches, a white blouse with flared sleeves and a neckline low enough to show a bit of dark lace, and a red vest that would have been more at home under a circus tent. A necklace weighing at least two kilos was rubbing the skin of her neck raw. This riding-to-hounds look rarely failed to draw a comment around the office, at union meetings, at the front of a class, at the cinema, the opera, and the cafeteria. Emma Magy had been six in 1956 when she crossed the Austro-Hungarian border at night on her father's shoulders. She was fond of saying that the Soviets had been stopped in Poland by the Catholic Church, in Czechoslovakia by the intellectuals, in Romania by poverty, in Yugoslavia by Tito, and in Hungary by the people's *joie de vivre.*

Shortly after Samuel earned his master's, in the late 1980s, the Literature Department underwent a veritable theatre of back-stabbing. In the space of two or three years, the top echelon of professors, veterans from the Collège Sainte-Marie, survivors of the series of heroic strikes that took place throughout the seventies, were decimated as surely as old Bolsheviks during the Stalinist purges. Not all of them had been let go, but none of them lasted long. It was as though they had disappeared under the table, victims of one vice or another: alcohol, cigarettes, boys, garlic butter, poker. It was a kind of poetic justice that they had perished by the same swords that had been their principal sources of pleasure for most of their lives. The most erudite of them had even died of brain cancer. The silent survivors moved in the corridors like damned souls, kept alive by lithium and antidepressants.

And now, Chevalier...But the woman who had just come through the door with a raucous, Valkyrie-like "Hi!" that echoed from one end of the corridor to the other was different. None of the excesses inventoried in the King James Bible and *Sister Beatrice's Manual of Corporeal Hygiene* seemed to have done her any harm.

With an imperious gesture she signalled Sam to remain seated, then broke into Homeric laughter while managing to be extremely feminine.

"Hey, there, sweetie pie. We wondered who was going to be sent to clean up this mess..."

"No kidding."

He invited her to set her muscular thighs on a chair. They had to clear a path through the stacks of books and mountains of paper that covered every flat surface of the office, as though they were cutting a trail through a forest.

She said she was surprised not to have seen him at the funeral.

"I was there. Last row, just like in kindergarten..."

"Not just there," she said, winking. "That's where you sat in my classes, too."

"I don't know what was worse, the protestations of posthumous friendship from his colleagues, who avoided him like the plague all these years because of his supposed 'chronic conspirationism' the well-oiled public-relations blitz coming from the propagandists in the premier's office, or the family's pious attempts to whitewash him. In fact, I think it was the culture minister's deep tan..."

"Let's talk about something else," Emma said, casting an eye at the muddle in the office, the over-stuffed bookshelves spilling their burden of books, bristling with bookmarks like an old sofa losing its stuffing, the piles of papers, and learned journals that rose from the floor around them.

"How are you getting on?"

"All right, I guess. Keeping my head above water," he said, indicating the office. "A bit of this, a bit of that. As a matter of fact, I'm considering a salary of seventy-five thousand for fantasizing over eighteen-year-old girls while explaining *Madame Bovary* to them. I can see myself doing that."

"Why *aren't* you teaching in a CEGEP somewhere?"

"Whenever I have to send in my CV, I go blank. I don't know why."

"So what are you doing?"

"Translations. Or working in the white slave trade, writing for newspapers. Writer of all trades."

They talked about the dearly departed. His rages, his passions, his infatuations. His mania for psychocriticism, picked up in the early eighties while sharing pills of all colours with Gérard Bessette, the author of *Semester*.

Eventually they came back to the funeral service. Laughed about the premier's return to single life. The surrealistic tint of the culture minister's forehead.

"He died alone," Emma declared. "It's a scandal, what happened there at la Pérade."

"Maybe. It's always dangerous to attack the heroic versions of a people's history. But with *Elucubrations*, they really didn't have any choice, they had to celebrate it. They couldn't just shove it aside. Thanks to Chevalier, Quebec has its national anthem."

"No, you're wrong there. What made him untouchable was that he was imprisoned during the October Crisis. He didn't actually bear arms, but being arrested is like being issued a passport to seventh patriotic heaven, in certain people's eyes."

"Yes, that's as may be, but these nationalist questions aren't always easy to follow . . . Good old Chevalier. At least he managed to get the premier out of his bunker!"

"Stop. He died in deep intellectual solitude . . . All these young people he liked to surround himself with, his Socratic side, where did they all go when he lost his health?"

Sam made no reply. It had been Emma who came up with the name for the group that used to get together at the White Horse after classes, and then later at Lavigueur's, farther east. One fine afternoon at the beginning of the fall term, she'd run into Branlequeue and his little band on Saint-Denis, coming from a course on Hubert Aquin and the Revolution. "Hey, what's this, Oktoberfest?"

"But it's not even October," Chevalier called back.

"Ah, but with you people it's always October," Miss Magy had shot back cryptically.

And so they'd been baptized the Octobrists, a play on Tolstoy's Russian Decembrists. Then, on account of the rivers and rivers of beer that flowed in their drinking establishments of choice on rue Ontario, the word "Octobeerists" eventually insinuated itself on the group.

"What became of all those people?" Emma asked.

"CEGEP profs. Proofreaders. One's a stand-up comic. Another's picking wild mushrooms in the Yukon."

"Well, not one of them came to the funeral."

"I know."

"Are you working on anything at the moment?"

"A novel on the go," he lied. "A kind of thing . . ."

He kept his eyes down as he spoke, drawing squares and oblongs replicating themselves to infinity on a blank page on the desk.

"He had faith in you, Samuel. I feel it's my duty to tell you that, now that he's not here any more. He saw you going far . . ."

"I write little squibs. I send reviews to newspapers. I run around after freelance assignments."

"What I'm saying is that he counted on you a great deal. He told me so. Chevalier . . . saw something in you."

"Chevalier was always seeing something, Emma. Maybe he was a visionary. But maybe not. Maybe he was just mistaken. All those years . . . There was never any plot. And the second part of *Elucubrations* is lost, and that's a damned shame."

"Too many keys and not enough locks, was how he summed up the Lavoie Affair. He was sitting right where you're sitting now. I can still see his big gleaming eyes, his sad old face, and the amused and sorry look on it when he said to me: 'You know, Emma, in all this I find myself confronted by people who are a lot stronger than I am.'"

"He said that?"

"He was never able to follow the path to the end. It was his biggest regret, and he took it with him to the grave. I wanted you to know that ..."

Embarrassed, Sam turned to look out the window. With a sudden, diminishing clatter, a pigeon detached itself from the sill.

THE BOAT

HE WAS BORN IN COTEAU-ROUGE, in a tarpaper shack. The doctor had had to tramp through an acre of snow up to his knees to bring him into the world. His mother cursed like a trucker. The only other witnesses to the event were two goats, huddled in a corner, their faces masks of fundamental and archaic vindictiveness.

In Jacques-Cartier, the working-class district that had spread across to the South Shore around a simple crossroads in the region known as Coteau-Rouge, career opportunities were divided neatly into two categories (unless you counted providing flesh for the good Brothers of Christian Instruction to fiddle with): crime and the police. Before even reaching the age of majority, Jacques Cardinal understood that between those two spheres of activity there existed intermediary zones that weren't always as watertight as everyone pretended. One of them was politics.

He was one of those schoolyard jackals who hunted in silence. Later, he would be seen hanging around with a small gang at the billiard hall. Waiting for something to happen.

The inhabitants of this semi-rural slum were unacquainted with the benefits of running water. Those who had wells shared them with neighbours, others emptied their chemical toilets where they could, for example, in the washrooms of service stations. Coco's brother, industrious and resourceful, put a fifty-gallon drum on a wagon and dragged it with a friend into one of the better-equipped neighbourhoods, like Longueuil-la-Bourgeosie, where they filled it from a fire hydrant, dragged it back along unpaved streets to Jacques-Cartier, and sold it for ten cents a bucket. One afternoon they came back in tears, their drum empty, boot marks on their asses. Big kids, they explained.

Coco Cardinal was fourteen.

"Stop your snivelling and come with me," he said. "We're going back."

There was a stop sign in a stretch of the road, but no intersection. The sign was Longueuil's way of saying: "Stop, stranger. If you're Black, Chinese, Indian, or even just poor, go somewhere else."

They passed it, leaving the poor district, and stopped at a fire hydrant on the other side of rue Chambly. Without looking around, Cardinal signalled to his brother, who took a monkey wrench he'd stolen from a construction shed, went up to the hydrant, and stood there while four young toughs casually walked out of a nearby yard. The one in front had good shoulders and a pack of cigarettes tucked under the sleeve of his T-shirt. He also had a length of steel wire in his hands, which he played with like a Greek fingering his worry beads. Coco surveyed them from the corner of his eye.

The kid with the wire loosened his jaw, found a bit of saliva at the back of his dry mouth, and spat.

Cardinal stood his ground in front of the hydrant, and the kid came up and squared off. He stretched the wire to its maximum extent between his fists.

"Hey. You got no business being here . . ."

"We just came to get some water."

"Didn't you get what I just said, Fatso?"

"Water belongs to everyone."

The tough stopped playing with the wire and put it in his pocket.

"Not this water. This here's good, clean water. It's not for pigs."

Coco never saw the punch coming. He took it full on the mouth and felt a cottonlike thickness spread through his jaw, taking the full weight of the punch on the lower half of his face. Staggering backward, he felt for the pipe wrench but couldn't reach it. The tough fell on him, and they rolled around on the ground.

Managing to break free from his adversary, Coco stood up. Someone had snatched the pipe wrench from his brother, and now Coco took it full in the stomach and slowly fell to his knees. For a moment that seemed much longer, he did nothing but stare at the pavement and try to get his breath back. The wagon was kicked upside down, and he heard the heavy, metallic roll of the drum until it hit the curb somewhere far off. The same kid who'd sawn his insides in half with the wrench now used it to unscrew the cap on the fire hydrant. A large powerful jet of water flooded the street and turned the gutter into a dirty torrent. He could hear his brother bawling somewhere. He was grabbed from behind. He looked up and saw the grimacing face of the little tough above him, outlined against the blue sky.

"You want water? Help yourself . . ."

A few years later, when he was old enough to drink, by chance Coco came across the guy in a tavern in Longueuil. The tough was completely pissed, sitting at the bar staring at a large jar filled with a greenish liquid and a few hard-boiled eggs floating in vinegar. He was drinking a large Dow, his shoulders slumped forward. Cardinal took a seat a few stools down from him and watched him for a long time. No doubt about it, it was the same guy.

He got up and went for a piss. There was no way the mug had recognized him. The stalls were filthy, the smell of urine suffocating. The blue ceramic urinal down the centre of the room looked like a watering trough for animals. Coco turned on a faucet and watched a stream of rusty brown water run into the sink, then turn yellow. The towel was a grey rag that had been tossed into a corner. There was no soap. He took a small bottle from his pocket and shook two capsules of Benzedrine into the palm of his hand, tossed them into his mouth, and washed them down with a few sips of tap water cupped in his palm. Then he patted his face with his wet hands, dried them on his pants, turned on his heel, and went back into the tavern.

He sat two bar stools down from the only other customer in the place and ordered a draft. He took a dime out of his pocket and, before sliding it over to the barman, held it up between the thumb and forefinger of his left hand.

"See that?" he said.

The barman, in his fifties, white shirt, top button undone, sleeves rolled up, dark patches of sweat under his arms, looked at Coco's hand.

"What I see," he said, "is a ten-cent piece, and in the thirty years I've been working here, my boy, this isn't the first one I've seen come my way."

"Take a closer look."

The barman furrowed his brow.

"All I see is an old cow, why?"

"The other side," Coco said, noticing his mistake. He flipped the coin over in his fingers. He picked up his draft with his other hand and took a big swallow. The bennies were beginning to work their magic.

"A boat..." said the barman.

"A schooner," Coco corrected him. "A two-master. Built in Nova Scotia for fishing cod. But then they started racing it, and it won every race. You never heard of the *Bluenose*?"

"The only sailboat I know is the one on the Molson's label..."

Coco rolled the coin between his thumb and index finger. In the yellowish light it flashed like gold above the bar.

"Yeah, well, when I get my boat ... a two-master, just like this one, you won't be seeing my face in here again. You know why?"

Look at me closely, Coco's smile said.

"Because I'm gonna have a bar on it."

The barman shrugged and took the coin, looking annoyed. Two stools down, the other customer broke into a shrill, almost demented laugh. Slowly, Coco turned on his bar stool and looked at him without laughing. From somewhere in the depths of his drunkenness, the other man rolled his eyes and shook his head with a knowing look and smiled up at the ceiling.

As though reluctantly, Coco turned away from his neighbour and back to the barman.

"Believe me, it's gonna be one helluva fine boat..."

In the corner of his eye, he saw the steel-wire man weaving his way to the men's washroom.

With a dreamy smile on his lips, Coco drained his glass, got up, and went into the toilet. When he pushed open the saloon-style swinging door, he saw the other man urinating with some difficulty. Coco grabbed him by the back of his neck and smashed his nose against the wall, then cracked his skull a few more times until the tiles were covered with red spray, like a slowly descending burst of fireworks. He threw the man on his back in the urinal, his cock in the air, his bladder continuing to spurt itself empty, let him look around for a second to get his bearings, then bent under the ancient, rickety, rusted sink, closed his fist around the drain pipe and, yanking it free, brandished it like a club. Water began shooting out from under the sink, wetting his pants and running down his legs, flooding the filthy floor around him. Coco went back to the urinal, raised the pipe above his head, and brought it down hard on the body slumped in the blue ceramic basin. Blood flowed and mingled with the piss and the mothballs scattered in the urinal as a disinfectant. Bubbles formed, and he pounded away and kept pounding until his arm was tired. Then he threw down the pipe and grabbed the man's gurgling head by the hair to make sure his nose and mouth were well down in the mixture of blood and piss at the bottom of the urinal. Then he left the washroom.

"Water damage," he said in response to the barman's questioning look.

At election time, Jacques-Cartier was always taken over by the mob, from petty crooks to big leaguers. Any elections — school board, municipal board, provincial, or federal. Organizers wanting a little extra muscle found all they needed at the local pool halls. On polling days, groups of these little bantam roosters could be seen driving around, five or six to a car, going from polling station to polling station, as in a Western movie. For a few dollars, the streets belonged to them. Windows were broken, cars were sunk to the ground, all four tires slashed. Fires broke out in garages and garden sheds. Filthy messages in DayGlo red were painted on the sides of houses.

The small gang that gravitated around Coco had their unofficial headquarters in the pool hall in the new shopping centre, next to the five-and-dime. The hardware-store owner Dufour had made a bundle from the land the shopping centre was built on, and he knew Coco from having seen him sniffing around his daughter, a pale, dreamy-eyed blonde a bit on the thin side. The gang watched Dufour drive up in a white Lincoln Continental Mark II, a real boat of a car. They went out and had a good look at it, smoking and spitting, then went back into the pool hall to finish a game, the hardware-store owner at their heels.

"Seems you taught that Duchesnay kid a lesson or two."

Dufour acted as chief organizer for the candidate for the League of Social Vigilance.

"I guess I did," Coco replied.

Then he turned away and became absorbed in contemplating the complicated network of potential trajectories on the pool table.

The hardware-store owner lit a cigarette. Ordered a round of Kik Colas. Indicating the Lincoln in the parking lot, one of the most expensive models in the history of the automobile industry, he said he needed a hand getting people to change their minds on the day of the elections.

"But careful, like," he said. "I don't want to see a scratch on it."

"Why not?" Coco wanted to know, sincerely intrigued as he chalked the end of his pool cue.

"Because I might want to resell it."

Coco looked at him without saying anything. More and more interesting.

"It's politics," said the hardware-store owner. "Don't ask too many questions."

Coco leaned over the table and sent the eight ball hard into the corner pocket.

The municipal elections in 1957 pitted the "mob candidate," Big Raymond Girard, a jovial and skilled man whose methods apparently didn't meet with unanimous approval, against Gilbert Giguère, who was running for the League of Social Vigilance. Giguère had vowed to put an end to the "reign of terror" that he said had been imposed on municipal democracy by organized crime. It is now known that the League was a front for the Order of Jacques-Cartier, better known as "La Patente," a secret society that was an enemy of the Orange Lodge and worked in the background for the advancement of the French-Canadian race. In Montreal, the editors of the daily newspaper *Le Devoir*, infiltrated by La Patente and under the pen of its municipal affairs columnist Paul Lavoie, the future member of the legislature and Liberal minister, led a vigorous campaign against Girard, his Mafia ethics, and his dubious team of cohorts.

A Lincoln Continental was found with its four wheels in the air in the driveway of a bungalow in the suburbs in the small hours of the morning. It took a dozen men to do it: five to lift it up by its chassis and flip it over, the rest to catch it and let it down gently on its roof. They looked like a bunch of ants clustered around a piece of immaculate, white flesh. They deposited the beauty almost delicately on the driveway's asphalt.

Coco gave the rear fender an affectionate kick to ease his conscience. He looked up at the house and thought he saw the curtain move. The hardware-store owner was right. It would have been a shame to damage the car.

The others had already taken off, but Coco held back, took his time walking away, his hands in his pockets, and after a few paces stopped and turned around. For a moment he stood in the middle of the road, legs spread defiantly. The living-room curtain opened a little farther. A single blonde braid.

Later that day, Coco saw a patrol car parked at the sidewalk in front of the hardware store. Inside, Dufour and two police officers were examining the store's plate-glass window, which had a small, round hole with striations radiating from it, like a star. Coco stopped on the sidewalk and also looked at the hole in the glass from his side. When the hardware-store owner saw him, he gestured for Coco to move on. But instead of leaving, Coco motioned to the police officers to come outside. The two policemen knew him. After a moment, they came out, followed by Monsieur Dufour.

"Looks like a .303," Coco told them.

"Yeah, it does. Why, do you know something?"

"No, except that the shot was fired from *inside* the hardware store," Coco said, nodding his head. "But I guess you already knew that."

"What? What makes you say that?"

Coco met the hardware-store owner's murderous look. The man was livid. He looked away and lowered his head.

"Did you find any bits of glass inside the store?"

"No," admitted the officers, their curiosity piqued.

Coco squatted on his heels and pointed to several small pieces of window and a small amount of powdered glass on the sidewalk.

"See that?" he said. "It ain't complicated: the debris fell outside, therefore the rifle was fired *inside* the store."

The two police officers turned toward the hardware-store owner, who had turned green. They waited for an explanation.

But Monsieur Dufour stuck to his story: the rifle shot had come from a passing car. The officers had to choose between the eyewitness account of a respectable citizen, a pillar of the community, and the ravings of a juvenile delinquent.

Coco was walking down the street when the patrol car pulled up beside him. The officer who was driving rolled down his window.

"Where are you off to, Coco?"

"To fuck my girlfriend. You okay with that?"

"You got something you want to tell us?"

"Not here."

"Why not?"

"Don't feel like it."

"The street's all right as far as it goes, Coco, but you can't stay a fuckin' bum all your life."

"That's none of your Christly business."

"You should come back into the Force."

On voting day, the provincial authorities proclaimed the Riot Act. The situation on the South Shore seemed to have got out of control. As well as the usual clashes at the polling stations, this time there were direct attacks on members of the League. Cars overturned, death threats issued. Someone even fired a rifle through the window of a downtown hardware store. The owner of the establishment, a Monsieur Louis-Georges Dufour, publicly vituperated against the young thugs who had dared to vandalize his brand-new Lincoln Continental Mark II. He noted that his position as a League organizer, as well as his irreproachable standing as a citizen and parishioner, had made him a target in the eyes of the bandits. "You'd think we were living in the Wild West," he concluded.

It was generally thought that Quebec's reading of the Riot Act led to the restoration of law and order, and favoured the re-election of Mayor Giguère, the candidate for the League of Social Vigilance.

Three days later, Coco knocked on Dufour's door. The hardware-store owner wasn't happy to see him.

"Not a good idea, coming here like this..."

"After paying my guys," Coco said, "there wasn't anything left for me. I need more money."

"I don't have any more work for you. The elections are over, Coco..."

Coco looked over the man's shoulder, toward the hall. The hardware-store owner's daughter was walking down it to the brightly lit kitchen. Her father saw Coco looking at her.

"I don't have anything for you, my boy."

"I don't want money..."

Coco looked him in the eye with a tight smile on his wide face. He was a head taller than the master of the house.

"The Lincoln."

"What about the Lincoln?"

"How much?"

The hardware-store owner burst out laughing.

"I don't think it's in your price range."

"It would be if you gave me more work."

"Come see me before the next elections, okay?"

"No. I'll be paying a visit to Big Raymond Girard before that."

His smile equalled that of the hardware-store owner, who was the first to look away.

"I just want to try it out," Coco said quietly.

"You just … what?"

"The Lincoln. Just for a spin. Afterward I'll bring it back. I'll be careful with it," he added as the hardware-store owner handed him the keys.

Dufour didn't like the smile he saw flash across the face of this good-for-nothing with a bright future ahead of him.

The second time he took the Lincoln, he also laid claim to the owner's daughter and a quarter of the owner's chromosomes. They went to a Western, with John Wayne, at the local drive-in. It was early June and the evening was warm, much warmer in the car after the film was over. They drove south along the road to Chambly and then took the Eastern Townships autoroute to the Acadie River. In Quebec, there are as many places called Îles aux Fesses as there are Green Lakes and Long Lakes. Somewhere between Île aux Lièvres and Île Goyer, they found one where, after crossing a small bridge, they stopped in front of a clutch of cottages.

The Acadie is a flat river the colour of mud because of all the farms it runs through. Clumps of trees and shrubs extend down to the gentle riverbank. Just after midnight, Coco drove into a narrow meadow and pushed the nose of the car into the tall grass between two ruts until it was barely visible from anywhere.

Ginette guided his hand. Her breasts were like two loaves of bread fresh from the oven, bursting with life, and he told her so. Not long after that, the white Mark II began rocking between the cattails and the stars.

Afterward, they smoked a cigarette.

"I saw you the other morning," Ginette said. "You with were those guys who turned Dad's car upside-down. What I don't get is how he could lend you the car after that."

"It's just politics," Coco replied. "Don't ask too many questions."

He rolled down the window and threw his cigarette butt into the wet grass, then opened the door and got out. She saw him tuck his shirt-tail back into his pants, then walk back to the trunk. She heard him open it. When she got out on her side, she felt swallowed up by the sky and the night. The sound of frogs. A few feet ahead of her, Coco was holding a rifle, a .303 Lee Enfield, army issue, fitted with a scope. He raised it to his shoulder and peered through the cross-hairs into the dark.

"What are you doing?"

"Looking," said Coco, aiming the rifle at something on the far side of the river.

He cocked it. A sharp, almost joyful sound came from the mech-anism, metallic clicks slightly muffled by the heavy wooden stock. It pleased him.

"It's his deer-hunting rifle," Ginette said. "He goes every year."

"He uses it for other things besides deer hunting," Coco said in a mocking tone, the rifle still raised to his shoulder.

He told her about the incident with the window.

"I still don't understand why he lent you his car," Ginette remarked.

Next to her, Coco could see invisible frogs in the tumultuous river-bed. He lowered the rifle and smiled to himself.

"Because I've got him," he said, then said it again, for emphasis: "I've got him by the balls."

Ginette would never admit it, but she was impressed.

There were many Saturday-night drives to the Île aux Fesses. They played with each other, made love in the back seat, being careful, as much as they could, not to start a family, and then, sitting up in the big Detroit boat of a car, smoking cigarettes, they watched the river flow by them through the darkness.

"One day," Coco said, "I'm going to have a boat and I'll take you out on it. I'm not talking about a little rowboat either, I'm talking about a two-master, a real sailboat, Ginette, my own, sweet Ginny. I'm talking about a boat we can sail around the world . . ."

Three months later, when the hardware-store owner showed up at the pool hall, it wasn't to give Jacques Cardinal another cushy job, it was to tell him that he had to take responsibility for his actions. The ceremony took place on a day of wet snow, slush, and ice. After a night of drinking, Coco had to swallow half a dozen bennies just to stand up. He forgot to bring the marriage licence. As it turned out, he'd just misplaced it: he found it stuck between the cushions in the back seat of the Lincoln. They drove off in the car after the wedding, through freezing rain and a hail of confetti, accompanied by the traditional concert of horns, their faces split by Pepsi smiles.

Honeymoon in the Laurentians, at Colford Lodge, near Lachute. Ginette went into the bathroom to take off her wedding parapher-nalia. She had a brief moment of panic when she saw how young she looked in the mirror above the sink. She decided against the negligée that her mother had given her and returned bravely naked to the bedroom. Coco lay stretched out across the bed, snoring like a chainsaw.

The father-in-law had connections in the Montreal police. That was one thing being in La Patente was good for. Coco joined the force.

There was the sound of something smashing and a string of curses coming from the kitchen. As she lay awake, waiting for the next crash, he came into the bedroom and fell onto the bed. And stayed there without moving, fully clothed. She could smell his rough, heavy breath filling the room. She shoved him with both hands.

"Wake up."

Eventually, he opened one eye.

"What..."

"I'm having contractions...Take me to the hospital."

He tore three buttons from her pyjama top getting it open, exposing her heavy, swollen, expectant breasts. She gasped as, his breathing cutting through the silence broken only by the clicking of his metal buckle, he knelt above her on the bed and undid his pants. He roughly grabbed the two sides of the pyjama top, tearing them apart, the bottom button flying off into the air in an arc, at the apex of which it seemed to hover for a fraction of a second, like a woodcock over a thicket.

"Jacques, no ..."

Cardinal grabbed the elastic waistband of the pyjama bottoms and with a grunt exposed the incredible moon that rose in the room, as solemn as marble beneath his fingers. The strong biochemical smell rising from her did not deter him. Just the opposite: the intense mucousy emanations seemed to excite him.

Afterward, he slept where he fell, on the floor, alone, like a dog.

Before daylight she tried to wake him. At the word "hospital," he closed his eyes and went back to sleep.

Her contractions were coming in constant waves when Coco, still drunk, climbed behind the wheel of the Mark II and drove them into the night.

He was promoted to the morality squad. He eventually gave his wife three more children, alternating girls and boys. Work was a universe of illegal houses, gambling, and debauchery, long nights in Montreal. The mayor was a reformed sinner, incorruptible, who had built his reputation on an immoderate passion for decency and upright behaviour. While a young lawyer, he had attacked the Augean stables and accomplished the notable achievement of pad-locking the red-light district, then had himself elected mayor and extended his heavy-handed crusade to city hall, where someone was put in charge of explaining the realities of life to him.

The essential services rendered to Director-in-Chief Salaberry by a certain madame whose establishment in the quarter had re-opened, its façade spruced up and its suggestive sign made more discreet, was an open secret in the force. Tenants in cat houses were warned in advance of police raids by telephone calls from a high-ranking officer, as was only right. The men brought in a few hookers to show that they were not turning a blind eye to the corruption that was gaining ground, spreading like gangrene into the legs of the city's politicians, while the turgidity of the mayor's speeches increased in direct proportion to his secret and shameful lubricity. So they would bring in a few girls and lock them up for the night.

Bouncing like a pinball between alcohol and pills, Coco soared up mountains of euphoria and plunged into pits of despondency as he wove from party to party. He'd bring friends home, couples. One

night, Ginette went to sleep hoping that the shouting and the breaking glass wouldn't wake up the children. When she opened her eyes,
a young colleague of her husband's had slipped into bed with her
and was grinning like an idiot, wearing only his boxer shorts and
socks. She went after him like a mother dog protecting her pups.

"What the fuck do you think you're doing?"

"Well . . . Coco told me it would be all right."

The speedometer registered 110 miles per hour. On the seat between
Ginette and Coco was a case of Molson's Ex. He was driving with his
foot to the floor, a bottle between his legs, charging up behind cars
until their fenders were nearly touching, then swerving out to pass,
racing toward trucks coming in the opposite direction before cutting back into his own lane at the last second. Laughing at his wife's
terror, ignoring her pleas to stop.

Somewhere near Berthier he turned a corner too sharply, and
the case of beer flew off the seat and crashed onto the brake pedal.
The Lincoln flew across the road, crashed through a fence, and carried on for a hundred metres before coming to a stop in the middle
of a field. Eventually, Ginette stopped screaming. Coco sat staring
in front of him, eyes bulging out of his head, fists clamped on the
steering wheel, jaws squeezed so tight Ginette could hear his teeth
grating.

Another time, they were driving through some woods not far
from Morin-Heights when Ginette, gripping the dashboard, had a
nervous breakdown. Unable to make her shut up, Coco threatened
to put her out of the car and leave her by the side of the road. Thirty
miles farther on, he'd had enough. She was still crying her eyes out.
He stopped the car, calmed himself, then got out, walked around
the front of the car to the passenger side, opened the door, grabbed
his wife by her wrist, and yanked her out of the car.

She watched as the car burned rubber on the pavement and vanished around a curve. Then she sat down and waited for him to come back for her. But he never did.

The exact reasons for Coco's ejection from the Montreal Police Force are not known. At the time, there was talk of fraud, of irregularities with union funds. The fact remains that in the mid-sixties, Good-Time Coco left the force. What he said to his wife was that he'd quit of his own accord. All there was to it. Case closed.

Not that she thought of complaining. The squad had been a bad influence on him, but its effect receded with time. The new Jacques was free to spend some quality time at home. He looked after the youngest child, told stories to the older one. He cooked, an apron stretched around his ample girth. She became pregnant with their third child. They had no television, and so he spent his evenings after dinner reading books he'd borrowed from the library. The big *Reader's Digest Atlas of the World* reawakened his dreams of travelling. He memorized the names of all the seas and sailed them in his imagination: Azov, Marmara, Barents, Aral, Aegean, Oman, Kara.

They were living beyond the business section of town, where well-nourished rats scuttled through the breeze-blocks. The end of their street opened onto a field. The only thing Ginette had brought to the marriage was the Lincoln Continental Mark II, and it was now worth a small fortune, but Coco would rather be run over by a Volkswagen until he was dead before he would sell that car. When creditors outnumbered the mouths he had to feed, Coco began looking around for a connection or two.

He could usually be found in the Vegas Sports Palace on boulevard Taschereau, on the South Shore. The establishment belonged to Luigi Temperio, right-hand to the Montreal Mafia boss Giuseppe

Scarpino, who was related to the Bonanno family in New York. Coco's police contacts gave him access to some new friends. He started coming home late again, went back to drinking and chewing amphetamines like they were those candies threaded onto necklaces they sold at Labelle's in Coteau-Rouge when he was a kid. When deliveries from Labelle's Self Service Store had been made in a horse and wagon. The milk truck had also been drawn by a horse. And the chip truck . . .

And for running water, for running water, there had been that little wagon.

But today he drove around in a Lincoln Continental, while princes of darkness paid for his cognac.

Coco felt he had the soul of a patriot. He joined the separatist group Rassemblement pour l'indépendance nationale. Impatient for action, factions within this movement tinkered with bombs that rattled the symbols of power as well as the walls of barracks. Radical separatist groups formed, expanded, and disappeared faster than it took to name them, and history was made. Coco participated in meetings of the Comité indépendance-socialisme started by Francis Braffort, where he also met members of the Intellectuels et ouvriers patriotes de Québec, a workers' party founded by two former police officers. It was bizarre, two cops putting together a Marxist group, but in those days anything could happen.

One evening, Richard Kimball showed up at the apartment.

Kimball was a twenty-one-year-old from northern Michigan, Marquette, or somewhere around there. He had left the States out of idealism, so that he wouldn't have to do what was expected of him, which would have meant letting himself be eaten alive by insects and, if possible, killing a few Vietnamese. A draft dodger. He was a strange case. Kimball told Coco that in 1967, when President Lyndon Johnson opened the United States pavilion at Expo 67, he'd hidden in a tree on Île Sainte-Hélène and taken a potshot, not at the president but at the young fellow whose job it had been to raise the American flag during the ceremony. He later told Coco that the protocol office and the secret service had had the bright idea of having the flag raised by a Boy Scout, because they were convinced that no potential assassin would shoot at a child. Kimball added that the kid wore a bulletproof vest when he raised the goddamned Star-Spangled Banner. Those were the kinds of stories Kimball told.

Sometimes Coco believed him, sometimes he didn't. There were some things he could do without knowing.

Kimball was blond, gifted with a winning smile, and had a dangerous sense of humour. He apparently considered his rural accent from the Upper Peninsula to be a superior form of speech, and everyone around him had to bow down to it in the interest of maintaining good relations between civilized peoples. Ginette took an immediate dislike to him. He brought girls over. He lived on avenue Mont-Royal, in a huge five-and-a-half-room apartment. When he showed up, Coco and Ginette's place filled with smoke and a mental fog that lasted until the next morning. The first time Kimball brought Lucie, she climbed up on the table and took her clothes off. Someone took photos. Then Richard carried her into the bedroom, laid her down on the bed, and went to work on her. The other guests talked among themselves, while Coco, who had a ringside seat next to the bedroom, didn't dare stand up.

One morning, after watching Coco swallow a couple of bennies with a glass of water from the kitchen tap, Kimball took from the pocket of his vest a mirror like the one Ginette used to powder her face, a razor blade, one edge of which was covered with tape, and a plastic bag containing maybe a gram of cocaine. He poured some of the cocaine on the mirror, spread it out, and worked it with the razor blade. Coco's eyes never left Kimball's hands; he watched with the rapt attention of one observing a sacred ritual.

Kimball scraped the cocaine into two parallel lines, each about five centimetres long.

"This is the good stuff," he said.

"How … how good is it?" asked Coco.

In the bright morning light that filled the kitchen, Kimball looked at Coco as though he'd never really bothered to look at him until then. He smiled.

"Too good for you," he said.

One night after Coco took a swing at Ginette, Lucie brought her into the bathroom while Kimball turned a blind eye, muttering that as a matter of principle he never interfered in Canadian domestic affairs. Lucie pressed a wet facecloth to Ginette's black eye and promised to help her with the children as soon as the men went out.

"How old are you?" Ginette asked her.

"I just turned eighteen."

"I don't understand what you see in a guy like that."

Lucie smiled.

"And I don't understand what you see in a guy like your husband."

Ginette felt herself turning bright red.

"What does Kimball live on?"

"He works for a company. That's all I know, and it's best if you don't ask questions."

"But seriously, aren't you afraid of him?"

She seemed to think about it.

"Come with me," she said. "I want to show you something."

They left the building by a side door that gave onto the alley and took the spiral, wrought-iron staircase down to street level. Kimball's Z-28 was parked in the gravelled backyard.

"Come take a look," Lucie said.

She opened the trunk and pulled back a blanket. Ginette knew nothing about weapons. In the weak light from a neighbouring balcony she saw barrels, gunstocks, triggers, cartridge clips, an entire arsenal jammed into the back of the trunk, against a row of boxes.

"Do you know what's in those boxes? Look at what's written on them."

DANGER EXPLOSIVES

Kimball was driving around with cases of dynamite in the back of his Camaro.

The front doorbell rang. A little girl was crying in one of the bedrooms. Ginette opened the door, still holding the butcher's knife she'd been thinking of using to slit her wrists. From the door, water could be heard running in the bathtub. She found herself looking at two police officers.

They told her that the neighbours had called the division because of some noise and asked her if everything was all right. The one who'd spoken kept his eyes on the knife. Ginette assured them as best she could. As they were turning to leave, she felt she had to say something and told them she was going to murder her husband.

They thought she was joking. They asked her a few questions then advised her to put the knife away.

That night she slept soundly. The bathtub overflowed.

The sex was good. Household Finance had them by the short and curlies. Coco would disappear, phone her and tell her to have supper ready, then not show up. One night she saw the Lincoln drive by the building without stopping; she threw her coat over her shoulders and found the car parked in the field at the end of the street with her husband at the wheel and Lucie, looking a bit embarrassed, with her T-shirt rolled up above her breasts. Ginette swore it was the last time. She became depressed. A doctor came and gave her some injections. According to him, all she needed was some peace and quiet.

Then Coco tried to kill her. In a rage, he started breaking everything in the kitchen, split open bags of flour and flung their contents everywhere. He grabbed his wife by her hair and forced her to the floor. She fought him off until the neighbours broke down the door. Coco chased them off, throwing anything at them that came to hand, including their four-slice toaster.

When he turned back to her, he was holding the toaster cord in his hands, a strange smile on his lips. He looked at her coldly, still moving toward her.

"Are you afraid of me?"

She couldn't speak, her voice had given out. Someone pounded on the door. The police.

Coco knew them.

"Hey, Coco, what's the score?"

"He's trying to kill me," Ginette told them.

She did, in fact, have two or three bruises that were hard to explain.

"She's crazy," Coco assured them. "I was just roughing her up a bit."

"All the same," said one of the patrolmen, "you should be careful."

"What'll you do if we leave you here with her?" asked the other one.

"Finish the job," said Coco.

They had to admire his honesty, but they took him in anyway. They didn't use the cuffs. The next day the hardware-store owner went to the apartment without calling first and left with his daughter and the children.

But guess what. She went back to him. Rolled up her sleeves, went back to work. Sex. Reconciliation. Barbecued chicken from St.-Hubert every Sunday. Little notes left on the table in the morning, almost poems. Her sister took the kids for a week. They drove to New Brunswick with a little camping stove in the car and fifty-three dollars in their pocket. Two footloose lovers. Coco had always wanted to see boats. They slept in the car. He'd stopped driving like a suicidal maniac, had become quite the charmer. He drove with one hand on the wheel and the other around his wife, the Mark II turning heads all the way from Mont-Joli to Shippagan. They crossed the gulf of the Baie-des-Chaleurs on the bridge to Campbellton then followed the coastline. Small, dun-coloured villages, a few pulp and paper mills. Across the water were the red cliffs of Miguasha. At night they ate lobster on picnic tables. Walked on the pebbled beaches holding hands. Coco talked to fishermen on the wharves. Got himself invited onto their boats. Learned about knots and currents, the secrets the horizon held. Long-lined a two-hundred-pound halibut. Bouncing over the waves, the smell erasing everything, a new start from square one. On clear days they could see the Gaspé coast.

It was dark when they pulled into Shippagan, at the very tip of the Acadian peninsula. Coco drove right out onto the beach and they made love on the same back seat as the first time. "I love you, wife of mine," he said to her. Said it again. Then collapsed into tears. Ginette couldn't stop herself either. She'd never been so happy.

That night she dreamed of whales ridden by sailors wearing pea jackets and sou'westers, sitting in submersibles attached to the whales' backs, and when they left port they glided between a myriad of islands on the surface of blue-green waters, infused with light, like a gold lamé dress studded with diamonds stretching over the whole world. And the whales talked to one another as they swam with the same slow, peaceful, oscillating motion as the majestic swaying of elephants carrying tiger hunters in India that she had seen in a *National Geographic* special on TV. Or sometimes they dove and swam playfully like otters, without worrying about the boats tied to their backs.

As the first glimmer of light filtered through the grey crack of dawn, Ginette opened her eyes and sat up in the grip of a strange sensation. It didn't take her long to figure out why. The Lincoln was completely surrounded by water.

"Jacques! Wake up ..."

He slowly emerged from sleep and looked around the car in amazement. The sea was halfway up the doors.

"One day, Ginette, you'll see ... I'll have it. My boat. One day ..."

They returned to Montreal with little more than a can of beans between them, the genetic make-up for a fourth child conserved in a safe place. They were three hundred metres from their apartment and they had enough money for gas to get there.

CHICKEN

SAM PICKED UP THE LARGE yellow envelope marked CHICKEN AF-
FAIR from his desk. Tidiness had never been Chevalier's strong suit.
The orderly filing cabinet, the cardboard folders with their contents,
subjects, and reference numbers clearly visible on little tabs sticking
up from their tops weren't for him. He'd been more the stack-of-
newspaper-clippings type, aficionado of the random page covered
with illegible scribbles, folded in four and stuffed into an envelope
like the one Samuel was holding in his hands at that moment.

Thick and worn though it was and stuck among stacks of what
seemed at first to be uninteresting paperwork, the envelope had attracted its share of attention at UQAM. Maybe it was because of
its title, written on the flap in ballpoint: a reference to the famous
chicken ordered from a local rotisserie by the kidnappers of Paul
Lavoie during his time of captivity — it had, after all, become part
of the folklore of the October Crisis. When the pencil-pushers at
the BN weren't looking, Sam had slipped the file into his briefcase.

There would be plenty of time later to send the whole thing on to the Fonds Chevalier Branlequeue at National Archives.

Nihilo was a bachelor. He lived alone in a condo in a renovated building in a section of the city that seemed to have slid downhill from the Plateau to the South-Central, between Sherbrooke and Ontario streets. His neighbours were students and gays, one of whom was dying of AIDS, a Chinese family, and a man with Down's syndrome.

That night he reheated a plate of pasta with puttanesca sauce, a concoction of black olives and anchovies prepared according to an old recipe developed by whores in Naples, and ate it while watching a nature documentary on Télé-Québec. He learned that during the mating session, male rhinoceroses spurted literally buckets of semen in a more or less continuous ejaculation that could last for several hours without losing their erections, because their penises were covered with tiny hooks similar to the barbs on fish hooks.

When he finished eating, he took his glass of wine into his office and sat down again in front of the yellow envelope.

For Chevalier, the death of the labour minister, Paul Lavoie, at the hands of the FLQ kidnappers was the apotheosis of the October Crisis. That bloody death caused a spectacular *volte-face* in public opinion: the event dramatized the separatists' cause and projected them onto the world stage. At first it had elicited a certain sympathy from the populist left that hadn't been there before. Socialism and separatism had been seen as two separate options. But with Lavoie's murder, the kidnappers became regarded as unscrupulous killers, ready to do anything to get what they wanted. Quebec citizens found that act of pure barbarism so repellant that they turned against the separatists and accepted the presence of the soldiers as a necessary evil.

Chevalier always maintained that, thanks to a federal cabinet document leaked to a reporter at the *Globe and Mail*, it was known that the government in Ottawa had, as early as the spring of 1970, formed a special committee charged with studying the ways in which the War Measures Act could be applied in Quebec. In other words, the suspension of civil rights and calling the army in were far from being a spontaneous show of support on the part of a strong central government. The call for help from a local power overcome by events was actually part of a plan, part of a long-term plan.

Chevalier Branlequeue did not believe that the FLQ had assassinated Paul Lavoie, since they had no interest in doing so. According to the official story, when the authorities refused to agree to the terrorists' demands to free political prisoners, their response was to execute one of their hostages in cold blood. Others held to a different theory: that Lavoie had died as the result of an accident. Chevalier was of the opinion that strangling a man required a certain amount of premeditation. "Who profited from the crime?" he kept asking, before adding, with an almost imperceptible wink, "as Karl Marx used to say…"

The Lavoie case lacked neither conspiracy theorists nor suspects. For some, the hostage had been liquidated by a commando in the Canadian Army; for others, it was accomplished by a double agent controlled by the RCMP's Security Services; still others had organized crime stepping in. The fact that responsibility for the execution had been claimed by a new terrorist cell baptized Royal 22nd Dieppe, and that the car containing the body had been found in a parking lot beside a military airport, barely a grenade's throw from the headquarters of the Mobile Forces, had merely served to deepen the mystery.

And as Branlequeue pointed out, there was no need for the police to look outside the membership of the FLQ to find plenty of lost souls capable of carrying out the dirty deed.

Those were the Years of the Chicken in Montreal. Every Sunday night, the streets of Montreal and Laval teemed with little yellow Volkswagens that had illuminated St.-Hubert BBQ signs on top of them. On the South Shore, Baby Barbecue ruled the roost. Its delivery people drove Datsuns the colour of a turgescent coxcomb.

In the envelope, Nihilo found a bundle of newspaper clippings dating from the coroner's inquest in November 1970. It was in these that one of the members of the Chevalier Cell (the recurrence of the name Chevalier was pure coincidence), a certain Ben Desrosiers, arrested the night before, first alluded to the business of the chicken.

Samuel also found an account of the chicken episode written by Chevalier himself, on a sheet of loose-leaf paper, lined and crumpled. He quickly read the cursive script, written in Branlequeue's elegant if affected handwriting:

According to what the guardians of Lavoie themselves said, they hadn't thought of going to the grocery store before going into action, and quickly found themselves short of provisions. Fed up with eating canned [sic] spaghetti, their leader, who was in a good mood that day, suggested they order some chicken, and he would pay for it out of his own pocket. He gave them twenty dollars. In a long interview given to Temps-Presse *when he got out of prison, Richard Godefroid said when the chicken breasts in question arrived, "they all more or less devoured them ..."*

On another sheet of paper (this one torn from a notepad) were extracts of notes taken by Chevalier during Jean-Paul Lafleur's murder trial in the winter of 1971. Among other things, they recounted that at the inquest, expert witnesses called upon to comment on the photos taken at the scene of the crime testified that they had discovered, among the boxes of takeout chicken littering the kitchen, pieces of "unconsumed meat." This sheet was attached, by a no. 1 paperclip, to a photocopy of a police report; years later an excerpt was reproduced in the report of a specially designated investigator assigned to the case by the government. Dated the end of October, the report outlined the various avenues of investigation followed by the antiterrorist squad and offered theories on the significance of certain evidence found at the scene of the murder. *While investigating the suspect house,* read report SAT-904-35E, in characteristic constabulary prose, *the investigators state that several chickens and other foodstuffs were found intact, not having been eaten, which led them to conclude that something very important had killed the suspects' appetite.*

In the margin, in red ink, Chevalier had written:

Come on, guys ... Did you eat the chicken or didn't you?

Digging deeper into the affair, Chevalier discovered that there had been two deliveries of barbecued chicken to rue Collins during that fateful week, the first taking place *before* Lavoie was kidnapped. In their depositions, the drivers, named respectively Rénald Massicotte and Henri Dubé, both stated they arrived at 140 rue Collins on the 10th and 16th of October, respectively, between 11 a.m. and 12:30 p.m., so sometime around noon. On a sheet of paper, Chevalier reproduced the details of the bills presented in evidence at the trial.

Bill no. 10079. 10/10/70. Three club sandwiches. Six Pepsis.

3 x 1.60 = $4.80
6 x 0.15 = $0.90
Tax   = $0.46
Total   = $6.16

Bill no. 12232. 16/10/70. Three club sandwiches. Two whole chickens. One pack of cigarettes, brand Export "A."

3 x 1.60 = $4.80

2 x 3.50 = $7.00

1 x 4.85 = $4.85

Tax $0.95

Total $17.60

Samuel got up and poured himself a glass of wine. As far as he could see, everything up to this point was more or less old hat. During their meetings at the Cheval Blanc or Chez Lavigueur, the Octobeerists had had ample opportunities to ponder the pluses and minuses of the October barbecue.

But the notes written in pencil on the next page were something new:

One is a chicken, the other a chicken delivery man: the story of the Massicotte cousins . . .

Attached to this sheet by another paperclip was a photocopy of an article that had appeared in *Statut particulier,* in the Fall 1990 issue, on the twentieth anniversary of the October Crisis. The text, a kind of playlet imbued with the vague literary pretensions found in most radio dramas, bore the signature of Gilbert Massicotte, who, according to his biographical note, was a retired detective from the antiterrorist squad of the Montreal Police. The antiterrorist squad had been integrated into the Combined Anti-Terrorist Squad (CATS) in 1970; it was the joint organization that combined the expertise of the Montreal police, the Quebec Provincial Police, and the RCMP. The officers assigned to CATS had baptized themselves "the Combatants."

The first chicken delivery man, the one who came on the Saturday, was the one named Rénald Massicotte. Feeling a bit dizzy, Sam riffled through the rest of the envelope's contents without finding any more references to the Massicottes. The trail ended there.

In the Montreal telephone book, he found five G. Massicottes.

The Chinese corner store down the street sold single cigarettes. Sam found a quarter under a pile of bills on his desk, put on his coat, and went out into the winter night to buy a smoke. But first he pretended to examine the hunting and fishing magazines on the newsstand, letting his eye slide over to the shelf containing *Club* and *International*, the designers of which apparently had their own idea, and he stopped thinking about the difference between what the chef at Baby Barbecue thought was a sandwich and what was actually a sandwich.

He smoked the cigarette as he walked back to his apartment and arrived slightly out of breath.

In bed, he thought again about all those super babes with their silicone breasts as round as saucers, and masturbated, which helped him fall asleep.

But he didn't sleep for long. He got up an hour and a half before dawn and made a pot of coffee. At ten, after having drunk the whole pot, he dialled the first of the five numbers and hit the bull's eye on the first try.

He explained who he was to Massicotte. A university professor and, he added, a writer. He was interested in a brief bit of dialogue that Massicotte had published a decade earlier in *Statut particulier*, and could they perhaps grab a coffee together in a café somewhere?

"Sure," replied the former detective lieutenant.

"That was too easy," Samuel said to himself as he hung up.

He was sitting in the Taverne Fameux, near the glassed-in bay window, looking out at the mixture of artists, pseudo-artists, para-artists, and semi-artists, or perhaps just the young and cool, and the usual figures of the quarter, the characters who kept coming back, people who'd slipped through the cracks in the social services, all being swept along by the current toward the corner of avenue Mont-Royal and Saint-Denis. Then he turned to the sports pages, which occupied his attention for a few minutes until a series of raps on the window made him look up.

It was a short, stubby woman. He remembered her name: Marie-Québec. Her parents were hippies, which explained the name, but when he thought about it, it was no worse than naming someone Charles de Gaulle or Pierre Mendès France. Marie-Québec had been one of the few women to take part in the small group that had sat at Chevalier Branlequeue's feet, at least at first, a sort of Octobeerist hanger-on. But at the White Horse, and later at Lavigueur's, the talk had become sharper and the stakes higher, a kind of I'm-the-king-of-the-castle competition, with the discourse as the castle and everyone using their oratorical strengths to keep everyone else out of it. The loudmouths dominated, and Marie-Québec, who was the self-effacing kind, didn't hang around for long. He remembered the last time he'd seen her, sidling along rue Ontario, almost invisible except to him and the inevitable drivers who cruised the corner for hookers and stopped when they saw any vaguely feminine shape. He might well have forgotten her this time, too, except that after tapping on the window and continuing on her way, she did a one-eighty and pushed open the door of the restaurant.

Samuel had once read a novel in which the author took particular pains to inform the reader that the woollen skirt worn by his hero-ine was of a pale aquamarine colour, with corn-yellow panels and a large knotted belt. You won't find that kind of thing here. Simply put, Marie-Québec was dressed like any twenty-seven- or twenty-eight-year-old woman of the time, that is, in the fringe between two millennia. She wasn't tall. Her skin was dark. Let's say she had the eyes and cheekbones of an Indian. At first glance there wasn't anything remarkable about her. The way she walked did not cause men's heads to turn when they passed her on the street. Her neckline, visible beneath her unbuttoned winter coat, did not remind him of the foothills of the Rockies.

Standing beside his table (she had asked point-blank if he was expecting someone and he had said yes without thinking), she told him she had a part in a Camus play, *The Just*, being put on by the Loblaw's Happy Times Theatre in Maldoror, a town in the Abitibi region, where she was from, she explained. "Two of the actors live in Montreal," she said, "so the rehearsals are being held here, a bit like when one person speaks English the whole group ends up speaking English."

At that moment, a man in his early sixties, wearing a Mackinaw jacket and sporting a very full moustache came through the door, pausing just inside and scanning the restaurant.

"I think that's my friend," Samuel said.

She gave him an excuse-me smile but didn't move.

"Would you like to have a beer later, say four o'clock?" he heard himself ask her, speaking quickly, even breathlessly, as though he'd been running after a moving train.

"Where?"

"At the Quai des Brumes? The Barbare? Wait, I have an idea: at Lavigueur's, on rue Ontario."

Massicotte was the kind of police officer who had flourished during the 1970s. The cool cop, pipe stuck in the corner of his mouth. He was the cop equivalent of the with-it priest. He'd even studied sociology at UQAM, and the police department paid for him to get his master's in the legal aspects of environmental protection. Which, it has to be said, makes him stink to high heaven of an undercover cop.

A few years before his retirement, he served as president of the Police Officers' Brotherhood, an organization whose main function was to protect trigger-happy and overzealous cops from suffering the legal consequences of their actions.

"You know, I'm writing a novel, too . . ." Massicotte said as an opening gambit.

Samuel offered him a coffee but he opted for a beer. They hadn't exchanged three sentences before the beer was two-thirds empty. And now Sam understood why it had been so easy for him to arrange this interview. A budding novelist! They existed even among cops? He was probably looking around for a publisher, like everyone else.

"Your own version of the events, is it?" Nihilo asked.

"Events? What events? No, it's a story of redemption. An alcoholic police officer infiltrates a criminal organization formed by a biker gang who's gone in with the Russian mafia. Do you know any publishers?"

"If I find you one, will you talk to me about the October Crisis?"

"About the . . ."

Samuel nodded. Massicotte shook his empty bottle at the waitress, who brought him another beer. Watching the former CATS officer drink beer on his tab, Sam found a whole new meaning for the phrase "the long arm of the law."

"I'm tired of talking about that," Massicotte said after chugging half the beer and putting it back on the table. "What exactly do you want to know?"

"Okay, why don't we start with the guy who delivered the barbecue chicken to rue Collins? You're cousins, right?"

This produced a surprising result: Massicotte didn't say a word. For a long time nothing came out of his mouth, not the slightest sound.

Then: "I have a witness."

"What's that? What did you say?"

"A witness. Call Mr. Brien, in Gaspé."

"Mr. Brien? You mean the famous lawyer? The FLQ lawyer?"

"The same. He'll confirm everything."

"Confirm what, exactly?"

"The story I am about to tell you."

"Great, that's all I ask. But how do you know Brien?"

"I ran into him in court, you know? Our paths crossed. We talked a bit."

"And what do you need a witness for, if I may ask?"

"It's just a figure of speech."

Massicotte stopped and took another swig of Labatt's 50. A long chug. He'd already finished three-quarters of his second bottle.

"Brien," he went on, "was at the courthouse the morning those three kids who kidnapped the American consul were brought in. We'd nabbed them in June in a cabin somewhere up near Saint-Colomban. I was in charge of the investigation..."

He stopped again and burped, then, as an afterthought, covered his mouth with his closed fist. He grimaced, rubbed his stomach with his free hand.

"Brien was their defence lawyer. That's why I was at the court-house on the morning of October fifth. There's no doubt about the date, because it was just after the opening of the trial, the same day we found out that the British Trade Commissioner had been kidnapped..."

"You were in court that day?"

"Yes. And suddenly there was this fucking asshole in the court-room who took a kind of hammer, something like a judge's gavel, out of his coat pocket and started creating a disturbance with it, banging it on things, making a ruckus, and the judge had no choice but to throw him out. I sent one of my men out to make sure he left, and that's when I found out that the fucking asshole in question was my cousin, Rénald. Obviously, I hadn't recognized him. I hadn't seen him for so long I had no idea what he looked like ..."

"What was he doing there?"

"The trial was open to the public."

"Yeah, but ..."

"He had a personal interest in it. He didn't know the accused. Or anyone else in the FLQ. We made sure of that."

"So, you're telling me ..."

"Yup."

" ... the guy who was at the trial on the fifth of October, the trial of the three FLQ members ..."

"Yup."

" ... was the same guy who delivered chicken to their buddies on the South Shore *five days later*? Was that pure coincidence?"

"Call Mr. Brien. He's in the Gaspé. Tell him you've spoken to me."

"Mr. Brien. Your witness."

"Like I said."

"You're damn right I'll call him."

Massicotte raised his empty bottle and looked around for the waitress.

"It's not that I'm not having a good time," he said, "but could you tell me your name again?"

"Nihilo, Samuel. I've got your phone number. Speaking of which, do you have a number for Rénald?"

"For who?"

"Your cousin."

"Guess what? I haven't the slightest idea where he is. I wouldn't be surprised if he was dead."

"Huh. Not under tragic circumstances, I hope?"

"An angel passed over Montreal."

With that, the former antiterrorist cop stood up. "Thanks for the beer," he said.

"Maybe we can do it again sometime."

"I doubt it."

"Maybe at your book launch?"

"The book has nothing to do with the October Crisis," Massicotte said. And turning on his heel, he left the restaurant.

"I believe you!"

After paying the tab, Samuel walked out of the Fameux feeling elated.

He turned west on Mont-Royal with the idea of spending some time in the journalism archives housed in the old Aegidius-Côté Building, at the corner of Laval. A commotion drew his attention, and he turned to look down a narrow alley, where he saw Gilbert Massicotte sitting at the wheel of his car, having just backed up into a hydro pole. Two young police officers, big, burly, and belligerent, were talking to him, their patrol cruiser parked in front of his car with all its lights flashing.

Samuel could see that they wanted him to take a Breathalyzer test and that the retired sergeant was refusing to do so. He was trying to explain to them, more or less coherently but loudly, that he had had almost nothing to drink and that an accident can happen to anyone and that he was "the former president of the Police Officers' Brotherhood, which fought for your hard-earned rights, you ignorant, dribbling idiots, what the fuck's your problem?" One of the younger officers grabbed him by the arm and lifted him out of the driver's seat, pulled him out the door, pushed him brusquely ahead, and shoved him up against the side of the cruiser. After that he sent the sergeant face-first into a snowbank, whereupon his colleague knelt on him, putting all his weight into it. The sociology graduate squealed like a pig.

"You should have stuck to the two-beer defence," Samuel murmured, but no one heard him.

"Call towing!" shouted the officer squatting on their suspect.

Then he plunked his one-hundred-and-ten kilo body containing zero trans-fat directly onto Massicotte's face.

THE HOLE

THE BEIGE STATION WAGON STOPPED. Gode pushed a corner of his sleeping bag back and risked a peek through the window. The first thing he saw was the top half of a police uniform and an officer in three-quarter profile, his face cut off by the top of the hatchback. At almost the same time, he saw that the flashing light atop the patrol car parked a bit farther down had been turned off. Slowly he lowered the sleeping bag over his face.

"Don't move, guys."

They stopped breathing.

There was a whirring sound, like that of a winch, and the front of the car began to lift with a slow, steady movement.

"Tow truck," René whispered under his breath.

The car tipped up as though trying to pour them feet-first onto the diner's frozen parking lot. It was at about a forty-five-degree angle. They clutched the blankets and sleeping bags to keep them from sliding off, and Gode moved his right leg a bit to feel the metallic rigidity of the rifle. He inched his arm out until it touched the butt. The winching noise stopped. He thought about what he would say to the cop when he smashed the back window open with his boot. He took his hands out of the sleeping bag. *Don't even touch the rifle. Go to sleep.*

Abrupt exclamations, see-you-laters, car doors slamming shut, motors starting. The station wagon, still at an angle, started swinging, its thin metal sides jolting amid a clanking of chains and couplings. They were on the move once more.

Marcel and Ginette, the future Mrs. Corps, had been taken to the cabin by the bearded young separatist. This time they had brought their friend Saint-Laurent with them and a box of provisions. Above their heads, between the leafless maple branches, the sky was an unidentifiable colour.

Ginette would remember what she saw for the rest of her life: three men, filthy and frightened, forced to live underground in the middle of a forest, like hunted animals.

Marcel Duquet told them that they couldn't stay there. "You'll freeze like rats," he said. And they agreed with him.

The thin veil covering the moon meant snow.

Two days later, Duquet woke up in the house he rented in Saint-Marc-sur-Richelieu and looked out the window at a blizzard. He couldn't see the sky or the ground. He was in his late thirties, but he looked older. Thick moustache, thinning hair, a nice-guy look. His fingers hooked around his coffee mug like the talons of a bird of prey, he watched the snow piling up on the banks lining the access road. The window shook under the wind's ululating assault. There was nothing around the solid old farmhouse to provide shelter from it. The wind blew horizontally across the landscape, up from the St. Lawrence Valley, shaking the wisps of corn stalks left standing in the fields.

Marcel looked at Ginette.

"We can't leave them out there..."

Ginette agreed. The children were with Coco's mother in L'Acadie.

"The other thing I worry about," Duquet added, "is that they'll be shot like rabbits."

They'd left the station wagon at the edge of the woods. Leaning into the wind and the driving snow now mixed with pellets of freezing rain, the five of them came out of the woods with their teeth chattering. Marcel got in, his woollen toque with its pompom pulled down over his head. The road was covered with fresh snow, and the only other visible mark on it was the bluish double track made earlier by their car when they came in. The engine started, the heater was set at high. Sitting in the passenger seat, Ginette listened to the radio and smoked a cigarette.

The station wagon became stuck while Marcel was trying to turn it around, and the tires spun on the ice. The heavy, wet snow, packed by the spinning tires, also turned into ice. Duquet went down the list of every ecclesiastical swear word he knew, then shrugged his shoulders.

"Someone has to get out and push," he said.

The three men, who had already wrapped themselves in blankets in the back of the wagon, found themselves outside again, pressing against the fenders of the car as huge wet snowflakes settled on their eyelashes. Crystals sparkled in the air and fell about them like tracer bullets through a thick cottony fog. The car leapt forward, and Gode fell full length in the slush. There was laughter and another string of church-related expletives.

Gode stank like an old wet dog on their return journey. He calmed himself down, glad to be finally moving, even though it was down a road covered in ten centimetres of wet snow. He covered his head with the edge of the sleeping bag and closed his eyes.

Later, when the tow truck took over and the jolts became more regular, Gode's head had knocked when they went over a bump. On the autoroute, somewhere between Bois-Francs and the old Patriot Road, the snowstorm had turned into freezing rain.

Duquet's house in Saint-Marc boasted an enormous central stone chimney that drew so well it made the split cherry logs roar and crackle. Unaccustomed to the warmth, Jean-Paul Lafleur sat in a sofa chair sipping gin from a glass; he had refused to let anyone put even a single ice cube into it. There was a limit to how much cold he could take, and he had reached it.

Jean-Paul slipped into a fond reverie that took him back to the previous summer, when he and a few others had helped Coco build his boat. Twenty-six years old, built like a brick shithouse, head full of ideas, some of which weren't entirely idiotic, he had the tranquil air of someone born to be a leader of men.

At Cardinal's place in L'Acadie he'd gone to the fridge to get a beer or, even better, a cold Kik Cola, and Ginette had come up behind him, turned him around, and pressed her body against his on the fridge door. At thirty-five, she had reached the peak of her sexuality. He could tell she was aching for it and for him, wanting to be taken like a whore against some alley wall, her hormones in orbit after a couple of beers. With all the young helpers hanging around the cottage, Coco couldn't keep track of who was doing what and he didn't always keep an eye on Ginette, who was horny as a bitch in heat. You only had to look at the noses and ears and eyes of their kids to see that what she had inside her wasn't so much a womb as a box of Cracker Jacks, a different surprise each time.

Jean-Paul had let her go on with her flirting for a while before breaking away and joining the others. But later on he regretted it, not hard to believe, and the next time she tried it, on the Île aux Fesses, between the handrails of the new boat's reptilian ferroconcrete skeleton, he didn't make the same mistake. He rose to the challenge, gave in to temptation for a bit of the old rough-and-tumble. And now that same Ginette was sitting listlessly on the sofa on the other side of the fireplace from his chair, her breasts pressing against her woollen pullover.

"Jean-Paul," she said quietly, turning her glass of gin in the glow from the flames, "what are you in all this for? Love?"

"What's love got to do with anything?" he asked, half-jokingly.

"At least tell me you weren't the ones who . . ."

"What are you talking about?"

" . . . who killed Lavoie."

"And why couldn't it have been us?"

"Because it wouldn't have been safe, you could never have pulled off a thing like that. We're not talking about holding up a *dépanneur*, for Christ's sake. Everyone knows you're in the FLQ!"

Jean-Paul was about to reply when a shout from Marcel cut him off:

"Police!"

An unmarked car with its lights turned off had burst into the front yard, which had turned into a skating rink, and braked hard, causing the car to skid around like a top. When it stopped, a man got out, and as soon as his feet touched the ice he did the splits, his legs formed a perfect ninety-degree angle before coming sharply together like the point of a compass, then he spun around about a metre in the air and came to rest as he fell heavily to the ice. He lay there for a full minute without moving.

In a way, it was kind of like the police. At least it was piglike. It was Coco Cardinal.

While Gode got out the 12-gauge, the others listened to Coco's careful footsteps coming up the ice-covered porch stairs. Followed by an impatient tattoo of loud knocks on the door.

"Open up! I know the Lafleurs are in there..."

Everyone looked at one another, then Marcel opened the door.

It was Cardinal, all right, no doubt about that. Dripping wet in his midnight-blue quilted coat and fur hat. A coat of ice encased the zipper slide on his chest, which dangled with the rhythm of his movements. Cardinal seemed to use his imposing bulk to shove Duquet out of the way without even touching him. He advanced into the room, his rubber boots clip-clopping across the floor, paying no heed to the chain of small lakes they left behind.

He was beside himself with agitation. Breathing like a racehorse, he marched up to Jean-Paul.

"What are you doing here?"

"News travels fast... How did you know we were here?"

"None of your business. But they're expecting you in the States..."

Maybe he was high on coke. Something seemed to have spooked him, but it wasn't Jean-Paul.

"Calm down, Coco. Why shouldn't we stay here, as long as you keep your mouth shut?"

"You have to leave for the States," Coco said again, sounding stunned. "If you don't, you'll be shot... Can't you understand that?"

"We'll have to discuss it," replied Jean-Paul, looking at his two companions.

Coco turned to Ginette.

"Come outside, I want to talk to you..."

"Suppose I don't want to go outside?"

Coco raised his hand, but Jean-Paul moved between them, followed by Marcel, who was brandishing a poker.

"What the fuck..."

"Coco, you are so totally uncool."

"It's all right," said Ginette. "I'll talk to him." Her hand lingered on Marcel's arm momentarily as she passed in front of him, then she turned and followed her husband outside.

Standing before the flames from the yellow birch log, Gode drained his gin and turned to his friends.

"It's always the same, isn't it?" he said. "It's the history of Quebec. It always comes down to same goddamned question: Go to the United States, or stay here...?"

Coco pulled a small Ziploc bag from his coat pocket and stuck a short straw up his hairy nostril. He took a deep snort directly from the bag. The flesh on his face underwent a series of malarial vibrations and palpitations like brief seismic shocks. He filled his lungs and exhaled loudly.

"Ginette," he said, "you have to help me convince them..."

"Why the States? Why are you so keen on them going there?"

"Because they can't stay here..."

"Why not?"

"Because it'll go badly. I know how it will end: two or three passes with a machine gun. And anyway, you ask too many questions..."

"It would help if I knew what you were talking about..."

"They won't get out of this alive," Coco predicted in a low voice. "Gigi?"

"What?"

"Find some way to get them to go to sleep, okay?"

"Excuse me? Exactly how am I supposed to do that?"

"The Lafleurs. If they won't cross the border, then we have to find some way to get them to go to sleep, and we'll bring them across ourselves. It's the only way."

"You poor dumb Coco. What do you think I'm going to do, put some kind of drug in their gin? Don't you think I'm a little old to be playing a spy in some James Bond film?"

"Gigi?"

"What now?"

"I want you to come home."

"No, that's out of the question."

"Your place is with your children. Don't you think you've whored around long enough?"

"No, I don't!"

"The mother of my children is not going to stay here and expose herself to a hail of gunfire. It's not right! It's going to get too dangerous here, Gigi. Come on ..."

He grabbed her by the arm and she struggled with him, pushed him away.

"Jesus Christ! If I have to ..."

But his feet went out from under him, once again they flew up into the air, and he fell heavily on his back with a dull thud. The impact of his body on the porch seemed to shake the whole house to its very foundations. He stayed down, an elaborate string of curses issuing from his mouth, his face twisted by spasms, and his eyes blinking against the freezing rain.

"Ginette, if I have to smash your ..."

"You're not in any condition to try anything like that."

"I can't get up," cried the Fat Cop.

Ginette stood looking down at him.

"If I stay here, Coco, what can you do about it?"

"What do you think I'll do? I'll go to Parthenais and pocket the hundred and fifty thousand buck reward."

He tried to get to his feet, but he was as helpless as a giant cockroach flipped on its back. She could have crushed his skull with a few kicks of her boot.

Duquet turned and hit the side of the fireplace with the poker as hard as he could. But the fireplace had been there for a hundred years and the stones it was made from were a lot older than that; it would take more than a whack from Marcel Duquet to change what couldn't be changed.

"Marcel, calm down..."

Duquet was still holding the poker, which had a pronounced curve to it. He held it in both hands, like a baseball bat. Ginette watched him, impressed.

"If he ever lays a hand on you..."

"Don't worry about me. I'll be fine."

"Don't tell me that son of a bitch found some way to make you feel sorry for him again?"

"I can see through him pretty easily, Marcel, if that's what's worrying you."

"Guys, I don't know what's stopping me from..."

"I told you, I'll be fine, okay?"

"Where'd he go?" asked René.

"He's on the porch, trying to crawl over to a bench. It'll take two of you to help me lift him up."

"Why?"

"He hurt his back when he fell. If we don't hurry, we'll have to break the ice off him in order to talk to him. But once we get him in the car, everything will go much better."

"Tell him we have no intention of leaving," said Jean-Paul.

"You guys be careful."

She began picking up her things and stuffing them into a bag. As she moved toward the door, Jean-Paul followed her with his eyes.

That woman has had my cock in her mouth, he thought. That creates a bond between us.

In Marcel's kitchen there was a large stove, a L'Islet, made in Mont-magny, with gas burners and, above them, several compartments for keeping pies warm. A real piece of furniture. Every morning, Gode crumpled up newspapers and put them in the firebox with some kindling and struck a match. He read the headlines as they went up in smoke:

AUTOPSY REPORT PUTS END TO HORRIFIC RUMOURS
THE HOUSE WHERE PAUL LAVOIE SUFFERED HIS LAST AGONY
NEIGHBOURS SUSPICIOUS BUT DID NOTHING

He found some buckwheat flour in a cupboard and made bis-cuits the way his father used to in the bush in Villebois, on top of the woodstove. He let a pat of butter melt on the dough, then rolled it up like a cigar. No need for maple syrup.

Up there, in the North, Gode's father would tear off a sheet of newspaper and use it to wipe the stove top before making the pan-cakes, as though the ink on the paper were the only cleanser they needed.

The basement was divided in half, with a kitchenette and the fur-nace room on one side and a kind of family room on the other, fur-nished with a card table, a TV, a sofa, a bar, a pool table, a stereo, which was a Marantz, and a green shag carpet.

Jean-Paul let out a cry, and René turned just in time to catch a can of Kik Cola that had been tossed across the room at him like a hand grenade. When he opened it, it nearly exploded.

"How did Coco know we were here?" Gode asked.

René took a long drink and burped.

"From Saint-Laurent?"

"Coco has feelers out everywhere," Jean-Paul said, going behind the bar. "The question is, what'll he do with the hundred and fifty thousand dollars?"

The other two laughed.

"Seriously. You don't think he'll turn us in?"

They looked at each other.

René was drawing blueprints on a sheet of paper with a large carpenter's pencil. Off to one side, Gode was fiddling with the radio dial.

"Why did the Lafleur brothers and Richard Godefroid travel to Texas at the beginning of October?" said the announcer. "Who is the mysterious Pierre? These are some of the questions that were asked yesterday at the coroner's inquest into the death of Paul Lavoie, and which were raised again this morning at the . . ."

They couldn't get away from themselves. They were everywhere.

Behind the house was a barn, and beyond that, fields of corn stretched to where the farm ended at a narrow fencerow of trees. Between the barn and the house was a pond. In the summers it was home to tadpoles and bullfrogs and occasionally a pair of wild ducks, blacks or blue-winged teals. Muskrats traced their peaceful Vs across its surface in the evenings. Once, Marcel saw a painted turtle sunning itself on a half-submerged log.

They started digging between the house and the pond. They worked at night, breaking up the frozen earth with a pickaxe, working like moles in the snow and the mud and the meltwater that ran into the trench. It was back-breaking labour. They dug from sunset to morning, always two at a time, the third resting in the house by the front window, keeping watch.

As Gode dug in the dark, all kinds of thoughts passed through his head. He thought about a novel he'd read about the Spanish Civil War, in which prisoners were forced to dig their own graves. The epitome of power that one human being can exercise over another is to force him to dig a hole six feet deep before shooting him in the head with a pistol, or cutting him down with a machine gun, or running over him with a truck to save bullets.

And those prisoners in that Eisenstein film, *¡Que viva Mexico!*, who were also made to dig holes in the desert sand, then were buried in them with only their heads exposed, their wild eyes that seemed to jump out of their sockets when they saw the horses being made to gallop toward them. Their skulls exploded like pumpkins.

Gode didn't want to dig any more. Perhaps any man who burrows into the earth is creating his own grave? But they kept on, Gode, the Lafleur brothers, kept on digging, as blackened and stained as coal miners, too tired to wash before going to sleep, cleaning off the worst of it in the morning.

Cardinal returned once, to make fun of them. They looked up to see his bloated, blank face hovering over the edge of the hole, like a rising moon. One arm in a sling. A broken elbow or something.

"What are you looking for, guys? Buried treasure?"

"Worms. For fishing. Can't you see?"

"You'd be better digging in the manure pile."

"Each to his own," remarked Jean-Paul.

Gode stopped digging, slightly out of breath.

"If you really want to know, we're building a cottage."

"Where? In China?"

"Exactly. Chairman Mao's our new trip."

"Yesterday I talked to a guy in the Black Liberation Front."

"Like I said, we're all Maoists here."

"Well, you can do what you like."

"That's right."

The trench they dug was a metre wide, two metres deep, and about six metres long. It ran out from the wall of the house. At the end of it, they enlarged and deepened it to make a room, two metres by three. At the house end, they knocked a hole in the foundation wall with a sledgehammer, then made a floor with cement from the basement between the wall and the furnace.

Marcel couldn't take it. He'd been living somewhere else for a week. On one of his visits, René came up and handed him a sheet of paper. He glanced at it and decided to take the afternoon off. According to his calculations, he would have to make at least two trips to the lumberyard.

They propped up the sides of the excavation along its entire length with wooden beams, to which they nailed two-by-fours and chipboard panels to complete the framing. Then they built a roof and floor in the main room, which ran continuously with water. Finally, they covered their work with some of the dirt they'd dug out of the hole and spread the rest around the yard as best they could. Their well-supported trench was now a tunnel. To get to it, they went into the basement and squeezed behind the furnace, lifted a concrete slab identical to those that formed the base of the furnace. They ran an electric extension cord into the tunnel, camouflaging it carefully, and installed a lighting system and a heater. The tunnel entrance was about thirty by fifty centimetres. They had to slide in feet-first, then shuffle on their backs until they cleared the hole in the foundation wall, where the tunnel proper began. From there, they could crawl on their hands and knees until they reached the subterranean chamber.

It was December, early afternoon. Outside the air was cold, still, and bright. They had slept, as usual, in sleeping bags on the rug in the common room. They had finished the hiding hole the previous night and planned to use it only in emergencies. A bolt-hole for creatures in desperate straits. Gode made coffee and turned on the radio. Then stopped dead, his empty coffee cup in his hand. He tumbled down the stairs and turned on the TV. It was December 3, 1970. A special report was being broadcast over the airwaves of the CBC.

"Hey, guys! Come and see this..."

They spent the entire day in front of the television. They saw a cordon of soldiers in helmets carrying rifles that stretched across the screen and down a street lined with three-storey brick buildings. A bit farther down, the street was blocked by a bus. Army helicopters criss-crossed the sky throughout the area.

The camera followed a uniformed soldier carrying a rifle over his shoulder, bayonette fixed, courteously escorting a citizen who lived in the quarter to the corner of the next street. The newscaster explained that the authorities had ordered the evacuation of the entire sector. Armed forces were supervising the combined operations. The cordon of soldiers that kept the curious away stretched along several blocks of houses and disappeared into the distance.

"Holy fuck! I've never seen so many soldiers! I don't think the Germans had that many when they invaded Russia."

"Rue de la Compagnie-de-Jésus. That's in the north end."

The CBC camera kept returning to the façade of an ordinary-looking brick apartment block: main entrance surrounded by a projecting portico surmounted by a rectangular awning. The apartments inside would all open onto a central corridor, and those on the street side had doors that gave onto balconies with cast-iron staircases leading up to them. The balcony of Apartment 1 was over the door of the garage, which had been converted to a kind of sub-basement with access from the inside.

Since their co-conspirators in Rebellion Cell had respected the rule of autonomy and the strict separation of operations, Gode and the Lafleurs were discovering, at the same time as millions of other television viewers, the hiding place in which John Travers had been kept for two long months. Someone had scrawled the letters FLQ on the windows of the ground-floor apartment with a can of spray paint.

After a while, they saw a grey Chrysler emerge quickly from the garage, back onto the rue de la Compagnie-de-Jésus, bang one of its fenders against a low concrete wall, come to a stop for a moment, as though suspended on a thread of time, while an escort formed in front of and behind it. Negotiations had taken place. The journalist on the scene was Claude-Jean Devirieux, whose usual impish voice and thin, weasel's face encased in a huge pair of earphones lent the event an air of pomp and circumstance as he conjectured about the destination of the kidnappers. The word "Cuba" was bandied about.

Then, at the centre of a cavalcade of police motorcycles, a convoy consisting of the grey Chrysler, several unmarked police cars, and patrol cars with their lights flashing, began to move. Corbeau was at the wheel of the Chrysler. The lawyer who'd negotiated the release of the hostage was riding shotgun. Between them, in glasses and long hair, was Pierre, also known as le Chevreuil. Lancelot was behind the hostage. In Saint-Marc, emotion and irritation were running high.

"They'll be working on their tans in Cuba while we spend the winter buried like moles," René commented.

"I'd say more like ondatras," Godefroid corrected. "That trench with a chamber at the end of it looks more like an ondatra's bank-lodge."

"What the hell's an ondatra?"

"A muskrat."

"Then why didn't you just say muskrat?"

"Because ondatra is the Indian word for it and I've always wanted to say ondatra. You can fuck your hat if you don't like it."

"You mean my muskrat hat?"

"Okay, you two, give it a rest . . ." Jean-Paul said without taking
his eyes off the screen.

"So Pierrot's going to Cuba. Unbelievable . . ." said Gode, shaking
his head.

"For now, it may look like they got the best deal. We'll see if they
find it so funny having a coconut palm for a Christmas tree."

René climbed the basement stairs, stopping at the top.

"Anyone want a beer?"

"Yeah."

"Jean-Paul?"

"A Kik for me. With rum in it . . ."

"One Kik with . . ."

"Yeah. It's called a Cuba Libre."

Marcel placed the bucket of Kentucky Fried Chicken on the table
beside the paper bag holding four large bottles of beer.

"Merry Christmas, guys!"

"Hey, great! Compliments of the Colonel . . ."

They'd been in a good mood all day. They'd ticked off their fifth
week in Duquet's house in Saint-Marc. The first two they'd spent
building the hideout. Then they spent a few days discussing organization and finances. The next holdup. Duquet had found them an
abandoned scout camp beside Lake Brompton. The access road was
closed in winter. They would wait for spring to move their stuff in.

The army had finally pulled out of their area. It wasn't needed
after the Big Show in Montreal, when they'd rounded up the Rebellion Cell. And it was probably better if the silencing of their heavy
boots didn't coincide with the repeal of the War Measures Act and

its replacement by a piece of legislation that vastly extended the powers of the regular police. The new law received Royal Assent the very day that an armed-forces Yukon carried Lancelot and his buddies to Castro's island. Apparently, the whole operation was a well-oiled machine.

Richard Godefroid and the Lafleur brothers were preparing for their next move when the winter solstice fell. Darkness from four o'clock on. The side road was blocked by snowbanks that looked like huge frozen pillows. The fields everywhere were covered in snow. And now Christmas, and the memories of reunited families. The three moles took to brooding.

But now, thanks to Marcel, they had woken up to the sight of a bucket of Colonel Sanders and four large Molsons.

"Too good for Baby," René said, licking his greasy fingers.

His remark was greeted with silence, which didn't mean it had fallen on deaf ears. Duquet got up from his chair and produced four large cigars.

"Merry Christmas, guys!"

Gode felt a lump in his throat.

"Marcel, you're ..."

"A real ..."

"Good ... guy."

"Are they Havanas, at least?"

The first police search took place the next day.

JEAN-CLAUDE GOES TO QUEBEC (FALL, 1973)

MY NAME IS JEAN-CLAUDE MARCEL. My role in these events was small, one you will no doubt soon forget. At least I don't pretend to be someone I wasn't. It's been almost a year since we got together in Albert Vézina's basement in Outremont — Little Albert, as we already called him. In another time, that was the name of a popular book, a kind of almanac or encyclopedia. . . . By "we" I mean a handful of politicos, small fish in a big pond, who thought that every informal meeting was the beginning of a revolution. Every month for almost a year: meetings. Without his being aware of it, the Old Lion had shown that it was time for him to step down: he'd passed out, completely drunk, in the middle of an executive meeting. It couldn't have been a big surprise to anyone — no one fell off his or her chair when it happened — because for months the whiff of gin had begun to spread beyond his circle of intimates. His laboured speech, his

105

flushed cheeks that had once earned him the title of the Handsomest Man in Quebec, and the network of red veins on his big schnozz, had become the talk of the town up and down the Grande-Allée. From the day he collapsed in front of his dumbfounded ministers, though, his handlers were no longer able to maintain a wall of silence around him, and the corridors of power began to ring with the sound of knives being sharpened. Which is what we were doing that night in January 1969, three or four unknowns who found ourselves having monthly meetings in Vézina's basement in Outremont, his little band of supporters. Vézina was our man. He was the logical choice to replace the Old Lion: a graduate of Jean-de-Brébeuf College; a Ford Foundation scholar; degrees from Oxford and Harvard; a master's in political economics and another in international law and corporate finance. The guy may not have been a heartthrob, but he had done all right for himself in the skirt department, too. His wife wasn't exactly the queen of the ball either, but she came with one of those bonuses that made "going to bed" rhyme with "hitting the jackpot": she was an Allard from Saint-Romuald, the daughter of the local Onassis, a shipowner opposed to flags of convenience, a maker and defender of governments, the owner of naval dockyards that received lucrative contacts from the Department of National Defence. He sat on one of the largest fortunes in the country. He was *old French-Canadian money* in all its splendour. As you can imagine, he welcomed a specialist in corporate finance into the family with open arms. And so our little Tuesday-night gatherings were suddenly blessed with a new member. Tall, held himself stiff as a steel girder in his sensible suit, lantern jawed, grey hair kept in a brush cut, a man past his mid-forties. His name was Bob Lapierre, alias Uncle Bob, the Party secretary. Sorry: *Colonel* Bob Lapierre. Wounded in the field of battle during the Second World War, at least so they said. Which would explain his stiffness, anyway. Others spoke highly of his work in army intelligence, which, if true, would mean he was still in the Reserves at the time. In any case, just looking at him made us want to salute him, right? According to some, his war wound had made him a veritable workhorse. His reputation was that he slept four hours a night and spent the rest of the time shouting at people. It seems he also liked to go salmon fishing in the Gaspésie, treated himself to trips to Acapulco, and was passionate about plants: he was flower power, a man who cultivated his own garden, you get the idea. Frankly, I can't see the Colonel with a watering can in his hand, but that's what was being bruited about around the high tables on the Grande-Allée. Anyway, there he is that night, in the flesh, or more accurately in the bone, a new arrival among us. He never says a word all night. He listens. You can cut the tension with a knife. The meeting ends and he still hasn't said a thing. He hasn't even taken notes, at least not on paper. So what was Uncle Bob doing there? Checking out Vézina's team, evaluating his chances? Spying for another candidate? Or did the Old Lion send him? Rumour had it that like four-fifths of the caucus, Uncle Bob supported Paul Lavoie. We had our answer a month later: it wasn't the distinguished and proper Allard daughter who stood in our way, it was Uncle Bob. Arms crossed, he literally blocked the doorway when the bell rang, his face rigid and closed, grey eyes cold as ice, a gleam of steel in his look, his mouth an expressionless slit. I'll never forget the phrase he uttered then: *You three, I don't want to see you around here again. Get lost....* And you won't believe this, but that's exactly what we did! *And don't bother coming back,* the Colonel shouted at our backs, practically making us shit ourselves. But we already knew what was what. We'd been aware of who we were dealing with. We knew the man, the Lapierre method. We'd been in the front row when he crushed René Lévesque and his future separatists at the Liberal Party convention in 1967. The tone of that conference was established well in advance, when the Lévesque delegates discovered that they were unable to reserve rooms in the Château

Frontenac; the federalist faction was installed there and had to be kept under observation and away from any separatist contamination. "We're fully booked," they were told when they called, after their names had been checked on a list of black sheep provided by Uncle Bob (whose other nickname was Papa Boss). His men were all over the floor of the Convention Centre that weekend, walkie-talkies clasped to their ears, waiting for the slightest informal discussion, the tiniest rumour, shifting agents from room to room, infiltrating one committee after another, all to keep the balance weighed to the proper side. After that, Lévesque, who knew which way the wind was blowing, dragged his feet to the microphone like a lamb to the slaughter. He delivered his speech and hurried to the exit, through the great doors of history that opened before him. He passed Vézina on the way, and Vézina remained seated, staring into the middle distance like someone trying to see a wasp buzzing a few inches from his nose and waiting for it to fly off before breathing normally. A member of Lévesque's faithful saw Vézina sitting there and called to him — "Albert! Come on!" — and made as though to help him get to his feet. But Little Albert did not stand. He had already seen the writing on the wall. He'd wanted to be premier since he was fifteen years old, and now, twenty years later, when he had to choose between being head of a provincial government or the finance minister of an independent state, he made his choice without the slightest hesitation. And we saw the result in Outremont: Uncle Bob Lapierre had risen in Little Albert's ranks and taken charge of his campaign. Which meant that Vézina had been given the Old Lion's blessing and the entire party machine to back him up. The rest of us who had climbed the steps of Vézina's house in Outremont quickly got the message and made our peace with it. But not me. After a long, sleepless night I decided to scurry off like a rabbit at the sight of the shotgun, telling myself I would sell my skin more dearly than that. My wife, you know what wives are like, advised me to get out of politics altogether and concentrate on making a decent living for my family. By "decent living" she meant working nine to five. Generally speaking, women don't appreciate any emotion that can't be expressed with roses and chocolates. As though agonizing until dawn over the wording of a speech, high on nicotine and coffee and the exaltation of seeing the vision that was in your brain being transferred into words on paper, was just so much time stolen from the great, cuckolding novel of love. Speaking of which, why do you think "cupidity" and "Cupid" have the same root? But I digress . . . Apart from the steamroller, there were two candidates: Denis Müller, minister of justice, workaholic, expert at sending out frenzied cavalry charges to disperse any and all demonstrations, described by pollsters as the candidate most liked by the majority of citizens concerned with law and order. And Paul Lavoie, a man of the earth, tireless weaver of lines of connection, former editor of *Le Devoir*. Despite what for mere mortals would have been a handicap — having had his name connected with several infamous corruption scandals — or perhaps for that very reason, Lavoie was able to count on support from the most influential members at the heart of the party from the very beginning. I never did like Müller. Colleagues had heard him speak privately about the possibility of sending in police to end the strike in Shawinigan with a few bursts from their machine guns, to deliver a message to the rest. I aligned myself with Lavoie's organization. And what I found was a totally devastated candidate. He and Lapierre had known each other in that 100 percent Canuck freemasonry known as the Order of Jacques-Cartier, yes, the old Family Compact. Lavoie's ambitions had been obvious for a long time. What I didn't know, personally, was that Colonel Lapierre had promised to put at his service the all-powerful electoral juggernaut that was under his control. So Uncle Bob's going over to Little Albert's camp had been, in effect, a betrayal. Day by day, Lavoie proved to be leadership potential with neither a campaign nor a manager to run it. I rolled up my sleeves and took on the job, and my first move was to set up the Circle of Friends of Paul Lavoie in preparation for a counterattack. But between you and me, by letting me go after the Colonel, Little Albert pulled off the trade-off of the century. We learned through the grapevine that Lapierre had gone to the U.S. to learn the new politics, that a *scientific* poll conducted by an American firm could convince the Liberal establishment that Vézina was the right man for the job: young, numbers coming out his ears. The response from the big shots to disturbances on the street and threats from bearded anarchists. Focus on the economy as a remedy for chronic insecurity among the poor, that was Vézina. A total android. They got him a hairdresser and gave him a Kennedy-style campaign, a virile Irish smile, the whole enchilada. What can I say? They pulverized us. We weren't even in the same league. Uncle Bob got hold of one of the early computers and used his position as party secretary to compile the first complete, systematic list of members in the province and used it to get first crack at the postal services. The other two candidates got access to it when he was finished, but by then the budget was used up and they had to pay for their own postage! Uncle Bob liked adding insult to injury. While the very mention of the name of Vézina's father-in-law, Allard, was an open-sesame on the purse strings of the Rhodesian clique of barons of finance and the newer industrial upstarts that made up the local elite of the business world, Little Albert's rivals saw that the traditional backers of the FLQ dramatically turned off the taps. Lavoie was a man who ran up debts, who quickly got in over his head. More precisely, $175,000 before you could say Bob's your uncle. The race was over. Three days before the leadership convention, I was with Paul in his house in Saint-Lambert, helping him rewrite his opening speech. We were sitting around the kitchen table, sleeves rolled up, papers spread out among empty cups and overflowing ashtrays. Suddenly the doorbell rings. He gets up and goes to answer it and finds himself facing a bailiff who'd come to seize his furniture. The creditor in question was the printer who was claiming $10,000 for printing his campaign material. The print shop belonged to the *Orford Clarion*, and the *Orford Clarion*, it turned out, was owned by a media empire in the making, the owner of which was someone named Durivage, a man who had interests in the form of a daughter-in-law and a packet of policies connected to the Allards of Saint-Romuald. Okay. It would take more than that to wipe Paul Lavoie's name off the slate, but when he handed me the affidavit that day hoping that I would run my eye over it and find some way to raise the $10,000 in a hurry, I heard him curse between clenched teeth: "This is the Colonel's doing!" But there was more than simple rage in his voice; there was admiration there as well.

THE ASSEMBLY

THE LAVIGUEUR TAVERN ON RUE Ontario was an institution. The perfect place to wait out a bout of insomnia while checking out couples of a certain age, prudently entwining on the dance floor to the sound of an orchestra typical of Montreal's east end: a gay man playing saccharine chords on a Hammond organ, a man with a huge moustache and a Hawaiian shirt scraping his brushes over a snare drum as if scrubbing out a pot, and an aging crooner in a tight-fitting leather vest and a cowboy hat who specializes in transforming old Johnny Farago tunes into treacle. The waiter, six feet tall, built like a former NFL linebacker, took in the patrons with equanimity mixed with sullen friendliness, whether they were students, avant-garde artists, or penniless intellectuals who came in mainly for a change of scenery but who sometimes tipped with suspicious generosity, as if to apologize for not belonging to the ordinary world.

The establishment's four walls displayed a collection of unbelievably bad art: portraits of cultural giants from a long-gone era who had witnessed the closing down of the cabarets, the red-light district, and the Empire of the Night at about the same time as the rise of TV. At Lavigueur's, after having shaken the salt shaker like a censor over your glass of draft, you sipped it under the converging gaze of a company of legends straight from the forgotten nightspots of the 1950s, the western bars of the East End and the studios of Channel 10: Michèle Richard, Ti-Gusse and Ti-Mousse, Léo Rivest, La Poune, Oscar Thiffault, Jacques "Patof" Desrosiers, Paolo Noël, Marcel Martel and his daughter Renée, Bobby Hachey, and Willie Lamothe, Olivier "Ti-Zoune" Guimond, flanked, even in this fake resurrection, by his straight man with the flesh-eating grin, Denis Drouin, the real crook of the collection. There was Raoul Bonnard with his thick mug as deeply grooved as a winter tire. All of them were immortalized by the primitive brushwork of the same untalented hack, up there between two humming female singers, two dirty jokes, and two below-the-belt one-liners.

You could ponder for a long time the size of the tabs that these canvases represented, given in payment while the artist waited for his next UI cheque. Could it be that this permanent exhibition, a sort of Pantheon of the Poor, had replaced the old autographed photographs of local punch-drunk boxers, of Rocket Richard and Jackie Robinson, who once played for the Montreal Royals, a farm team for the Dodgers, in the park next to the tavern? They were the immortals of a nation that had forgotten how to amuse itself. Guardians in charge of watching over this lugubrious collection of horse-piss drinkers and compulsively drugged players of electronic strawberry-banana-kiwi combos that formed Chez Lavigueur's faithful clientele.

In the mid-1980s, the small band of university types who migrated here once a week after Branlequeue's lectures on Hubert Aquin and the Revolution had, as the weeks went on, successfully passed all the stages of tacit acceptance necessary to be admitted to the inner circle of the tavern's largely proletariat clientele. These sessions took place on Tuesdays. They arrived on foot, passing en route such monuments to popular patrimony as the scrap man, the treasure-hunter, the Panet Tavern, placed like obstacles on the course to middle-classism. Not to mention the sawn-off hookers hanging out on every street corner.

There was no membership, attendance was informal and spontaneous, based on individual interests and a desire to share truth. The Octobeerists' format was therefore identical, in a way, to that of every revolutionary *indépendantiste* group active in the 1960s. A stable solar system gravitated around Chevalier Branlequeue: Alexis, the little comic destined to make stacks of money under the name Alexis-the-Man-of-Rubber, Humorist; Alexander, the cursed, trigger-happy poet who drank like a fish, got all the women, and was the future soul of the Group Alexandersen, of piercing and painful memory; Frédéric Falardeau, a.k.a. Fred, who was working on a great Joycean novel that absorbed him to such an extent that he ended up being transformed into the spitting image of *A Portrait of the Artist as a Young Man*. And there was Samuel Nihilo.

Women seemed condemned to remain at the periphery of the circle, assigned the role of simple observers, mainly because they (though not their clothing) were invisible as far as Chevalier Branlequeue was concerned. He quite simply ignored them. Among such creatures, Dogsbody's spouse exhibited a kind of misogyny that looked a lot like distraction; their simple presence was something to which he seemed completely oblivious.

Another explanation for the fragile and provisional status of female students who risked turning up at Lavigueur's (they usually lasted about three weeks) had to do with the very nature of the themes of the meetings: if the October Crisis in Quebec was going to accommodate the rising and powerful feminist ideology over the next decade, then women, in this male-dominated milieu, would have to develop their own idea of liberty, just as the Senegalese and Algerians driven to disaster by their colonizers resurrected the holy spirit of democracy on the battlefields of Europe. But you had to ask the complex question about how many human females were really interested in the secret services, outside of Mata Hari, femmes fatales (most often Russian), and other Bond Girls, whose roles were assigned to them by tradition. "No doubt we are dealing here," Branlequeue remarked, "with one of the last authentic private hunting reserves of the male condition."

Chevalier opened each session by tapping several times on the table with some object of his choice, brought from his home for the occasion: a cap pistol, an authentic Mohawk tomahawk, and even, once, a coyote femur. The agenda was, as a general rule, chaotic to a fault; the president of the assembly was elected according to the principle of deepest pockets, and sticklers for procedural refinements had to content themselves with Moron's Rules of Order. Example: the adoption of the meeting's agenda was carried more often by raising a glass than by raising a hand.

"What you are holding in your hands," Branlequeue announced, his voice quivering slightly as he passed around photocopies of a press clipping made on the department's Xerox machine, "is an article from the *Montreal Sun* dated November 25, 1970. I'll give you a moment to read it."

KEY WITNESS DETAINED

SECRET FLQ MEETING HELD ON NIGHT OF NOVEMBER 3–4

BY PAUL CHARLEBOIS

The two FLQ cells claiming responsibility for the kidnapping of British diplomat John Travers and Minister of Public Works Paul Lavoie joined forces on the night of November 3 to hold a meeting that went on until the early hours of the following day, two reliable sources have separately informed a *Sun* reporter.

The accuracy of the information already furnished by these two sources, as well as their professional honesty, have never been questioned.

"The man who organized the get-together remains in custody," revealed one of the sources.

"He has already given a statement, and we didn't learn very much, but we do know that he still has a lot to tell us. And he doesn't know that we know.

"We're holding him for now in isolation from numerous other individuals who have been detained as witnesses.

"He now believes that we have no other questions for him. And that's precisely what we want him to think.

"But at the proper time we'll bring him back into Court, where he'll have to answer to some pretty direct questioning.

"He won't be expecting that. We're going to surprise him by getting him to lower his guard, and he'll confirm everything we already know.

"Such a corroboration of all the facts already in our possession will be very, very useful to us.

"The only problem is that we have to wait for a while before putting him on the witness stand. But we can't help that, for reasons that, when they are able to be known, will be self-evident," affirmed one of the sources.

"We've made mistakes so far. No investigation is perfect. But we are at the point of making up for lost time," added the second source.

Information furnished by these two separate and well-placed sources is to the effect that the man (AKA "the liaison man") who originated the meeting of the two FLQ cells (the Rébellion Cell in the case of Mr. Travers and the Chevalier

Cell in that of Mr. Lavoie) was so designated by FLQ members trained in Jordan.

"We have reason to believe that the terrorists trained in Jordan are not presently residing in Canada, but that they keep in contact with their Montreal organizations. How they do that exactly we can't say," said one of the sources.

"We know the identities of the two FLQ men in training in Jordan, but the time is not ripe for us, that is to say, Canada, to go to the Middle East to look for two men, important though those two men be," confided the second source.

"We have no assurance that Mr. Travers is still alive. What we do know, however, is that there are important frictions between the two cells.

"Of the two groups that have taken hostages, one is radically opposed to the infliction of the death penalty, no matter who would be involved: them, or their hostage," added the source.

Chevalier let his glance sweep around the table.

"Those who understand what's going on here, raise your hand ..."

One of them picked up the pitcher of beer. Another cracked his knuckles.

"Now," Chevalier continued, "we're going to do a textual analysis. In literature, what is the very first question we always ask?"

"Who's doin' the talkin'?" said the big guy, Alexis.

"The identity of the narrator," Chevalier agreed, imperturbable. Eyes sparkling, he took a drink and put his glass back on the table.

"I've not been able to trace this Charlebois whose name appears above the piece, but he seems to practise an odd kind of journalism. At first glance his article is a tissue of anonymous quotes and allusions that are quite shocking for the pages of a reputable publication. So, what's the next question to be asked?"

"Point of view," said Fred Falardeau.

"And whose point of view are we getting here?"

"That of the two sources," replied Fred and Alexander in unison, the latter slightly out of sync thanks to the two glasses of beer he'd poured and drunk for every one taken by his companions. He was beginning to show signs of being seriously tanked.

"And who are they, do we know?"

"Unidentified Canadian officials," risked Samuel Nihilo, placing his finger on the sheet of paper and drawing his neighbours' attention to the eighth line from the bottom: " ... us, that is to say Canada ..."

"Officials, or perhaps ... unofficials," Chevalier observed with a smile. "Okay, let's look at the characters. What do we know about this so-called liaison man?"

"We know who he is," Fred said. "François Langlais, alias Pierre. It's in the Lavergne Report. Page 53, I think ... And, in fact, the episode of the meeting on November 4 is extremely well known. It's mentioned in about three or four reports. And the name Pierre came up at the coroner's inquest. ... The real question is, why did these sources say he was detained in November 1970, when it's known that he was not arrested before his departure for Cuba?"

Fred drew the looks of mild hatred always levelled at those at the top of the class. In the battlefield of sheer intellectual virtuosity, he and Samuel engaged in a muted competition for the Master's approval that was no less ferocious for being subtle. Le Frotteur and Alexander were several rungs below them on the ladder leading to such emulation.

"Yes, the mysterious Pierre Chevrier," Branlequeue agreed. "The childhood friend of Richard Godefroid, and his companion during a trip to France. The most discreet of all the FLQers, from what we can gather. I think I'll assign one of you to come next week with a complete dossier on this guy ... Sam?"

"Okay, I'm on it."

"We must also turn our attention to two other important characters in this little unhistorical history," Chevalier continued. "You've no doubt guessed that I'm talking about the two fellows who went to Jordan to train with Palestinians from the Popular Democratic Front for the Liberation of Palestine in August of 1970. The Algerian option. Code names: Zadig and Madwar. Both were graduates of Collège Sainte-Marie, the precursor to UQAM, and therefore they had the same alma mater as you, in a way. You're practically brothers-at-arms. Does anyone wish to continue?"

Frédéric raised his hand.

"They were found near Javesh, in Jordan, by the journalist Yves Lépine when he was writing an investigative report of the FDPLP training camp in the middle of the desert. They let themselves be interviewed and used the occasion to announce that a campaign of selective assassinations was to be carried out in Quebec. As far as I know, the *Sun* article was the first to suggest a possible link between the famous fedayeen in the FLQ and the Travers–Lavoie affair."

"Excellent . . . really, excellent," murmured Chevalier. "My dear Fred, you will report back on these weird fedayeen and their mysterious delegation to Algeria."

Falardeau and Nihilo exchanged smiles above the empty pitcher. Chevalier, at the head of the table, embraced the group with his beneficent regard, like a scholar from Greek antiquity.

Falardeau, apparently having decided to deliver the *coup de grâce*, raised his hand once again.

"Yes, Fred?"

"This Charlebois, it's beginning to come back to me . . . he collaborated with the police. His double game was revealed by a commission of enquiry in the seventies. He was an officer in the Reserves, with connections to military intelligence."

"Better and better." Branlequeue beamed appreciatively. "Good. I think we deserve another round after that . . ."

As always, the tone mounted slowly, the voices became thicker, the discussions grew more heated, more chaotic, the entire table seeming to dance on a thin line between scandal and genius.

Taking advantage of the fact that he was still reasonably sober, Branlequeue refilled his glass and resumed control of the seminar.

"In this newspaper article there is probably more mystery and human drama than in a dozen pages of Shakespeare. The text you hold in your hands reveals a few things, but it hides a few things from us as well. In fact, it hides as much as it reveals. The mask betrays its real function: it shows us the very thing it would hide from us..."

The Octobeerists hung on his every word.

"We are literary scholars. Our vocation is to decode texts. And it is my belief that this strange example of prose contains the key to many of our preoccupations. Read it again carefully, keeping in mind that the police controlled a great many journalists. Their exaggerated overstatements are the oil in a machine that creates atmosphere and fabricates public opinion. We are looking for the subtext, the infrastory.... We should read it as if we were defusing a bomb, opposing our intelligence to theirs. Disinformation is nothing less than the bastard child of the union of literature and publicity. In brief, we are swimming in a pool of semiotics, my friends. The text that you have before you may well be a kind of minor masterpiece..."

"Maybe, but in any case it isn't addressed to me!"

Everyone turned to Marie-Québec, who was sitting at the opposite end of the table, the only hanger-on to have turned up that day.

"Excuse me?" asked Chevalier.

Marie-Québec squirmed in her seat, then leaned forward.

"All I said was that I didn't understand a word of it. And for a very good reason: because it wasn't written for me. That's obvious."

Fred turned toward Chevalier:

"The question of the intended reader ..."

Chevalier, pensive, nodded silently. As for the young woman, a first-year drama student, she was so uncomfortable with all the looks she was receiving that she did her best to be forgotten again, and at the first opportunity she put on her coat and fled to the door.

Sam let the silence continue for a few seconds, and when the meeting erupted once again in a contained euphoria of cackles and crazy laughter, he took his own leave.

Stepping out onto the sidewalk, he saw her hurrying through the rain, making her getaway, perfectly discreetly, as untheatrical an exit as anyone could want, he thought. Then, seized by a sudden impulse, he almost ran after her, but changed his mind and let her go.

VILLA GRANDE SECTOR, ITALY, 1943

THE COMPANY HOLDING THE position had established its advanced command post in the carcass of a tank that had driven over a mine. The message came over the radio in the middle of a German counterattack: machine gun almost out of ammunition. Bédard, the brigadier-general, ordered two cases of cartridges to be loaded onto a donkey and two men to go with it. *Poor beast,* he thought as he watched them leave, *nothing of what's happening here is its fault.* But when he thought about it, that was the case with them, too, wasn't it? With each shell that exploded, they could see the donkey stiffen, plant its hooves in the ground, and flatten its big ears, and the two men had to pull it harder each time to get it to move, one pulling, the other pushing from behind to take up the slack. The rest were able to follow their progress from a distance thanks to the Boche flares that kept going up and coming down, slowly burning themselves out above the incredible confusion of battle, the close combat, sometimes at point-blank range in thick shadow saturated by explosions and lights, tracer bullets, and the smell of gunpowder and burnt flesh, the dry rattle of the machine gun still holding its position, and the muffled sigh of mortars followed by the exhalation of shells and the shaking of the earth all around. Halfway to the machine gun's position, the donkey stepped on a mine.

A huge orange geyser filled with bits of donkey and steel rose from the ground into the illuminated night. Clots of earth and sharp explosions were still peppering the roof of the shelter when the brigadier-general's voice resumed yelling — "Stretcher-bearers!" — as though he really expected anything in that heap to be still alive. A stretcher-bearer, identifiable by the red cross on his arm-band, grabbed one end of the stretcher and caught his colleague's eye. The colleague nodded, and it was clear they were thinking the same thing. They set off at a light trot, leaning forward, heads drawn down as far as possible into their shoulders, in the direction of the cloud of sulphurous dust that filled the entire space ahead of them and was spreading slowly over the battlefield and into their lungs until there was nothing else to breathe where they were. Their route looked impossibly long to them as the mortars continued to explode, making the mud quiver around the bombed-out assault vehicle below them. At the spot where the donkey and the two men had last been seen was an enormous crater into which they almost fell, smoke rising out of it as from a huge volcanic mouth that had been hidden from view. They crawled into it and began their search. By patting the ground ahead of them in the darkness, they came up with several bits of skin, three or four pieces of donkey hide, and one hoof. That was it.

Meanwhile, the situation on the hill had become critical, and the brigadier-general ordered the men to make a second attempt. When the stretcher-bearers appeared at the shelter with their empty stretcher, they were met by General Bédard, hands on hips, standing as straight as an I. "Where are the wounded?" he thundered. "Up in smoke," came the reply. But the man who made it could see that this response was not going to make the brigadier-general's day. Surely he wasn't going to send them back in there? He hadn't even had time to formulate that thought before he felt himself being grabbed by one arm, and before he could understand what was happening he had been turned precipitously around and, still clutching the stretcher, was doing his best to avoid a series of swift kicks to his backside delivered by the brigadier-general. "Follow me!" cried the latter, and he meant it, overtaking the two men and leading them back into hell. They could see the general's gigantic silhouette rising up out of the smoke at the lip of the crater, hands on his thighs like a tourist peering over the edge of a cliff. The scene was illuminated by the flares and explosions that continued to rain down around them. When they saw their commanding officer doing their work, the stretcher-bearers felt foolish and began to look around as well, groping their way through the burning shadows in a kind of frenzy. They found one of the men ten feet away, missing two legs and an arm; blood was spurting in huge, burbling jets from the stump.

The brigadier-general came up to them. One of the stretcher-bearers, who was on his knees beside the body, looked up and shook his head: dead. "Are you quite certain of that?" shouted Bédard. Just at that moment there was a momentary lull in the roar of battle, and the man who had just been declared dead opened his eyes and said: "Not sure ... I'm quite dead yet ... commander."

They put a tourniquet on him, then hoisted him onto the stretcher, and while they were doing so the general found the other soldier a few feet away, in no better shape than his fellow soldier. The general lifted him across his shoulders like a sack of potatoes. And so they headed off into the night, completely soaked in blood from the stumps of the half-dead man who, admittedly, was easier to carry because he was missing two or three limbs. Whenever the pair at either end of the stretcher stumbled with their load over bomb holes, the good general found some way to keep them going. If anyone had predicted that night that the two donkey attendants would make it, he would have been laughed out of the regiment. But that's what happened: they both survived, costing the government a fortune in prostheses.

In the 22nd regiment this story was often told. It was like a glorious wreath around the brow of the regiment and its mythic commander, to show to the lowliest orderly stationed in Cyprus what sort of stuff Brigadier-General Jean-B. Bédard was made of.

DORA OF THE JUST

SAMUEL WAITED FOR MARIE-QUÉBEC in the Lavigueur Tavern, sitting at a table near the window. When he looked up from his beer, he recognized the portrait of Raoul Bonnard, the former comic and crooner, the Channel 10 man, his face swollen like that of an overstuffed gargoyle covered with make-up that cracked when he smiled. Powder-blue suit, red bow tie, white chrysanthemum in his lapel. Thick Brylcreemed hair of a dubious colour. Le Bonnard from the heyday of cabaret.

Across the street, between two tattoo parlours, was a pile of boards and rubble that had once been a Hells Angels hangout before it was destroyed by a car bomb. Just to the left was the window of a pawnshop, a favourite with the local petty thieves, and a store selling old clothes whose owner, wearing his perpetual cowboy hat, lit a candle for Kurt Cobain every day in the church next door, which had been taken over by Latinos. At the corner, the masculine silhouette of a homeless person spun like a top at each passing car.

"Hey! Psst..."

Sam raised his eyes to the king of entertainment's painted mug, looked around, and then looked back at the painting. He hadn't been mistaken: Raoul Bonnard had indeed tried to attract his attention. Above the bow tie, his bloated face resembling the physiognomy of Thing, one of the Fantastic Four superheroes, softened suddenly and spread into a sly, astonishing smile.

"How's it goin' there, young fella?"

Samuel looked around again, then back at the portrait.

"Are you talking to me?"

"No, I'm talkin' to the wall. Hey, kid! What do you call a Negro buried in the sand with his ass in the air?"

"No idea."

"A bicycle rack!"

Samuel looked quickly over at the waiter.

"Mr. Bonnard...that's not funny at all."

"Maybe not, but you got a face on you like a bloodhound with a head cold. How come you're sittin' here fuckin' the dog all by yourself?"

"I'm waiting for a woman."

Raoul leaned out of the canvas and gave him a twenty-four-carat wink accompanied by a truly lecherous grin.

"*Attaboy*! What're you drinking there, my son? Scotch? Cutty Sark?"

"Why not make it turpentine? What are you trying to do, kill me?"

Then Samuel gave a start: the waiter had come up to his table and was looking at him curiously.

"A Cutty Sark," said Sam.

Marie-Québec ordered an apricot beer. The waiter gave her an uncomprehending look, and Sam went to her rescue.

"I'd be surprised if they have that here."

"Okay, I'll have a Belle Gueule, then."

The waiter still didn't move.

"They don't have Quebec beers, either," Sam whispered.

Looking up, she favoured the waiter with a forced smile that seemed the essence of charm.

"Right. Got it. I'll have a draft."

"Excellent choice, Mademoiselle," said the waiter, before he moved away.

Sam asked Marie-Québec a few questions about her work. She had just spent two weeks in Montreal filming a couple of scenes from *The Just* and was leaving the next day. When Sam asked her what character she was playing, she realized he hadn't read the play. She supposed she might have been playing the Grand Duchess, but did she really have the kind of head that would be a Grand Duchess?

She tried to sound Samuel out on the character of Dora.

"I'll have to reread the play," he told her.

"Because you've already read it?"

"Oh, sure I have. Camus, a must-read."

The lie didn't convince her and they both knew it. The conversation trailed off. After a moment, Marie-Québec got up and went to the bathroom.

"Hey!"

Samuel looked up at the painting.

"Yes, Raoul..."

"Nice piece of ass. Play your cards right and it'll take you three, maybe four sentences to get her from here to your bed."

"I'm not completely obsessed with sex, if that's what you think."

"Yeah, go tell that to someone else, I ain't buyin' it. And stop tryin' to make her think you've read all them French philosophers. Keep that up and she'll be out of here in ten minutes flat."

"No, she won't, Raoul. She's an actress ..."

"Yeah, I've known a few actresses in my time. They don't get lips like that from suckin' lemons."

"What do you think of her? I mean, seriously?"

"Well, to be honest, I prefer blondes with bigger tits. And I gotta ask myself what she's got against high heels. But listen, she's got a nice little heart-shaped ass on her, and ever since she got here she's been tryin' to rub up against your knees under the table, so I'd say ..."

"What's with the knees?"

"Yeah, keep playin' the innocent. What d'ya think she's doin' in there? Crossword puzzles? She's gonna come back with her face all made up and perfume on her, and then we'll see what kind of stuff you're made of, my man."

"Marie-Québec isn't like that."

"Hey, listen up, Happy Face. I'm advising you to take my advice, otherwise you ain't gonna get nowhere."

"Dream on!"

"Yeah, well, what else can I do, jump into a cab? You gotta score for both of us ..."

From the corner of his eye Sam saw the young woman in question coming back. Walking silently in her running shoes, she moved with a graceful modesty and simplicity that could not have been put on, even though her self-assurance and a certain tightness in her gestures spoke of effort and self-consciousness. Sam imagined the former stars of the music-hall stage, like Denis Drouin and Ti-Zoune Gimond, salivating as she walked past their portraits.

He cast a final glance at the painting. The old straight man gave him a spicy eyeful, the whole Bonnardian gamut. The facial equivalent of an all-dressed with extra anchovies.

The last thing I read of Camus's ..."

Samuel stopped himself. Bonnard, from his frame, was holding his head in both hands.

"What's going on?" Marie-Québec asked.

"Nothing. The last thing I read of Camus's was his defence of Don Juan in *The Myth of Sisyphus*."

"Oh? And what did Camus think of Don Juan?"

"First, he was a pretty good Don Juan himself. By which I mean he was someone who knew he was mortal and believed in holiness down here."

"And is that what you are? A Don Juan?'

"Not yet. But I'm working on it."

"Not very hard, from what I can see."

"When I was fifteen, I wanted to be an engineer. At twenty, a biologist. At twenty-five, a writer. But when I turned thirty, I really understood what I wanted to do with my life. It was Don Juan or nothing."

"Well, in my case I didn't get off to much of a start."

"But you're an actress. Your goal in life is to seduce."

"No. My goal is to change the world."

"I don't believe it. You've been put on earth to give pleasure. Changing the world, that's something else altogether. You need an AK-47 for that."

"What's an AK-47?"

"An assault weapon. Soviet made."

"So you're a nihilist."

"I may well be."

"It's people like Dora who change the world. With their love. And me, when I'm being her."

"I adore Dora."

"But you don't know her."

"I've read the play. But it was a long time ago."

"If ever. And you haven't read *The Myth of Sisyphus*, either."

To prove to her that he had, Samuel launched into a long harangue about reconciling the Casanova and the actor/actress in the Camusian absurd, which quickly embroiled him in a web of conflicting ideas, a total cerebral miasma in which, in the end, every possible position was abolished by its opposite, and from which he extracted himself only in time to see the young woman stand up and hold out her hand.

"I think I'd best be gone."

Samuel looked at her hand with a stupid expression on his face. He took it with as much enthusiasm as if it was a venomous snake or a baited marten trap.

"Are you staying here?" she asked him.

Fully aware of the immeasurable inanity of the only word that he could bring to his lips, he said it anyway.

"Yes."

She gave him a fixed look, turned on her heel, and left.

"Bravo."

"Not you again."

"My boy, it's not as though it's your face on the marquee, you know what I mean? You gotta work at it a bit!"

"I'm socio-affectively maladapted, is that what you're saying?"

"Look, that wasn't a pole she was handing you when she left, it was a whole goddamn Hydro-Québec pylon. What are you waiting for? Get off your ass and run after her. I'll pick up the tab."

"Thanks, Raoul ..." Sam murmured as he jumped to his feet.

When he emerged onto the street, he had to run barely thirty metres to catch up with Marie-Québec at the next corner, apparently waiting for someone. She looked up at him.

"Do you want me to come with you?"

Here I am, sitting at the kitchen table nibbling at the heel of a baguette and reading, for the third time, a paragraph in an article by Réal "Real Life" Poirier on the Pavlovian Saga — Sergei Pavlov, the hockey player that is, the Red Light, the Russian Missile, recently acquired by the Montreal Canadiens, and whose mysterious upper-thigh injury and his eight-million-dollar-a-year contract are the hot topics of the day. In a few seconds the coffeepot on one of the burners on the stove is going to explode. Through the open bedroom door, I can see her stretched out on the bed, at the foot of which the rumpled sheets make a kind of elongated lump, and I think: cat. She has that suppleness of body, nervous and languid at the same time. And I remember when I entered her last night and again this morning the sound that escaped from her lips and her chest could only be described as a growl. The impression of having spent the night fucking a cat, and having shared enough secrets to last a thousand years, and of not having felt this good since Christ knows when.

"What do you want to do later?"

"I'm almost thirty years old. This *is* later."

"I mean in your life. By today's standards, you're still an adolescent."

"I want to live alone, in a cabin, in the woods. In voluntary simplicity and truth. That's it."

"But that's no ambition for a young woman like yourself..."

"What's an ambition for a young woman like myself? To be celibate?"

"Among other things."

"And why is living in a cabin not a legitimate ambition? Too difficult?"

"Yes, for a woman living alone."

"But if it's so difficult, is it not therefore a legitimate ambition?"

"You have a point."

"And to be celibate, is that difficult or isn't it?"

"Not so difficult, it would seem. But all right, I just can't see you doing it."

"Doing what? Living alone in a cabin or being celibate?"

"Both."

"You don't have enough imagination."

"And you, you have absolutely zero ambition."

"I do what I can. I'm in a play in Abitibi."

"Dora. That's a really nice name."

She had a small, striped kitten inside her that growled when he opened her up and brought her to the end of herself and raised her up like a feather a fountain a full moon, and it became her gravitas, her risen rose.

The Mazda, or Colt, or Corolla pulled up behind a taxi in front of the bus station on rue Berri, and Samuel put on the four-ways. He turned to Marie-Québec, who was huddled in her winter coat.

"Funny, but I have the feeling that what I'm going to say now is bound to sound stupid, not that it matters."

"Ha!"

"What does that mean?"

"It means you don't have to say anything."

"No, I know. See you soon?"

"I don't think so."

"No? Why not?

"You see, I was about to say that if you wanted to see me again you would drive me to where I'm going, but of course that's crazy."

"You mean . . ."

"Yes, up there."

"How far is it?"

"Seven hundred kilometres. But I was kidding."

"Seven hundred kilometres from Montreal to Maldoror."

"It's not far."

From where he was sitting, by stretching his neck a bit he could see a small piece of the Judith-Jasmin Building. If he worked at it, he could probably pick out the window of the office in which he'd been sorting papers a few days earlier.

"I've got a lot of work waiting for me. A pile of things to do . . . Research . . ."

"It was a joke, okay?"

He managed a smile.

"One of these days, though. Why not?"

"You just said that because you felt you had to."

"I didn't say it like that."

"You even said *that* like that."

"Hang on, I'll park a bit farther up."

"No. Don't bother."

He watched her get out, her large backpack trailing in her hand. A homeless man dressed like a lumberjack held the door for her and bowed as she went into the station, as if she were a princess.

At five in the morning he was listening to the Chinese couple quarrelling in the next apartment while he took four crackers at a time out of the box and stuffed them into his mouth. He chewed the dry purée while standing on one foot in the morning light, remembering Marie-Québec perched, rather than sitting, on the sofa chair he'd inherited from his grandfather, and that she'd dragged over to the sliding glass doors in order to catch the first light of day coming in from the alley, naked, her knees drawn up to her chin, letting her body soak in the sun's warmth as naturally as the pot of herbs on the neighbour's balcony. And the perfect curve of her breasts, their self-assured line, the way they pointed toward the sun like phototropic fruit. The delicate, precise outline of her darkly pink nipples, as if they'd been carved from coral.

He remembered the way she talked about a film or a play, un-ravelling the narrative without paying the slightest attention to the main dramatic line. She would pick a thread and pull on it, and a single episode would go off in a dozen directions at once. She put works of genius and complete dogs through the same mill, Lelouch and Fellini, treat them all the same, and have them come out totally indistinguishable from one another.

He surprised himself by smiling at the memory, his lips frosted with white soda-biscuit dust.

He called the lawyer, Mario Brien, the next day. The preacher fa-mous for his fire-and-brimstone defences seemed much less dis-posed toward writers than his cop friend had been. Sam never got a word in edgewise. The conversation left him feeling like he'd gone three rounds with George Foreman in his heyday. When he heard the phone go dead at the other end of the line, he realized he had just let himself be harangued like a stinking fish for twenty min-utes and that Brien, apparently a pathological motormouth and a consummate artist at drowning out the opposition, hadn't made a single reference to the antiterrorist squad or to the deliverer of the chicken. Hurling a string of insults at his interlocutor, he said he was doubly bound, not only by the pact of silence he'd made with the members of the Chevalier Cell, but also by his professional oath, and that's the way it is, monsieur, and so I'm going to hang up now without wishing you good luck or good day or good anything.

Samuel was depressed for a day and a half after the call. He finally decided that feeling sorry for himself wasn't going to get him anywhere, so he made some coffee and sat back down at his desk. He took a sheet of paper and wrote "pact of silence" on it.

The next day, he went to the public library and took out *The Just*, a play in three acts by Albert Camus.

AN EVENING IN THE COUNTRY

IN HIS DREAM, THE RINGING telephone was the alarm that sounded the general alert in the Parthenais Prison. He'd climbed up a ventilation shaft and was standing on the prison roof, the village illuminated at his feet. Then he grabbed a rope of knotted sheets and, with its aid, started to lower himself hand over hand down to rue Fullum.

Instead of which he woke up at the bottom of the bed, tangled in a different set of sheets. His own. Foolish man, thought Chevalier Branlequeue. He was thirty-eight years old, his children were asleep, the news program had ended hours ago, and the pulsating, sonorous heap under the sheets beside him was La Grosse Éléonore.

It was December 28, 1970. Chevalier was wide awake and the bloody phone was still ringing. He struggled to untangle himself, managed to get his feet onto the carpet beside the bed, stood up,

137

and left the bedroom, heading toward the telephone table at the end of the hall. It was a black contraption, fitted with a round dial made of clear moulded plastic and a handset that had bulges shaped like shower heads at each end. It was a time when the only function required of a telephone was that it convey the human voice from one location to another. He picked up.

"Chevalier? Prosecutor Grosleau here. Sorry if I've disturbed you..."

"My dear sir, do you have any idea what time it is?"

"What time it is, no. What time it might be, yes."

Chevalier had to admire the classical education that could impart such linguistic exactitude. Grosleau represented the Crown in the coroner's inquest into the Lavoie Affair.

"I took the liberty of waking you," added the man at the other end of the line, "because your presence, so I am informed, is required in the Valley of the Patriots."

"Where's that?"

"In Saint-Marc-sur-Richelieu. Where the three sparrows that everyone has been looking for have been found hiding like rats at the end of a kind of tunnel. Corporal Huet is there."

"I see. But why is my presence required?"

"They've asked for you ... They are in the midst of negotiations, as I understand it. They have been attempting to agree on a mediator, and it seems your name has been put on the table. You are the government's concession to the FLQ, Chevalier. And they need to make it, because yours is going to be the only name that will come up."

"Mr. Grosleau, you're an intelligent man, surely you're not going to drag up that business of..."

"Of a supposed link between the author of *Elucubrations* and the Chevalier Cell? Come on, you have the right to a family name. Not even the police think the Lafleur brothers would be low enough to compromise you so callously. We know our Quebec history. We know that Chevalier de Lorimier was the notary with the hemp tie. Are you reassured?"

"Somewhat."

"But we also know that you had at least two of these dangerous terrorists in your class at Saint-Ernest. And that, when you were running as an independent in the 1970 elections, we know whose campaign they worked on."

"You are well informed."

"Does that surprise you?"

"I'd be lying if I said it did."

"I don't have the authority to force you to go."

"I know."

"But you're the one they want, Chevalier . . . The train of history has been set in motion and it's stopping at your station. The lives of three men hang in the balance, not to mention that as a writer you'd be a damned fool to pass up this opportunity! They're surrounded. It's all over. And they want to give themselves up with honour and dignity, which is where you come in, my friend."

"Saint Marc," said Chevalier. "Is that the port next to . . ."

"Take a cab to the Parthenais Prison. We'll put a driver at your disposal. Can I count on you? Not a word to anyone?"

"My lips are sealed."

"Good. Oh, and, er, Chevalier . . ."

"What?"

"Don't forget to get a receipt for the cab."

He'd published *Elucubrations* the previous spring. Despite obvious references to Lamartine, Hugo, and Rimbaud, the book was neither a collection of poems nor a novel nor an essay, but contained elements of all three genres, appearing in the form of an epic divided into a series of stanzas, like the poems of Homer. He blended in historical material as if the book were so much soup in a pot. The Rebellion of 1837–38 was his Trojan War, and Madeleine de Verchères his Helen.

When critics criticized his title for, as they believed, making light of his topic, Chevalier referred them to his dear Monsieur Littré: *Noun. Feminine. 1. Nightwork, the cost of such work. 2. A work requiring great effort and long nights. He presented us with his* Elucubrations.

Take that!

His real name was Laurent Chevalier. Chevalier Branlequeue was the pen name under which he had published his book, and the sobriquet had stuck. He didn't know it yet, but his book would represent a turning point in his career. The bulk of the second part of the manuscript for *Elucubrations* had taken off in October, and he was still working on it. And at the start of the year, during the worst of the parody of a trial that placed Richard Godefroid and Jean-Paul Lafleur in the shadow of the gibbet, Branlequeue, who had been awarded the Didace-Beauchemin Prize for *Elucubrations*, took advantage of this recognition and the media attention that came with it to ring the conspiracy-theory bell on the events of October.

"The Lavoie Affair," as Premier Albert Vézina would call it a few years later when speaking to a group of journalists close to the sources of power, "is our Kennedy mystery . . ." And it was Chevalier Branlequeue who was the first to sow that theoretical seed in the fertile soil of October 1970. The Didace-Beauchemin reception, with twenty years still to go in his after-lecture drinking bouts in the Faculty of Farts and Unopened Letters (another Branlequeueism), was the founding act of the Octobeerists.

"So, you gonna beat the shit out of those FLQ fuckers?"

The taxi driver thinks I'm a cop, Branlequeue thought.

The announcement of his destination had been followed by a heavy silence filled with innuendo.

"I can't say," replied Chevalier, both because he had to play the game, but also because he really didn't know.

"If it was up to me, I'd line the fuckers up against a wall and shoot the whole lot of them."

Chevalier was aware that this man was speaking for the silent majority, that he was expressing a widely held opinion. When the body of Paul Lavoie was recovered, police stations around the province were inundated with calls from people who had jumped to the phone to denounce a neighbour or a friend or a brother-in-law, most of whom had been guilty of nothing more than having hair a bit longer than the norm. And it wasn't only for the $150,000 reward. Hatred of longhairs, of threats to established order, had reached a fever pitch that coincided with the military presence in the streets. Even normally right-thinking people felt the threat. A publisher friend of Chevalier's, a man from France, spoke openly to him about a "purge." He recognized the mood.

From the Jacques-Cartier Bridge he could see the brightly lit city smoking under the snow. Chevalier thought of the nights of his youth, the book launches, the poems written at dawn on the corners of restaurant tables and read to the room while standing on a chair. Of the little politico-cultural world of the metropolis, now bludgeoned by the October Crisis. The luckiest ones had been thrown into prison early and released after a few days into the arms of a sympathetic Left, with a certificate of good revolutionary conduct that would follow them to the grave. The others did what they could. Two and a half months later, they could say to themselves: the deployment of troops in this beloved city was like siccing a vicious dog on militants and intellectuals of all stripes.

These days, Chevalier spent his time reading, correcting, and editing the work of people he knew, resented, or envied, to the detriment of his own writing. His children ate up the rest of his time. He had to believe that he'd done his best to be a good father, the best he knew how. At night, instead of shutting himself up in his office and pecking away at a manuscript while smoking Sweet Caps and sipping two fingers of scotch, he'd plunked himself down in front of the TV with the family and crammed his head full of beer commercials and the jokes of Marcel Gamache like a normal human, secretly disgusted with himself, the magnificent loser.

Most nights, but not tonight . . . The Parthenais Prison that welcomed the poet-publisher this night at the end of 1970 was no longer the heavily armed Bastille it had been in mid-October. Once he paid off the taxi driver, he walked into the prison as if into a mill.

"You came in by the main gate," the guard said, recognizing him.

"True. No more need for handcuffs. Now when they call for me I come running . . . wagging my tail behind me!"

He laughed heartily.

Behind his grille, the guard was reading a comic, paying no more attention to Chevalier than a receptionist at a resort in the off-season.

"You should put a 'Vacancy' sign on the door," the visitor joked.

"No kidding. Or we could organize a raid on someone, to fill up the cells."

"Really? What about the five hundred you rounded up in the fall?"

"Ah, that was different. We had our checklist, eh? Like those birdologists have."

"*Or*nithologists."

"Whatever. Where did you learn to roll your Rs like that?"

"From an old priest. I'm from Sainte-Anne-de-la-Pérade."

"Where they catch them little fish?"

"The same."

"I went there with my brother-in-law one time. We caught eight hundred fish in one night."

"Even better than the War Measures Act."

The driver was waiting for him in the car, a burly, plain-clothes inspector from the homicide squad who had came to take him the rest of the way. Not the talkative type, he stayed behind his bulletproof window and asked Chevalier to show some ID. Chevalier patted his pockets and then spread his arms to show that he didn't have a single piece of identification on him.

"I'm Chevalier Branlequeue," he said, "the author of *Elucubrations*. At your service, but only so far ..."

"*Elucu* ... what?"

"Never mind."

On the autoroute, where there was nothing to block the wind, icy gusts sent serpentine drifts of powdery snow across the pavement, from one lane to the other.

"My mother used to say snow like that was 'as deep as a dog.'"

Until then the driver had been content to stare ahead at the road, only occasionally glancing furtively at his passenger without unclenching his teeth.

"As a *dog*?"

"Yes, deep as a dog."

The officer looked at him briefly as though to make sure he wasn't being made fun of.

"It's just an expression."

When they turned onto 223 North, the driver breezed through a red light that swung alone above the deserted intersection. He'd also ignored the lights and stop signs that had come up between the prison and the autoroute. From time to time, the radio in the unmarked vehicle began to crackle. Once or twice he palmed the transmitter and gave their position. A short-barrelled automatic rifle lay between them on the seat.

Chevalier made a fresh attempt at conversation.

"You'll probably laugh at me for saying this," he said, "but I can't think of a single illegal thing I've done in my entire life. I've been a totally boring model citizen."

"You mean that light? I've got the right to go through them, and I'm the one who's driving. So you're still okay."

"Too bad."

A quick glance from the officer, followed by more silence. Then:

"You may be a model citizen, but you were jailed anyway, on October 16."

"Yes, but that was different. In that case, it was my arrest that was illegal."

"We could debate that."

"No, come on. Dragged out into the street, handcuffs on my wrists, you have to admit it would be crazy to debate that."

"I bet you've kept a couple of trout over the limit. Slowed down too late in a thirty-mile-an-hour zone. Declared your golf bag stolen and forgot to withdraw the insurance claim when your wife found the bag at the back of your closet. Innocence is like health: it only exists until there's proof that it doesn't."

"No. I don't fish for trout: give me pan-fried tommycod any day. I don't have a driver's licence, and as for golf, I've never played it in my life. See what I mean?"

Apparently the officer saw nothing at all.

They were close to Saint-Marc. They were in a white-out. To their right, the river tumbled between woods and fields. Snow blew up onto the road over the guardrails, and the cop had to let up on the gas because of the drifting.

"So, what was Lavoie's crime?" Branlequeue asked after a moment's silence.

"You won't get me going down that road."

"Maybe not, but his death is your business. If it isn't, what do we have? An army that invades a province without evidence of a single corpse? That would make everyone look bad. You need a death. Having a body changes everything. The feds finally have their martyr, and his friends in the party in power who didn't raise a little finger to save him can give him a national funeral."

"You won't get me going down that road."

"All right. What would you say to a battlefield instead?"

"I don't see it coming to that."

Chevalier pointed out a road less obliterated by drifting snow.

"We'll see the sign announcing the ferry pretty soon. In summer it takes three minutes to get across to Saint-Charles. Where our boys were cut to ribbons by the Redcoats under General Wetherall in 1837. As soon as they were charged by a regiment of Royal Scots, and saw their bayonets glinting in the sun, most of them took off. But a good many continued to snipe away at the soldiers, and others tried to surrender, and they were all massacred. What history doesn't tell us is if the Scots were accompanied by bagpipes..."

"If there'd been bagpipes, the whole lot of them would have been scurrying for the woods."

Chevalier tried to make out the river through the snowstorm.

"I'm trying to see the church where Wetherall's men lit their huge bonfire after the victory. They celebrated long into the night, with the bodies of their enemy stacked up in front of the altar. Dozens and dozens of corpses piled up to the foot of the cross like so much cordwood. Maybe twenty survivors were kept overnight in the sacristy. The guard who watched them described the scene: they knelt in the dark, lit by a single candle, silently praying while the *Goddamns* laughed and sang in the next room. The officers ate well that night: roast chicken, fried bacon, pancakes, baked potatoes, plain bread. The English came back to the church in the morning to get rid of the corpses. They discovered that pigs had somehow got into the building and were eating the frozen bodies."

"So what'd they do?" the inspector asked after a pause.

"What do you think they did? They shot the pigs, too."

Leaning forward, the inspector strained his eyes to make out the road through the maelstrom of whirling snowflakes that dimmed the light from his headlights.

"Eaten by pigs," he murmured, thinking about it.

Chevalier turned toward him.

"Yes, pigs ate them."

The inspector stared straight ahead.

"But I don't see it coming to that."

They arrived at Saint-Marc.

A solid farmhouse was flanked by a covered shed at one end that acted as a garage and, at the other, by a monumental fieldstone chimney that loomed over them as they waded through the snow that covered the driveway. To his great surprise, Chevalier had counted only two other cars on the road. Apparently the military police had been called off.

They were welcomed at the kitchen door by Corporal Huet and Captain Claude Leclerc, head of the homicide squad. Huet and Leclerc stood on either side of Marcel Duquet, who was visibly nervous. No fire burned in the woodstove. Below them, the furnace made its usual noise. Handshakes, the stomping of boots. Captain Leclerc described the situation briefly:

"They're downstairs. We have to make them come out."

"How many men do you have here, Captain?" asked Branlequeue.

"Just the three of us," Leclerc replied.

"So there's no one downstairs keeping an eye on them?"

"No."

"You don't seem to be very afraid of them, then."

"No, that's true," said the captain.

"Strange. I'd have thought the whole sector would be sealed off. I imagined coming through cordons of soldiers to get here. You've changed tactics?"

"Don't read too much into it, Chevalier," the captain said patiently. "What you saw going down in north Montreal, when they surrounded the Lancelot Cell, that was the Armed Forces' and the Mounties' show. Up here, we're investigating a murder, that's all. We're not playing politics."

"So, in other words, now that the English are out of the country, we can go back to doing things our own way, is that it?"

"Think what you like. Come on, I'll show you where they are."

The first time the provincial police had arrived, on Christmas Day, they came in four or five cars and contented themselves with searching the house from top to bottom. The three sparrows stayed holed up in their burrow, kneeling in fifteen millimetres of ice water and smoking cigarette after cigarette. After a few hours, the police left.

The second time, the police tapped on walls and ceilings and tore into the walls of closets and partitions with picks and crowbars. They smashed chairs and gutted mattresses. While all this was going on, two officers took Duquet for a car ride into the deserted countryside. Near a small stand of trees, they made him kneel in the snow at the edge of the woods and threatened to put a bullet in his head if he didn't tell them where the three men were hiding. Duquet swore at them copiously, then clamped his teeth and brayed like a calf, but told them nothing.

The next day, Corporal Huet turned up alone at the wheel of an unmarked car. He took Duquet for another ride. Marcel was almost beginning to get used to it. This time, Huet parked at the end of a dead-end road. In front of them, the snow-covered fields stretched to the horizon, marked here and there by sugar bushes as regularly as in a geometrical pattern. The wind howled around the vague shapes of buildings in the snowfields.

"Marcel," the corporal said quietly, "we know they're in there."

"How do you know that?"

While the corporal thought about it, he saw a snowy owl perched on a fence post a hundred feet away.

"We tapped your phone line, my friend. You don't believe me? When you talked to your mistress about your 'cousins,' you must have thought we were imbeciles."

Huet cast another glance at the immaculate raptor, immobile on its post. From this close he could make out the owl's cold, yellow eyes. The corporal had excellent vision. At training camp, he'd regularly placed nineteen of twenty shots in the bull's eye.

"And that's not all, Marcel, my boy. One night when you were out, the boys took a look around your house, and they noticed that even with all the lights off the disc on your hydro meter kept going around. And the furnace works on propane. See what I'm getting at?"

Marcel said yes, he understood.

"I did it to protect them," he said.

"What do they have in the way of weapons?"

"Just an old sawed-off shotgun."

"Any dynamite?"

"No, no."

"Good."

"I'm afraid they might shoot themselves..."

"Everything will be all right, Marcel, you'll see. You and me, we're going to speak to them calmly."

As he started the car, out of the corner of his eye Corporal Huet saw the snowy owl leave its perch and glide into the air, lifted by its momentum over the infinite plain of sparkling whiteness under the pale nugget of the sun. Half a kilometre off, the adventuresome vole returning to its nest in the snow under a cluster of wild grape vines never knew what hit it.

When Jean-Paul Lafleur crawled out of his den like a bear along the passage between the furnace and the sub-basement wall, Chevalier thought he couldn't be more than twenty years old. His voice was hoarse from shouting loud enough to be heard through the cement blocks. While he'd been killing himself trying to convince the three that it was safe to come out, the house had been filling with cops. There were at least a dozen of them coming and going, moving from room to room, armed with machine guns. The cold floors reverberated with the sound of their boots.

Gode and the Lafleur brothers were handcuffed as soon as they came out of the secret passage. Jean-Paul turned to Duquet.

"How did they find us?"

"They heard you coughing," Marcel said and looked away, embarrassed.

Captain Leclerc was waiting for Branlequeue at the bottom of the basement stairs.

"Do you want to speak them?"

Chevalier looked at him, caught off guard.

"Of course, but..."

"But what, Chevalier?"

"Why are you doing me such a favour?"

The captain seemed to think about it.

"Who says I'm doing it for your sake?"

A tired smile spread over Chevalier's face.

"Okay, tell me the truth, Captain. Is my presence here tonight meant to demonstrate that your men are not beating these three **dangerous terrorists up with billy clubs?**"

It was the captain's turn to smile.

"Beating people up with billy sticks is Martinek's method. He'll no doubt turn up here before too long. As for me, what I think is that there's already been one death too many in this affair. Another reason to treat these people humanely."

"When you say one death too many, you're implying that that death could have been avoided?

Leclerc paused on the lower step of the stairs.

"Come on. We'll go into the living room."

Many years later, Chevalier Branlequeue would once again ask himself how Corporal Huet and Captain Leclerc were able to keep journalists out of that neck of the woods, engulfed in snowbanks behind Saint-Marc-sur-Richelieu. It was a surreal scene: the living room full of police officers waiting, their patience bordering on angelic, considering the circumstances. And he, too, in the middle of the room, on a chair, chatting calmly with the three men, two of whom were on the sofa facing him and the other on a chair a bit farther off. The oldest of the three was giving him, despite the handcuffs shackling his wrists, an accelerated course in radical political action. That an episode precipitating an unprecedented national crisis, receiving media coverage the likes of which had never before been seen, could lead to this strange intimacy, without a single member of the press present, and that it was he, a poet, editor, former political prisoner, and an ex-candidate for an independent Quebec, who found himself caught up in the events, gathering the first proposals of the three most wanted criminals in the country, was something that would never cease to astonish him.

"We wanted to speed up history," Jean-Paul declared. "And history will be our judge. All I can say is that the Chevalier Cell did not act selfishly. It's our self-abnegation that distinguishes us from governments and gangsters, who amount to the same thing. If we'd blown up a Brinks truck instead of kidnapping a minister, there never would have been an October Crisis."

"But it's going to be harder now to distinguish yourselves from them, now that you have blood on your hands," remarked Chevalier.

"Lavoie's death is another story. It wasn't good politics, killing Lavoie. It's obvious that Paul Lavoie was a lot more useful to the FLQ alive than dead. But to be honest, the death of a construction worker makes me feel a lot worse than that of a Liberal minister, and I won't shed a single goddamned tear for him and his kind. But we have to stick to politics. What's certain is that by calling in the army and stirring up the baser instincts of the population, power has finally shown its true face. But we're ready to take responsibility for the violence that took place. We'll pay the price."

He started to say something, but Marcel Duquet chose that moment to cause a fuss.

"Stay outside, you dirty dog! Outside!"

One of the police officers tried to calm him down, while the other turned to the great, hulking brute in civilian clothing who had just appeared at the door to the living room. Small moustache, glasses, Mackinaw jacket, tweed cap.

"Ah, Martinek! What good wind blew you here?" asked Captain Leclerc, with a sidelong glance at Chevalier.

The colossus rolled his huge eyes and shook his head, as if he couldn't believe what was unfolding in the living room. In a way, he looked like a habitant come to spend a quiet night in the country. He'd even forgotten to bring his machine gun.

"What the fuck is going on here?" he said in English.

"Everything's under control, Martinek," the captain assured him.

Still shaking his head, Martinek turned his back, and it was like a panel of the wall had turned and taken several steps down the hall.

Without speaking, Leclerc looked questioningly at his prisoners.

"We're fighting for the same things you are," Jean-Paul said, addressing Chevalier, "except we're using different methods. That's all we have to say."

"All we ask of you," his brother added, "is that you speak on our behalf every chance you get. We need you to be our voice..."

Chevalier said he would. He was overcome by emotion. He turned to Richard Godefroid, who had not as yet spoken and who was shivering, his hands shoved between his thighs.

"Gode..."

"Chevalier... I'm as frozen as a side of beef in Matagami. Can't someone get that furnace going?"

Dawn crept into the room. Captain Leclerc stepped forward.

"We're going to have to go now."

ELDORADO

AT THE NORTH END OF the park he saw vultures circling, and then a few crows and a large harrier rising up from a wolf carcass stretched out on the side of the road. The wolf had been flattened by traffic like an ordinary groundhog.

The forest had taken on the features that remained consistent from here to the Arctic Circle. The only variation would be the size of the trees, which would continue to diminish with monotonous and predictable regularity for another two thousand kilometres. The forest was dominated by conifers, and wherever streams created a bed of moss and humus, the drowned areas formed by beavers made a gap in the woods, the austere, dried-out trunks of trees poked up from the forest floor. Low mountains sprouting from the spinal column of the continent seemed content to spread peacefully along the horizon.

After climbing a series of hills covered with a mixed forest of black and white spruce and paper birch, with the occasional white pine that had survived the nineteenth century, the Nihilomobile tipped down into lowlands.

It cruised among huge reservoirs with innumerable bays bristling with black trunks that looked like fence posts coated with tar. The horizon vanished. Everywhere there were lakes. Sam found himself in a picnicking mood, so he stopped, took off his clothes, dove head first into one of these lakes, dried himself off as best he could, and continued driving north. After a while, muskeg and its immense peat bogs, covered with thick spongy cushions spiked with spindly tamaracks, lined both sides of the road. A bald eagle flying six hundred metres up watched him pass, its wings spread out to catch a thermal, its head as white and dazzling as a snowball thrown by the sun. If it could read, from that distance the bird could have made out the numbers on Nihilo's licence plate.

Ahead of him, the continental plateau tilted toward Hudson Bay.

He paid thirty-five dollars for a room in a motel on the outskirts of town, TV but no cable. He fell onto the bed without undressing and slept until late afternoon. When he woke up, he lay for a long time without moving, scraping his memory for an image or a thought that would correspond even vaguely with where he was. The roar of tractor-trailers opened huge corridors in the silence and brought him to some semblance of reality. One of them drove him from the bed to the window.

It was early May. Across the highway, on the flank of a hill, was another motel, possibly even more dubious looking than the one he was in, but crammed to the rafters. It looked like a rubbish heap in the middle of a huge parking lot. Beside it, a neon sign for an equally decrepit gas station rose above the roadside, but one of the letters had burned out, so that it said -HELL. Farther down the road, a car cemetery was surrounded by a wall from which sheets of rusted corrugated metal hung like the hem of a dress. The whole scene was set in a yellowed wasteland strewn with dead machinery and trembling aspens. The grizzled nudity of it would have made a great advertisement for antidepressants.

He took a shower. The floor sloped noticeably toward the bathroom door. The shower stall made him think of a hamster cage without the bars, and the mysteries of the crude plumbing gave the impression that he was in some remote Siberian laboratory, the subject of an experiment conducted by a pharmaceutical company studying the effects of sudden, extreme temperature swings on the human psychology. He could have used the single towel to sand a hardwood floor.

Apart from that, everything seemed fine.

Maldoror. He drove between two rows of car and truck dealerships to the shores of the small lake, Lake Makwa, and stumbled onto the main street almost by accident. He found what he was looking for on the door of a Pizza Delight and decided to go in for a bite to eat. The weather was still too cold to eat on the terrace, which was deserted. The sign taped to the door showed a bomb exploding — it was reproduced from a single frame of a cartoon strip, a kind of bowling pin with a fuse sticking out of it. On each star given off by the explosion was a photograph of one of the actors in the play, with their names underneath. The predominant colours were red and black.

Sam washed his two slices of Neapolitan pizza down with a glass of red wine, thinking how lucky he was to be on his own in an unknown town with a reason for being there. He paid, left, found the theatre, and bought his ticket.

Saturday night in Maldoror. Family dinners at the Cage aux Sports. Couples, groups of friends, chicken wings. And me, the stranger, elbows on the bar, writing it all down in this notebook, drinking beer between two slam dunks and a wicked backhand. You can't look anywhere without seeing a TV screen, bathing suits, numbers, floats, balls, bats, clubs, logos and jerseys in the colours of rival teams. Or hunting trophies on the walls: caribou, deer, bears, grouse. Or fishing: northern pike, lake trout, Arctic char. Or trapping: beaver, otter, and even, perched on a narrow, artificial ledge, its startled face about as lifelike as an old shoe, a lynx. The dark mahogany wall panelling also holds a great horned owl wearing a baseball cap, and a red-shouldered hawk.

More convinced than ever that the ex-cop Massicotte had made a huge mistake by trying to put me off the scent by dodging my question with his story without beginning or end. I've compared my notes on the Chicken Affair with those taken by Chevalier Branlequeue in the early 1970s. The author of *Elucubrations* had been right there, attended all the court proceedings. On Saturday, the Baby Barbecue rotisserie had had no fewer than fifteen delivery men on the go. And among those fifteen guys it so happened that the one who made the delivery to Lavoie's future kidnappers was the same one who, five days earlier, was in court following the trial of his clients' accomplices! The thread was a bit obvious. If he'd wanted to get rid of me, all Massicotte had to do was deny that there was any family link between him and this Rénald guy, and that would have been that! Did he think I'd check into it? Putting me off with his long, dragged-out story succeeded only in arousing my curiosity...

Yeah, except that the hypothesis that the second cousin was, as Branlequeue believed, a police undercover agent doesn't explain why Rénald delivered his club sandwiches to the occupants of the bungalow on rue Collins several hours *before* the kidnapping took place...Think about that.

Maldoror rose from the mud in the Abitibi gold-rush days of the 1930s. Barely a single human lifespan separates us from that gloomy, copper-bearing agglomeration of a frontier town whose wooden storefronts on its single street welcomed wagonloads of call girls and poor devils belonging to two dozen different nationalities, from Russians of all stripes to American Negroes, all ready to go at the rock with their bare hands until they'd dug themselves to China if they had to. A crowd as varied in gullibility as it was in depth, exploitable as hell, while on the face of it the town continued to grow, a crazy, gluttonous pyramid whose base rested on gold dust and nuggets.

Today, the rutted mud on the main street was gone, buried, like everything else, under the usual amount of concrete and asphalt. But enough vestiges of the former Babylonian mushroom remained to be shaken like a rattle in the ears of tourists. The thirst for gold had been recycled into a more plebian greed, its dangers and prestige traded in for an industrial incinerator that swallowed old computers and spat out leather. The call girls were long gone, replaced by down-market escort services, home-video stores, high-speed Internet connections, and an immoderate love of horsepower. The old ways of burning gas couldn't hold a candle to the $2,000 Toro snowblowers that filled in the gaps left by the hookers.

If someone took all the internal combustion engines off the streets and out of the parking lots and driveways of Maldoror, there wouldn't be much left to look at. Its wind pump, its lake, its hospital, its naked, brownish-pink hills covered in graffiti, its foundry chimneys. At any hour of the day you could fit its visible pedestrian street traffic into a delivery van. As for architecture, it had always owed much of its inspiration to the unbridled Western film. The result, American to the hilt, was a typical strut-your-stuff decor with a bit of Soviet realism thrown in by the foundry and the old workers' quarter, where dilapidated white stucco houses were sinking into a cocktail of toxic tailings.

SKURATOV — *Listen. I arranged this meeting with the Grand Duchess so that tomorrow we can publish it in the newspapers. It'll be an exact transcript except for one thing. It will contain your confession and repentance. Your comrades will think you've betrayed them.*
KALYAYEV — *They'll never believe it.*
SKURATOV — *I'll withdraw the article if you'll make a confession. You must decide tonight.*
KALYAYEV — *They'll never believe it.*
SKURATOV — *Why not? Have they never done anything wrong?*
KALYAYEV — *You don't know their love.*
SKURATOV — *Maybe not. But I know that no one can believe in brotherly love for a whole night without a moment of weakness. I await that moment. There's no hurry. I'm a patient man.*

The theatre was a former cinema. Sam perched on a stool with his elbows on the bar that had been set up at the back of the theatre. Emma Magy had been right: here, sitting behind everyone, he was in his element. Unobserved, looking over the backs and the necks of the audience, he watched Dora go through her lines. Then he gauged the reactions of the audience. A play by Camus in May, Marie-Québec had explained, was a calculated risk. In Maldoror, audiences were used to laughing first and thinking later. They went to plays to show off their artistic sensibilities, like their good clothes, and they were more accustomed to summer-theatre farces. There were always two or three laughers in a crowd, educated by television and the sort of crude humour you get at fifty-dollar stand-up comedy shows. They laughed at the first somewhat ambiguous lines, sucking a joke from them like juice from a lemon. Here, going to the theatre and laughing your head off were natural synonyms, like coughing when you had a cold.

In the minds of these admirers of contemporary, unhistoric farce, confusion was no doubt encouraged by certain choices the director made when mounting *The Just* — for example, refusing to use costumes that identified the time of the action. Tsarist Russia as it was seen in the Loblaws Happy Times Theatre seemed pretty similar to Quebec in the 1960s; all it would have taken would be to alter a line here and there and dress the Grand Duke up like the Lieutenant Governor. Dora wore a man's sweater and a pair of work boots. Around her, the men were wearing jeans, T-shirts, and mackinaws.

Sam went back the next day, and the next, and the next. He loved the play. He loved Dora. He thought she was great. Magnificent. He vanished after the curtain call and went back to his motel room, where he drank beer from cans and watched the news on television. He did not try to go and see her in her dressing room after the performance. Didn't try to contact her. And Dora couldn't see him from the stage. Marie-Québec didn't know that Sam was in Maldoror. He simply went back and sat in the same place every night.

DORA — *Do you love me in solitude, tenderly, without egotism? Would you love me if I were unjust?*

KALYAYEV — *If you were unjust and I could love you, then it wouldn't be you that I loved.*

DORA — *That's no answer. Tell me this, would you love me if I wasn't in the Organization?*

KALYAYEV — *Where would you be, then?*

DORA — *I remember when I was a student. I laughed. I was pretty. I spent hours going for walks and dreaming. Would you love me if I were light-headed and carefree?*

KALYAYEV — *I am dying to say I would.*

DORA — *Yes, say it, my love, if you think it, if it's true. Say yes, never mind about justice, never mind misery and all the people in*

chains. Say yes, I beg you, forget the suffering of children, forget those who are hanged, or whipped to death ...
KALYAYEV — *Shut up, Dora.*

During the day, he drove out of town, through aspen woods where soft, luminescent green buds were just beginning to open. The forest edge was sprinkled with houses set well back from the road, one in every three of them sporting a For Sale sign. He would park the car at a trailhead and go exploring, stopping to listen to wood thrushes and warblers, walking on, and finding himself surrounded by hunt camps, beaver dams, bear scat, raised blinds set up to look out over marshlands. Once, in an old burn, he found morels.

Another time he stumbled onto an old abandoned mine site, in an area of peat bogs filled with black water, like open-pit oil wells. He stopped for a moment by the gutted carcass of a metal tank, half-eaten by rust, half-buried in gravel that spread to the edge of the surrounding muskeg.

Concrete foundations rose from the ground like monstrous molars busily chewing on the trunks of poplar trees. A signpost riddled with bullet holes. Silence.

He returned to his car and followed a road that ran for some twenty kilometres through stands of mature conifers and zones of reforestation beside lakes that formed a chain stretching down to the south. The broken pavement finally disappeared altogether, as though swallowed by sand and gravel from a hundred-metre-thick esker, along the top of which the car made its way like a flea along the spine of a dog. He saw a lot of rabbits. Black spruce, Jack pine. A hand-painted For Sale sign near the end of the road, stuck in the shadowy forest.

He turned up the access road and found himself above an inclined, brush-covered plain, at the centre of which was a large brown house, all angles and squares. It looked almost sinister, with the huge lake behind it and the distant, wild shore. As he sat there contemplating the scene, he saw a crow flying low above the trees, carrying a long, dry stick crosswise in its beak.

On his way out, Nihilo saw a lynx crouched at the centre of a small sandy patch by the side of the road. He stopped and backed up. It was the first time he'd ever seen one. The animal lounged on the sand, its head up, like the Egyptian Sphinx in the desert. As Samuel slowed down, it was observing the movements of a rabbit romping about some twenty metres back. The rabbit went on gambolling at the edge of the woods, but the lynx lost interest in it and turned its attention to Nihilo and his car, watching him intently but without the slightest sign of fear. Sam detected no nervousness. Its disquieting face seemed to express only cautious curiosity tinged with indolence. After a moment, the lynx returned its gaze to the rabbit, and Sam continued back along the road.

Maybe. It's absolute love, pure, solitary, a joy that actually burns me. At certain times, however, I wonder if love isn't something else entirely, if it could stop being a monologue and become a call-and-response once in a while. I imagine that, you see: the bright sunlight, heads tilted gently together, hearts empty of pride, arms reaching out . . .

As she says the lines, Dora is standing at the front of the stage, and finally sees him. In the eternity it takes for her to stop, feel her voice weaken, then remember her lines, Sam feels her eyes travel the entire length of the room and light upon him.

It was the play's second-last night. Once again he leaves after the curtain. Afterward, Skuratov bought a round of Goldschlager shooters at the White Wolf, but Sam was nowhere to be seen. He was sitting in his car under a rising, postindustrial moon about a kilometre away.

The next day, he spent the equivalent of two nights' stay in the grotty motel at a florist's shop on rue Drummond, almost beside the foundry. When she got to the theatre, Marie-Québec found a dozen roses waiting for her, with a small card that read:

WOULD YOU LIKE ME TO COME WITH YOU?

TWO

THE LYNX
CONSTELLATION

CAMP EL SOUF, JAVESH (JORDAN), SUMMER 1970

"HE'S IRAQI," DECLARED ABOU DINNAH.

Or rather *Comrade* Abou Dinnah, as he insisted on being called.

Thirty metres from them, a man in fatigues stood up, took several long, loping strides, and threw a hand grenade. They followed its arc with their eyes and, twelve metres away, saw a spruce-like shrub pop into the air, its branches splintered by the blast, the pieces falling to the earth in a brief shower of vegetation from a yellow cloud.

There was shouting, and someone clapped. The Iraqi walked back to the sixty or so men gathered in the hills in the middle of the desert. He was tall, well built, and the way he walked indicated that under the circumstances (with sixty pairs of eyes staring at him, watching his every move as he pulled the pin from the grenade, tossed the bomb in his hands two or three times before running like a cricket bowler and straight-arming the thing into the shrubbery)

165

he was happy with the way he'd landed it just where he'd wanted it to go.

"Iraqi," Comrade Dinnah said again.

"Apart from Lebanese and Iraqis, do you have other foreigners among you?" asked the journalist.

Abou was Lebanese. He spoke fluent French, which was why he'd been selected to guide the three journalists around the camp. They were sitting in the cool shade of the pines, separate from the group formed by the fedayeen and their Iraqi instructor. The three Westerners were a team: one worked the microphone and handled the script, another the camera. The third was taking still photographs for a magazine. The dazzling light, the incandescent nakedness of the stones, the biblical hills.

"Yes," Abou Dinnah replied. "There are Saudis here, and Egyptians, and Turks . . . And even some Canadians, North Americans, who are fighting for the French there . . ."

"What? Québécois, here in el Souf?"

"That's it, from Quebec. Yes . . ."

A second grenade exploded a hundred feet from them, and the journalist looked up instinctively. Then they fell silent as a fedayee, his head wrapped in a checkered keffiyeh and his eyes hidden behind sunglasses, passed close to them after detaching himself from the main group. He'd slowed down as he approached the four sitting in the shadow of the bush that sheltered the tents of the FDPLP, as though curious about their presence in this place.

The journalist jumped to his feet and went up to the fedayee.

"Are you Québécois?"

"Huh? How did you know that?"

"You're the only one wearing Ray-Bans."

Then the journalist saw a second revolutionary coming toward him, his features hidden under a keffiyeh even though most of the others were bareheaded. Waving madly, the journalist signalled his cameraman to join him. The second fedayin's eyes were deep blue and his hand, when he held it out, was white and slender, a student's hand.

"Hello! It's good to see you somewhere other than on television ..."

"The Kalishnikov is a good assault rifle," Zadig was saying. "I'd even go so far as to say that the AK-47 is far superior to the American M-16. But for carrying out guerrilla warfare in an urban setting, it's not so practical ..."

"Why?" asked the reporter, moving the microphone a bit closer to Zadig's mouth, which could be seen moving through the fabric of his keffiyeh.

"Because after a while it becomes difficult to find ammunition for it."

"I see. But if the training you're receiving here isn't appropriate to conditions in Quebec, what are you doing in el Souf?"

Zadig hesitated. The journalist and the two terrorists were standing at the foot of a hill at the end of the valley. The camera was rolling, the photographer clicking away. Target practice and hand-to-hand combat training had just ended.

It was Madwar who answered.

"The FDPLP is the most radical, the most leftist Palestinian resistance group there is, and that's what interested us from the beginning. But while we quickly saw that the commando training they provide is good, they're not all that strong on the politicization of the masses. The priority here is clearly military instruction. The other problem is that they spend a lot of time each day discussing Marxist and Leninist dialectics, and we can't understand a word of it because it's all in Arabic."

"Comrade Abou Dinnah helps us a bit," Zadig said.

"So what you learn here, basically, is how to kill people?"

"More that than mobilizing the worker masses, anyway."

"And when you return to Quebec, what will you do?"

"Begin a campaign of selective assassinations," Zadig said calmly.

"Those who are responsible will pay," added Madwar.

"And who are they, the ones who are responsible?"

"The premier, top businessmen, people like that."

"And you won't be going to fight in Palestine?"

"I think I will be," said Madwar.

"Not me," said Zadig.

"And where did you get your code names? Because these are code names you're using, are they not?"

This journalist could be a real pain in the ass when he wanted to be.

"I took mine when I was studying literature at . . . I almost gave the name of the university. We have to be careful not to say anything that could be used to identify us," Zadig explained, with an indulgent smile.

"And what about you, Madwar?"

"I have nothing to add to that."

The photographer asked them to pose for a portrait: combat position, Kalishnikov held in both hands.

"Try to look fierce," he told them. "That's-good-hold-it-like-that."

Like lambs to the slaughter.

At the end of the interview, he shook their hands.

Zadig: Long live the socialist québécois and international revolution!

Madwar: Long live proletarian internationalism!

Zadig: Long live Comrade Nayef Hawatmeh! Long live the FD-PLP!"

Madwar: Long live the FLQ!"

SAINT-COLOMBAN, JUNE 1970, AROUND THE SOLSTICE

WHEN ARE WE GOING TO arrest those pieces of shit?

That question keeps coming up, believe me. Because that's what they literally spat in our faces when they came out of the cabin, the sons of bitches. And the night before that, we'd even bugged their place and could hear everything they did, even when they were fucking, because there was nothing at all between us and them. The sound board was in the shit hole we rented next door to theirs, and the two cabins were connected, like a camera with a zoom lens. We heard everything.

I seen one of them come out. Sideburns, glasses, hair combed on the side, turtle-neck, looked like a faggot. There were these big pine trees in the yard, their shadows were over everything, and you could hear these little birds in them. Sparrows. And when there's nothing

169

else to listen to and nothing to do but swat mosquitoes, you end up listening to sparrows, take it from me.

The guys that came out were carrying two shoeboxes under their arms. I took their pictures, if I took one I took ten. They put the boxes on the back seat of the Acadian, careful like, like they had their mother-in-law's Bohemian crystal wine glasses in them. I don't know if there are such things as Bohemian crystal wine glasses, but I think there are.

While they were in the yard, Patenaude called our guys on the walkie-talkie. Sound of the motor drowned out his voice and a good thing it did, too, because the shack we were in didn't even have any windows. There were lots of us out on the highway, and a few more not far from there, in a house on the river. That's where the sergeant was. He ate there, slept there sometimes. So he could take charge, direct traffic. We had guys everywhere.

The next day I was cruising around the bottom of Sainte-Scholastique and I saw a gopher right in the middle of the road, its two front feet practically on the white line. I stepped on the gas and the gopher sort of froze, then it tried to turn around and run back but it was too late, I felt my tire go over it. There, you little prairie dog, that'll teach you to make holes in farmers' fields for cows to step in and break their legs and farmers to break their machinery in, gopher holes, they're nothing but dirty vermin, but there was one less on the earth that day.

Right after that I heard Sergeant Massicotte's voice on my radio, we made fun of him behind his back, him with his pipe and the fucking smart-assed way of talking he always tried to pull off, like he wanted to sound cool all the time, like he thought he should understand them before he arrested them or something, which must be why they put him in charge of the investigation into the holdup at the university. He belonged there with those goddamned sons of bitches. I guess he wouldn't have been too happy if he'd known we called him the Doormouse.

He told me to get back on the 158 at Saint-Canut, and to drive slowly east, until I see a green Valiant come up behind me and to stay in front of it maintaining visual contact until we reach the autoroute, and from there take the 15 South and make sure the Valiant was still behind me. Yes, sergeant.

Everything was green around me, the woods, the fields, the bushes, dark green, so green that I thought to myself that a green Valiant could get lost in a place like this. It looked okay from the car, except don't forget it was full of mosquitoes.

I did what the sergeant told me, and drove slowly, in radio contact with the guys in the other car that was behind the Valiant, who told me they were coming but not fast, and I told them I couldn't go thirty miles an hour on the autoroute, so I'd pull over to the side of the road and let them pass, and after that all they had to do was pick up the Valiant and I'd follow them. All in all, there were about thirty of us on the job, no need to be nervous about it. I pulled off onto the shoulder. The river was to my left, hidden by trees in the fields. Farther off were the foothills where my brother-in-law goes to hunt deer. I saw white smoke coming from the mill in Saint-Jérome. I took the napkin that I had from lunch and was still on the back seat, and I got out of the car, raised the hood, and checked the oil, all innocent like. I craned my neck and checked out the cars passing on the autoroute, all the time wiping the dipstick with the napkin.

At a certain point the Valiant passed by, and the young guy at the wheel looked at me the same as he'd look at anyone stopped by the side of the road with the hood up. Sympathetic, but like he had other fish to fry. As for me, I met his gaze and made a sign that everything was okay. Which was funny, because in fact the car was down half a quart.

"Those goddamned pieces of shit, when are we going to bust their asses?"

"Tomorrow," the sergeant said. And we closed on them at six a.m. sharp after completely surrounding the cottage. We even had guys who go around and cross the river farther upstream, and let me tell you they got eaten up pretty bad. Inside the cottage we seized four FLQ, one of them a real pussy. And three rifles, a few handguns, a cache of weapons, hoods, handcuffs, detonators with dials on them made in China and illegal mechanisms inside them. Plus a big stack of bills from the university holdup. The rifle barrels had been sawed off. At the same time, other commando teams had seized a Gestetner copier in an apartment in Ahuntsic and three hundred pounds of dynamite from the basement of a house on rue Meunier, in Laval. The boxes of dynamite had been wrapped in polyethylene garbage bags. We let the bastards jump into their clothes before we handcuffed them. Got a good look at the babe's tits when she was trying to get dressed in one of the rooms. She tried to close the door but we kicked it open because we had to keep an eye on her, bra or no bra. Massicotte wasn't interested in her tits, though, or in the sawed-off shotguns. Go figure: he took out his reading glasses and puffed away at his pipe while examining the papers he found on the desk!

When the tit-show was over, I went into the bathroom and looked at myself in the mirror, saw a good-looking guy, then I opened the bathroom cabinet. Aspirin, Band-Aids, and something else that caught my eye: a syringe, with a dozen extra needles in plastic bags and three small vials of some kind of liquid, no labels. I took them to the sergeant, but do you think for one minute that he gave a shit? He hardly looked at it. Don't bother him. He was reading!

"Next time," he said (*puff puff*), "wear gloves when handling evidence."

"What's that you're reading, sarge?"

He looked up as he puffed away on his briar and squinted at me through a cloud of Old Dutch. He had a stack of *The Old Patriot* and some drawings of old guns with the FLQ Manifesto written underneath. One thing that struck me was that the Old Patriot was smoking the exact same pipe as the sergeant.

"Literature, Bobby," Sergeant Mass said. "Literature . . ."

His breath smelled like old pipe juice.

Two days later, in Saint-Romuald, a shoebox exploded in the lobby of an office building that belonged to the premier's brother-in-law. Expert analysis later confirmed that bomb fragments recovered from the site came from the same source as the material that was seized from the cabin in Saint-Colomban.

In the seized papers, there was also a communiqué calling for the kidnapping of the American consul in Montreal, a Mr. Green. I didn't even know the Americans had a consulate in Montreal.

A second shoebox went off three days later, in front of a Department of National Defence building in Ottawa, the only fireworks celebrating St. John the Baptist Day in that city, believe me. It killed one employee on the spot. Some sort of secretary.

ARCHAMBAULT BEACH, 1976:
GODE'S POINT OF VIEW

THEY CAME FOR BUCK YESTERDAY. He called them. His death cries
kept everyone on the range awake. You'd think he was a wolf chewing off his leg that was caught in a trap. We heard doors rolling
open automatically. Steps in the corridor. They asked him what was
wrong. He told them: Get me out of here ... No one inside could do
anything for him. They had him taken out, they left. Buck walked
between the rows of cells, looking at his feet. Two hours later he
hanged himself with the strap from his artificial leg. In the nursing station. He was what, forty-five years old? Thirty of them spent
inside.

I have a pencil and paper. Buck, he had nothing but his voice.
Didn't know how to write. He had me. We called him Buck, the
Buck. When I was on cleanup in the corridor, I'd sit down with my
back against the door of his cell and we'd talk. Him sitting in the

174

same position on the other side of the door. We must have looked like two bookends, with a door between us instead of books.

He'd had thirty years to build up his shell. He lived in a mental Hilton compared to our doghouses. He'd been through everything, from corporal punishment delivered with power hoses, to the eager fingers of the good Fathers. When he was fifteen, Juvenile Court sent him to Bordeaux Prison, which was like dumping a sack of fresh meat into a lion's den.

They couldn't break him there so they threw him in the hole. Light bulb left on twenty-four hours every day, hang the expense. To help him get his head straight, the prison warden offered him the job of washing the hanged men. That way he could at least eat steak at the banquet they held after an execution, with the hangman sitting at the head of the table. The condemned cells began at the end of a hallway. The convicts shared their cups of milk and their egg sandwiches with him, their little privileges. Sometimes he had to stick a broom handle up their backs and between their shoulder blades to help them walk upright behind the priest holding up the Eucharist. The Buck had to stand under the gibbet, wait for the hanged man to stop jiggling in the air and shitting himself, then wait for the doctor to take the man's wrist and look at his watch and nod his head, and then he had to take him down and wash him.

"You know what?" he once told me. "The rope isn't made of hemp."

"What do you mean, it isn't made of hemp?"

"Nope, it's made of parachute silk."

"Of para..."

"Yup. Parachute silk. What're you laughing at?"

This is maximum security, nothing but one long, endless present. You forget the future and you avoid thinking about the past. It's like living in an open bar, except all the bottles are empty. I'll crack one day, just like Buck. I'm not going to blow a fuse. Or die, like Marcel Duquet, in an accident so stupid it had to be a warning. I'll bide my time, set my alarm. With my paper and my pencil. My escape kit.

Father Gamache's face was as fat as a backside, his whole head was bloated, shaved above the ears and topped with a kind of tuft that made him look like a Mohawk warrior in a soutane and decked out with a pair of large glasses. Thick lips. To look at him you couldn't tell if he was a humanist or a pervert.

He oozed grease like a pan of bacon. He called us in that day, the kids in the choir. He told us he'd just learned that his predecessor used to give us a quarter for each high mass and the same for a marriage or a funeral, and ten cents for a small mass!

It was too much for him, emotionally. He let go a high-pitched fart that smelled like methane. *Amen!* I sang in a low voice. Langlais spluttered with laughter. Father Gamache was as ugly as a chamberpot. But it was obvious that such hijinks wouldn't go down well with him. He told us that the Baby Jesus was getting low on money, and from now on we'd be getting only ten cents for a high mass.

"And your ten cents," he continued yelling at us, "my boys, I will personally make sure that your ten cents is not spent on bubblegum, candies, chocolate drops, or jawbreakers...for the very good reason that each week it will go directly into the pocket of Our Lord to be used to light candles for the souls of little Chinese communists!"

François Langlais was my best friend. I called him the Little Genius. After the meeting in the church, we walked out along the railway track, trying to walk on the rails, side by side, our arms stretching out from time to time to keep our balance.

"I kicked a stone that went bouncing into the dorm."

"I went to ask for my dollar-a-week anyway ..."

"Not me, I'm never setting foot in that place again!"

"Me neither!"

A groundhog was sunning itself on the tracks. I picked up a good-sized rock and snuck up on it. When I was thirty feet away, I rushed at it like a linebacker rushing a quarterback. The groundhog disappeared into his hole in the middle of the track, making a series of piercing little whicks that sounded like he was trembling with indignation. I never even got near him.

François and I went over the entire arsenal we'd acquired over the previous year or two: bows made from alder branches and a bit of string; some slings; two crossbows; slingshots made from forked tree branches; and an old bicycle-tire inner tube.

"What we need is a rifle," said Little Genius.

"I'd get one if I could," I said, "but I'd have to pay for it out of my own pocket."

We walked on in silence. On the railway track there was always lots to do. We could put pennies on the rails and pick them up afterward as thin as leaves. We could find detonators, and some even said they'd found dynamite, but we never did. And there were lots of gophers, but our chances of ever killing one would have been much better if we'd had a rifle.

The old school bus picked us up in the morning, with our lunch pails, our Pepsis, our Paris Pâté or peanut-butter sandwiches, and our Joe Louis, or maybe a Half-Moon or even a Mae West, or some Lady-Fingers, or those little caramel squares. We hulled strawberries in a kind of hangar belonging to the Val-Pie canning factory. They hired mostly women and children. Fourteen hours a day, six days a week, and at night when you went to bed and closed your eyes, it wasn't Bonhomme Carnival you'd see in your dreams, or the strawberry cheeks on one of his queens. It was real strawberries, nothing but strawberries. Half a cent a case. Fact.

The overseer who paced up and down the rows was paid to make sure that fingers reddened by haste didn't crush too many berries. I'll never forget the older kid, maybe fourteen, who looked at us oddly between two bites of his baloney sandwich and said:

"Half a cent a case, that's not enough..."

"You're right, but what can we do about it?" a woman said, coming up to him.

"Go on strike," said the fourteen-year-old, taking a drink of Kik to wash down his baloney.

He spoke louder so that the people sitting near him could hear.

"What could they do, do you think, if everyone went home this afternoon? Sell their jam with their tails? Are you afraid Duplessis' cops'll shoot us, like they did in Murdochville? Do you think Val-Pie is going to send in scabs with baseball bats supplied by the company, like what happened in Noranda? Who'd fill these cases for them?"

He said, "Follow me," and stood up and left the hangar. No one had ever seen that before: a parade of angry hullers in the middle of the workers' suburb. Eight-year-olds and mothers with ten children carrying three or four handmade placards.

The Val-Pie owner didn't budge when he saw some fifty women and street urchins from the South Shore occupying his building. But he did fold when Jean-Paul Lafleur (that's who it was) said he was calling in the media from the big city, and newspaper reporters and radio crews started showing up. People started talking about a public enquiry into the exploitation of children by the agri-food industry.

They settled for a penny a case.

✣ ✣ ✣

Léo Godefroid, Gode's father, was one of the unemployed workers the government thought they could get rid of by shipping them up to the low, burnt-out lands around Abitibi, where the blackflies, mosquitoes, and minus-forty winters gradually did them in. When they returned south, they found themselves joining the masses of workers being chased out of Montreal by the housing shortage, and who crossed the Jacques-Cartier bridge with their broods of kids and established themselves on the south shore of the St. Lawrence, in the countryside surrounding the Montreal ports. The local farmers sold them land for a few hundred dollars and they built their shacks with whatever they could scrounge. In Abitibi, at least they'd learned how to build cabins. At night, they tore apart abandoned railway cars and used this "wagon wood" to make their houses in the fields.

The cabins were simple affairs, for the most part, with no foundations or running water, made of wood covered with tarpaper. In front, where there should have been sidewalks, flowed open sewers that they had to cross by walking on two or three planks thrown across the ditch.

Léo shovelled sugar for Redpath in the port of Montreal. He spent the rest of his time with a hammer in his hand and nails in his mouth, working on improvements to his own and his neighbours' living conditions. By the end of the 1950s, this cluster of vagabonds had become a residential district, with small, properly built houses, attractive, some of them, and almost comfortable.

When the first wave of baby boomers hit the schools, the clergy found itself short of unctuous but domineering Sisters and ancient, drooling priests to whom to entrust the task of sensitizing youth to the dangers of solitary sin. They had to call in the laity. One fine morning in September, a young man of twenty-six or twenty-seven found himself standing in front of the grade seven class; he was thin to the point of emaciation, stood straight as a fence post despite being stooped at the shoulders. Face like a knife blade, high fore-head, Coke-bottle lenses in thick, horn-rimmed frames. His name was Laurent Chevalier. He sat on the desk before thirty gamins from the workers' world and, for a full hour, talked to them about the novel *Le Survenant*, by Germaine Guèvremont. He recited whole passages from the book, which he apparently knew by heart, ex-tolled the virtues of its prose style, with its vigorous populist flavour and its extraordinary poetic quality. Before those thirty pairs of eyes he felt like a missionary sailing into the Manchurian interior. He listened to himself. The pupils looked at him like a herd of cattle being played music by Mozart.

François and Gode read everything they could get their hands on: Jules Verne, Arsène Lupin, Sherlock Holmes, *Reader's Digest*. But it was always François who got ten out of ten in dictation. Sitting with their piles of books on the edge of the sidewalk (they had sidewalks by then), they waited for Mr. Poulin, who drove the Bookmobile sent around by the local Optimist Club. They read *Le Survenant* and stuffed their heads with images of white geese and other flutter-ing wildfowl forming floating islands on blue rivers.

François Langlais was small and was called a fairy, a faggot, a limp-wrist, in the schoolyard. Nonetheless, when Mr. Chevalier suggested he run for class president, he was elected as smoothly as a letter passing through the post office.

"This is probably the first time," Chevalier remarked, "that an intelligent person has been elected to any position whatsoever in Jacques-Cartier, but don't tell your parents I said that..."

When the bell sounded and the school corridor reeked of pot and school bags spun through the air like weapons, whistling dangerously close to ears, the new teacher signalled Gode to come up to his desk. Young Godefroid's ears stuck out a bit, his hair less and less blond and bristled in a brush cut. With his thin, somewhat angular face he looked like one of the field mice that made their nests under the boards left lying in the tall grass behind the school, where he and his friends released neighbourhood mutts.

Chevalier put on his best smile in an effort to put the boy at ease. From the bottom of a pile he took a lined sheet of notepaper covered with sloppy, cursive writing and smelling like ballpoint ink.

"Your homework . . ." said Chevalier. He smiled. "I don't think there are many lynxes in the woods around these parts, so tell me: where are you from, Richard?"

"From Villebois."

"Villebois. Well, well, there's an oxymoron for us. And where is Villebois?"

"Abitibi."

Chevalier knew the story. Lots divided up on a map and distributed to unemployed workers from the south, spongy soil soaked in black water where nothing lived but pitcher plants and pale, un-compostable sphagnum moss. An image crossed his mind of the Abbé Félix-Antoine Savard, the author of *Menaud*, striding into the Promised Land at the head of his future parishioners, his biblical dream tucked under his arm to protect it from the whirlwinds of blackflies and mosquitoes.

"You'll have to tell me all about it some day," Chevalier told the boy.

He raised the paper to his eyes.

"You don't make mistakes..."

"My mother was a schoolteacher. She used to take me with her, put me in my crib under the blackboard. She says my first words weren't words but the alphabet: A, B, C, D, E, F..."

"That explains it."

Chevalier shook the paper gently between his fingers.

"Is it true that the way to kill an otter is to give it a good smash between the shoulder blades with a stick of firewood?"

"That's what the trapper said."

"'*For every animal*,'" Chevalier read, "'*there is its own way to kill it*.'"

He raised his eyes from the paper. Godefroid nodded.

"'*The fox, you have to take its hind legs and press them against its chest until the heart stops.*' Hmm…'*A rabbit cries like a newborn baby. You hold it by the legs an' whack it with a hard karate chop to the back of the head.*'"

Chevalier raised his eyes from the paper to the student standing before his desk.

"I've docked you a point for the 'an,'" he said, "and another for 'whack.' Try to avoid using words from common speech whenever possible. I have one more question for you: did you really watch a man strangle a lynx with his bare hands?"

"Not his bare hands. He was wearing gloves."

"He was wearing gloves," Chevalier repeated, transfixed. "That's good. That's not bad. It's a good story. All you need is a title for it…"

The boy shrugged his shoulders.

"A text without a title is like a majorette without a baton. The baton doesn't define the majorette, but it announces her. What do you think of *Ecce Lynx*?"

"What does that mean?"

"It means 'Behold the Lynx.' It's from the Latin," he hastened to add.

"I know what Latin is. I was a server at mass. My mother says it's a dead language."

"She's right."

"Then what good is it?"

Chevalier looked at him with a pensive air.

"This lynx of yours, is it possible it's not dead?"
Gode opened his eyes wide. He didn't answer.
"You can go join the others now."
But when he was at the door, he stopped and turned around.
"Monsieur?"
"Yes, Richard?"
"What's an oxymoron?"

In 1960, François enrolled in the Franciscan day school, whose mission was, theoretically, to encourage boys with religion vocations to pursue them, but to which certain sympathetic teachers directed promising young minds. They didn't have to dive into a font of holy water at such an early age, it was enough "not to oppose the idea of submitting to the influence of the Holy Spirit" to have the purse strings of the Works and Vocations Fund opened like magic, as well as the doors to the study of the classics. In other words, playing the game paid huge dividends.

For François, the main difference between the day school and the public school was that whereas formerly the brothers questioned him about his "nocturnal practices," the new brothers were more interested in what he was reading, in particular if he was reading "forbidden" books by authors like Flaubert and Balzac who, in Quebec, were still circulated more or less on the QT. One of the freethinkers at the centre of this trafficking was none other than Professor Chevalier, whose reputation as a social miscreant was already beginning to be taken seriously by the clergy. Gode had gone into the technical stream, received his electrician's licence, and was working for the Canadian National Railway. How many workers did it take to change a light bulb at CN? Nine. One French-Canadian and eight English bosses to tell him how to do it. Gode grew tired of filling out forms in triplicate every time he needed to fart. He handed in his resignation and became a cook in a chip wagon, working out of an old Coteau-Rouge bus in Jacques-Cartier, selling *"hotdogs stimés."* In the 1962 federal election, Chevalier ran under the banner of a tiny democratic party that was pretty much socialist, and the collared pack hounds leapt at the opportunity to sack him from teaching.

Gode and François took to hanging around the offices of Top Step Editions, which had just been founded by Chevalier, who had been practically reduced to poverty and whose offices were situated in the "Placard," a two-bedroom apartment he shared with his wife and their offspring (one little branlequetee and two small branlequeettes) above a hardware store on Chambly Road.

Using shoe polish, Gode disguised his windbreaker and vest and turned himself into a kind of poor man's James Dean at the new shopping centre. He read all the poets: Giguère, Chamberland. At the same time, François was working his way through *Nausea, Lost Illusions, The Human Condition, The Plague,* and *The Guermantes Way.* In the Placard, Chevalier supplied them with cigarettes and talked to them like grown men.

"There's a paradox in Malraux's heroes," he said to them. "For all their metaphysical pessimism, they take part in a revolution in the name of hope. Maybe revolutionaries are unhappy because they believe in happiness more than they appear to ..."

To François, Sartre was a god. Then he favoured Camus over Sartre. Then it was Hemingway, whom he had just discovered, over Sartre and Camus, then Steinbeck and Hemingway over Sartre and Camus and Malraux. Faulkner he found heavy going.

Sartre had written that for Hemingway, style came from ethics rather than from metaphysics, Langlais told them, to show that he, too, knew how to use the word "metaphysics." After that he kept quiet, as though he had said all that needed to be said on the subject.

"I think Malraux and Hemingway had a lot in common," Chevalier suggested. "A fabulous talent for personal advertisement. But when we're talking about writers, as opposed to, say, soap brands, then we have to talk about myths. Don't we run into Malraux at the end of *For Whom the Bell Tolls*?"

"No," François corrected him. "There's a French guy who fights on the Republican side and who calls himself André Marty in the book, but he really existed. I checked..."

"In fact, it was André Malraux who didn't exist," Chevalier said, exhaling a cloud of smoke.

"He might well have existed, but he no longer had the time to liberate the people. He was too busy strutting around the Mona Lisa in Washington with Jackie Kennedy on his arm."

"No different from your famous Hemingway as the liberator of Paris. We have a better idea now of his military objectives: the wine cellars at the Ritz and Marlene Dietrich. Of course, not everyone has the chance to hug a plane tree in full bloom," conceded Chevalier, with a bored air.

And he gave Godefroid a completely obvious wink that said:

"He's a tough nut, isn't he?"

Chevalier lived like a hermit at home in the Placard. La Grosse Éléonore, his implacable goddess, ruled over the other four and a half rooms. She would have made a great prison guard, but such are the fortunes of life that she became the head nurse in a new hospital built without under-the-table dealings with the Mafia and a handful of federal ministers. She was now the sole breadwinner, and the household was feeling the pinch. It was she who gave her head-in-the-clouds husband the name Branlequeue, which means tail-wagger, a sobriquet he remembered when he came to pick a nom-de-plume. The children, Martial, Pacific, and Vénus, wandered from one realm to another, according to their needs: order, the call of nature, and their stomachs dominated Éléonore's world;

Canada notebooks, washcloths, and toothbrushes drifted into the Placard, where games and the imagination, freedom and beauty could be found among the incredible clutter, in the middle of which the *pater familias*, silhouette outlined in a fog of nicotine, red pen in hand, glasses on the edge of his nose, feet up on a desk entirely carpeted with ink-smudged papers, coffee cups and Saskatoon-berry jam, officiated. Chevalier let them push their little cars and walk their dolls among the shadows of skyscrapers and mountain chains represented by piles of books and manuscripts. Perched at the peak of one of the piles, an ashtray overflowing with butts smoked away with the majesty of a domestic Etna.

It was in this smoke-filled Placard that Gode and François first heard about Quebec independence. The idea was a child of the right, but socialism took it and ran with it and impressed it in the minds of the province's progressive thinkers. Oppressed nations were the powder keg, the ideology of decolonization the lit match. Chevalier wanted their opinions on the situation in the Congo. On the Algerians drowned in the Seine. Everywhere on Earth, people were shuffling off the chains of the old imperial domination and embracing the cause of freedom.

They joined the RIN, the Rassemblement pour l'indépendance nationale. They volunteered their time. The Montreal office was next to a coffee house called The Patriot. On the South Shore, the soul of the separatist movement took bodily form in the person of Marcel Duquet, the man with the accountant's moustache and the checked suits. He was said to be of the right, but that didn't matter. In the RIN, Gode and François met Jean-Paul Lafleur, a large young man in his early twenties, built like a bear. Through him, they got to know his brother René. Patriots and revolutionaries of various plumages joined their circle of friends. There were people like Jacques Cardinal, the ex-cop turned political agitator, a genius at fraud whose supreme ambition was to "fuck the system." Bad eggs like him were legion, on the left and on the right, scrambling, scheming, and scribbling between the St. Lawrence and the U.S. border.

Between scorching puffs shot up by the fryer in the chip wagon, I saw the neighbourhood where I'd grown up change. Once a workers' eyesore stuck under the nose of the big city, the western outskirts swiftly became part of the urban conglomeration. You could get there by subway now. There were still vacant fields, but you no longer ran into the dog catcher, hired by the municipality, who advertised his prowess by stringing garlands of dogs' ears like bandoleers of bullets across his chest. He was said to have killed three thousand dogs in a single year. And Weston Bakeries no longer distributed free loaves of sliced bread on the street corners, as if we were in Africa. That was mostly around boulevard Taschereau. The only thing that hadn't changed was on election days the streets belonged to the mob. Yes, there were open sewers, but don't think for a minute they still reached as far as the mayor's or the deputy mayor's offices.

One night I knocked on Chevalier's door. He came down in his dressing gown, his little girl hanging onto his neck. He told me to come up.

To give me something to do while he finished correcting a chapter, he took a slim volume from a box on the floor and handed it to me. It must have been about sixty pages long. I read the title: *Damnedamerican*. It was Pepe Bourguignon's latest collection, the new darling of the poetry-of-engagement set. Hot off the press. It smelled funny.

"Pepe told me," Chevalier said without looking up, "they've printed a thousand copies, can you imagine that?"

I watched him correcting a typescript with his daughter. He had her sitting on his lap, and she was the one holding the pen. Three years old. Chevalier would indicate the word or words or lines he wanted cut, and she would take the red pen and strike through them, scritch, scratch, screech. From where I was sitting, I could see the huge, red lines: the page looked like the back of someone who'd been whipped.

"Vénus is a more severe critic than I am," Chevalier said complacently.

"Whose work is this?" I asked, pointing to a manuscript on his desk. A huge stack of papers, maybe a foot thick. He didn't reply right away.

"Mine."

"You wrote all that?"

He looked at me.

"It was easy. Simply put, I've rewritten our history."

He went to put the child to bed. When he came back, I'd found the courage to take a sheaf of papers folded in thirds from under my jacket. He took them without a word, sat down, offered me a whisky, and looked at the title page.

"*Hot Doggerels*. Hmmm."

He read it while I was watching. To pass the time I chain-smoked and refilled my whisky glass. Then I started examining the manuscripts piled on the chairs and even on the floor around where I was sitting. I picked one up, placed it on my lap, and read:

Click Beetles
A Novel
By François Langlais

I was floored. I counted the pages: three hundred and seventy-seven!

"He took the title from *Le Survenant*," Chevalier said, barely looking up from my manuscript. "Guèvrement used the term to mean something like 'a strong man'...It's a Québecism, like 'boulé,' which means almost the same thing. Do you want to know if it's any good?"

What could I say? That if it wasn't completely awful, a piece of shit, I would kill him?

"Umm."

"Your friend François is a very intelligent young man, but that's not enough to make him a writer. He's written a kind of detective novel, in which thugs rule the roost. There's a local Sherlock Holmes, a clone of Arsène Dupin, who likes to don disguises...There's a bit of Proust in it as well: in the end, we discover that every character is ...no, not a homosexual: a spy. It's brilliant, actually, very nuanced. Needs to be rewritten top to bottom, of course. So, now, shall we talk about your poems?"

He poured me a slug of whisky in a waterglass covered in finger-prints, then lit himself a cigarette, and offered me one.

"There's something you need to know, Richard, and the sooner you know it the better. 'Many are called, few are chosen ...' You'll thank me one day."

Touché, Chevalier. My first taste of whisky.

Nineteen sixty-eight arrived. It was spring. "Everything happens in Paris ..." Langlais told me, and so we pooled our money, got our passports and tickets, and left. Student unrest had sprung up in Nanterre and spread to the Latin Quarter, and those in power had reacted by shutting down the Sorbonne. On boulevard Saint-Michel, two thousand students had confronted the riot police.

The minute we arrived in the Place de l'Odéon, we started crying like babies, not because all the old grey stones that surrounded us were impregnated with literature, or because we were treading on the same cobblestones as Marcel Proust. It was because the students had been tear-gassed and Boulevard Saint-Michel was blanketed by an acrid pall that was blowing our way. We stepped on broken glass and all kinds of other debris. Someone had overturned a Peugeot: it lay on its back like a beetle on top of a pile of ripped-up paving stones. Farther along, men were busily tearing down a barricade: cobblestones, wooden beams, bags of cement, wire fencing, metal grilles, tree trunks, upside-down cars. Red and black flags flew over everything.

Ambulances were parked in front of the Sorbonne. A line of overturned, blackened cars stretched along the rue Gay-Lussac. Protesters had torn up trees and built barricades all around the Latin Quarter, and fought off the forces of law and order until six o'clock in the morning. They'd thrown bricks at the riot police, and the police had charged at them with billy clubs swinging, and blood was running in the streets. It looked as though the police had also used the kind of grenades known as crickets, which gave off a disabling nerve gas. And the students, joined by the young unemployed and the broke and homeless denizens of the suburbs, had returned the police fire with Molotov cocktails and blasts of sand jets from compressors stolen from the work crews trying to take down the façade.

Just before we left Montreal, someone gave us the address of a Parisian willing to rent us a room for next to nothing. His place was on Saint-Germain, between the Café Mabillon and the Café de Cluny. One bed. One dresser. One heater. Cold water and Turkish toilets at the end of the hall. We took it. It gave us front-row seats to the arrival of the revolution.

In the morning, François let me sleep in and went down to the Café Flore to nibble on a croissant and drink a cup of coffee served in a cup the size of a thimble. I found him immersed in the novel

A Sentimental Education and pulled up a chair and asked him the obvious question:

"Seen Jean-Paul Sartre yet?"

It didn't get a rise from him.

"He doesn't come here any more..."

We'd read in the paper that Sartre had addressed the students in the occupied Sorbonne. Rumour had it that the author of *Nausea*, taking his place at the podium, had found a message to him scribbled on a piece of paper: SARTRE, BE BRIEF! Our spies reported that the "little father," Charles de Gaulle, had also talked about "democracy run wild" and "a liaison between socialism and liberty."

"You know," François said, holding up *A Sentimental Education*, "the events taking place under our noses will go down in history and will find their place in the books exactly like those of 1848."

"What happened in 1848?"

"The July Revolution, of course!"

"I thought that was in 1789..."

"That was only the first. They never really stopped after that. They have an average of one a century."

François read *L'Humanité*, which in those days was calling for a GGI, an unlimited general strike. Pompidou had reopened the university, but the unions and student associations were still out and a huge cortège stretched from Place de la République to Place Denfert-Rochereau. This time, there were almost as many workers as there were students, all marching under the banners with arms linked. The floodgates were opened: factory workers were out, strikes were spreading like a contagion over the entire the country.

Once again, the red and black flag waved above the Sorbonne. The lecture halls were full to bursting with young men and women working to upset the establishment, to have their say, to hand the reins of power on to someone else. They were making placards, printing tracts and manifestos and broadsides, forming human chains, smoking unfiltered Gitanes, electing committees, representatives, delegates, naming those responsible, voting for programs and resolutions, picking up followers from the extreme left, from the far right, and bottling them all up in Paris with such ... You'd see them with their feet sticking out of sleeping bags, couples making love or just talking quietly about the importance of approaching the question of sexual politics from a dialectic perspective.

I met a girl from the Britanny Liberation Front, but it didn't work out. I lacked nerve. I hadn't yet understood that the trick was to lay it on as thick as possible. I was more the laid-back type. Everywhere you looked you saw kids with their hair falling down over their eyes holding cigarettes like they were characters in a Truffaut film.

"The more I make revolution, the more I want to make love," shouted one signpost. Another, in blood-red letters two feet high: "Fuck Who You Want!" Easy for them to say.

One day I saw the Notre-Dame Cathedral, the Louvre, the Place de la Madeleine, and the Eiffel Tower. After that, in the early evening, I met up with François at the Old Navy. He was almost finished *A Sentimental Education*. The night before, the General had addressed the nation. All of France had tuned in. And all of France agreed: "He doesn't have a clue what's going on." Pathetic.

"It's bizarre, though, don't you think?" François said.

"What is?"

"Less than a year ago he was announcing Quebec's liberation from the balcony at City Hall. And now he's the incarnation of the most reactionary power. What do you make of that?"

"That maybe Malraux should step down."

"You're forgetting Chevalier's theory: Malraux doesn't exist."

"I'll drink to that," I said, and ordered two more espressos.

One of François's friends dropped by, someone he'd recently

met. He looked interesting. As though lurking behind his eyes was the missing link between the post-war hip cat and the hippie. Mick Jagger with half the testosterone, give or take. Quite androgynous. His name was Luc Goupil, and he was French from France, a Quebecker by adoption, and was now living in London. He was part of the first wave of the FLQ. He had been arrested in 1963 for allegedly throwing a Molotov cocktail at a barracks. Imprisoned. He wasn't yet twenty years old. When he got out, he went underground.

"So, you think the Communists are going to take over?" he asked us.

"Civil war. Anything's possible," replied François. It was the phrase we'd been hearing everywhere: Anything's possible.

"I like that," Goupil drawled.

"The Americans would never allow it," I said.

Goupil leaned over the table and looked at me earnestly.

"The Americans?" he said. "They love all this shit . . . The old General said he wanted his own nuclear bomb, and look what he gets: a bomb up his ass!"

He laughed.

"I hear that Pompidou is complaining that his usual sources aren't reporting to him, his pools of spies aren't keeping him up to date with what's happening. Poor Pompy . . . What does he expect? Students are hard to keep an eye on, hard to infiltrate. You agree?"

I was beginning to understand François's fascination with the guy. With Goupil, a conversation always seemed to be taking place on two levels at the same time.

"What do you mean? That the French secret service . . ."

"The secret service works for the secret service, and if their interests happen to correspond with the interests of the government, then so much the better. The Communists don't have a snowball's chance in hell of seizing power, but in the meantime the Old Camel has a nice little revolution on his hands. Nothing too serious. But the next time he'll think twice before pulling out of NATO," Goupil said with a gracious smile. And ordered drinks. And more drinks.

Long before dawn I managed to drag myself toward the exit.

"Stay with us, Gode," Goupil said. "We're going to get some breakfast — stuffed crêpes smothered in Calvados."

"Makes my stomach heave just thinking about it," I said. "I'm going to bed..."

But we ordered one for the road. We drank to our little maid's room on Saint-Germaine-des-Prés, and to the health of maids in general, to their disappearance in a classless society of the future, and also to the health of Karl Marx, who liked maids well enough.

On the afternoon of May 29, hundreds of thousands of people marched from the Bastille to the Saint-Lazare station. Jean-Luc Godard was rumoured to be among the demonstrators, as was Aragon, and, of course, Elsa. The union and Communist leaders had signed the Grenelle Agreement with the government, but their members were refusing to vote in the factories, and the country's equilibrium was hanging by a thread. De Gaulle was finished. Power seemed to be up for grabs, at the business end of a rifle, ideally one with a flower in the barrel. If you could believe the rumours, groups of citizens were arming themselves and forming militias, waiting only for the order to switch to the offensive and liberate the Sorbonne and the Odéon. But de Gaulle had not had his last word. The French were cattle, and the Old Camel still had a trick or two up his sleeve. Under complete secrecy, he had himself helicoptered to the general headquarters of the French occupational forces in Germany, where he met with General Massu. Later, it was revealed that he'd envisaged a reconquest of France, starting with Alsace, to prevent the ripe fruit of power from falling into the Communist hands. He'd even considered borrowing combat helicopters from the Americans.

The next day, I took the subway to l'Étoile so I wouldn't have to say later that I'd been to Paris without seeing the Arc de Triomphe. I'd really had it up to here with everything, and I was flying home. Put it down to home sickness. I wanted to be in my own house. But first I would walk down the Champs-Élysées. And as I walked, I heard a noise crescendoing ahead of me, in the distance.

Traffic had stopped. Motorcycles roared past bearing policemen, there was a nervousness in the air, a wind charged with electricity whistled down the most beautiful avenue in the world, and, like an idiot, I continued walking down the middle of the street toward Place de la Concorde, because the cars had all disappeared. I was walking into the teeth of the parade! In one moment, flowing into Place de la Concorde and completely filling the vast avenue, pouring in from every direction, a million French citizens, from veterans in wheelchairs to young hippies in miniskirts, they formed a compact mass several kilometres long and moving toward the Arc de Triomphe. And there I was, stuck in the middle of them. I froze. The crowd was coming toward me like a tsunami. I waited until it was thirty metres from me before moving out of the way, and it was then that I saw him, arm in arm with the Gaullist big shots who'd begun the walk, singing *"Allons enfants de la patrie . . ."* at the top of his lungs. Malraux.

RED SQUARE, MOSCOW, MAY 1, 1946

FOUR ENORMOUS PORTRAITS, of Marx, Engels, Lenin, and Stalin, dominated the paved square where Marshal Koniev's T-34s, the heroes of the defence of Moscow, passed by in a continuous parade. With a low rumbling and a metallic clatter, these were the tanks that pierced the Panzer flanks at Stalingrad and Koursk. On the platform, the Little Father of the People, looking old and sunk into himself but still capable of annihilating ten million human beings with a snap of his fingers, showed the impassiveness, the almost cadaverous rigidity, that is the proper comportment of Soviet dignitaries below the exhortations and official slogans on the flurry of banners and insignia.

More impressed than he was willing to admit, the young Canadian military attaché turned to General Guillaume, his counterpart at the French embassy. "I sure wouldn't want to have to order my troops to dig in before these bloody things..."

The Frenchman smiled. At thirty-two, General Bédard still had the impetuosity of youth.

"But you know what?" added the Canadian. "The Allied High Command made a mistake. A very big mistake..."

And he went on to elaborate.

"Three years ago," Bédard continued, "Europe could still have been saved. The Allied strategy should have been to stabilize the Italian Front and throw massive troops through the Balkans into Europe. With the help of the Turks, we could have marched on Vienna and stopped the Communists from getting into the heart of Europe. Now it's too late..."

General Guillaume continued to smile. *Ah, these Canadians...*

"My dear Jean-B, you Anglo-Americans always think you know what's good for Europe. But the truth is that your deaths and ours were nothing compared to the twenty-five million who died in the Soviet Union. The Reds paid a high price for the spoils of Yalta."

"Behind the spoils of Yalta, as you put it, lies the shadow of a new terror creeping over our dear old civilization, and now there's nothing to stop it. The Red Army occupies half the continent. Marxist tyranny threatens the Acropolis. And by the way, I'm not Anglo-American. I'm French-Canadian."

"My apologies, my dear sir. But I still find you unduly pessimistic..."

"There is only one buffer left between Paris and the Mongolian hordes: the American troops. If I were you, I'd pray that they don't pull out too soon."

"You're forgetting the atomic bomb..."

"Stalin is going to want one for himself."

"Jean-B, my friend, you mistake them. These marshals, with their chests wallpapered with ribbons and medals, are walking museums. Under their uniforms, they are still peasants."

"Maybe, but they brought back French masterpieces and syphilis from Berlin, didn't they? And a few German scientists, as well. They already have their own program for producing heavy water, did you know that?"

"We'll see. But meanwhile, what a show!"

"Yes, they seem to have pulled out all the stops. And the day they receive their orders to roll on to the Atlantic, you'll find yourself cosying up with the British once again!"

General Guillaume erupted in a frank and friendly laugh.

"Please don't take offence, but you remind me of our collaborators, with their famous Christian rampart against Bolshevism."

General Bédard said nothing. General Guillaume drew his attention to the parade.

"Look! The famous Katiouchas," he said, indicating the esplanade. "Stalin's Organs."

They watched them approach in silence, pulled by trucks, the celebrated multi-barrelled rocket launchers that were the terror of the German, Romanian, and Italian infantries. They didn't know it, but they were witnessing the end of the myth of the Second World War.

SAINT-JEAN-BAPTISTE
DAY, 1968

HE TURNED AND SAW SEVERAL dozen protesters massed between Sherbrooke, Amherst, and Cherrier. They were hoisting fleur-de-lys and shouting, "Quebec for the Québécois!" and "Tru-deau no go!" Across from them, a cordon of helmeted police lined the north side of Sherbrooke Street, creating the single lane the marchers would have to use. Other protesters occupied the grassy slopes of Parc la Fontaine. Fresh police troops kept arriving.

Jean-Paul returned his attention to the platform that had been erected for dignitaries on the steps of the library. He was on the north side of the street, near the enclosure reserved for journalists. The sidewalk around him, and behind him the slope leading up to the Normal School, were crowded with spectators who had come to watch. Squinting, he made out the prime minister of Canada on the platform, waving at the crowd, all smiles, surrounded by body-guards and official invitees.

There was a small commotion in the crowd, and Lafleur saw Bourgault, the intellectual of the independence movement, lifted onto a sea of shoulders on which he floated like a coconut on the tide. The police, marked by their white helmets, tried to contain the throng of militants distributing tracts to the people crowded in front of the platform. The president of the RIN was not lacking in panache. He had alerted the newspapers that the presence of the prime minister at this Saint-Jean-Baptiste Day parade, in celebration of Quebec's national holiday, on the eve of the federal election, would be considered a provocation by the separatists. Trudeau having ignored the warning, Bourgault showed up, too, and now it was as though the two men, the extravagant Liberal on his official platform, and the eloquent agitator perched on his human dais, each one as conspicuous as the other, were facing off against each other from opposite sides of Sherbrooke Street.

No sooner had these thoughts flitted through Jean-Paul's mind than a ripple stirred in the crowd and spread in nervous waves around him. From the demonstrators' side, which continued to shout slogans, he saw an onlooker in a red T-shirt shoving and shouting at a young, long-haired man who remained unprovoked. Others in civilian clothing attacked the protesters, pushing them toward the line of uniformed police who, ready with their truncheons, joined in the action. He watched as two policemen grabbed fleur-de-lys from the hands of the demonstrators and tore them up, definitely putting a match to the powder keg.

Without warning, the four horsemen who, a moment before, had been carrying Bourgault in triumph, made a sudden rush toward the platform, broke through the police cordon, and burst out onto the street. There they were quickly grabbed by uniformed policemen, who also seized the separatist leader and carried him like a sack of potatoes toward a paddy wagon parked nearby. They were still waiting for the bulk of the marchers. Police motorcycles came and went between the platform, flanked by the library's Greco-Roman pillars and Parc la Fontaine. Still stunned by the suddenness with which Bourgault had rushed into the arms of the police, Jean-Paul felt himself being pushed from behind. He tried to resist it. Ahead of him, the police were charging through the park, bludgeoning anything that moved. Panicked spectators rushed the barriers, pushed through the police cordon, and surged into the middle of Sherbrooke Street.

Jean-Paul started to run. All around him, billy clubs were rising and falling as the guardians of law and order clubbed men, women, and children at random. He stopped across from the dignitaries' platform, blinded by searchlights and the Corinthian columns, and raised his fist.

"Quebec for the Québ—"

A flashing pain cut through his shoulder, his arm fell to his side, and a hard object whistled through the air, tracing a horizontal arc and hitting his inert arm at the elbow. It was as if someone had shut off the nerve with a tourniquet.

"Oww, Jesus!"

He began running again, sprinting east, fleeing before the parade that, in the distance, was descending the hill with its fanfare and floats. Around him, young people were being grabbed by the police and thrown to the ground and held down while other cops bashed at their heads as though they were baby seals. Then they were dragged toward the fenced-in compounds with the billy clubs still lashing them. There was a whistling sound, and the first beer bottle shattered like a grenade on the pavement ten feet from Jean-Paul. More bottles rained down. The sharp explosions sounded strange, different from the dull thud of clubs on flesh. A clamour arose on the street, the police were trying to clear the area in front of the platform. Jean-Paul leaped to one side to avoid being hit by a sidecar attached to a motorcycle. He turned and saw a demonstrator take several quick steps and throw an empty Molson's bottle toward the platform, then run back, quickly chased by white-helmeted police, their billy clubs raised at the ready.

Then Jean-Paul saw stars. A hardwood truncheon had struck him just above the ear, and for a second he lost consciousness. He quickly came to, his face squeezed in the armpit of a police officer who had him in a headlock and who should have been wearing more deodorant.

"You goddamn piece of shit," said the cop, his head bent close to Jean-Paul's.

The cop was regulation size, but Jean-Paul was built like a logger. He shrugged off his assailant, helped him lose his footing, pulled his head from the vise of the cop's arm encircling his head, and ran off without looking back.

He ran up the grass in front of the Normal School and headed back towards rue Cherrier just as the parade was arriving at Sherbrooke Street. It was blocked by the tangle of motorcycles, human forms milling about, and a row of idling ambulances. Police chased the demonstrators into the ranks of a marching band, the musicians standing at attention silently holding their instruments. He could hear music from another band mingled with shouts, slogans, explosions, the nervous revving of the motorcycles coming and, from the direction of the platform, the popping of beer bottles and windshields and the sound of sirens slicing through the air. Jean-Paul slowed his pace to catch his breath. He could see that fires had been lit in Park Lafontaine. The smell of smoke floated toward him, it tingled in his nose. *Molotov cocktails*, he thought. On rue Cherrier, a police scout car left unoccupied was being pushed backward by rioters. Then a second, and a third, and then a private car. Jean-Paul was heading toward it when he was stopped by the spectacle of three policemen animatedly beating a young man in the centre of a circle of indignant citizens slowly closing in on them. He shoved his way between their shoulders. The young man had stopped defending himself, and the blows continued to rain on his face, his legs, his testicles. A fountain of blood spurted from his bare head.

Jean-Paul went up to the policemen.

"Hey!" he shouted.

"He was throwing bottles," explained one of the officers, who kept Jean-Paul at a distance with his billy club dripping with blood.

But the spectators began closing in, and the policeman seized the young man by his arms and began dragging him onto the grass while the other two kept on bludgeoning and kicking him.

"We need weapons..." Jean-Paul said to himself, stunned.

Then, looking around at the crowd, he repeated it out loud, almost shouting:

"We've got to arm ourselves!"

He was standing there, incredulous, when someone near him shouted, "Look out!", and through the storm of panic that was blowing over that section of the park, Lafleur turned and saw them coming. It wasn't the charge of the Cossacks from *Doctor Zhivago*, or young Winston Churchill's regiment launched with drawn sabres against the Bedouins at Soudan, but the Montreal Mounted Police charging through Park Lafontaine. They came six abreast on their beasts, equipped with wooden batons four feet long, and their white helmets with the short visors made them look like polo players, rigged out like a laughable colonial cavalry. They charged the crowd, falling on women, children, and old-age pensioners who had come to watch the parade, beating on shoulders and backs, and cracking skulls indiscriminately. Gaping holes appeared, disclosing trampled grass and those who in the general mélée had tripped and were trying to stand up, a forehead bleeding here, a nose smashed there, a cheekbone crushed, a shoulder blade cracked, all under the avalanche of blows amid rearing and prancing horses.

One mounted cop passed so close to Jean-Paul, who protected his face with his forearm, that he felt the heat of the beast on his cheek, and experienced an animal terror while the man above him shouted, his truncheon pointed ahead of him like a lance:

"Charge the French-Canadians," he shouted.

An officer, he thought.

All this time the tightly packed crowd was trying to escape by flowing back in a herd onto Sherbrooke Street, further paralyzing the parade. Jean-Paul zigzagged down the slope to avoid the horses that had been spurred into the mass of demonstrators like a tournament of truncheons. He turned again toward the officials' platform, clenching his teeth, rage in his heart. As he set foot on the street, he saw a young protester cornered between a reporter's car and a horse, the rider of which was pounding away at the young man's back, rhythmically and methodically, using both hands on his long club. Suddenly, the club broke in half, and the policeman continued to beat on his victim with the half he still clutched, until explosions between the horse's hooves caused the animal to rear, dumping the attacker beneath it. Onlookers' arms shot into the air as if Maurice Richard had just scored on a breakaway.

Lafleur heard more bottles whistling over his head. Ahead of him, young men and women were being arrested and dragged by the police along the broken-glass-covered street. Shards sparkled in the light from the spotlights. A clamour arose from the area of the platform, now being targeted by the bottle-throwers, and Jean-Paul raised himself on his tiptoes to get a better look at the mayhem: the frantic retreat of the diplomatic corps and the honoured guests from the bombarded dais, a chaos of chairs, and then the prime minister, evading the approaching guards and advancing to the front of the colonnaded portico, facing the enemy alone, the grand seigneur, a proud smile on his lips, his moment of glory broadcast coast to coast. All cameras on him, his parliamentary majority in the bag.

Almost at the same time, Jean-Paul received a billy club to the chest. When he was able to breathe again, he was surrounded by five police officers who jumped on him, calling him a "goddamned separatist" and a "flea-bitten dog" as they escorted him toward the nearest paddy wagon. Once they were screened from view, they made sure their client got its money's worth, going to work on Lafleur as he lay stretched out on the ground, no longer feeling anything, like a caveman being trampled by a wart hog. Then they grabbed him by the arms and legs and threw him into the van.

There were twenty others in there already, it was hot as an oven and the atmosphere was one of dejection. Standing, sitting, lying down. Gashes, broken ribs, a dislocated shoulder, a fractured elbow, a few eyebrows transformed into gushing faucets, and enough bruises to repaint half of one of the three Canadian oceans. One of the victims had slipped into unconsciousness. A rapid examination showed a possible skull fracture. Someone stood up and pounded on the side of the van with the flat of a hand.

"Someone is seriously injured in here!"

"He's dying!"

The police officer left behind to guard the van gave his opinion through the ventilation duct:

"Let him die like a dog, I couldn't care less ..."

Jean-Paul turned to the guy sitting beside him, a thin man in his early twenties. He had a scalp wound and his head was covered with coagulating blood. Fresh blood was flowing from one of his eyelids and covered half his face.

"Let me wipe that," he said, tearing off the sleeve of his shirt and folding it into a pad, which he applied to the man's temple as a kind of bandage.

"Hold it there. Have you been here long?"

"About an hour," replied the man.

"Water!" someone called out.

"Die!"

When the paddy wagon began to move, the young man held out his bloodied hand to Jean-Paul and managed a smile.

"My friends call me Lancelot..."

"As long as I don't have to call you Sir Lancelot, no problem." Jean-Paul shook his hand, took his own back with the man's blood on it, and said, "Jean-Paul."

"I never thought they were capable of such barbarity..."

They were driven west along Cherrier. They couldn't see the huge float stuck in the middle of a bunch of brawlers a bit farther down, between Montcalm and Wolfe streets, with its gigantic papier-mâché figure of St.-Jean-Baptiste suddenly decapitated by a beer bottle thrown accurately from a distance of thirty feet. Police charged the float and hopped up onto the truck bed amid a bevy of young shepherdesses who, in the general confusion, were screaming. An evacuation order was given.

The van followed rue Ontario to Division 4 and turned into the courtyard. The prisoners held their breath.

The door opened with a clang. Between the paddy wagon and the police station a dozen officers stood in a receiving line. Each had a billy club in his hand. Some of them fondled the tips of their clubs, grinning, while others pounded them impatiently into the palms of their hands. And all of them were shouting insults.

"What the hell are they playing at?" Lancelot asked.

He gave a sudden lurch and bent over to vomit, but nothing came out.

"Cowboys and Indians," said Jean-Paul. He was struck by a sudden inspiration. "Try not to fall down, okay? I'll go ahead of you. You hang on to me..."

"But..."

"Don't give them the satisfaction...Stay on your feet."

"Yeah." A smile cracked the dried blood on Lancelot's lips. Ten out of ten.

WITH MADAME CORPS

"IN YOUR ESTIMATION, why did Godefroid and the Lafleur brothers go to Texas a week before kidnapping Paul Lavoie?"

"I haven't the faintest idea, Samuel."

"According to one version, they went to buy arms. Others say it was to make contacts. Set up financing for future operations. Someone even suggested they went to avoid getting mixed up in the kidnappings and to establish an alibi. And do you know what their poor old mother told the coroner? That they had creditors up their asses (she didn't phrase it like that), and they went to the States to start new lives..."

"She may have been right about the creditors. Coco had taught them a trick or two. Credit cards, travellers' cheques. And loans. When you have no intention of paying anything back, being in debt can be a kind of business plan. They'd been maxed out for two years."

"Yes, and when their real names were no good any more, Coco got them false identification papers. I know about all that, Madame.

But what I'd like to know is why Coco was so keen on sending the guys in the Chevalier Cell to the United States in November 1970."

"That..."

"At least one other person, you see, had urged Gode and the Lafleurs to cross the border that autumn. Bernard Saint-Laurent. The man who'd smuggled them out of Montreal and hid them in a sugar cabin in the woods. Funny little bird. A pure product of the Company of Young Canadians, who worked as a cover for the federal government's spies in the Quebec community movement. Saint-Laurent, the famous mole who'd been thrown out of a Parti québécois meeting in 1971. Some writers make him part of Colonel Bob Lapierre's organization. Lapierre was the *eminence gris* of the Liberal Party..."

"You're losing me here."

"Too bad. Just when the trap was getting interesting. Do you know what Saint-Laurent did after the October Crisis? He opened a restaurant in Old Montreal and called it Le Chat Huant, which means great horned owl but it's a word we never use in Quebec. But in Vendée, there's *chouan*, which in Quebec is corrupted to *chouay-en*, which we call the *Chouan canayen*, and which we also use to mean 'counter-revolutionary.'"

"Don't you think you might be pushing the cork in a bit far?"

"Maybe. But when you don't have a corkscrew, sometimes pushing the cork in is the only way to open the bottle."

"You want to know if Coco knew Saint-Laurent, is that it?"

"It sounds like we're talking about French haute couture."

"Very funny. But the truth is, I don't know anything. Not a thing."

"Tell me about the boat..."

"Why? The boat has nothing to do with what you're interested in."

"I can still go fishing. You never know what's going to bite. If the boat is too small, I'll throw it back in, promise."

"He wanted to make it with his own hands. Sail it around the world... His dream."

"Was it really a schooner?"

"A two-master, yes. With a ferro-concrete hull. A fairly revolutionary technique at the time. He bought some land beside the St. Lawrence in Acadia..."

"At Île aux Fesses."

"That's what it was called. It had a couple of summer cottages on it, up on stilts. He built the boat in a hangar. Which was just a roof over his floating shack."

"Godefroid and the Lafleurs helped him?"

"They may have. Why?"

"On October 18, 1970, only a few hours after the body of Paul Lavoie was discovered, the police undertook a large-scale operation code-named Operation Rabbits, in the area of Île aux Fesses: army helicopters, combing the woods, road blocks, searching all the cottages and surrounding fields. Apparently they came up empty-handed."

"During the raids connected with the War Measures Act, Coco was arrested. You knew that, didn't you?

"Yes. What happened to the boat?"

"No idea."

"And Coco. What did he die of, exactly?"

"An overdose."

"An overdose of what, Madame Corps?"

"He ended up snorting himself to death."

"I see."

"Yes, and I was the mother of his children. The water under his beautiful big boat..."

"Your lover gets his head crushed under a tractor. And your husband dies of an overdose. More and more interesting. I didn't know about the overdose..."

"You can't tell me you find his death suspicious."

"I'm not going to tell you anything. Why weren't you a witness at the trial?"

"Because I was afraid. Everyone told me I should go into hiding ... But when Marcel's trial came up, I tried anyway. I went to the police in Pathenais to ask them if they wanted to take my statement. They told me I'd made the trip for nothing: they didn't need a statement from me. Later, when the case went to appellate court, I went to see his lawyer, *Maître* Brien, and practically begged him to call me as a witness for the defence. I could testify to something important: Marcel had been against killing Lavoie. He'd agreed to hide the guys in order to avoid a bloodbath until he could hand them over safe and sound to Justice ..."

"I guess that's one way to look at it. So what did *Maître* Brien have to say?"

"He took down my phone number. But he never called me back ..."

GODE'S TRIAL,
SPRING 1971

MAY WAS A MILD MONTH. In his cell on the fourth floor of the Parthenais Prison, Gode was allowed to see the few rays of spring sunlight filtering in through his iron bars. It was there that he ate and slept, slept and ate.

When he looked north, he could see De Lorimier Park, people playing baseball, couples walking hand in hand, a church. The Lavigueur Tavern.

One day, he was told he had a visit from his lawyer.

At the time of the October Crisis, *Maître* Brien had acted as the negotiator on behalf of the kidnappers before the authorities. Charges of sedition that had been levied against him had been dropped in February. When he'd been liberated with a caution, the Crown launched an appeal, and a charge of obstructing federal agents still hung over his head. Meanwhile, unable to practise, it was simply as legal counsel that he'd been authorized to see his client.

In January, several weeks after the departure of the soldiers, the coroner had detained René Lafleur, Jean-Paul Lafleur, Richard Godefroid, and Benoit Desrosiers for criminal responsibility in the death of Paul Lavoie. The basis for the charge was an unsigned confession attributed to Richard Godefroid describing an attempted escape by Lavoie, the serious injuries that had been inflicted on him, and the way in which he and the Lafleur brothers had, the next day, strangled him in cold blood using a silver chain that the victim had worn around his neck. The officers who'd interrogated the witnesses appeared in court to swear, with their hands on the Bible, that the statement had been given voluntarily on the night of the arrest of the three men, but that Godefroid had later refused to sign it.

The sound of automatic doors being unlocked. Footsteps in the corridor. Brien.

"What the hell's all this about a confession, for Christ's sake?"

His arrogance was untamed by his time behind bars, his thick hair was still wild and cut short. Upon his release, *Maître* Brien had gone back to the few comforts of life that remained to him: his motorcycle, illicit substances, and young women. He was his old, cocky self.

"I don't know," Gode replied. "I was expecting to get beaten up but goddamn it, he started talking to me! And while he was talking, the other one went and got me a coffee. Good coffee, too, and hot. I'd just spent three days freezing my ass off in that rat hole. The first thing I knew, I was telling them the story of my life."

"Never tell them anything. Never!"

"They asked me if I had a lawyer. I said yes. That's how I found out that you were in prison, too."

"Yeah, when I interviewed your pal Jean-Paul, they didn't have to go far to get me. They took me out of my cell and brought me to his. It was convenient."

Maître Brien didn't appear to be in a good mood. He kept pacing back and forth in front of Gode, who watched him as he sat on his cot.

"I didn't even sign their damned confession. It was just a story I told them."

"You didn't sign it, but you added corrections to it in your own handwriting! The Crown sees that as a form of admission. Would you kindly tell me what the hell you were thinking?"

"There were mistakes in it!"

The lawyer gently massaged his temples with the tips of his fingers.

"Jesus Christ . . . They really pulled a fast one on you, my friend. Do you want me to find you a good lawyer?"

"You're my lawyer. I'll defend myself . . ."

His look was that of the Musketeer at the Bar.

"But I'm going to need some books."

Jean-Paul had been the first to go to the chopping block in January. For security reasons, a room in the police headquarters building had been converted into a courtroom. Little-known fact, the suspects were therefore detained and tried in the same building, on rue Parthenais. It had its practical side. Jean-Paul, conducting his own defence, completely politicized his trial, which therefore degenerated into a judicial guerrilla war that concluded with his rapid expulsion from the courtroom and a first in the history of Canadian jurisprudence: a defendant conducting his own defence *in absentia*. "He's going to need an imagination . . ." the judge remarked in a memorable aside.

The public prosecutor could build his case in peace, with the help of an interminable line of cops assigned by the Crown. By mid-March, at the end of a trial tainted by numerous irregularities, Lafleur was found guilty of the murder of Paul Lavoie and sentenced to life imprisonment. The prosecution's summation of the case lasted ten minutes.

From their appearance before the coroner at the beginning of the year, the FLQers had waged a fierce battle, the burden of which had been insults aimed at the magistrate. By May, the cup had gone to René, who had scored twice at the coroner's inquest. Jean-Paul and Gode shared second place with one goal each, but Gode won on points because of the way he'd taken advantage of current events to score his goal: when he advised Coroner Bourdages to "eat a bucket of shit," only the most awake among the journalists noted that his words were a light paraphrase of the famous apostrophe that the prime minister of Canada had delivered to the unemployed workers in Rouyn-Noranda.

At the beginning of his trial, in the spring, Richard Godefroid shattered his comrade's record with a fully acknowledged grand slam: four contempts-of-court in less than two hours. His hair was shorter, he'd shaved his beard, and he wore an almost presentable moustache. *Maître* Goulet, *Maître* Brien's assistant, acted as second counsel for the defence.

Gode moved forward and seemed about to step out of the defendant's box.

"Where do you think you're going?" Judge Morel demanded of him.

"I'm just going to sit beside my counsel. Since I am conducting my own defence, I need ..."

"Get back to your place."

"Well then, I'll need a table to write on."

"Permission refused."

"But how am I supposed to take notes?"

"You can write on your knee."

"Maybe when they're as old as yours are, Judge, they'll make a good writing table, but I'm not there yet. Talk about a goddamned fair trial, for —"

"Sir, what you have just said is called contempt of court. And I am warning you that I have no intention of tolerating the slightest attempt on your part to turn this court into a personal stage or a public arena. Enough legal badgering, do you understand me?"

"Ten out of ten, Your Honour. We'll stay well within the letter of the law..."

Gode hadn't been idle in his cell. He'd amassed an impressive stack of paper covered with his grade-school handwriting, with its deep, rounded Os in lead pencil. He read aloud his request that the trial declare its jurisdiction invalid in this case because it was unconstitutional. He traced his request back to the battle between Wolfe and Montcalm on the Plains of Abraham in 1759, to 1867 and the Constitution imposed by the railway barons, passing en route through the Royal Proclamation of 1763, the Quebec Act of 1774, the American War of Independence, the Constitution Act of 1791, the 1837 Rebellion, and the 1840 Act of Union, concluding his argument with the illegality of the said Court of the Queen's Bench since its legitimacy was based on Articles 99 to 101 of the British North America Act, which had been illegally imposed on Quebec by a foreign power following an armed conflict.

The judge waited for an opportunity to interrupt him. When Gode seemed about to bring the dispute over the borders of Labrador into play, he jumped in.

"You express yourself with an astonishing facility, sir, but you have a tendency to drift into side issues. To the point, if you please!"

"And you are an old whore representing a repressive power established by force of arms. I am the one who's been wronged here, and I'm fighting to liberate my country from those holding its people captive."

"You are in contempt of court. Please take note of that, clerk."

Gode went on to talk about justice, a dubious term in a province that had the highest unemployment rate in the country, whose French-Canadian citizens trailed behind all others in education and led all others in heart disease and infant malnutrition. He switched to the Gaspésie, where fishermen were exploited from father to son by a pack of inverted Robin Hoods who stole from the poor and gave to the rich.

"You digress, you digress..."

"It's better to be off topic than to be off my rocker, like the Fathers of Confederation."

"Your request is denied, sir."

"For fuck's sake!"

"*Strike three!*" cried the judge, waving his gavel in the air. "Clerk..."

But Gode returned to his attack during the jury selection process. This time, his request for annulment was based on the notion that said process violated his right to be tried by a jury of his peers, a right guaranteed by the Magna Carta, which had been signed by King John at Runnymede in 1215, and ratified by his successors, up to and including Queen Elizabeth II. Far from being his peers, any jury in Quebec would be selected from among a small group of privileged citizens representing only 20 percent of Quebec society, because women (50 percent of the population) and male small-landowners (30 percent) were excluded from jury duty, which meant, in effect, that his case would be heard by a jury constituting only businessmen. Furthermore, according to the Canadian Bill of Human Rights, it was discriminatory to establish distinctions among citizens based on race or financial status, which is exactly what the Quebec Jury Law did. To bolster his argument, Gode cited the case of *Drybones vs. Curouk* and Article 538 of the Criminal Code, adding for good measure the commentary of Judge Lagarde.

Judge Morel listened with his mouth hanging open.

"Hmm. I congratulate you on the quality of your presentation, but I find no cause for objection under the terms of Article 538. Request denied."

"Thank you, future Senator Lemor."

"Why do you say that?"

"Because you're doing your job."

"And what name did you call me?"

"Lemor. It's an anagram of your name."

"I don't quite see why you would place yourself in contempt of court for ... for that."

"No big deal, I was just helping you out. What I wanted to say was: Fuck you!"

"Clerk, did you get that?"

Chin in hand, Gode's face expressed astonishment as he watched the long line of witnesses called to the bar. A significant number of them came from the ranks of the Mounted Police, most of them young men in their early thirties. Others were from the Montreal Police and the Quebec Provincial Police. Apart from the patholo- gist, whose questioning was purely pro forma and who gave the curious impression of having been caught in a wind storm, the wit- nesses were all police officers. Standing at the bar, masters of all they surveyed, they identified one court exhibit after another: the two modified M1 rifles (barrels shortened to five inches, sawn off, and fitted with sight extensions, for a total length of between twenty- two and thirty-two inches, as described in the doleful voice of the ballistics expert); cartridge clips, with a total capacity of thirty bul- lets each; cartridges, brand name Norma, soft-point lead tips, in one of the guns; in the other, Hirtenberger bullets with coated tips; two pairs of handcuffs purchased at an army surplus store; bills for same; a bill for the purchase of a military-type folding shovel; two rolls of tape; a chain of the type used for dogs' leashes; wigs; one khaki ski mask with holes for the eyes; one plastic false nose and eyeglasses; raincoats, brand names Wellington and London Fog; a rifle, Winchester Model 840; a 12-gauge sawn-off shotgun; cartridges for same, brand name Imperial, filled with No. 5 lead pellets; one sweater, stained with blood, that belonged to Jean-Paul; one blanket belonging to Mrs. Lafleur.

Then came photographs of items the experts had fingerprinted during the investigation and did not appear in court: a jar of jam; a jar of mustard; another of mayonnaise; a bag of sliced bread; a cardboard chicken box from Baby Barbecue.

Scraps of paper and fragments of communications found at the scene, with their truncated messages forming indecipherable puzzles as far as the public was concerned: Lima. Ditch. Cell. Rebel. Communiqué 1. No concessions. Ten-hour limit.

And typewriters. The old Underwood. The Remington with the smashed keyboard.

"State your name, age, and profession."

"Rénald Massicotte, forty-two. I deliver chicken for Baby Barbecue."

"Would you please tell the court, Mr. Massicotte, what you were doing on October 10, last fall, between the hours of eleven-thirty and one o'clock in the afternoon?"

"Sure. I was delivering chicken. Why?"

"What kind of chicken?"

"Club sandwiches ... Three club sandwiches."

"That was all?"

"No. There were also six Pepsis in the order."

"Tell us a bit about Baby Barbecue, Mr. Massicotte."

"It's the biggest."

"The biggest what?"

"The biggest chicken outlet on the South Shore. On a weekend a good delivery person can make maybe fifty deliveries. A good ten, fifteen bucks in tips, maybe even twenty. On weekdays it's almost as good. Maybe thirty deliveries."

"Good. And now, describe for us what happened when you arrived at 140 rue Collins, in Saint-Hubert."

"I parked in front of the house and I didn't even have time to open the car door when someone came out of the house."

"What happened then?"

"He came right out to the street to get the order. I stayed in the car and rolled down my window."

"Does this sort of thing happen often? That a customer comes out to the car like that?"

"No, it's pretty rare."

"How rare, Mr. Massicotte?"

"I'd say it happens maybe once every two hundred deliveries. No more than that."

"Thank you, Mr. Massicotte. Your Honour, I have no more questions."

Judge Morel turned to Gode, who seemed to have become prey to an erotic reverie in the defendant's box.

"Does the defence wish to cross-examine the witness?"

As though half-asleep, Gode swiped at a fly in front of his face.

"Nope, future Senator Lemor."

Since the denial of his last request for a reduced charge, he had hardly opened his yap.

Near the open doors of the courtroom, a uniformed officer lightly nudged a journalist who was standing, arms and legs spread apart, notebook in one hand and morning paper in the other. A bit farther on, a group of young long-hairs in bell-bottoms were talking and smoking. Off to one side stood a man with a gentle look, a high, pale forehead as shiny as a dome of ice, and a long, thoughtful face. He seemed to be in his forties. He was wearing a suit and cardigan and a tie. His hands, humbly held up before his chest, clasped the brim of an old-fashioned hat. Captain Leclerc, in civilian clothes, nodded to him from a distance and moved obliquely in his direction, passing close as though surprised to find the man in his path, even though their meeting was no accident. He held out his hand.

"Chevalier. How's it going?"

"Very well, Captain. And you?"

"A bit overworked these days, but not bad, not bad ..."

"I assume you're working in close collaboration with the Crown in this business, no?"

"We usually do in cases like this. Why do you ask?"

"Well, a trial like this must be expensive. The least the Crown could do, it seems to me, is to not waste its witnesses."

"Tell me what's going on inside that head of yours, Chevalier."

"That chicken delivery boy who was up there this morning, no one asked him if he was able to identify his customer. No one even asked him the question! I was a bit surprised by that ..."

"The prosecutor must have asked him that before and already knew the answer ... The Crown has the right to prepare its witnesses, as does the defence."

"Maybe so. But if I were a juror and I was told that a certain event happens only once in every two hundred deliveries, I'd be inclined to think that such an event would have a good chance of leaving some trace, some memory. And I'd be curious as to why ..."

The captain narrowed his eyes. A shadow divided his forehead in two like a vertical curtain, and he looked attentively at his interlocutor.

"To make his case, *Maître* Grosleau only needs to show that the occupants of the house acted in a suspicious manner that day. And the delivery boy must not have been able to identify the customer, otherwise the Crown would have jumped all over it, don't you think?"

"Maybe, but I do know one thing for sure: on the tenth of October, at noon, the occupants of the bungalow on rue Collins had no hostage inside. They didn't take action until six hours later. So where was the risk? What difference could it possibly have made if the delivery boy came to the door or if someone went out to meet him at the curb? They were safe, as long as they hadn't left their machine guns lying about on the dining table or their handcuffs on the kitchen counter. And even then, going out to meet the chicken man in his little red car would only make him think there was something odd about it."

The captain nodded slowly, as if he were dreaming, surprised and consternated.

"Where are you going with this?"

"I don't know yet. But there's something somewhere that doesn't add up."

"All I'm doing is investigating a man's death. I'm not interested in politics."

"Of course," said Chevalier, letting his eyes drift around the sixth floor of the vast polygon on rue Parthenais. "It must be handy, having the courtroom right here, with the prison cells and police headquarters all in one building. One-stop shopping, in a way . . ."

"Extraordinary times call for extraordinary measures, isn't that what some writer said?"

"Monsieur Chevalier, at the time that Richard Godefroid was working for you during the electoral campaign, he was already involved in criminal activities. My question to you is: Did you know about it?"

Chevalier Branlequeue had told the court, at *Maître* Grosleau's request, about his mediation on December 27 in the Valley of the Patriots, the night Gode gave himself up. He clearly saw the trap that was being laid for him, more from malice than anything else, by the Crown prosecutor.

"All I can say is that I had the greatest respect for his idealism. I still do. But at Saint-Marc, I was acting without idealism. I was simply following the instructions I'd been given."

"Given to you by whom, exactly?"

"I never found out who I was representing. Perhaps that was a professional lapse. Or perhaps it's the story of my life."

"Do you sympathize with the accused?"

"As I just said, I respect his ideals. And he has discovered that his ideals have been betrayed. It was the twisted electoral tricks of the political machine that drove him from idealism to action. When the group began to radicalize, last summer, he tried to keep his distance from it, up to a certain point. But he found what went on around him too depressing. He's a sensitive person. He wanted reality to allow him to dream. He's neither a weak innocent nor a dangerous idealist..."

"When we need a psychological evaluation, we'll let you know."

"You asked me a question, I tried to reply. Richard Godefroid gave democracy a chance, but it was the underworld that took him."

"Watch your language, sir..."

"That's exactly what I'm doing, *Maître* Grosleau."

"Good." The prosecutor smiled. "No more questions, Your Honour."

Judge Morel must have wanted a cup of coffee.

"Ahem. *Maître* Gode... Excuse me, I mean Mr. Godefroid. Have you prepared a cross-examination for this witness?"

Over the previous few days, Gode had listened to exactly 190 witnesses, almost all of them police officers, without opening his mouth once except to yawn. He had been the caboose on the train and the Crown prosecutor was the locomotive, the police were the cars, and the pieces of evidence were the cargo. And so now, in response to this purely routine question from the judge, he was seen to gravely nod his head, place both his hands on the railing of the defendant's box, get slowly to his feet, and turn even more slowly toward the witness box. Silence reigned in the courtroom.

"Yeah, Seigneur. I am going to do exactly that . . . cross-examine the witness."

"He's all yours."

Now, thought Branlequeue, *he's going to get even with me for what I said about his poems.*

Gode would have very much liked to be able to step toward his former professor and walk around him, hands behind his back, giving him an occasional sharp look, like an uppercut, like they do in the movies, but the combination of roles did not extend to allowing him to leave the defendant's stand.

"Do you know anything, Monsieur Chevalier, about the unsigned 'confession' that has been attributed to me?"

"I've read excerpts in the newspapers."

"And what did you think about them?"

"Ask a specific question," intervened the judge.

"Oh, for Christ's sake, back off . . ." Godefroid retorted.

Chevalier looked at the judge, who shrugged his shoulders.

"I can give you my opinion as an editor," he said. "It's total fiction."

The judge silenced the brouhaha that arose from the public benches with a bunching of his Jupiterian eyebrows.

"I said, confine yourself to precise questions. And that goes for replies, too!"

"Monsieur Chevalier," Gode began again, "do you recall the words that were exchanged on the morning of December 28 in the living room of the house in Saint-Marc?"

"Yes."

"Do you remember a promise you made on that occasion?"
"Yes."
Gode turned his back.
"I have no further questions, Your Honour."

After ten days and nearly two hundred witnesses, the Crown had constructed a proof that was now closing in around Gode. He found himself encased in a solid version of the story that had a worldly vision. When it was his turn to counter the steamroller, he called a single witness. The name Marie-France Bellechasse was met by a perplexed and interrogative silence.

She had already refused to be a witness at the coroner's inquest, arguing that she could not, neither in her soul nor in her conscience, participate in a judiciary process that persisted, against all human reason, in denying a woman the fundamental right to judge her peers, no matter their sex, as a member of a legally constituted jury. The coroner had admired the logic of her reasoning before sticking her with a charge of contempt of court and sentencing her to a month in prison.

When she advanced toward the witness stand, a tall, well-built blonde, her long hair in curls, dressed in light blue jeans and a dark green worker's shirt, unbuttoned, sleeves rolled up, over a green sweater, and workboots, the whole outfit fitting her perfectly, even graciously, a respectful murmur rippled through the room.

Gode turned his eyes toward the spectators as if to say, *Okay, agreed, a man has been killed. But are you seeing the same thing I see?* And suddenly it was as if he had sung, *In the month of May the girls are so pretty . . .*

"Your witness, sir."
Gode turned toward the magistrate.
"If you say so, Your Honour."

Then he clung to the railing with both hands and appeared to be concentrating.

"What do you do for a living, Mademoiselle Bellechasse?"

"I study law. At the University of Montreal."

She spoke with aplomb, her voice resting somewhere between vulgarity and a somewhat softened melodiousness.

"And I live with my parents, but I think you already know that..."

Embarrassed laughter from the public. Gode resumed his questioning.

"And you want to be, what, a lawyer?"

"Yes, a lawyer."

"And in the meantime, you have been accused of being involved in the events of October, and I am acting as a lawyer. Life is strange, sometimes. So tell me, what do you make of our great legal system?"

"It's short on women."

"I'll say. Especially in prison..."

"Monsieur Godefroid," the judge drawled, "you're getting nowhere with these questions."

"Right. Okay. So, what were you doing on the day of Paul Lavoie's death, October seventeenth, at around six o'clock in the evening?"

"Making spaghetti."

"Ah. The kind that has...meatballs, an onion, some vine-ripened tomatoes, a bit of garlic..."

"And a glass of white wine and a sprig of thyme. Yes, that kind."

"I see. And...if you don't mind my asking, what is it that gives it its delicate taste?"

"For seasoning, I use coarse salt and add a teaspoon of mild paprika, and some cayenne pepper, just a tiny bit on the tip of a knife."

"For spaghetti and meatballs?" asked the judge.

"Yes, Your Honour. The secret with any spaghetti bolognese, which is a meat sauce, is to mix in different meats. For mine I use ground beef with a bit of veal chop, some lamb or mutton shoulder, and of course some pork loin."

"That sounds absolutely delicious. Thank you. My wife makes it with just ground beef, carrots, celery, garlic, and a large white onion. And a bay leaf. Then she adds a spoonful of sugar to cut the acidity."

"When her garlic is nice and golden and the onion is soft, tell her to deglaze the pan with some white wine. Makes all the difference."

"I will. You may proceed."

By now, not only was Gode dizzy with desire, but his stomach was rumbling like the inside of an empty cathedral.

"In prison," he said, "we have something else other than bolognese on the menu, but it isn't spaghetti . . . Anyway, let's go back to the night of the seventeenth. It was a Saturday. Six o'clock. You were making spaghetti. Was Jean-Paul Lafleur there?"

"Yes."

"We're talking about apartment six, in the building at 3730 Queen-Mary Road, is that right?"

"Yes."

"Who else was there?"

"My friend Nicole Toutant and my brother Guy. We split the rent."

"How long had Jean-Paul Lafleur been there?"

"Since the night before."

"And he spent the whole of the seventeenth in the apartment?"

"Yes."

"So, you have just stated that Jean-Paul Lafleur did not move from the apartment on Queen-Mary Road the entire day of the seventeenth, is that correct?"

"I was there the whole day, and he was there the whole time. Yes."

Gode was no longer looking at Marie-France. He was facing the twelve businessmen who, the next day, after a good night's sleep and two hours of deliberation, would get up and declare him guilty of

premeditated murder. Gode looked calmly at the twelve good consciences that hung on the faces of these salesmen.

"I'll stop there," he said. "I've proven what I had to prove."

In his summation, *Maître* Grosleau reminded the jury that by the
terms of Article 21 of the Criminal Code, they were not obliged to
identify the precise way in which the person had perpetrated the
fatal act as such. But he did not completely succeed in dissipating
the unfortunate impression that the judicial apparatus had already
sent Jean-Paul Lafleur, a troublemaker nonetheless provided with a
perfectly valid alibi, to prison for the next twenty-five years.

The defence strategy employed by Richard Godefroid, which at
first glance seemed incomprehensible, ended up making the jury
feel uneasy. First he had reminded Chevalier of his promise to
"speak on our behalf every time you get a chance, be our voice ," and
he had then established the innocence of his close friend, Jean-Paul
Lafleur. After that, his own trial seemed to have been of absolutely
no interest to him.

When it was time for him to deliver his plea, Gode remained
seated, his mouth sewn shut. Later, he modified his indifference to
the point of applauding when his sentence was handed down: life
imprisonment.

THE GHOST OF KAGANOMA

SAM OPENED HIS EYES. For a brief moment he wondered where he was. But yes. He was upstairs in the big house shaped like the hull of a Spanish galleon, full of hidden recesses and obscure creakings, and engulfed in darkness at the heart of a forest at four o'clock in the morning. He could hear Marie-Québec breathing beside him. After a moment, he realized that she, too, was lying awake with her eyes wide open.

"You're not asleep?"

"No." A pause. "I heard something downstairs…"

Samuel listened.

"I don't hear anything."

"Someone's there, down there, downstairs…"

"Hmm."

She had gone from hearing "something" to hearing "someone," and the change was not lost on Nihilo.

The classic scenario left him with no choice. The shotgun was in the next room, where he had set up his office. It was leaning against the wall at the foot of the wardrobe, first door on the right. Moving on tiptoe, he grabbed two cartridges from the box on the table and slipped them into the double barrel. Pellets big enough for Canada geese. He made no sound except for the slight click when he closed the weapon. He crept along the hall as silent as a wolf and as naked as Adam.

And then he heard it, too.

Something had moved in the kitchen.

Motionless in the shadow of the staircase, the shotgun cocked and held in both hands, he searched the silence. Through the window, the faintest hint of dawn.

Slowly he made his way to the bottom of the stairs, holding his breath, and with a single motion pivoted and pointed the rifle in front of him.

And saw the cat, who without paying him the slightest attention, was batting at a masked shrew with its paw. The shrew slid along the tiled floor like a curling stone. The cat's tail swept dreamily over the squares in the silent dawn.

Noune then flipped its prey straight up into the air and seemed to juggle with it for a couple of dance steps. When the shrew fell to the floor, she grabbed it with her teeth and dropped it at the centre of the ring for the beginning of the next round.

Samuel leaned the shotgun against the wall and went to the woodbox. He picked out a log and tightened his grip on it as he returned to the kitchen. One knee on the floor, one swift blow, and the masked shrew, at four centimetres the smallest mammal in that part of the continent except for the microscopic pygmy shrew, was put out of its misery.

The cat examined the pulpy mass with a mournful eye, reached out a paw, nudged at the lifeless object, then lost all interest in the game.

"What were you doing?"

"I was helping Noune kill a mouse. That was the noise you heard."

Marie-Québec made no reply.

"You don't look all that convinced."

Still she said nothing.

They tried to go back to sleep, but the day was too far advanced.

This all took place in 1999, the summer in which they allowed themselves to go for several weeks in a row without thinking, moving only to the rhythm of the wavelets of blue silence on their lovers' bodies. It was the summer of Perfect Days. They had a way of pronouncing those words when evening came that made it clear they had capital letters. Glasses of wine on the pebbled lakeshore. Marie-Québec wrapped in a beach towel adorned with toucans and red macaws. The sun in their faces, setting gloriously into a postcard-purple image of 250 square kilometres of uninhabited forest, still wild, barely touched, dense as sheepskin.

It was the summer they rode their mountain bikes along an ancient portage route that had been converted into a hiking trail all the way to the Kino River, which ran wide and glacially slow, tinted a brownish-green by the reflection of the birch and white spruce forest that flourished in this part of the world, before joining the Ottawa River farther south. They picnicked on tuna sandwiches, feet up on the plank that served as a handrail for the narrow porch in the hunting camp they found in the tall grass above the clayey riverbank. Blueberries picked nearby. The summer of fresh walleye fillets dipped in Shake'n'Bake and pan-fried on a campfire in the gentle evening twilight. The plaintive calls of loons filling the warm nights, and the illuminated violence of summer storms. The lake alive, like a huge, indigo animal. They moved through its darkly transparent skin, writhing like midnight worms. Above their heads, meteors consumed themselves like matches flaring out in a sea of ink seeded to infinity. The summer they made love rolling on carpets of hawkweed and fireweed. The summer of Perfect Days.

Just below the 48th parallel, Nihilo, at the wheel of a rented truck with a storage space of sixteen cubic metres that contained most of his worldly goods (a dresser, an old sperm-encrusted mattress, and a TV that worked only when it felt like it), realized that he had crossed a border, literally and figuratively, when he saw a truck painted with a sign that said GAME and showed illustrations of caribou instead of the usual deer and moose.

He'd rented, with the option to buy, the large house on the shore of Kaganoma. All around it the filigree of black spruce, with their roots clinging so superficially to the soil they would crash to the ground at the slightest wind, and there they would remain until their trunks crumbled underfoot and their tops were methodically nibbled away by the larvae of insects. Shears in hand, he and Marie-Québec attacked the shrubs and long grass, the scrub pines, the scouts sent in by the boreal forest that waited calmly to reconquer the strip of land it had conceded to the chainsaw. The henhouse, the old greenhouse, the posts of the ruined dock sticking up through the reeds by the lakeshore: everything was in disrepair. The lake was a mirrored screen decorated with spruce and birch. They bought chickens and chicken feed and let the poultry wander freely at the edge of the woods. Silence filled with the whine of insects and the twittering of birds rippled in deep, concentric waves all the way to the horizon.

Marie-Québec's legs were exposed in her light cotton dresses. Here it was not unusual to get a thin screen of ice on shallow puddles in mid-June, and the next week enjoy ferocious sunlight and the intense, shimmering, Abitibi heat. The summer season was like a race against the clock, in which everything that lived and was driven to reproduction had to move fast. Marie-Québec's body seemed to soak in sunlight as though it were soft wildflower honey, and Samuel would spread his hands over her perfect breasts like a musician playing a harpsichord.

I don't call myself Nihilo for nothing. I'm as skeptical by nature as it's possible to be, but I'm no champion of rationalism. I consider UFOs, telepathic transmissions, and some form of posthumous survival of the consciousness other than that of the ego to be possible, if not probable. I believe, among other things, that the numerous cases of people returning from the dead can be explained by the persistence, beyond our knowledge, of a certain kind of vital force (call it the soul, if you believe in such a thing). But I stop at believing in little reptilian beings who live at the centre of the Earth and only come out to kidnap and rape motorists. What else? I prefer Nietzsche to Descartes. When faced with some object that is new to me, I have the simple good sense, inherited from my peasant ancestors and refined by my own skepticism, to approach it with an open but critical mind. I do not find a panacea in science, but it is also true that my brain stimulates the production of antibodies and begins to secrete them whenever it hears people talking about Reiki and the Cosmic Network, the turiya, mandalas, the energy of consciousness, reprogrammable kinesiology, the teachings of Ramtha and the magical properties of chocolate, fractal homeopathy, suling flutes and spending two days reharmonizing the angelic vibrations given off by the enigmatic Madame Houannannah (Germaine Trudel to her husband, three children, and neighbours). And if the aura is a common electromagnetic phenomenon that a photographic plate can render visible, as I believe it is, why not, I am not thereby convinced of the necessity to balance it as though it were a set of winter tires.

Marie-Québec was different. She was the universal believer. She kept her generous heart wide open twenty-four hours a day as a safe haven for any stray superstition or theory that came along. The existence of a paranormal reality was dogma in her eyes, and her mind functioned like an assembly line: in went the raw material of some foolish notion or other, and out the other end came gospel.

Her conviction that the house in Kaganoma was haunted grew the longer we stayed in it, and gradually it came between us.

In the morning, I would look for her wherever the house or the yard received the most sun. It wasn't unusual to find her curled up in a ray of sunlight, purring like a kitten. She was like one of those grass snakes that, in the spring, before the sun has sufficiently warmed the ground and raised the temperature of their blood, allow themselves to be picked up without showing the least alarm. The quality of her sleep was almost that of a coma. The night was a vast nothingness from which she had to return every time she opened her eyes.

That morning, I brought her her café au lait and found her sitting on the new steps of the henhouse: two flats, one on top of the other, on top of four cement blocks. Nature surrounded us like a freshly waxed parquet floor in the new light. A few metres away, Noune was stalking, centimetre by centimetre, ears back, crouched up as though auditioning for the part of a lion ready to defend herself to the death in a Hemingway novel, a rabbit busily eating its breakfast of corn that we'd scattered for the chickens.

"I was awakened again..." Marie-Québec announced.

"It's a big house. It's bound to creak a bit..."

I turned and glanced back at the house: square as the muzzle of a sperm whale whose tail formed the plateau that looked out over a perfectly calm Lake Kaganoma. And I said:

"Tonight, I'd like you to wake me up...when *it* happens."

But that night nothing happened. In the morning, though, Marie-Québec was still in her Wiccan mood. She wasn't the only one who had had a bad night. When I went out to collect the eggs for breakfast, I found the hens still in their coop, looking frazzled, their feathers ruffled, rolling their little black eyes wildly in the deep, odoriferous darkness of the shed. They seemed terrified.

Later that day, I was shuffling my papers about listlessly in the humid heat of my office when I heard my name being called through the open window. Marie-Québec, a book in her hand, was standing at the forest edge in a small peach-coloured summer dress and a large straw hat. She was signalling for me to join her. The afternoon was quiet, the lake as still as oil. I ran downstairs and out to her.

When I reached the part of the yard where she was standing and saw, twenty metres farther off, the animal she'd been watching, it took off down the laneway. I ran after the fleeing animal, past Marie-Québec down to the fork in the road, where I looked around, breathing lightly, and saw it, sitting on the roadside as if waiting for me.

It had a strange head, with brushlike muttonchops, and massive, muscular paws, almost as big as its body. Its shoulders were higher and more powerful than its hindquarters. Its summer coat was molting, a yellowish beige colour showing through the grey. It was the second time in my life that I'd seen a lynx.

The small wild animal stayed where it was, immobile at the edge of the trees. A sense of antiquity emanated from it. It showed not the slightest hint of fear. In its eyes, which never left me, I could read nothing but an intense and yet tranquil curiosity. And something that resembled infinite patience.

At the beginning of the 1980s, when the exiles returned and the others were released from prison, the trajectories of the former October kidnappers diverged considerably. Those who hadn't sought and found forgetfulness were for the most part recycled into perfect representatives of the left, ready to resume their parts in the speculative bubbles of the Reagan years, the shenanigans of Québec Inc., and the government subsidies to Canadian-style socialism. They sat comfortably on the ruins of the collective dream, keeping their speech politically cool, their goal nothing more than a decent retirement plan. Some of them even managed to live lives that could, at least in part, be called public.

Far from past ideological torments, a single trait continued to link them together after all those years: the silence surrounding the death of Lavoie. Explanations had been demanded but never given. Incredibly, the pact of silence sealed in that pit at Saint-Marc by three desperate men still held thirty years later.

Sitting in the stifling heat of the room that served as his office, Samuel was going over the file he'd painstakingly put together over the preceding months — he felt that he hadn't discovered anything but the tip of the iceberg of a story. Somewhere, under the thousands of tonnes of ice and language that constituted the iceberg, lay the body of a man in a perfect state of preservation: Paul Lavoie, victim of an improvised revolutionary justice whose corpse obstinately refused to die.

But the dozen men and women who'd formed the avant-garde of the Quebec revolutionary movement never did manage to reinvent their lives.

Jean-Paul Lafleur became a journalist, cinematographer, documentary maker, etc. He wrote a regular column for *Bélier*, the journal of the hard left. His brother René worked in renovations. He'd had the bright idea of setting himself up at the end of Lac-Carré as a contractor specializing in patching up old cottages for next to nothing. This was just before the company Intrawest moved in and, by placing a good bit of money in the right pockets, transmogrified Mont Tremblant into a gigantic, model Swiss village made of marzipan.

Richard Godefroid talked about films that were never filmed and formed his own production company: Lynx Sightings, whose films seemed destined, in most cases, to end up committing daily suicide on Télé-Québec. Apparently, he didn't have enough money to hire someone to answer the telephone.

Ben Desrosiers bred horses, or maybe organic raspberries, somewhere in the Gaspé region. Go figure.

Lancelot taught communications at UQAM, where rumour had it that he bedded one female student after another and hosted a program on garbage-radio in Quebec City. He had children in both cities.

Élise Francœur became a political writer and a feminist. Sam had no idea how she made a living. Her ex-husband, Justin, worked in advertising and had been given the famous "Good Genius" account, where Balzac is shown in rags, Hugo is shown starving in a commune, and Chateaubriand is standing in awe before Niagara Falls, all of them supposedly demonstrating who the creditors were, who owned the greasy spoon, who was the tour guide, who carried the symbolically plasticized Good Company card, and who received low interest rates with extendable margins.

The famous English member of the FLQ, Nick Mansell, made a fortune in electronics and lived in a $500,000 mansion on the side of Mount Royal.

Maurice Corbo, known as Le Corbeau, the Crow, was living out his dream in a hotel in Costa Rica next to Manuel-Antonio National Park.

And François Langlais, according to unconfirmed sources, was working as an attendant in a residential hospital or retirement home on the South Shore. According to others, he owned an extended-care facility near Joliette.

Sam Nihilo had already written to Jean-Paul Lafleur (care of *Bélier*) and to Élise Francœur (he'd found her name in the list of members of the Quebec Writers' Union). He hadn't received even a notice that his letters had been received. And the telephone in the offices of Lynx Sightings was never answered.

He then tried to trace Justin Francœur through his advertising agency. Two days later, he had him on the line.

"There's no way I'm going to talk about this on the phone," Francœur said right off the bat. A natural precaution whichever way you look at it, for someone who's had his telephone tapped. "If you came to Montreal," he added, "we could go for a beer…"

In his dream, a loon was eating his liver while he was chained to the bottom of his canoe, fighting it off and trying to scream but nothing coming out, only silence, was, in the cold light of dawn, Marie-Québec's elbow in his ribs. He opened his eyes. A white-throated bunting sang out its pure, solitary note, a strange nakedness and a living affirmation in the grey morning light.

"Someone came in through the window," said Marie-Québec.

"What's that?"

"I heard the sound of breaking glass, downstairs."

"What?"

"Someone's broken in."

"No, you were just dreaming again."

"I've been awake for the past hour. Why don't you ever believe me?"

This time the shotgun was in the bottom of the cupboard.

He did a tour of the windows. Nothing unusual. Standing in the panorama of the bay window in the living room, he paused a moment to watch the balsam fir and birch trees slowly separate themselves from the earth's brown shadow and attach themselves to the surface of the lake.

While recrossing the kitchen to get to the stairs, something caught his eye and he stopped. He approached the north-facing window and examined a tiny, downy feather stuck to the window glass by a few splotches of blood. He looked down and saw a still form lying at the base of the wall.

"It was a grouse," he told her. "It flew into the kitchen window. It couldn't have chosen a better place if it was trying to land in the stew pot."

It felt good to be getting back into the warm bed.

"What about the window?"

"There's nothing wrong with the window. It took the hit."

"But I heard glass breaking."

Another time she maintained that she'd heard a man crying somewhere in the house during the night.

And while Nihilo that night cleaned the suicidal grouse in order to cook its fillets sautéed in butter and olive oil and mix it with penne noodles alla puttanesca, she told him the following story while sipping a glass of Cahors:

"Yesterday, when you went into town to run some errands, I went out to pick blueberries."

"Where did you go?"

"Just around here, not very far. Along the roadside . . . I had just passed the old greenhouse and was ready to turn into the woods when I felt I was being . . . watched."

"What did you do?"

"I turned around. And . . ."

"And what? Tell me."

"Someone was there . . . standing in your office window. I could see him clearly. It was a man. He followed me with his eyes."

Samuel looked at the carcass he was holding in his hands. He'd been planning to make soup stock with it.

"So, the house is haunted ... Is that what you believe?"

"Yes. Why are you laughing?"

Samuel thought about their house, cast up like a shipwreck on the shore of several hundred square kilometres of savage forest. And in it, the two of them, trapped in their obligatory prison.

"Because if I didn't, I'd be afraid."

On paper, it was perfect: back-to-the-land, life of the pioneer, simple, self-sufficient, neo-hippie philosophy. Composting. Free-range chickens. Catch a fish for supper. His lady kneeling in her peasant skirt in the middle of the sandlot-sized herb garden. But eventually you discover that the only thing Nature is able to grow here are carrots two centimetres long and a few lettuces surrounded by more fencewire than a Jewish colony on the West Bank, which in any case proves useless because there is always a newly weaned baby rabbit that can slip through the wire and eat everything in the garden down to ground level. And to the idyllic image of your lady in straw hat and peasant skirt you have to add netting hiding her face about as sexy as a hijab, to prevent the hordes of blackflies, mosquitoes, deerflies, horseflies, and any other kind of flies from picking her up and carrying her off.

As far as the neighbours were concerned — that mixture of villagers, retirees who'd converted their summer cottages into year-round residences, and suburbanites shunted out to the extremes of Maldoror by the centrifugal force of urban sprawl — Sam and Marie-Québec were artists, and people didn't generally ask what they did for a living for fear of upsetting them: a freelance writer doing contractual piecework and working on "a serious book," and his actor partner. Marie-Québec had decided to stage a production of Chekhov in the Loblaw's Happy Times Theatre, and to direct it herself. She also took on other projects: picked up an old Westfalia camper van from somewhere, for example, and founded Four-Wheel Theatre, an itinerant troupe of actors whose mission was to bring Camus, Shakespeare, Lise Vaillancourt, and Daniel Danis to villages surrounded by forest and ugly, mono-industrial agglomerations on the fringes of the 49th parallel, to show the idle youth of the North that there were other things to do in the summer than making suicide pacts.

One day, going in to Maldoror to buy supplies, Sam saw a seagull sitting squat in the middle of the road. The roadway had been cut into the red sandstone between two lines of Jack pines studded with patches of white birch. Although the lake was only a few hundred metres below, a gull was still an unusual sight in such a spot, where the usual congregants were pine grosbeaks and spruce grouse. The gull was trailing one of its wings, which had been torn half off. Sam took his foot off the gas to assess the damage, but he knew from experience that there was nothing to be done for the creature except to deliver the *coup de grâce*, which the bird in any case seemed to be asking for, to judge from the way it offered Sam its bravest profile. And so he pressed on the gas pedal and drove over it. A loud POOF! from under the vehicle and, in his rear-view mirror, a pile of crumpled and more or less flattened white feathers was the only evidence of death that Nihilo needed.

Upon his return two hours later, the carcass was gone. He attributed the cleanup to some wild animal intent on giving the lie to the old adage there was no such thing as a free meal. Marie-Québec had taken a part-time job at the White Wolf, a bar in Maldoror, to help pay expenses, and her shift that night ended at nine o'clock. At ten, Samuel was banging away at the tiny black-and-white television set that had come up through La Vérendrye park with the rest of his junk, when he suddenly heard someone kicking frantically at the front door. Since they never locked the place, he wondered who it could be as he hurried across the room.

In the porch lamp's weak light, the scene that leapt into view was that of Marie-Québec, looking like Mother Teresa of the Forest, holding the gull in her arms like a suckling child. The bird was staring at Samuel with a baleful, accusing eye. The sight of the revenant brought a cry to his lips.

"Aaaaaaaaaahhhhhhh."

The bird had sprung into Marie-Québec's headlights as she'd been driving home, apparently still looking for someone to put it out of its misery. As Marie-Québec held it to her body, Sam bent over and looked at its wounded wing. Under the feathers, which were dirty and smeared with blood and road dust, the wing was held on by nothing more than a thin filament of shredded tendon. The bird nodded its head threateningly.

"What do you intend to do with it?" he asked.

"Take care of it ... Save it," she added after a moment's reflection, in case she hadn't been clear.

"But look, its wing is completely broken off. No autumn migration. And it can't spend the winter up here in Abitibi. Believe me, it's pretty well fucked."

"Not if we take it to the Pageau Refuge ..."

"The Pageau Refuge? They take wolves and moose there. This thing is a dump rat with wings."

"You should be ashamed of yourself, speaking like that."

Nihilo received a fierce peck from the topic of their conversation, which made him think of scenes from the Hitchcock film.

"All right, what do you propose we do with it?" she said.

"Put it in with the chickens for tonight."

"And tomorrow?"

"A painless treatment. Number 4 lead shot."

That night was the first time they slept in separate rooms.

That's how it started. The next day, Jonathan Livingston Seagull disappeared from the yard, where we'd put him before going to beds (plural intended). The wire fence was in shreds and the bird took advantage of the fact: by the time we discovered it was gone, it was probably already in some fox's or lynx's belly, a happy ending for a bird that had probably lived on Big Macs all its life.

In the following days, Marie-Québec's insomnia continued as usual, except that now she experienced her dazed, nocturnal meanderings in a separate bed. I slept in my office, on a mattress on the floor. I buried myself in the October business and worked even harder.

One day, apropos of nothing, I asked Marie-Québec what Chekhov play she was doing.

"*The Seagull*. Why?"

"Nothing," I replied, "except that some strange things are happening in this house."

Two days later at first light, I stuck my nose outside the door. The night before, I'd left a garbage pail by the corner of the house intending to take it to one of the Dumpsters along the road into Kaganoma. And who do you think I caught going through my garbage? Him. His wing was in an even sorrier state; he was dragging it behind him on the ground at the end of a knot of nerves as he scurried out of my way, flapping on his webbed feet like a tragicomic clown. I went back inside to get the shotgun. Quietly, on tiptoes. I came back downstairs putting a pair of shells into the double barrel. I went through the door and advanced, barefoot across the dawn's wet grass, shotgun at the ready.

PERCÉ, SUMMER 1969

THE WATER AROUND THE *Miloiseau* was churning. Birds swam
over from the base of the cliff and fought each other for the capelin that were rising from the blue depths of the sea. Gannets cut
through the air like swords, necks straightened, wings tight to their
bodies. Waves exploded on the brick-red rocks below the cliff, where
a puffin stood with three smelts in its colourful beak. Higher up,
razor-billed auks were lined up along a ledge. On the boat they had
to yell to be heard above the roar of crashing waves, piercing bird
cries, squawking and shrieking, as though the red cliff face was being bombarded by explosions of feathers and webbed feet. Griffin's
face was the colour and consistency of the rock. Godefroid and the
captain didn't need words to understand each other. It was enough
that their gazes met from time to time. The way they tried to match
their movements to the violent but regular rhythm of the sea was a
kind of intimacy. The net flying through the air, then falling, then
flying again, the long-line quickly hauled aboard with both hands,

and shaken, the fish unhooked . . . In the middle of the boat was a pile of glistening guts and thick, moustachioed heads. The day's take must be around three-quarters of a tonne, according to the captain. Since they'd found the school of cod that had been going after the same capelin the gannets were spearing in their frenzied chase to the surface, they had caught fish after fish without a break.

Wilfrid Griffin's eyes, with their hint of Ireland set deeply in the crazed network of grooves in the burnt leather of his face, fixed on a point somewhere behind Gode. The latter followed the captain's glance. Griffin was the sole master of the *Miloiseau*, one of those solidly made Gaspé fishing boats, decked and graced with an elegant line and a forward cabin; this one was twelve metres long, with deck planks of hemlock spruce and a hull of Nova Scotian white oak. Squinting into the sun, Gode saw a sail, an immaculate white triangle, rounding the island's tip, leaning into the whitecaps that broke and lapped appealingly against its hull.

He followed the apparition for a moment, then turned back to the captain. By way of response, the captain threw out the net again, drew in another twelve kilos of cod with smooth, alternating movements of his arms. With a simple flick of his wrist, he detached the three-pronged hooks from the fishes' gullets and finished the motion by throwing the fish onto the heaving pile behind him. Then, after again throwing in his jigger line and wedging it, the coastal fisherman spat into the sea.

The lobster boat was pulled up alongside the *Miloiseau*, a line of empty beer bottles trailing in its wake almost all the way to the horizon. The newcomers had a propane stove on board on which they'd set a pot of seawater to boil, and the boarding consisted of a typical exchange of freshly caught and cooked lobster for a few sun-warmed Labatt 50s. Gode grabbed the dripping, bright orange-red lobster that was tossed to him, cracked the shell of a large claw against the boat's side and chewed the aromatic flesh. When he was finished, Captain Will passed him another beer. He applied the neck to the boat rail, polished by the incessant rubbing of lines, and hit the cap with his fist, letting the foam spurt out. While he went back to working on his lobster, a shout made him look up. The lobster boat was about twenty metres off, heading into the wind. The excited fishermen scrutinized the distance between the island and the shore. Gode followed their gaze. A tiny sailboat was coming straight toward them, giving the impression that it had taken off from the red cliff face to dive like a gannet on the two boats.

It was a Sunfish, about four metres long. About thirty metres separated the *Miloiseau* and the lobster boat. They were running parallel to each other, and the Sunfish, without even changing course, passed directly between them. A tall blonde was at the helm, navigating by herself, her body leaning completely over the side so that her long, curly hair blew in the wind and touched the water, the air ecstatic in her white sailing pants and sailor's T-shirt with navy-blue stripes. The men watched her go by, mouths hanging open. It didn't matter where this rig ended up, they knew they had their conversational topic in the tavern for the next month.

Gode took time to read the name painted in red letters on the tailboard: *Those Were the Days.*

The captain spit into the water.

"I'd haul that one below."

They called us outsiders, bums, crud, fleabags, hippies, beatniks, filth, students. According to the chief of police, Big Tony Tousignant, we were always having orgies at our place, between "persons of both sexes aged thirteen to thirty," which delighted the journalists when things got hot and the press started showing up. The mayor

(Gill Fournier, who also sported a huge beer belly) was quick to say that our presence in his little fishing port encouraged the consumption of drugs, the corruption of minors, theft, and murder. The whole village was on edge ever since the owner of a motel had been villainously assassinated at the beginning of the summer. Percé was a colony of artists, motels, campgrounds, and a few souvenir shops: shell ashtrays, agate necklaces, *Made in Japan* junk. A fishing village for whom the principal catch was tourists, and the season lasted two weeks. Local businessmen filled their pockets as long as the manna kept coming and the hole in the famous rock stayed where it belonged. Millions of Kodak moments had turned it into one of the most famous nature postcards on the continent.

After spending nearly a year getting ourselves organized, the Lafleur brothers and I simply wanted to take a vacation. The Fisherman's Hut was a dilapidated shack filled with old fishing nets, but it was a few feet from the dock, and we rented it and turned it into a café. A few tables, the fishing nets now hanging on the wall with a few crab shells and half-rotten starfish stuck in them. Someone showed up with an old jukebox, and the party was underway.

Mayor Gill Fournier's Pontiac hurtled down the Three Sisters, the triplet of low mountains that blocked the horizon to the north. Seen from this angle, the famous rock didn't look so remarkable, with its hole demurely hidden by several million tonnes of limestone. As if the local cash cow was protecting herself from the prying eyes of anyone who'd come from the direction of Gaspé, which is what Fat Gill was doing. He had just bought himself a hunting rifle at the sports shop in the regional capital and was dying to try it out. The beautiful, brand-new 12-gauge pump-action was sitting on the back seat, still in its case.

Crossing through the village, he noticed the cluster of tents around the new Fisherman's Hut at the end of the quay. The owners of the motels, campgrounds, and restaurants were already complaining to the municipal council. Not to mention the grumbling from the local population, him included, that could be heard over beers in the hotel. Not hard to figure out why: the hippies were charging nothing, zero, free, gratis, to pitch a tent in the field full of crabgrass, dandelions, and thistles adjacent to their café. They sold food for what it cost to make it. He could even name one or two fishermen who were providing them with fresh cod for no better reason than that it gave them an excuse to hang around with the hippy chicks with eyes as blue as those of a northern gannet. And if that wasn't a case of high treason, you had to wonder what was.

From Highway 132, which when it went through the village became the main street, you could see a few of them hanging out, barefoot, their hair down around their shoulders, lounging in the sun with nothing to do but lean back against the old rail fence or sit on their asses on the steps of the Hut, or on the ground, like savages. No ambition at all.

Just before the road headed off up Surprise Coast, Gill parked his car, took the shotgun out of its case, and started walking along the beach. Bird Island rose up across from him. The shore at Percé, with its swaths of beached kelp rotting under the July sun and swarming with sand fleas, gave off, in the mayor's opinion, a rotten stench. His vocabulary was somewhat limited, and for him "briny," "salty," "humid," and "rotten" all pretty much described the same smell.

He reached into his pocket and took out a shell filled with a number 4 buckshot and slid it into the chamber of his new shotgun. He figured there was plenty of space around here for trying out the gun. A movement caught his attention, and he looked up and saw a gull coming toward him, its wings flapping confidently and regularly in the light sea breeze. The palmiped was flying in a straight line parallel to the edge of the seashore, about twenty metres up. Gill released the safety, shouldered his shotgun, quickly took aim at the moving bird, and fired a fusillade of pellets. The gull spiralled down like a struck fighter plane. It hadn't even reached the silvered surface of the wavelets before Gill turned and walked away.

Marie-France was tall and sinuous, her plump ass leaving harmonious waves in the wake of her undulating walk. The way she filled her bell-bottomed Wrangler jeans was the very height of eroticism. She had a devastating smile, a few spots of rouge, a voice that ranged from simpering to guttural, and an easy laugh, a sort of throaty bray that added a destabilizing touch of vulgarity to her personality, which was far from disagreeable.

Gode was twenty-two, and his crippling awkwardness had allowed him to get through Expo 67 and May '68 practically without a hitch. He'd come out of those two great laboratories of free love more or less intact but more confused than ever. He was still incapable of seeing opportunities with the girls who moved around him, the silent signals woven into the coded thickness of the nights. And then along came Marie-France. No separatist had ever held a bomb like her in his hands.

She was touring the Gaspésie with her friend Nicole. The car belonged to Nicole, the sailboat on the trailer behind it was Marie-France's. Nicole, a petite brunette, was a nurse in Rivière-des-Prairies and no sailor. She was much too busy to cruise around on a boat. Marie-France was different. Among all these good little women in bell-bottoms who seemed happy to have exchanged a seduction code involving patience and ritual for another that centred on simple sexual availability, she had a character in which inclination and a moral sense seemed to be able to exist at the same time. She was studying to become a legal secretary, but hastened to add that that was only until she could afford to study law at a university.

René cast his net for Nicole first. The youngest of the Lafleur brothers broke the ice, and Gode threw himself into the water after him. They were a dozen or so sitting around a bonfire on the beach, driftwood crackling like the poles of a tipi on which someone had thrown some old tires. A thick, oily smoke filled the hot night, or rather the early morning, in the small fishing port cum tourist trap. A guy named Latraverse, a tall, bony type, was scraping on a guitar in the light from the flames and sang like he was chewing on sandpaper.

Gode stood up, a small O'Keefe in his left hand, and walked around the fire to sit beside Nicole, Marie-France, and René, who already had the two women laughing uproariously. I'll jump through the flames if I have to, but there's no way I'm going to stay sitting down. He hummed Dalida's *Those Were the Days*.

After opening on the twenty-sixth of June, the Hut became a café, the café a restaurant, the restaurant an inn, and the inn a colony. On any given weekend, there could be a hundred people packed into the place. On the evening of July 20, a Sunday, René had disappeared into the guts of an old black-and-white television he'd found some-where, emerging in time for them to catch the dark, shadowy figure of Neil Armstrong's boot setting down on the surface of the moon. Some among them were awed by the magnitude of the historical event and suspended their critical faculties and political opinions. Others saw in it an extreme example of Manifest Destiny, and it fed their fierce resistance: Vietnam, salmon rivers, and the Sea of Tranquility, just different aspects of the same fight.

The next day started out as a true summer day *à la Gaspésie*: wall-to-wall wind and cold rain with no relief in sight. About thirty of them were hanging around, minding their own business, when a police officer presented himself at the door at about nine o'clock in the evening. The following is the official version of the order of the events that followed:

- Officer states that the establishment named The Fisherman's Hut was operating without a permit and was, moreover, situated inside a residential zone;
- Jean-Paul Lafleur points out to the officer that the establishment named The Fisherman's Hut was in the same zone as an art gallery, a restaurant, and a craft boutique, and if that wasn't commercial then he didn't know what was;
- The officer states that no operating permit, then no operating, and that was that;
- Jean-Paul Lafleur replies that the Village of Percé only issues permits to exploit the people and fishermen of the Gaspésie, and the members of the Hut collective want nothing to do with all of that;
- The officer states that he will take the matter up with a higher authority;
- Jean-Paul says the officer can take the matter up with whoever he damned well pleased, there is no higher authority, and so good riddance to him;
- 9:30 p.m.: the officer's chief, Tony Tousignant, presents himself at the door to the premises, accompanied by two unidentified individuals;
- Gros Tony Tousignant senses they're at the bottom of the barrel;
- Gros Tony Tousignant repeats, though not in the same words, the message delivered by the officer a half-hour previously;
- Jean-Paul opens his mouth and . . .
- Jean-Paul closes his mouth, or at least his mouth is closed for him, because Gros Tony Tousignant has just smashed his fist into Jean-Paul's face;

- Jean-Paul falls backward and lands in the arms of his friends, girlfriends, etc., and remains in this position while consulting with them;
- Rubbing his jaw, Jean-Paul returns to Gros Tony Tousignant and says, in more or less these words: "We're not leaving..."
- Gros Tony Tousignant leaves, swearing loudly, followed by his two acolytes, in the direction of the hotel, promising that this is not the end of the matter by any means.

How I love you
Allelujah, in pajamas
Eyes wide open
My sweet summer love
I know what I want
Qué-bécois, we are all qué-bécois...

That was playing on the jukebox. There was also a piano. And sitting at the piano that night, Marie-France played *Clair de lune* with Gode sitting beside her on the bench, rain drumming on the roof, their thighs and hips and sides touching but their hands not, their hands keeping their distance, hers making music and his down on his knees, gripping his thighs to prevent them from flying up to rest on her shoulder as she played the sonata. Or to hold her by her waist. And Marie-France pretending to be concentrating on the genius of Beethoven when in fact all she could think about was how much she wanted something to happen, and Gode was beginning to look like a desperate case.

A woman will forgive a man for rushing an opportunity, but never for missing one. She'd read that somewhere, maybe it was Cocteau, while flipping through a dictionary of quotations. She decided that if nothing had happened by the time she finished the last bars of the sonata, she'd give up on this Godefroid, *this cold goad* (the audacity of her little play on words brought a smile to her lips).

She played the final notes of the sonata and looked at Gode, but he wasn't looking at her, apparently being more interested in what was happening at the front door. She opened her mouth to say something to him, but just at that moment a furious gush of white foam smashed into her chest and took her breath away. Then she was flying across the room on a roaring geyser that smashed everything in its path, and her hand closed around another hand that was closed around hers, holding on with all its strength. Gode, at last.

If I thought a flock of northern gannets made a deafening racket on the red cliffs of their island, that was before I heard Marie-France having an orgasm in the wheelhouse of the *Miloiseau*. I was sure the entire village of Percé was following our every move on its municipal seismograph. She came oceanically. It was as if she wanted to shout to the whole world that yes, she was coming and it had only taken seven seconds, and it wasn't going to stop any time soon. I was sitting with my pants down around my ankles and this magnificent blonde impaled on me with her dress hiked up above her navel.

Later, we stood on the bridge. There was the smell of fish. The sea rocked us gently. We couldn't go back to the Hut. They'd destroyed everything.

The wrecking of the Fisherman's Hut perpetrated by the police, with the assistance of the volunteer fire department, which had furnished the truck and the fire hoses, and of a dozen or more thugs wielding crowbars, marked the beginning of what became known as the Fisherman's Hut Affair.

The day after the showdown, the young people who had dispersed during the night ripped off the padlocks on the door and gathered in the Hut with eight superficial wounds in their ranks. To that total they added the nervous shock suffered by one of the women, the destroyed furniture, water damage, and the wrecked piano.

For a few days it seemed that life would go back to normal. Gode worked in the café, spent his nights with Marie-France, got up before dawn to go out in the boat with Griffin to furnish the Hut with fresh cod. After a week, he looked wasted.

On Saturday, Gill Fournier called a special meeting of the municipal council and had them vote in a resolution denouncing the permanent scandal visited upon their village by the presence of professional agitators and drug addicts in the persons of the Percé hippies, and ordering said young people to vacate the premises by Monday at five o'clock. And so they were back to square one.

Jean-Paul hired a French-from-France chef. He was a magician. You gave him plaice and he turned it into Dover sole. On Monday, when the ultimatum ran out, there were snow crab claws on the menu, which no one on the entire peninsula regarded as human food. During the night, the firefighters' truck drew up in front of the Hut and the boys from the brigade were back at it. Earlier in the day, Gros Tony Tousignant had enlisted a couple of dozen citizens, transformed them into keepers of the peace, and sensitized them to the hippie problem. Some of them had had a few drinks . . . And it was this pack of hooligans from the corner tavern, generously armed with baseball bats, Johnson bars, axe handles, and bicycle chains, that the mayor and the chief of police unleashed on the Fisherman's Hut at the expiration of the ultimatum.

This time, the deluge lasted a good fifteen minutes, during which time jets of water smashed whatever furniture and chinaware had survived the first onslaught. After that, the auxiliary forces broke into the Hut, shouting and swinging clubs and whips and other improvised weapons.

"Time for your baths, you pieces of shit!"

"We're gonna drown you like the dirty dogs you are!"

"We're gonna kill you!"

In the ensuing confusion, Wilfrid Griffin was seen standing up to Gros Tony Tousignant. He dropped the chair he'd been using as a shield and grabbed the police chief's head in his huge, calloused hands, crevassed by years of handling lines, and held him in his unbreakable grip as though he was going to give him a big, wet kiss. Then he smashed his big, Irish forehead between Gros Tony's eyes and the chief went down like a ton of bricks.

Shortly after that, Jean-Paul, trying to avoid a massacre, entered the fray waving a white napkin as a flag. Falling in behind him, the young people left the building, fists raised, soaked from head to foot, with the word "Freedom" in their throats.

They had nowhere to go. From the direction of L'Anse-à-Beaufils came a distant rumbling sound that made everyone's head turn. A few minutes later, a rolling as of thunder came down from the Surprise Coast Road and spread throughout the village. Everyone, virtuous citizens with a few beers in them, young rebels stoked to the eyeballs, was now looking in the same direction.

The first motorcycle was followed by a second, then a third, then ten, then twenty, until a whole pack of Harleys suddenly surged out of the night. At their head was the most improbable apparition: the lead biker wore no helmet, had hair flying back like a musketeer's in a windstorm, but was dressed not in the leather vest painted with the Sun Downers colours, as those behind him were wearing, but in the flowing robes of a lawyer, its long, black cuffs flapping behind him like a vampire's cape.

Maître Mario Brien seemed incapable of addressing any young woman without resorting to such endearments as "my sweet," "my beauty," "my heart," "my dear," and so on. Before a week was up, the first graffiti praising the lawyer and his famous cigar began appearing on the bushes in the area of the Hut. His role in the defence of placers of bombs vaguely associated with the FLQ was well known, but his flamboyant arrival at the head of the Sun Downers was a simple coincidence: two members of the gang had been beaten up during the first assault on the Hut, and the Sun Downers had decided to roll down to the Gaspé to take a look. At Mont-Joli they'd run into *Maître* Brien: the bizarre lawman was also out on a run down the lower St. Lawrence on his Harley, and his generous distribution of goodies at a pull-off beside the highway (Benzedrine, mescalin, hash, coke, a bit of pot) had been so appreciated by the bikers that they'd allowed him to ride in their company.

That night there was another great party aboard the *Miloiseau.* The next day, the hippies once again cut the locks off the Hut's door and reoccupied the premises, while the municipal authorities deliberated afresh on how to put an end to it.

When Gode saw Marie-France sit down at the piano to assess the damage, and the lawyer get up, follow her, and sit down facing her astride the piano bench, about as subtle as a dog in heat, he knew he was in trouble. What chance did he have against a silver-tongued devil, a lawyer no less, with a growing reputation?

"What are you playing, my sweet?"

"*Clair de lune.*"

"Ha! That's something else the Americans have stolen from us..."

Marie-France gave him a quick glance, then played a chord.

"That's a stupid thing to say," she said.

"What do you mean? Who's stupid? Me?"

"Loony," she said, casting a final look in his direction.

And that was the end of that conversation.

Later that summer, the group staged a sit-in at a salmon-fishing club on the Bonaventure River, to denounce the club's exclusively American membership, which was not uncommon in the area. They forced the gourmet fishermen to fish at night with nets or with spotlights and pitchforks. Operation Bonaventure succeeded in disturbing the halieutic activities of a high-ranking hero of the Vietnam War, a certain General Gore, since he'd been looking forward to flogging the smaragdine waters of the Bonaventure with his favourite Black Bomber: a number-one hook garnished with golden pheasant and black hen feathers and a tuft of black squirrel.

Maître Mario then had the protesters march from the prison in Chandler, a sleepy little village dominated by the smell of rotten eggs, shouting at the tops of their lungs. He kept them busy. Cheques signed by the members of the collective had an annoying habit of bouncing. A girl belonging to the group was caught emptying the collection box at the church. She said she was simply financing her political activities. The rest of that summer was spent more or less going back and forth from the Hut to the police station to the Percé prison to the courthouse.

The police harassment intensified. Penniless youths caught panhandling were rounded up and escorted to the outskirts of town.

Passing through Percé, René Lévesque held a spontaneous press conference on the dock. Around him, men up to their chests in cod were forking piles of fish out of their boats with manure forks. A trawler was unloading mullet. A political attachée held the umbrella under which the thin little man in the wrinkled raincoat spread his hands, cigarette dangling from his mouth. It was raining cats and dogs.

"If you ask my opinion of the Fisherman's Hut," he said in a voice that sounded like a sour lime grated on pewter, "and the so-called [apologetic smile] hippies, and this business that is so much in question here at the moment, and not just here but elsewhere as well, I would say that I, when I see what's going on, as does the whole world, I ask myself questions. Because when we see the young who are engaged in these things, it's natural that we ask ourselves who's behind all this goddamned stuff. A handful of professional agitators, who come down here to be fair-weather friends [pout], okay, well, if they want fair weather they'll have to come another day [apologetic smile], but to me, in response to your question, it seems obvious that these so-called Percé hippies are being supported, either locally or from afar, by someone who has the means to finance their let's call it bloody..."

A hand reached out of a boat like an oar and Chrome-Dome grabbed it and went over to the *Miloiseau.*

"How's the fishing?"

"Not bad. We've got problems with the goddamn draggers..."

"The *what?*"

"Draggers. When they come here for scallops, they turn over the seabed. They cause a lot of devastation..."

"Okay, thanks, that's good," said Chrome-Dome.

Gode and Griffin watched him move away.

"What the hell?" asked Gode.

This time, Griffin didn't spit into the sea.

While looking for sand dollars, Gode and Marie-France found a seabird carcass cast up by the tide. It was already beginning to stink. Gode kicked at it with his foot. It looked something like a puffin, about a foot and a half long, with a heavy, compressed bill grooved laterally by a white stripe.

"*Alca torda,*" a passing tourist told them, binoculars slung around his neck. "Razorbilled auk. Around the Gulf of St. Lawrence they're called *godes...*"

Gode found Jean-Paul talking to a girl, an English girl, on the dock in front of the Hut. Jean-Paul had just gotten out of jail for trying to bounce a rubber cheque in one of the local shops. While in the clink, he'd met France's future public enemy number one, a fellow named Jacques Mesrine, who was suspected of having strangled a motel guest earlier that summer. Mesrine was at the start of a career that would claim thirty assassinations and, before ten years were up, would end with him receiving eighteen slugs shot from a canvas-covered truck in central Paris. The two hit it off immediately. Mesrine took Lafleur under his wing and, to teach him a trick or two, beat the shit out of another detainee before his eyes, without giving him a chance. Lesson number one: no pity.

By the end of the summer, Jean-Paul had changed. They'd all changed, but Jean-Paul had changed more. His brilliant eyes now shone with a harder light.

"It's beginning to get pretty hot around here," he confided to Gode.

"You mean the girl?"

From the Hut's porch, they looked at the young woman lying on the beach.

Jean-Paul shook his head, smiling wanly.

"No. This place. We're getting to be too well known, too much under surveillance. Too many people passing through..."

"Yeah, well, there's too much bickering going on in the Hut for me. I could use a break."

Jean-Paul's gaze settled on him.

"Where to?"

"Camping on the island with Marie-France."

"Yeah, don't go getting fed up with us, eh, buddy..."

He gave him a friendly shove.

"Who's the chick?" Gode asked.

"What chick?"

"The English chick."

"Oh, her. A real aristocrat," said Jean-Paul with a shrug. "Janet Travers. Her father's some kind of British diplomat, I think ..."

Those Were the Days rode the waves with Gode crouched in the hull, terrified by the force of the wind and the height of the whitecaps, the steep slope of the rudder as Marie-France, hanging over the edge grinning like a cartoon whale, steered the boat toward Île Bonaventure.

They walked along the island's deserted shore, drank muscatel from the bottle and had sex on a woollen blanket that made a bright red splash on the pebbled beach. The gannets that earlier in the summer had covered the top of the cliff like a living duvet had all but disappeared, dispersed along the coast and up the estuary and out to sea. Gode's penis was still buried in the warmth beneath Marie-France's blonde pubic bush when he fell as sound asleep as a rock.

When he awoke, Marie-France was looking through the binoculars at an excursion boat full of tourists that was just rounding the point, en route for the cliffs on the opposite shore. It was called *The Island Gannet*, according to the name she read on its side.

Fat Gill's company. Business was booming. Percé was on everyone's itinerary, it seemed. All the motels and campgrounds were full. Vacationers were having to sleep in their cars. In the early mornings they could be found walking on the beach near the extinguished bonfires, in the hopes of surprising a nude sleeper. The mayor himself had had to admit that hippies had become a tourist attraction.

NINA

IT WAS THE BEGINNING OF autumn, 1999. After Labour Day and the departure of the cottagers, tranquility had returned to the shores ringed by the forests of Kaganoma. A concert of shrill voices filled the yard where the chickens roamed at will. The yard, about a hectare in area, formed a vague parallelogram, one side of which was the lake. It had been only partially cleared by the previous owner, and fallen black pines had been left to rot among their own saplings, ferns, yews, blueberry bushes, and Labrador tea.

Nihilo wandered to the edge of the clearing, passed under some chickens that were roosting in tree branches, as passive as old biddies. A bit farther on, he came face to face with a feral cat that must have weighed forty pounds, reddish feathers sprouting from its mouth as it sat contemplating him, unperturbed. The feline moved off unhurriedly through the striations of sunlight that slanted through the understory.

It came back later that day, the same or possibly a different cat. Nihilo went out, aimed his shotgun at its huge round head framed by sideburns, raised his line of sight a good metre, and fired. The beast disappeared in a few bounds.

The next time he saw it, Sam fired two shots at it, again aiming over its head through branches of spruce, three metres from the chicken coop. Stretched out like a sphinx on the carpet of spruce needles, his visitor continued to look back at him with the same air of suicidal indifference and fathomless consciousness. This time it didn't even bother to move off.

At the municipal library in Maldoror, across from the hockey arena, Sam cruised the bookshelves for anything he could find about lynxes. He sat at one of the tables near a window and went through the pile. He read about the Spanish lynx reintroduction program, and about another in Colorado, releasing individuals captured in the Yukon and near Abitibi.

The Canadian lynx consumed an average of two hundred hares a year. The kits, usually two in number, spent the first winter with their mother.

Old French trappers had called it the *pichou*, a word derived from the Algonquin *pesheen*. At one time the term was also used to refer to snowshoes made from deer or caribou hide.

In a book on animal symbolism in Amerindian cultures, he read that the lynx was considered a kind of "holder of secrets." Another work, entitled *Discover Your Animal Totem*, confirmed that to penetrate the deepest secrets you needed to resort to the medicine of the lynx. According to writs of this medicine, the Egyptian sphinx was obviously not a lion, as had always been assumed, but rather a lynx. "If the lynx knocks on your door, pay attention!" concluded the authors, who then went on to issue this advice: "Become a lynx and smile like Mona Lisa!"

Sam met Phil Baron at the White Wolf, where Marie-Québec had four or five shifts a week waiting on tables, usually from three o'clock to nine. Phil was one of their neighbours on Lake Kaganoma, a balding man in his fifties with a long, uniformly silvered ponytail who had dropped everything and blown six thousand bucks on his dream: a hunt camp, rough as they come but with a lease from the Ministry of Natural Resources tacked beside the door. Phil lived with Joey, a young groundhog that accompanied him wherever he went, nestled under the hood of his ancient Dodge Chrysler, curled up on the chassis. Phil liked lifting the truck's hood to show you the brownish red lump huddled up against the engine block. Joey had come into Phil's life during a spring fishing trip when, after drinking half a case of beer, he'd parked his truck above the animal's burrow to take a piss. It took him a while to figure out why, when he was leaving, the fat groundhog had taken refuge in his truck; the engine, well known by his friends for its musical talents, made a noise like a groundhog: a shrill whistle followed by a tremolo.

Now, whenever Phil parked in the town, he looked for empty yards and vacant lots with plenty of clover and dandelions.

From customers at the Wolf, Sam also learned that during the mid-1980s, Richard Godefroid, the former FLQer, had spent a few summers in the area. Once, he'd even rented a cottage on the next lake down from Sam's, Salaberry Lake. Phil Baron had known him well, his informants added, and could maybe be persuaded to talk about him.

Baron's hunt camp was about a kilometre north of Kaganoma. There was always a fire burning somewhere in that corner of the dense forest — dead leaves, branches, slash, old boards, bits of broken shingle — among the slanting "cypresses" (black spruce) that served as his backyard. An open case of twenty-four was always within reaching distance. A chainsaw that could use a good sharpening had been left out in the trees. The yard was a dump. Inside, the camp was a minefield. The dock was a work in progress.

Helping to make a dent in a six-pack of Miller Lite, Samuel listened to Baron tell him that Gode, as he'd been called, had been
from the area, from Villebois to be exact, a tiny village pretty much
smack on the 49th parallel, just above La Sarre. When he needed to
make himself scarce after his release from prison, Gode had gone
to Abitibi and worked for a few summers as a brush remover in
the forestry concessions of the Northwest. That's how Phil knew
him. They'd removed slash together out by Joutel, and it was Phil
who'd provided him with the tiles for his cottage on Salaberry Lake.
They'd hunted together, drank together. When Gode left, they'd arranged to keep in touch from time to time. If he was passing anywhere near Maldoror, Gode always stopped in at the White Wolf
around four o'clock, where he was sure to find his old bud in his
usual state of alcohol-induced stupefaction. Once, he even came
to introduce a documentary he'd co-produced at the film festival,
but his arrival had coincided with a period during which Phil had
had a maddening tendency to get himself so pissed he could fail a
Breathalyzer test from a metre and a half away, and then conduct a
perfectly straight, two-hour conversation with a line of coke in his
nostrils as big as the Kaganoma esker. He didn't remember a single
thing about Gode's visit.

While Phil was talking, Samuel Nihilo was thinking that, for the
second time, their paths had almost crossed, his and Godefroid's, in
fact, somewhere on this sandy terrain sprouting severely malcon-
tent pines, the future had turned into the past. It was as if he and
Gode occupied the same home range, a territory bigger than that of
a cougar, on which they circled warily around each other, distancing
themselves, coming closer together, without being aware of it.

"You wanna hear a good story?" Baron blurted out, crushing an
empty Miller can with his fingers. "In 1969 or '70, I don't remember
exactly, me 'n' a few friends broke into the local firehall and took
off with a half-dozen FN and some walkie-talkies. Nothing to do

with the FLQ. The stuff later ended up being used by a poaching outfit specializing in moose meat, but that's another story. Except that when the War Measures Act came in, they hauled me in from the room I rented by the week above a stripper bar, and I became the first political prisoner to be arrested in the history of Maldoror. A few years later, the police chief bought me a beer by way of apologizing, and so I got the last laugh on that. He told me that two days after the special law came in, he received a phone call from the head of the QPP. The guy'd called to warn him that from his perspective in Montreal, the guys who drove around Maldoror with a cherry on top of their cars were spending too much time in the doughnut shop. Three arrests in the whole of Abitibi? That wasn't good enough. They needed more. He said he was sending up a few helicopters. Make it look ugly up here, he said, the big kahuna, and then he hung up."

"That's really what he said? Make it look ugly?"

"Yup. With helicopters."

"Did Gode ever talk to you about the death of Lavoie?"

"Never."

Sam read *The Seagull*. Then he read it again. He thought about it. "When Trigorin sees Nina and the seagull that had just been shot," he wrote, "he instinctively perceives it as a symbol, he imagines the whole story right there: Nina free as the air beside the lake, seduced by Trigorin's idleness, condemned to a death of the soul by something as useless as Treplev's gunshot. The idea of the 'short story within the play,' which takes the place of the 'play within the play,' means that Trigorin, thanks to his creative compulsion, foresees both his liaison with Nina and its aftermath. But Chekhov's vision is larger than that: it isn't Nina's seduction that provokes her actual or symbolic death, but the fact that the writer immediately conceives their idyll in the form of a narrative, a story. Something that aligns with real life, but which, unlike the great, romantic love stories, contains its ending in its beginning. In fact, Trigorin doesn't seduce Nina from idleness. On the contrary: he seduces her through *activity . . .*"

Maire-Québec was fading. She didn't like her job. The regulars at the White Wolf mistook their bar stools for a shrink's couch and drained all the energy out of her, not to mention that if she had a dollar for every time she heard the words "tits" and "ass" she'd be a millionaire. But a job was a job, and a kind of social standing (however mediocre and libidinous) came with it. Whereas being in a Chekhov play in Maldoror didn't count for much. Because of their precariousness and their isolation, regional troupes saw themselves prevented from participating either in the travelling provincial circuit or on the stages of Montreal, so that being booked for four, five, six, or seven nights maximum, in places like the Loblaw's Happy Times Theatre, was the most they could hope for by way of success, despite all their hard work: the slow approach to the text, the ever-deepening reading, the memorization, line by line, the rehearsals, the blocking, the body movements, the putting on of this second skin of words, the mastering of the role, the dress rehearsal, the performance, the exaltation, the exhaustion, the labour and the stage fright, and then the return to darkness.

At the beginning of autumn, she seemed to oscillate endlessly between chronic fatigue, bouts of insomnia, PMS, polymorphous flashbacks to an old case of mono, and black thoughts that could drag her into something resembling postpartum depression but wasn't. *What's eating you, anyway?* he wanted to shout at her. But he held back, as though he feared provoking an irreparable breach. Waking up the sleeping cat. And it was as though the characters she inhabited during the production prevented her from showing her true self other than to make it die again in the soft glow of the footlights.

He found her sitting out on the deck. As the autumn advanced, her inner unhappiness had become a mask that she could put on or take off at will.

Samuel drew up a chair, sat down, and leaned his elbows on the table.

"I have to go to Montreal . . . I have work to do there. People I need to see, archives I have to consult."

"When?"

"Tomorrow. I'll be leaving first thing."

"And by three o'clock you'll be in Montreal while I'll be here listening to Phil Baron making propositions that would make a porn star blush . . ."

"He does that?"

"They're all the same. You should hear them."

"Not sure I'd like that as much as you do."

"Ha!"

"But I don't want you to stay here alone."

"And where would you like me to go?"

"Why not visit your parents?"

"No way. I'll stay here. The Ghost of Kaganoma will keep me company."

"Okay. But I want to do you a favour first. I want to show you how to use the shotgun."

"Are you out of your mind? If you feel guilty about leaving me alone here, that's your problem."

"Maybe, but a 12-gauge aimed at the gut is a universal language."

"Don't waste your time."

"What if a bear tries to get in? What would you do?"

"If you think it's so dangerous for me to stay here, then why are you leaving?"

"To work."

"Yeah, right!"

Sam got up and went into his study. A rifle is a strange tool that gives birth to a threat even as it averts it. He went back out onto the deck, the Baikal broken and hooked over his arm. Marie-Québec turned her back, looked out over the blue lake and, superimposed on it, the great forest that stretched all the way to Maldoror. She shook her head. No.

KOREA, HILL 187, SPRING 1953

THE GENERAL HAD LIVED UP to his reputation as a solid trencherman, but now he regretted his momentary weakness in the matter of the Armagnac, having taken one too many for the road. He sent General Libby home, already quite tipsy from the three bottles of Romanée-Conti they'd drunk from his personal reserve, requisitioned in Dijon less than a dozen years ago, and brought with him to Seoul. It was an excellent Pinot Noir, thanks to the predilections of the monks from the Abbey Saint-Vivant, and made even more precious by the phylloxera epidemic that had halted its production after 1946. In the jeep that was taking him to the front lines, Bédard, trying to keep down the acid reflux rising from his stomach on the rough road, did his best to interpret the snatches of information related to him by the short-wave radio tuned to the regimental QG frequency. The bad reception, the confused feverishness of

269

communications from the front to the rear, and reports from advance posts certainly didn't help to give him a clear picture of the situation on the ground.

As expected, the Chinese were concentrating their fire on the sector occupied by C Company, on the right flank of the third battalion. As Bédard well knew, that was the most vulnerable point of his plan: a high ridge making an overhang from which a line more than a quarter of a kilometre long, held by the Canadian brigade, was exposed. Over the past few days, the Chinese had increased their patrols in that direction, kept up regular bombardments, and the section had received more than its share of attention. Another detail bothered the general: he was operating with two battalions of the line and another in reserve. And the reserve, consisting of a contingent of the newly arrived 22nd Regiment, had had to be placed under cover of the battalion deployed on the left flank, where there was a dangerous hole in his defences. His room to manoeuvre was drastically restricted.

At night, the communists behaved as if the no-man's-land belonged to them. The Canadians occupying the sector were green, and the Chinese were surely aware of that. Their units were constantly under fire. Bédard had had shell fragments recovered from the area expertly examined for several days. Most of them came from canons that could be used if their positions were attacked. Lots of good reasons to slip away from General Libby.

Bédard leapt from the jeep before it stopped rolling and shot into the officers' mess. He found himself in the middle of a small farewell party in honour of a lieutenant-colonel who was returning home. The men froze when they saw him, glasses in hand. The heavy sound of shelling shook the ground, illuminating the Asian night in the background. The front was barely eight hundred metres away.

"I want everyone at their posts," the general said, his voice a bit breathless but calm.

The first two patrols sent on reconnaissance by the third battalion, a dozen men in each, were engaged across from the rocky overhang and practically annihilated. Shortly before midnight, the bombardments intensified, still aimed at C Company.

And then came the attack. At the stroke of midnight.

The Chinese flares had done their job well, and the successive assault waves swarmed through breaks in the lines of barbed wire cut by their sappers. They swept into no-man's-land and rushed the advanced positions where they were immediately engaged by a foolhardy squad. Bédard placed the canons from his brigade under the command of Lieutenant-Colonel Taylor, who commanded the third battalion, then hurried to the radio phone and called for artillery from the army corps deployed on the heights of land. At exactly 0005 hours, United Nations shells began raining down on the small silhouettes bent double and galloping to meet their enemies in the smoke-filled darkness of the battlefield. And behind them, line after line of replacements from the Chinese army. Bédard listened to a report from American intelligence, charged with the task of intercepting and deciphering communications from the Reds: apparently, the Allied shells were making them eat dirt, but no one was finding it funny.

Bédard went outside to assess the situation. As soon as he got to the observation post, he saw friendly planes flying low over the battlefield, dropping incandescent bombs that lit up the scene as if it were midday. The general squinted several times through the sharp smoke, finally saw them: wave after wave of small, yellow, grimacing soldiers in the blue uniform of the People's Army, fanatics, revenge-seekers, little mechanical toys, he thought. Look at them, columns of warrior-ants charging from an anthill as though it had been kicked with a boot. Numberless hordes, intent on submerging the entire world.

THE FIRST HOLDUP

THE POLICE TOOK THEIR TIME getting there. Kilometres of Gaspésian winter and mountains and bad roads separated them from Clo-
ridorme, a village squeezed between the flanks of the Chic-Chocs
and the open sea. The alarm had been going off for a good five minutes by the time they ran out into the ice-cold air, balaclavas over
their heads for masks. Attracted by the alarm, people had gathered
on the sidewalk in front of the credit union to gawk at them as if
they were some kind of alien life form. Embarrassed, Ben tried not
to point the shotgun in their direction. Gode's feet slid on the icy
street as soon as he began to run, and he went down, holding the
brown paper shopping bag full of money against his chest. On his
knees in the snow, he tried to stuff the small and large notes back
into the bag, but it was torn. He got up and ran, cradling the bag in
his arm like a football, cursing under his breath as the money kept
slipping out and flying onto the snow behind him. The car took off
as soon as they reached it. The last thing Gode saw when he looked

back in the rear-view mirror was the village diminishing behind him at full speed and people on their knees in the snow, gathering up the money.

PIERRE

LOOKING UP FROM HIS BEER in the Berri-de-Montigny Tavern, Gode saw François come in from the bus station. He was wearing a London Fog raincoat, his feet stuck in galoshes, and he was carrying a suitcase. Now his best friend was sitting across from him with a glass of beer, and it was like they were picking up a discussion they'd started maybe two years earlier, in the Flore or the Mabillon or the Rostand. Except that now they were talking less about literature and more about revolution. His big, soft eyes lit up behind his Coke-bottle lenses. Langlais wore his hair longer and was calling himself Pierre Chevrier. He'd kicked around Paris and London for a while before travelling to Switzerland, Spain, Morocco, Algeria. Luc Goupil, the pretty boy from Old Navy, had introduced him to other exiled FLQ members. Some of them were busy getting a foreign delegation together that would get training in Algiers. Others were in Cuba. Pierre had met up with the group from the Fisherman's Hut at the exact moment when they'd decided to get away from the

274

Gaspé winter and establish a base of operations closer to Montreal. It was the beginning of 1970 ...

"Call me Pierre," François said every time Gode called him François. He'd always been tight with words, and now more than ever looked like a deer caught in the headlights of a car. The Little Genius.

"I've got a book for you," he said suddenly, and leaned over to rifle through the dirty laundry and magazines crammed into his suitcase.

"I think my suitcase was searched at the airport," he said.

"Oh, yeah? Why do you think that?"

"It took a hell of a long time for me to get it. Don't you ever feel like you're being watched?"

Gode shrugged his shoulders. Pierre shoved some malodorous socks aside, brought out *The Urban Guerilla Manual* by Carlos Marighella. He put it on the table.

Gode raised two fingers to the waiter.

GOLAN

THE ISRAELI CONSUL IN MONTREAL was named Moshe (or Moïse) Golan. Three years after the Six Day War, having that name was a bit like a French diplomat being called Clovis Alsace-Lorraine.

The rented Econoline van was pulled over at the curb on Saint-Denis, across from the Carré Saint-Louis. Behind it, the flashing light on top of the patrol car shot splashes of bright red light on the park benches on which poets had once declaimed.

"I need you to get out of your vehicle and unlock the rear door," the cop said after glancing at the driver's licence. He was standing beside the door.

"Why?" asked Lancelot.

"Because. I want to see what you've got in there."

"But why did you stop me?"

"Your left-turn signal light is burned out."

"You're supposed to give me forty-eight hours."

"I said get out and unlock the door."

"This is an abuse of power," Lancelot shouted, to gain time. They knew what they were looking for, he thought. And they know who I am...

Having complied with the officer's request, he watched as the cop bent the top of his body into the Econoline's storage space while his partner examined certain documents in the glove compartment. The partner soon found a sheet of paper on which had been pencilled a series of telephone numbers and radio-station call numbers. The names of known journalists were written in parentheses, and the word "Golan" was written in capital letters at the top of the page.

The first officer had just seen the wicker basket about the size of a coffin, big enough at any rate to hold a man. He knew an illegal weapon when he saw one, and he took a marked interest in the sawn-off 12-gauge Remington shotgun, first making sure that the thing wasn't loaded.

"So I suppose you're going duck hunting, are you?" he said to Lancelot.

"How did you guess?"

"In the middle of February?"

"No, rabbits..."

With the shotgun in his left hand, the officer opened his holster with his right and ordered Lancelot to place both hands flat on the side of the vehicle, keeping them in plain sight, and to spread his feet. His colleague came around waving the sheet of paper.

"Looks like he might be a journalist or something..."

With his fingers freezing on the cold van, Lancelot endured the other's hands on his sides.

"What does this mean, 'Golan'?"

"It's a plateau, like this one..."

"A plateau where?"

"Under your feet. I'm talking about the Mount Royal plateau. Golan Heights is in Syria, but for the past three years the Zionist state has been occupying it illegally."

"What the fuck's he talking about?"

"I don't know, but he can explain it down at the station."

MOSSAD

AFTER SPENDING THE NIGHT in jail, Lancelot weighed his options and called *Maître* Brien, who hurried down and in no time obtained his release with a caution. Brien assured him he could have been charged with possessing an illegal firearm. They went drinking in Old Montreal to celebrate.

The next day, the list from the glove compartment landed on the desk of Detective Lieutenant Gilbert Massicotte, head of CATS, who examined it with interest. It took him thirty minutes to connect the word "Golan" with the Israeli consul.

"Good God, it looks like the bastards were cooking up a kidnapping," he said to himself.

It was a good thing he'd tipped off the Montreal Police about Lancelot and his rented Econoline van.

By the time he could procure a warrant to bring him in for questioning, the cockroach had had time to disappear back into the woodwork. He was already well known to the police; he had a kind of gift for being recognized, and his dossier with the antiterrorist squad was a thick one. Arrested in 1963 for throwing Molotov cocktails, he'd been photographed at many demonstrations since then, and by the winter of 1970 had achieved the status of a wanted revolutionary. The plot against the Israeli consul catapulted him from Robin Hood to Punchinello among the secret police. Surveillance teams were put on his trail, and he was soon reported to be hanging around with several local members of the Mossad, *the* benchmark in the terrorist profession.

MARCH

THAT SPRING IT WAS Coco Cardinal who found them in their bungalow on rue Collins, in Saint-Hubert. Gode and the Lafleurs knew him from their days in the RIN. Jean-Paul had convinced his girlfriend at the time, the beautiful Lou Ballester, to pretend they were married, and they signed the lease as Jean-Paul Hamel, a university professor with no references, and his young wife. The scene: two parallel streets not quite a kilometre in length, dropped as if from the sky into the middle of flat fields peppered with woodlots, fencerows, and overgrown rubbish heaps.

There was the full range of habitations, from rundown cottages to typical suburban ranch houses, with mobile homes somewhere in the middle. The bungalow Jean-Paul rented bore the street number 140. You entered through a foyer with the living room to the left, the kitchen on the right, and a second door facing northwest, toward the neighbouring house. A short hall led to the bathroom and the two bedrooms. A garage had been added beneath an extension of the roof.

With help from René and other members of the group, they spent a weekend repainting the place. Then they bought furniture on credit from Woolco. They had no intention of paying for it. For a long time, systematic and perpetual indebtedness had been the principal mode of financing their activities.

A few hundred metres from them was Savannah Road, and a bit beyond that was the beginning of the airport. It was a military base. The main headquarters, which accommodated the mobile force, was less than a kilometre to the south. The airfield and hangars were visible from the bungalow's bedrooms.

While Lou and Jean-Paul whiled away a grey afternoon in March by making love on a mattress on the floor of one of the rooms, jeeps came and went in the distance, like beetles filing across the dirty snow.

MILAN, SUMMER 1970

THE VILLAGE HAD BEEN FOUNDED by the Scots, but bore the name of an Italian city. The main street led straight to the church, which stood on one of the Appalachian spurs that undulated all the way south to the White Mountains of New Hampshire. Beyond the church, the road passed in front of the school, went through a wooded area and debouched into hilly countryside consisting of fields, most of them lying fallow, and stands of dark woods. At the end of this road was a farmhouse made of wood and covered in cedar shingles. The barn was farther back, its ancient boards turned as brown as animal fur with age. To the west, in clear weather, one could see smoke rising from the mill in East Angus. And to the south, the face of Mount Mégantic seemed both distant and yet near enough to touch, like certain islands.

In May, birdsong, warm wind in the hair, clusters of trilliums and dog's-tooth violets in the understorey. Nests. Marie-France had never been so happy, Gode never in such good spirits. As far as the village was concerned, they were a couple of hippies who spent all their time naked, taking drugs, and holding sexual orgies with a bunch of their like-minded friends.

In fact they spent their afternoons repairing the buildings and mending the fences that Brutal, their lascivious mountain goat, butted down at will, and discussing plots, compost, and couples.

And the People's Prison.

Marie-France had seen the drawings on a sheet of paper left lying around: a rectangle representing the tow truck destined to be buried at the bottom of the field, to be used as a cell.

René had asked Nicole to sneak a bottle of chloroform home from the hospital where she worked, because even though he'd be put to sleep at the beginning, a man waking up in the trunk of a car could struggle, and that would be a problem.

Officially, they were raising goats.

THE PART

IN APRIL 1970, LITTLE ALBERT, thirty-six years of age, became premier of Quebec. It looked as though a hairdresser followed him everywhere he went. His hair always in a mess, Ti-Poil, as he was called, had been defeated in his own riding and had to content himself with a caucus of only seven members, even though his Indépendantiste Party had received 23 percent of the popular vote. Chevalier Branlequeue, who'd run as an independent indépendantiste in the riding of Taillon, received three thousand votes. Richard Godefroid and the Lafleur brothers, willing to give democracy one last chance, had put up posters and gone door to door and made phone calls for him, turning his electoral committee into a kind of progressive Trojan Horse, a last attempt to legally bring about change. It ended in pure defeat. In Boucher, Paul Lavoie, the unfortunate rival of Vézina for the party leadership, had slipped in like a knife through butter.

In their little local office that smelled of stale pizza, felt-tipped pens, and cigarette smoke, Gode and Chevalier were the last to stay to watch the large, snowy, black-and-white TV screen showing the election results. They watched Little Albert give his victory speech in a voice whose pathetic rises and falls sounded like the bleatings of a goat.

"The mob wins again," Gode said dully.

"Don't go there," Chevalier replied.

They were drinking Molson's and savouring the bittersweet taste of catastrophe.

"Go where?"

"Hiding your head..."

"You know damned well what I'm talking about. On the ground, the election workers for the Liberal Party were lent to them by the construction mafia, and they did their campaigning with baseball bats and crowbars! Even the Parti Québécois were obliged to toe the line and align themselves with the mob just to be able to hold meetings. And if any of that had disgusted Bourgault enough to make him pull out of the race, you wouldn't have needed to run to uphold the honour of the Indépendantiste forces, isn't that true?"

"Twenty-three percent of the popular vote, Gode . . . You don't seem to have grasped the significance of that! Four short years ago the RIN weren't even in the running. Twenty-three percent in 1970 means 34 percent 4 years from now, 45 percent in 8 years. That means coming to power..."

"Eight years of baseball bats, that's too long. You can go on having faith in the system if it turns you on, but in eight years there won't be a single piece of the country big enough to plant your Kébek flag in. The Holy Trinity will have taken over the rest."

"The Holy Trinity?"

"The Mafia, the Liberal Party, and the Americans. You know what I mean."

"You know what, Gode? Working to liberate a country is like pissing on a fire when you're facing the wind. The best thing you can hope for is that you don't put out the flames..."

"Yeah, well, Chevalier, I know what I have to do next."

JEAN-CLAUDE
GOES TO QUEBEC CITY
(PART II)

I DON'T KNOW WHO you are. Really no idea. I'm telling you this because when I'm alone in my car like this, it never fails: I start going over it all in my mind, the events of that autumn, certain details in particular, they all come flooding back to haunt me, and as soon that happens I take out my little tape recorder and put it up to my lips and try to imagine who you are, you out there somewhere in the future, and this whole story, assuming that it even holds any interest for you, must seem unbelievably complicated. So. We were at Monday, a little before six in the morning, October 1973. Somewhere on Highway 20 between Montreal and Quebec City, about to cross the Richelieu River on, you'll never guess, the Paul-Lavoie Bridge. Rebaptized two years before. An ordinary piece of

288

highway construction; cement is a safe way to preserve a person's memory. I'd say that that's the main difference between politics and organized crime: the Mafia buries its victims in cement, the government, only the names of its victims. And now, I need to explain a few small things to you. Again. What I would like … Wait a minute. What I would most like you to understand is why Little Albert, after only two years in office, is going to call an unexpected election, perhaps this autumn, and to campaign on the backs of the separatists, instead of against the mob. And why he is going to win.

In the run for the party leadership, you will recall, poor little Paul Lavoie was lambasted by the electoral machine run by Colonel Lapierre, Uncle Bob, who grabbed Albert Vézina by the seat of his pants and set him down on the throne. In the meantime, Lavoie, flat as a pancake, was completely washed up. His coffers were empty. He owed $175,000. And Vézina had no reason to wait until he'd returned to financial health before calling an election. The election took place in April 1970. Lavoie could have bowed out. Everyone would have understood. But he was a determined little scrapper, and he decided to stick it out and carry on the fight within the party. Oh, he'd rally around the newly elected chief, no doubt about that. He'd hasten to assure him publicly of his loyalty. He'd swear on a stack of Bibles that he would place his experience at the disposal of the victor: Dear Albert, let me be your right arm … Ah-ha! Lavoie was in no hurry, and he was no fool. He had three-quarters of the delegates on his side and he wasn't yet fifty years old. Vézina was the outsider, tangled up in his diplomas, dressed to the nines. And Lavoie was still green enough that it was worth his while to wait to see if the tree was going to break or bend. *Bend over, Albert …*

Lavoie ran again in his old riding, but now he knew what he had to do to win it. He had to get rid of any weak-kneed supporters, no more choirboys in his organization, no sir. The leadership struggle had taught him a thing or two, or rather had confirmed in capital letters what he'd always known: in order to hold on to your sword in politics, you need to be willing to have dirty hands. He was a man who had always had debts, the hazardous combination of a spendthrift temperament and the provider of a growing family. He loved ostentatious watches, gold or silver chains, those little signs of material comfort that he could unobtrusively wear in public. He had the mentality of the parvenu, if you like, but in the 1960s all of Quebec was like that. After having passed his bar exams, Lavoie wanted to see some action, but his skill with a pen diverted him from his high ambition and landed him at the *Devoir*. Where, falling victim to a kind of economic civil war, he was condemned to grab any passing devil by the tail. Financially speaking, being a correspondent with the *Devoir* placed you somewhere between a Biafran native and a minor colonial civil servant.

Parachuted into the position of parliamentary correspondent in the Old Capital, our friend discovered he had a certain genius for augmenting his income. On one hand, he denounced the weakest of the scandalistas (the "assholierthanthous," as he famously neologized) that rose from the practice of power, and he learned how to operate this marvellous machine for making money that is to any politician what mud is to a pig. He perfected the art of situating himself as a go-between between the politicians with whom he rubbed shoulders on a daily basis in the corridors of the Assembly and around the high tables on the Grande-Allée, and the businessmen of his acquaintance. Understand me well: the commissions he received for his good offices, he needed them! Suits to buy, mouths to feed, the whole nine yards. Everyone knew the Liberal Party existed only to stay in power and allow the greatest possible number of friends of the regime to fill their pockets and their bellies up to their eyeballs. So when people gave him the sign, their boy Lavoie didn't

hesitate for a second. Renounced his quasi Maurrasian nationalism, gave up his Basque beret and leapt on the train of the Quiet
Revolution. The train of progress and big money, of elevated ideas
and under-the-table payoffs. And I'm going to be very clear on one
point: if you think Albert Vézina, with his first-class airs, was, from
this point of view, more proper (or cleaner) than his future rival for
the party leadership, you're sticking your finger so far into your eye
you'll be able to scratch between your shoulder blades. When you
join the Liberal Party, you become what the Liberal Party tells you
to become, and when the last trumpet hath sounded, money hath
no smell, not even if it comes from a baron of tainted meat who
wants to increase your chances for the leadership.

Speaking of the daily paper on the rue Saint-Sacrifice, I'd like
to read you something that was in it this morning. Yes, you who
are sleeping in the future, who perhaps are driving down this very
Highway 20 and crossing the Paul-Lavoie Bridge to overlook, in its
happily amnesiac way, the Richelieu River and its Chemin des Patriotes. Perhaps you are on your way, on this marvellous October
day, the sky pure and cold, to hunt woodcocks in the farm woods
around Saint-Glinglin. There, I've slowed down, I'm pulling onto
the service lane, I've put on my four-ways for extra safety, and now
I'm getting my good old *Devoir* from my briefcase. The guy who
signed the article is a first-class shit-shoveller and we love him for it
— except when the shit's on the tips of our own shoes from stepping
in it, obviously. And if, way off in the future, you've never heard of
the second Lavoie Affair, well, open your barn doors wide, that's my
friendly advice to you.

RCMP REPORTS INCRIMINATE PAUL LAVOIE

That's the title of one of them. Now, I'm going to read you an
excerpt from the police report that is quoted extensively in all four

articles, no less, that have to do with this affair: this one appeared under the byline of the (admittedly) courageous Louis-Georges Laflèche:

On April 2, 1970, we were informed that a meeting was going to take place that day at 6 o'clock in the evening in the apartment of Jean-Claude Marcel, secretary to Paul Lavoie, between Lavoie and Giuseppe Scarpino F.P.S. 354448 and Luigi Temperio F.P.S. 348015. A certain Louis-Gilles Gauthier would also be present at this meeting.

According to information received, the apartment was situated in a building on boulevard Saint-Joseph East, in Montreal. Apartment number 4.

A check was made of the building at 5145 boulevard Saint-Joseph East, and no name appeared on the list of apartments for number 4. It was later established that the apartment in question was situated on the top floor of the building.

That same day, at 5:40 p.m., in the presence of Corporal Maurice Vachon, regimental number 3347, we observed a v.a. 1970 Oldsmobile, colour grey, Quebec licence plate 5P-2024, registered under the name of Paul Lavoie, park across the boulevard from 5145 boulevard Saint-Joseph East, in Montreal. The v.a. was driven by an unidentified man. Mr. Lavoie got out and went inside the building situated at 5145 boulevard Saint-Joseph East.

At 6:00 p.m. we observed Louis-Gilles Gauthier enter the building at 5145 boulevard Saint-Joseph East. Photographs of the subject were taken.

At 6:10 p.m., we observed a v.a. Cadillac, colour dark blue, roof black vinyl, Quebec licence plate 2M-9898, registered in the name of Giuseppe Scarpino. The latter, accompanied by Luigi Temperio, interred [sic] the building situated at 5145 boulevard Saint-Joseph East. Photos of the subjects were taken.

At 6:50 p.m., we observed Paul Lavoie leaving the building at 5145 boulevard Saint-Joseph East. He was alone. He got into the Oldsmobile and drove away.

Surveillance was terminated at 7:00 p.m.

Factual note: It has been verified that a telephone was installed in apartment number 4 on 30-03-70 and was terminated on 30-04-70.

That's the kind of thing that happens when you're in power and you try to stick bats in the spokes of investigators of good faith (there are some). Somewhere in town, a journalist wakes up with an anonymous manilla envelope shoved through his mail slot. And now I'm going to start the car and merge with the traffic, otherwise I might draw attention to myself. Standing between the ditch and my car, both feet on the shoulder, one door open like the door of a shitter as if I were taking a piss in the open air, it might look like a normal thing, but it's not normal for me. I mean, for me to whip it out on the side of the road? My wife would say it lacks class. There, I'm back on the highway, left signal light flashing, exiting the service lane — get it? *La voie de service*?

I hope you know that what you just heard, you out there in the future, that piece from the *Devoir* I read at the steering wheel of my stopped car is a bomb. You do? No? But perhaps by the time you're hearing this it is all common knowledge. If so, so much the better for you, but now, in 1973, in Quebec, not Sicily, it's hot shit! An apartment that has a phone installed one month before the elections and then has it removed the day after the votes are counted, okay, so far no big deal. They were in an election campaign and soliciting funds. That two big names from the Scarpino family and a Liberal member and ex-candidate for the party leadership were there at the same time, what can I say? It isn't exactly the kind of thing you'd want to become public knowledge. Scarpino controls the entire North American distribution of heroin, and his organization serves as the link between the Corsican clan in Marseille and the big New York families. The only problem for Paul Lavoie, and it wasn't his fault, was that he was dealing with two gentlemen who were at the centre of a wiretap operation set up by the RCMP as part of their Operation Plain, a huge international investigation into the trafficking of heroin. The contact between us and the Scarpinos was through Gauthier, a supporter who owned a tavern in Saint-Léonard and a good friend of mine, who was chief treasurer for the Lavoie campaign.

The day after the psychological triumph of the wallet that was the Liberal victory, when Little Albert was busy constructing his cabinet, he was told of the dubious connections of his new right arm. Either he received a visit from some higher-ups in the civil service or else he was put in the picture by his special adviser, Uncle Bob himself, who knew everyone from the head of state to the lowest echelons of the public service. Uncle Bob, who wagging tongues were saying had access to the collection of tapes gathered by the intelligence services of the Quebec Provincial Police, and who had only to snap his fingers to have at his disposal any relevant hardware belonging to military intelligence. Papa Boss and Big Brother all rolled up into one person, imagine it . . . The result? Paul Lavoie, whose secret financial backers expected to be made Minister of Justice, found himself relegated to the sidelines once again, given the portfolio of Public Works as a kind of consolation prize. What was worse, now Uncle Bob had him by the short and curlies. So why wasn't he simply kicked out of the cabinet altogether? Because Lavoie would have taken half the party with him. He still had too much support to be confronted head-on. The scandal would have blown the whole party to smithereens, and most of the shit would have fallen on the premier's well-coifed head.

But behind the scenes, the confrontation went on. I know that at one point Lavoie went to Vézina and told him, regarding the special counsellor: "It's him or me . . ." Ha! Vézina gave him the usual runaround, and before my unfortunate patron could cut a path through the bullshit, Uncle Bob, the Shakespearian character hiding behind the arras, had once again consolidated his power.

And once Paul Lavoie was no longer around to defend himself, people began opening the floodgates and covering him with all the crud that rose to the surface. And we, his friends, stood there without saying a word while he was stabbed in the back again, forced to watch the shit-spraying in silence, because if we didn't, the whole apple cart would have tipped over. In politics, there's nothing better than a scapegoat with his mouth full of dirt. And just between you and me, it wasn't the Mafia who pulled off this coup. At bottom, the business between Lavoie and Uncle Bob Lapierre was a war of succession. And if, boys and girls from the distant future, you wonder how I'm doing, I'd say that J.-C. Marcel isn't doing too badly, thank you for asking. I was elected in a supplementary by-election at the beginning of autumn. I'm the new member of the National Assembly for the riding of Vautrin, and the parliamentary secretary to the Minister of Revenue. It's not exactly the red carpet, but with a bit of luck that will follow. All is well. I don't regret my choices. I've sworn allegiance to Uncle Bob.

THE FOUR PS

WITH LA VÉRENDRYE PARK displaying its melancholic golden tamaracks around him, and the fall rocking in from the far side of October, Sam, at the wheel, remembered his last meeting with Chevalier Branlequeue, the previous year, toward the end.

In the mid-1990s, as Branlequeue was sliding quietly toward retirement as professor of creative writing at UQAM, like Tolstoy deserting the conjugal foyer late in his life, he abandoned La Grosse Éleonore and took a tiny apartment on rue Saint-André, in Montreal's South Central district, a two-minute walk from the university and smack in the middle of the Gay Village. He freely confessed that he aspired to nothing more than to minister to the humblest of the humble and signed on as a volunteer in the care of AIDS victims in their terminal phase. It was unexpected, a late-blooming and a very touching return to the rejection of that homosexuality he'd been carefully keeping under wraps, but which must have continued to exist in a state of pure latency. Desire he'd never had the courage to acknowledge, that he'd let desiccate like a skeleton in the closet of his books, the author of *Elucubrations* (Didace-Beauchemin Prize, 1970), disowned by wife and children and eyed with growing suspicion by his university brotherhood, as well as by his two true adopted families, literature and politics, he was now going to sublimate himself in a twilight homage to adepts being decimated by AIDS.

His kidneys gave out first. Nihilo, who under Branlequeue's tutelage had started his master's in creative writing, visited him during his dialysis. They discussed books almost as though nothing had changed, but Sam watched as Chevalier's body emptied and refilled with blood and felt like one of those shades who buttonholed Ulysses at the mouth of the Underworld.

Next it was his lungs. The doctors took a huge chunk out of him, but the cancer had metastasized to his liver. These were organs that, once transformed into killers, weren't known to take their sweet time about it.

"You should have come yesterday," Chevalier told him with a weak smile. They were in his room in the Palliative Care Unit of Nôtre-Dame Hospital. "You'd have run into someone who would have interested you, even here."

Samuel, standing beside the bed, had just handed him a paperback of *Le Survenant*, which he'd bought earlier in The Exchange, on rue Saint-Denis. The beautiful cover on the new French-Canadian Library edition showed a man with his back turned, standing on a point of land, one hand deep in his pocket, collar turned up, a small bag thrown over his shoulder. In front of him flowed a river, and farther off a shore and island, a cluster of trees casting dark blue shadows on the green water. Chevalier had taken a moment to hold the book in his hands and turn its pages, his eyes shining.

Sam was privately shocked by Chevalier's thinness. His colour was a kind of ash yellow. He'd always spoken, even in class, in soft, luminous tones, but now using his own feeble voice seemed to tire him out. They could hear car horns sounded by drivers on Sherbrooke Street, demonstrating their support for the nurses on strike, who were picketing in front of the old hospital entrance and whose angry signs were held up and shaken in their faces as they passed. From the hospital-room window, they could see the irregular, phallic shape of the obelisk raised in memory of Charles de Gaulle at the edge of Park La Fontaine, the same park in which, thirty years before, mounted police had charged and beaten the crowds assembled along the parade route up Saint-Jean.

"Oh, yes?" Sam asked. "Who was here?"

"Richard Godefroid ... Do you want to sit down?"

Sam shook his head, as though taking a chair was getting too close to the position held by the man in the bed. He preferred to stay on his feet.

"Godefroid was here?"

"Yes. Why, are you surprised?"

"You publicly called him a liar. I thought he was nursing a grudge against you."

Chevalier smiled.

"To him, I'm still the old twenty-five-year-old prof who read his work to the class."

"And ... what did you two talk about?"

Chevalier's eyes continued to smile.

"What do you think we talked about?"

"October? The Lavoie Affair? No, I guess not ..."

"It wasn't the time to talk about that. But still, he didn't come here to talk about the weather. I told myself he wouldn't dare continue to deceive his old mentor on his death bed. So I asked him a question, just one: why did he go to Dallas? Why Texas, one week before the Lavoie kidnapping? But he gave me his old song-and-dance about financing themselves by pretending to have lost some travellers' cheques . . . 'Go tell it to the marines,' I said, and he just laughed and shrugged his shoulders. But do you know what? As he was leaving, standing in the doorway over there, he stopped. He kept his eyes down. He knew it would probably be the last thing he ever said to me. We both knew it. And he said: 'You were right . . .' I waited for him to go on, and he said: 'About my poems . . . They really were crap.'"

So that's how it ends, Nihilo thought. Alone in a bed that doesn't belong to you, wearing a skimpy johnny-shirt that's as thin as paper, with your insides being devoured by your own cells that want to know nothing about you.

And, in Chevalier's case, abandoned by everyone but a handful of the faithful: students, minor writers, more or less unknown poets, a few profs, all of them very much alive and caught up in their own activities: full schedules, necessary vices, amorous trysts, tennis matches, weekends up north, conferences at the University of Ithaca on textual genetics in the works of Joyce, articles to write about the time Hubert Aquin spent in the library in Buffalo. So much to do, so many pretexts for spending less and less time in the Palliative Care Unit of Nôtre-Dame Hospital, their hearts shorn of pity and affection. Chevalier's bedside table was notably less encumbered than the ideological benches of the nation. Illness was approaching like a high-speed train, and the tunnel was opening up before him all too quickly.

Toward the end, he continued to write his famous letters to editors, poking at the clay feet of our statues, discrediting our great heroes. His feverish missives were aimed at everything from the huge cars driven by the bigwigs of the left-right nationalist movement, to the private jet flown by the Kid-caïds in Québec Inc. He'd never been good at the art of making friends, but in these latter years Chevalier perfected, often to the point of no return, the ability to turn his back on the world. And when reproached for shitting in his own nest, he replied that he didn't have a nest, he had a goal.

If he'd been content to rest on his laurels for his work in the prisons that October, even though it meant making his patriotic skin crawl every fifteen years — the years of the referendums on sovereignty — he probably would still have had some visitors. And even without accepting the epic (which is to say, heroic) version of the October Crisis, in which the terrorists were collected and recycled as productive and enlightened members of society, just like the cops and their political masters, and limiting himself to denouncing the duplicity of the federal government and the wheeling and dealing of the War Measures Act over a pint of local beer or a glass of Chardonnay, as most of his colleagues did. But Chevalier needed more than that. He couldn't stop trying to understand what had *really happened*.

It occurred to me to wonder if La Grosse Éléonore didn't see him the same way that Marie-Québec had regarded me, those last few months in Kaganoma. Not like a fool, exactly, at least not yet, but as someone who was in the process of crossing to the other side, passing through a border that was supposed to be kept reassuringly clear and watertight, like the line that separates the world of reality from that of the novel. In fact, it's not so much a border as a grey area between multiple possibilities. Above it lies a parallel universe, a world in which every step forward is simultaneously a step back, where the Kennedy brothers and Martin Luther King, Jr., and Elvis and Jimmy Hoffa and Hitler and the little extraterrestrials found at Roswell in 1947 are all alive and hanging around the same cloning factory in an extinct volcanic crater on an island in the South Pacific.

Chevalier's problem had become mine: we both lived in an age of so many plot-seers and conspiracy theorists that any Machiavellian notion we might entertain was automatically reduced to a permanent caricature of itself, discrediting any sustained attempt to reflect a little on the theme of political manipulation. The incessant communicational bombardment of the Web had erased the last permanent markers for distinguishing between the ridiculous and the serious.

Chevalier would die before reaching his Promised Land, but in any case his tribe had dispersed and no one had the slightest confidence that the Promised Land even existed.

"Have you had any news from your confrère, Falardeau?" came the nasal voice from the bed.

Sam replied that he hadn't seen Falardeau for a long time, but he'd heard that Fred was living in a bedroom community on the South Shore and worked as a researcher for a television station. He'd seen his name in the credits for *L'Enquêteux*, the new documentary series on Télé-Québec. Sam wondered what Fred's reaction would be to seeing Chevalier in this condition, nothing but skin and bones under the thin johnny-shirt.

Chevalier smiled at him.

"You were my two best..."

His old professor took his hand. Sam gave it to him but refrained from shaking it, as though his existed outside himself. The sick man feebly held his left hand as he spoke. Nihilo suddenly found the situation ridiculous. Then he found ridiculous his finding anything ridiculous concerning this dying man. He tightened his grip, enclosing Branlequeue's hand firmly in his own.

"Sometimes, Sam, it seems to me that the light of fact comes to us from a long way off, like light from dead stars. And that we are swimming in a sea of arbitrariness when we call on facts to give us a plausible explanation.... Maybe the explanations we're looking for can never be anything but approximations, mere outlines that we fill in with meaning, like constellations: we draw dogs and huntsmen and dippers on places where there is nothing but eternal ice and extinct suns."

Samuel took his hand more firmly in his own. There was a pause, and then Chevalier went on:

"We know from the coroner's inquest that someone in the Lafleur cell made three calls to a firm in Houston, James Engineering, during the summer of 1970. It was confirmed that that enterprise had offices in Laval from February 1970 to March the following year, apparently without having landed a single contract. But there the trail ends. Disappears in petrol smoke somewhere on the gulf coast of Mexico. The CIA is like God in the Old Testament. Either you believe in Him or you don't. But if you do, it's everywhere... But Texas is too far, too violent, for me. Which means we have no choice: we have to go back to rue Collins."

"Yes."

Chevalier took a sheet of paper from his bedside table. He had scribbled some notes on it.

"What's this?"

"My theory of the four Ps. Let me explain..."

"What are the four Ps?"

Chevalier read:

Pieces of chicken
Prosecutions
Pierre
Police warrants

"There's something funny about the guys who delivered the chicken," he said, looking up at Sam. "Something doesn't add up about those deliveries... I followed the trials closely. I went to Jean-

Paul's and his brother's, I was even a witness at Richard Godefroid's. Have I ever told you about Captain Claude Leclerc?"

"No, I don't think so."

"He was the head of QPP's homicide squad. Not long after Gode's trial was over, I heard through the grapevine that Leclerc had given up his commission. From what I understood, he slammed the door but didn't let it make any noise. I wanted to talk to him, but he never returned any of my phone calls ...

"Then, at René's trial, the lawyer Brien saved his client's ass, and do you know how? By systematically stuffing the jury's head with two main points: one, the Crown had not succeeded in proving beyond a reasonable doubt that René Lafleur had been to 140 rue Collins during the week in question; and two, François Langlais, alias Pierre Chevrier, probably went to that address while Paul Lavoie was still being held hostage there ..."

"What?"

"Which brings us to the third P: Pierre."

Sam gave a faint but happy smile at seeing his old professor waving his sheet of paper as he spoke, whipping the air with it. Beware, you enemies of the truth! He was just getting warmed up. His final course ...

"Listen to this: a police officer told me that the night before the departure of the Rebellion Cell to Cuba, the Montreal police had traced the ownership of the kidnappers' car to a certain Pierre Chevrier, and from there connected it to François Langlais and the FLQ. But officially, it wasn't until a whole week later that the law enforcement agency identified 'a mysterious Pierre Chevrier.' Alias Pierre Guité. Alias Pierre Bousquet. The man changed identities more often than he changed shirts. Have you learned anything new about this guy?"

"Nothing that you don't already know, Chevalier. You gave me an assignment, but I'm sorry, I deserve to get a big fat zero ..."

"It's the final exam that counts, Sam."

"Tell me about the final P."

"Ah, the police warrant. In his famous interview in *Temps-Presse*, Gode said that while the members of the cell were holding Paul Lavoie, the police obtained a warrant to search the house right next door to theirs. Desrosiers told the coroner the same thing, and so I'm inclined to believe it. But when the police finally discovered their hideout, after the cell had abandoned it, no one said a word about having searched the house next door. Nobody said: 'Goddamnit, five days ago we were this close.' ... It was as though the search had never taken place."

"Yeah. According to Gode, the police rousted some long-haired hippies next door."

"Do you think it's an avenue worth exploring?"

"Maybe."

A nurse came in the door without warning. She was a kind of sympathetic shrew. If she would rather have been down in the street soliciting motorists with union slogans, she hid it well.

Samuel let go of the patient's hand and, once again, felt silly.

Chevalier murmured his own version of a song by Charlebois: "If I had the essential services of an angel / I would go to Quebec..."

"He's going to have to get hisself some rest ..." the nurse said as she arranged the pillows behind Chevalier's back. She spoke with a strong English accent.

"*Him*self," Nihilo corrected under his breath.

"We can go on talking," the sick man said, arching his back under the nurse's hands. "Georgina's as silent as the tomb," he added, grimacing.

"And he runs on like a leaky facet," the nurse shot back.

"You mean faucet."

"I promised Georgina I wouldn't cross the picket line when I leave here ... I think I'll be leaving by another exit, though, don't you, Georgina?"

"Would you please stop talking..."

The nurse began refilling the intravenous bag that was dripping solution into Chevalier's arm.

"So what do you think, was there a kind of pact of silence?" Samuel asked Chevalier, now suddenly eager to end the conversation. "They were covering for a comrade...?"

"They could well have been. But we still don't know the answer to the most interesting question: Who was Pierre Chevrier working for?"

"You should read the nice book that your friend brung you," said Georgina.

"I would, nurse, but with all these drugs you pump into me, I'd be lucky to finish a single sentence...When I think that I promised myself I'd read *Remembrance of Things Past* again before I died: *For a long time I used to squeeze my head early*, as the constipated man said. He-he-he."

Chevalier regarded Samuel from the cottony depths of a strong dose of morphine.

"Don't forget...the four Ps."

"Paper-pasta-potatoes-pain," the nurse recited.

Sam smiled, his chest tightening.

"Take this sheet of paper," Chevalier said. "Take it..."

He took it. Chevalier was a voice, a whisper.

Nurse Georgina helped Branlequeue lie back. She had the same physique as Chevalier's wife. And, to ease his final moments, an English accent to rub it in.

After passing Mont-Laurier, Sam Nihilo's Mazda or Colt or Corolla was surrounded by the archaic chain of the oldest mountains on Earth. Two weeks before, they'd given him a magical display of colour. But now all the leaves had fallen.

INQUEST

AS SOON AS I GOT to Montreal I headed straight to the Fameux, no
doubt for sentimental reasons. Then I spent the night in a small,
European-style hotel a few steps from there, bathroom down the
hall, window overlooking Place Gérald-Godin. The Fameux was a
good observation post during Indian summer, at the heart of a sat-
isfying concentration of cool young couples, artistic mothers yoked
to baby strollers, French passing through, French entrenched, odd
characters, self-caricatures, talents of all genres, from builders of
doomed bridges to punctilious, semi-planetary superstars.

I was sitting near the window, in the same booth I was in when
Marie-Québec had appeared to me the winter before. The restaurant
was straight out of Michel Tremblay: forty-something waitresses
who called you "honey" and a faunal mixture of cultural nobodies,
young bums and bummettes from good families, clones of Shirley
Théroux straight from the taxidermist's, and Madame Balcon rushing from the pawnshop to the Dollarama.

Justin Francœur, formerly of the FLQ's Rebellion Cell, had just got up, shaken my hand, and left the restaurant, leaving behind a meniscus of pale coffee at the bottom of his cup on its white ceramic saucer. I didn't know what to make of him. He'd been quick to do his revolutionary *mea culpa* after the October Discomfort, publicly calling his former accomplices "manipulative assholes." And he'd included himself in the phrase. Somewhere between Cuba and Paris he'd been converted to Maoism. Then he'd seen his former comrade-in-arms and the mother of his children, Élise, take the populist path brightly illuminated by the burning bras of feminism.

During our talk, Francœur had constantly oscillated between a desire to exchange confidences between two troubled souls, and episodes of name-calling and cautious introversion. I could accept that he'd found listening devices in his telephone after his return from exile. But what to make of the three attempts on his life in Paris? Put them in a little file labelled Paranoia or in a drawer marked Megalomania? Did he really expect me to believe that professionals had messed up three times in their mission to liquidate this charming, bespectacled intellectual? From what I knew, the secret service of any country would consider Francœur a liability.

When I'd mentioned James Engineering, he shot back spontaneously:

"You mean the company in Houston that sold arms and was a front for the CIA?"

"Yeah," I said, "that James Engineering."

"I don't want to talk about it. I don't know anything about it...But one thing I never understood was why the money that was seized in Saint-Colomban, the money we got from the university holdup, was later returned to us."

"What? What are you talking about?"

"I can't say any more. But you know, the Travers abduction was really a kind of super publicity stunt, in the end."

"A publicity stunt? Are you kidding me?"

"That's how I see it. They left the financing to the guys on the South Shore. The gang of Jean-Paul's represented a new direction ... paramilitary, I'd say. If you're going to go there, I suggest you to make copies of everything and put them in a safe place, because your nosing around could start a fire."

I looked at him with interest.

"Really?"

"Really. Let me tell you a story. While we were hiding Travers, in the north end of the city, something bizarre happened. One afternoon, I went out to catch the bus and I ran into my brother at the corner of the street, quite by accident. I thought he was in France. I asked him what he was doing there, and he sort of shrugged off the question. We went for a beer in a kind of strip bar called the Wick. I still remember the name. At one point, I got up to take a piss, and when I came back I was feeling kind of woozy. Years later, I found out he was working for the French secret service. Goddamnit, he'd put something in my beer ..."

"Why do I get the feeling you're making fun of me?"

"Why do you say that?"

Francœur finished his coffee. Shortly after that, he left the restaurant.

Nihilo spent the afternoon a few streets west, in the National Archives' microfiche collection, browsing through the periodical section. After a few hours of putting up with the white noise from the antique photocopy-scanners rescued from the scrap heap, he read a story about rue Collins published the morning of the discovery of the hiding place of the assassins of Paul Lavoie, on

October 19, 1970. One detail in the piece leapt to his attention.

According to the first statements given to journalists, the bungalow next to the terrorists' hideout had also been occupied by individuals known to the police. Neighbourhood witnesses said the apartment had been vacated a month previously, but a few hours before the macabre discovery of Lavoie's body a half-mile away, neighbours had seen a familiar car parked in front of the house and a man loading things into it, then driving off.

This story was repeated in most of the papers, sometimes in the form of a CP wire-service report. In *La Petite Vie*, an abundantly illustrated popular daily that never backed away from wild speculation, they even put a name to the leasee of the neighbouring house: Lancelot.

Strangely enough, in the editions of the next few days, the story of this second house disappeared, *pfft!*, as though it had evaporated into thin air. It was never mentioned again.

There was nothing next to the two lots on the southeast side of the street but a vacant lot, and so this neighbouring house at 150 rue Collins was obviously the one for which the famous search warrant had been issued, where police officers had searched not twenty feet from where Lavoie's kidnappers were hiding. It made him wonder if the police had found someone on the premises after all, and if so, whom?

Samuel had read up to November 1970, following the trail of Pierre Chevrier, known as le Chevreuil, in accounts of the coroner's inquest. As the afternoon wore on, he lost the trail and was about to give up when, on November 24, he found this succinct and unsigned item in the *Montréal-Matin*:

FLQ MEMBER HANGS SELF IN LONDON

If the *Standard-Tribune* of London can be believed, a young French-Canadian, Luc Goupil, described as a sympathizer of the *Front de Liberation du Québec* (FLQ) hanged himself on the weekend in his cell in Reading Gaol, in England.

Still according to the article in this London newspaper, this young man of 25 hanged himself from the bars of his cell with the aid of his shirt at the very moment when Scotland Yard was preparing to question him about recent activities of the FLQ, in particular those involving Jean Lancelot, suspected of being one of the key figures responsible for the kidnapping of British diplomat John Travers ...

The name Luc Goupil vaguely rang a bell. Samuel put a quarter in the metal slot of the prehistoric and probably condemned apparatus and made a photocopy of the article, which he slipped into his briefcase. Then he left for his next meeting.

"The police can make mistakes just like anyone else. But it looks like that never crossed your mind."

So, here we are. I had the famous Lancelot seated across from me with a pint of beer. He'd agreed to meet with me at the Quai des Brumes. I wondered who he meant by "your," and then I remembered that he'd already had a run-in with Chevalier Branlequeue. In his eyes, Chevalier was at best a delirious innocent in the final stages of a terminal case of *conspiraciitis*. At Chevalier's death, on *Lancelot Standing,* his regular program on Radio-Trashcan, the former FLQer badmouthed the former writer without even waiting for the coffin lid to be lowered: "Your poor, flogged horse is dead, and good riddance, sausage meat!" he'd cried at the end of his editorial.

The man I saw above the foam looked like a sensualist from the Renaissance period, a subtle mixture of fat and refinement. Above the raised eyebrows, the bald pate and grey tonsure were those of a minor civil servant. But the full lips and puffy, reptilian eyes told a different story. There was logic in his rise from impoverished street urchin to grizzled rebel, idealist at seventeen, sybarite at fifty-five. His journey had taken him down blind alleys and right turns, but it had ended up with deputy seats and chauffeured limousines with the fleur-de-lys flying from the hood ornament. If Marie-Québec was ever looking for a fifty-something actor to play Casanova, I made a mental note that, despite the repulsion that the character inspired, I'd recommend Lancelot.

"I've thought about that," I replied to him.

When our beers came, I asked him about that neighbouring house. I knew that Lancelot had spent at least part of the summer of 1970 hiding out on rue Collins. His reaction was immediate and categorical:

"They weren't FLQ, the people living there. We didn't know who the hell they were. We didn't know any of our neighbours."

"Okay, let's agree on that. But when questioned by the police, other neighbours confused the occupants of the second house with photographs they were shown of the suspects from 140. Later, the police noted the error and the trail was dropped..."

"Sure. Do you have a problem with that?"

I took a mouthful of beer and glanced over at the bar. A few tavern philosophers were seated there, adherents to the allures of mad doctors like A. A. Painchaud, purveyor of rare books and used cassettes. And a few good musicians as well, unknown, depressed, uncontracted, sometimes all three at the same time. Lancelot was already a member of the local *nomenklatura*, thanks to his history as an impenitent kidnapper, and he was enjoying his second life as an on-air rebutter (he preferred the neologism to "debater"). His latest scandal had been unleashed when he'd called the Governor General the "Queen's bum-boy." It had not only thrust him to the foreground of the news, it had also brought him to the attention of the younger generation of bloggers, Web surfers, and cultists who'd been born after the October Crisis. But here at the Quai des Brumes, no one was paying him the slightest attention. But even if Jean-Paul II had walked into the bar, sat down, and ordered a large Black Label with a shooter of Jack Daniel's, it would have been accepted as the most natural thing in the world. I took up my questioning:

"Let's agree that the police made a mistake. What intrigues me, though, is that at least one element in the story of the neighbouring house, of this supposed false trail, corresponds to reality."

Lancelot raised his eyebrows and waited for me to continue. So I continued:

"The house had been abandoned for a month. Yes, because what happened on rue Collins a month before the third week in October? Richard Godefroid and the Lafleur brothers went on a trip to the United States, that's what. And the so-called young kids who lived next door vacated the premises at exactly the same time. Simple coincidence?"

He looked at me. I could see him thinking.

"Whatever it was, it wasn't anyone in the cell who rented that house. I never set foot in it. I was in the north end of the city. And let me tell you something, mister mystery lover: you are going to be disappointed. The guys in the Chevalier Cell were under a lot of pressure. Our action had caught them unawares. They improvised a kidnapping and the thing blew up in their faces. That's the whole story right there."

"I was twenty years old then, too, Lancelot. I marched with the ML on the first of May, I participated in an anti-Reagan demo in front of the Parliament Buildings in Ottawa, and watched Salvadoran exiles try to use a Bic lighter to set fire to the Star-Spangled

Banner. The lighter was out of butane and the television camera-
men took the time to wait until the flag began to burn. I have one
question: how could anyone who was twenty years old decide to
kidnap someone?"

"Have you ever been hit with a billy stick?"

"No."

"There's your answer. In 1968, in Saint-Jean, mounted police had
truncheons that were four feet long, made of hardwood. Two or three
hits with that and kidnapping a fucking British diplomat was suddenly a good idea. These days at demonstrations, you get about five
cops for every demonstrator. A revolutionary act for these little world-
changers would be a billiard ball tossed through a window. In those
days they let foreigners come in to sweep the streets, now they take
the broom handle and shove it up the ass of political rectitude, and for
every individual who complains there's someone else who takes a rifle
and shoots fourteen women without thinking twice about it! Without
thinking period! Me, I'm not ashamed of belonging to a generation
that wanted to change the world and who almost managed to do it..."

"You don't have to talk like I'm a SHIT-FM listener."

"Oh, yeah, I forgot I was on the Island — sorry, I meant the You-
land — of Montreal! You're all a bunch of sheep!"

"How can I get in touch with François Langlais?"

"I heard he's opened an old-folks' home somewhere out in the
Saint-Alphonse-Rodriquez area."

"What does he do?"

"Haven't the foggiest. He's a weird guy. You don't hear a word
from him for ages, then all of a sudden he opens up and says something outrageous."

"That's interesting. Other people describe him as intelligent and
extremely articulate. So which one is the real Langlais?"

Lancelot hunched his shoulders like a guy who's already halfway
out the door. Then he gave me his opinion of Justin Francœur:

"Son of a top-level civil servant, spitting image of his fucking bourgeois father, dipped his ladle into leftist politics like it was a pot of chicken noodle soup. I took him along with us so my little sister would have someone to play with. Submachine guns gave him a hard-on, not the grateful arms of the working class. And with that, my good friend . . ."

He jumped to his feet and put on his six-hundred-dollar suede jacket with a single motion.

"See you later!"

"Luc Goupil," I said, without looking up at him.

"What?"

He stopped in mid-stride on his way to the door. He didn't turn or move an inch.

"You knew Luc Goupil," I went on. "When you were that serious seventeen-year-old and throwing Molotov cocktails at the system. You two were arrested at the same time. You were compared to each other. And years later, while you were holding a certain English gentleman hostage in Montreal, he knotted his shirt and succeeded in hanging himself in a British prison, under somewhat suspicious circumstances. Talk about a stroke of luck . . ."

Lancelot said nothing. Then he turned and looked at me.

"I've got some advice for you," he said, "but you already know what it is."

"I'd like to hear it anyway. Coming from you . . ."

"Stop this. Don't go there. This is not for you."

He made a vague gesture with his hand. Then he made a somewhat nonchalant exit and slipped between my fingers.

THE BOAT (2)

COCO CARDINAL DREAMED OF HIS schooner in the area around Miscou Island, in Acadia, while on a belated honeymoon with Ginette Dufour. Now she'd made the sails and he was building the boat on the bank of the Acadia River, on a piece of land he owned on the Île aux Fesses, a dozen or so miles south of Montreal. The *Patriot* would be a twenty-metre schooner with a ferro-concrete hull. Thirty-five tonnes' displacement, a draught of eight feet, a teak deck, four twin cabins, two heads, and a wardroom big enough to hold ten people. And the deck would be big enough to hold two lifeboats: one inflatable and one made of fibreglass.

As well as the sails normally found on a two-master, Coco planned to rig a topsail to the foremast. The method of naval construction he chose — ferro-cement, an armature of steel rods supporting a coating of concrete — was the method of choice for first-time boat builders, and incidentally gave them an appreciation of the amount of work that had gone into building the great pyramids of the Pharaohs. For the amateur boat builder who wanted a craft longer than twenty-five metres, it was the easiest and least costly technique; in other words, the most accessible. And it required no specialized tools.

In the spring of 1970, Cardinal had been acting as a sort of coach for the organization Jean-Paul and his friends were trying to put together. He was the man you went to if you needed a used revolver. It was Coco who showed them how to saw off not only the barrel of a shotgun, but also the butt of an M1 rifle to make it as easy to handle as a pistol. It was also he who told them that the M1, a .30-calibre assault weapon sold in all good sporting goods stores, could be converted into a machine gun by the removal of a single spring.

Under Coco's patronage, the fraudulent financing system of the Lafleur-Lancelot network picked up steam. Preparing for a revolution was, they discovered, an all-consuming enterprise. Holdups weren't enough. Coco did business with a forger of genius who worked undercover in Montreal East. Cloned credit cards, illicit driver's licences, artfully retouched passports, false birth certificates: all impeccable work, discretion guaranteed. The Fat Cop had connections with all the useful trades. But Coco also had his nose in the powder up to his eyeballs, and this goddamned cement boat, to which everyone had to lend a hand, was not part of the bargain.

In May, the militants in Lancelot's entourage found that Jean-Paul was beginning to weaken. The time to make a grand statement, they said, had arrived. Some twenty members of the network met for a strategic planning session at a rest stop on Highway 40, between Montreal and Trois-Rivières. The spot overlooked the sandbars and flood plain of Lake St. Pierre, and they could easily survey their surroundings and spot any potential followers. Gode swept the horizon with his binoculars: not a cop in sight. Nothing but pintails, green-winged teals, northern shovellers, black ducks, and huge, noisy rafts of Canada geese.

That day, a first cell was formed and left the rest stop with the mandate to kidnap the American consul. A few days later, its members rented a cottage in Saint-Colomban, in the Lower Laurentians.

Sitting on a case of Labatt 50s on the Île aux Fesses, Coco took a long swig as he watched ducks swim past on the river. Beside him, Jean-Paul sipped a small can of cold Kik. The openwork skeleton of the schooner was reflected in the brown water at their feet, bearing a striking resemblance to the rib cage of a diplodocus in a natural history museum.

"Yesterday," Coco said, chuckling, "I saw a pig floating downstream with only its chest and feet sticking up out of the water…"

Jean-Paul had come to show him the green Chevrolet with a vinyl roof that he'd bought that day. The driver's licence he'd used was a fake, and Pierre had forged a signature on the registration. Cardinal had barely glanced at the vehicle parked under the trees above where they were sitting. After giving it a brief inspection, he started to laugh.

"Now I've seen everything…"

He'd slapped his thighs.

"They sold you a taxi. If this odometer showed the real mileage, it'd have the equivalent of about fifteen trips from Montreal to Vancouver and back on it. They really saw you coming, J.-P."

Coco took a snort off the vinyl top of the Chev.

Now they were back sitting beside the river, Coco on his case of beer, Lafleur on the grass.

"What you really need, Jean-Paul, are weapons…"

"Yeah."

"Enough to equip a militia…"

"Call it what you want. But a serious organization, with a solid structure, base camps, able to defend itself against attacks."

"I think I've found someone who could help you."

"Oh, yeah? Where?"

"Houston ... But they have offices in Laval."

"And they do what, these guys?"

"You don't want to know."

Jean-Paul drained another Kik Cola.

"Who cares? Anyway, I don't need help from Uncle Sam."

After a moment, Coco fished a wallet flat as a buckwheat pancake from his back pocket and took a card from it, which he handed to Jean-Paul.

ROBERT NILE
JAMES ENGINEERING

There was an address on boulevard Saint-Elzéar in Laval, and a telephone number.

"What kind of engineering?"

"Electronics. Doesn't it say on the card?"

"No."

A black duck swam slowly in front of them, followed by four ducklings pedalling in its wake. A skunk or rat must have eaten the rest of the eggs.

"Hey, Coco?"

"What?"

"What's your link with the Americans? The CIA?"

Coco squeezed out a laugh.

"You don't want to know. All you want are some weapons."

"Yeah, right, they furnish us with arms and then we use them to kidnap their consul. You think they'll thank us for that?"

"They won't give a fuck. And I'll tell you why. Maybe they don't like communists too much, but they respect people who fight for what they believe in. They understand that. They've been there..."

"There's a few people in Guatemala I bet would like to hear that."

"Don't lay your goddamned geopolitical trip on me, man. Selling guns is just business . . ."

Cardinal stopped and drained his beer. Then he raised his right arm, stretched it back, and threw the empty bottle into the middle of a raft of black ducks, where it caused an indescribable hullabaloo.

"Jesus, Coco!"

"What?"

"Sometimes I really think you don't give a shit about anything."

"I didn't hurt them. They're just ducks."

The mother continued to squawk while the young ones slapped their wings on the water and scattered off in all directions.

"Look, Jean-Paul, you need weapons. You don't have the means to buy AK-47s on the market. Let me introduce you to a few good people."

"But why Houston?"

"Because that's where they're based. They supply a few anti-Castro groups . . . people like that."

"Oh, I see. And where do they get these weapons from?"

"From our own military bases, where do you think?" Coco said, laughing softly. "Weapons and electronic equipment stolen from our good little soldier-boys over the past seven years. Where do you think they end up? Don't look at me like that. You know what I mean: storerooms emptied in broad daylight, real professional work. It's not like your friends in the FLQ could have pulled it off."

"You're telling me I'm naïve, is that it?"

"You've got a few things to learn."

"Okay. I'll buy myself a bazooka and I'll blast a few American fishing boats off the Cascapédia, how would you like that?"

"You can kill as many Kennedys as you want, but spare the higher-ups in the army and you won't have any problems."

"I'd just like to know one thing: what's the deal . . . ?"

"Talk to Bob Nile. Ask him."

"Hello, Houston? Can you hear me?"

"Fucking comedian."

"I don't need you guys. Is that clear?"

"What you need is to be snivelling enough for two. You can't be afraid to play in these guys' court. Because any way you look at it, they're there. We're stuck with them."

Coco took another deep drink and burped. Jean-Paul thought. Then he shrugged.

"I'd just like to know what game he's playing, this engineer of yours. Robert Nile and company."

"Call him and see."

They watched a large great blue heron skimming just above the waves, stomach filled with a plump-thighed bullfrog and a five-spined stickleback.

"And Jean-Paul . . ."

"What, Coco?"

"Did it ever occur to you that the Americans would like nothing better?"

"Nothing better than what?"

"Than to stick it to that socialist fag who's running the show in Ottawa."

FINANCES

IN MAY 1970, AT AROUND ten one morning, Mr. Ron Lamoureux, a man in his fifties, Second World War vet, sufferer of what was not yet called post-traumatic stress disorder ("The bombing made him a bit loony, is all"), was standing near a window in the Queen Mary hospital for former combatants, his back to the street, thinking about the uninspired adaptation of *Madame Bovary* he'd seen the night before at the Jean-Talon cinema, when the window behind him suddenly blew out. At the same time, a deafening roar shook the structure of the building around him and even the air he was breathing. The next thing he knew he was lying on his stomach on the floor, convinced he was back on Omaha Beach on D-Day, at Courselles-sur-Mer, to be exact. Even before making the slightest move to shake off the splinters of glass and the flakes of plaster that covered him, he realized that his sphincter had opened. "Mommy," he said, very distinctly.

Two kilometres away and exactly fifteen minutes later, in the parking lot of a building belonging to one of the Canadian branches

321

of General Electric (the American industrial giant), a powerful explosive transformed the lovingly souped-up Camaro of Ti-Guy Porlier, a Gaspésian exiled to Verdun, into a mass of twisted metal. For Ti-Guy, his car was his life. He raced it on weekends. The murmur that issued from its exhaust practically made him come in his pants. That of a Formula-1 literally made him faint. When he left the building with a few other employees to check out the damage and saw the smoking wreckage of his car in the parking lot, he simply said, "No..."

At the same moment, three hoods armed with machine guns burst into the Credit Union of the General Association of Students of the University of Montreal (GASUM), situated partway up the mountain on boulevard Édouard-Montpetit. They lined up the employees and clients with their faces turned toward the wall and their hands behind their heads, then threw $58,000 into a cloth bag and got the hell out of there.

Shortly afterward, three hooded gunmen showed up at a branch of the Canadian Imperial Bank at the corner of boulevard Saint-Laurent and rue Saint-Viateur. They made off with a cool $51,000.

At almost the same time, the Montreal-North Franco-Canadian Credit Union was hit by, you guessed it, three masked gunmen wearing nylon stockings over their heads. This time, however, Detective Sergeant Miles Martinek had been warned by an informant the previous night and had set up an ambush for the holdup men. In the midst of the prolonged gunfight that ensued, the hoodlums tried to get away by shoving a hostage out ahead of them, a twenty-nine-year-old blonde pretty cashier. Not in the least deterred, Martinek leapt from behind a nearby parked car and laid out one of the thieves with the Thompson machine gun he always used on important occasions. He'd got hold of this beauty during a raid on a gangster hideout. The two other thieves dropped everything — weapons, hostage — and, stepping instinctively away from their fallen comrade, who was pissing blood, raised their hands. Martinek later posed for the *Police Gazette* photographer who, alerted by a helpful phone call, had been listening in that day on the police radio band. In the photo, we see Miles Martinek, one knee raised, bald head glistening like a full moon, leaning on his rifle like a bwana who'd just shot himself a buffalo. With his free hand, he was picking a pile of blood-stained banknotes from a large pool of blood.

Only the holdup at the university and the two bombs set off as diversions were eventually traced to the FLQ. The two other robberies staged at the same time were put down to simple coincidence, just another day at the office in the holdup capital of North America.

Meanwhile, on the mountain, the holdup men evaporated into the woods that surrounded the university. The cash they'd made off with put a serious crimp in the golf season of Mr. Tim Burroughs, the United States consul in Montreal. The neighbouring cemetery resounded with the song of small birds.

VISIT

IN THE TEMPERATE LATITUDES of North America, the countryside is at its greenest in the days leading up to the summer solstice. The fields are green. The woods are green. The understory is strewn with green. The light is green. The mountains are green. The lakes are green with the reflection of all this greenery.

It was on this infinite green palette that, leaving the preparations leading up to the Saint-Jean-Baptist Day celebrations, one, two, three, four police cars showed up in the village of Milan, in Quebec's Eastern Townships. In the unmarked car at the front of this convoy, Detective Sergeant Miles "Machine Gun" Martinek rode armed with his inseparable Thompson. He had come from Montreal especially to lead the detachment of Quebec Provincial Police stationed in Lac-Mégantic.

The cars braked, raising clouds of dust; the officers jumped out, ready to charge; Martinek advanced with long, purposeful strides, his machine gun at his hip pointed majestically skyward like a thermonuclear warhead. Two days before the national celebrations, he approached the small farmhouse as though it were a ruined castle filled with fanatical warriors ready to die for their cause.

Inside, Jean-Paul Lafleur and his brother René, Lancelot, and Lou Ballester had no intention of dying for their cause, at least not then. They ran for shelter and disappeared into the attic. Richard Godefroid, with Marie-France and Momo Corbo — a communist taxi driver — welcomed the visitors at the front door. Lancelot's wife, Sylvie, was a few paces behind them, a child hiding behind her skirts.

"You've come to celebrate Saint-Jean-Baptiste Day with us, have you? Well, come on in: we've got lots of beer and plenty of people who know how to sing."

"Get out of my way, or I'll rip off your arm and beat you with the bloody end..."

The police pretended to be ferocious, but they were merely paying a courtesy visit. They appeared to swallow whole the fake names furnished to them by those in the kitchen and refrained from pushing their enquiries further. When they went upstairs and came within a hair's breadth of Lancelot, crouched in the attic and officially on the run, they went back down without breaking anything. Then they took up their tough talk again.

"You know why we're here?" one of them said. "Because your little friends in Saint-Colomban got themselves busted. And Martinek always finds a way to make people talk who don't want to talk..."

"We'll be back," Martinek predicted in a sinister tone.

Before leaving, the officers decided to look around the barn and the buildings.

"You should cut the grass," one of them called without looking back at the house. With his right foot, he kicked the head off a wild daisy.

That's when Gode, from his vantage point on the porch, saw Brutal, the goat, lying in wait at the edge of the ditch. He checked to see that Corbeau had seen it, too. The latter slowly raised a finger to his lips, which wasn't necessary since both men understood each other perfectly. Gode turned back to look toward the grassy ditch. Behind the goat, he now saw clots of dried mud flying in the air, kicked up by the virile caress of a split hoof.

The goat's rage sent up clumps of grass from the edge of the ditch, and then he charged, head down. The next instant, Sergeant Martinek dropped his machine gun and took off with his legs around his neck. From the porch, Gode and Corbeau saw him cross in front of the house, running, running, like Francis Macomber in the Hemingway story being chased by the lion. Behind him came the stinking goat, hot on his heels. A car door slammed and there came a loud BOING! that must have been heard all the way to the top of Mégantic Mountain. Brutal charged the cars twice more before making a dignified retreat. That winter, Lionel Arcan, the man who owned the body shop in Lac-Mégantic, had his trip to Florida paid for by the Quebec Provincial Police.

SHORT TRIP

THE CHIC-CHOC MOUNTAINS rose above the sparkling sea. The Chevrolet clung to their flanks with Justin at the wheel. Jean-Paul was in the passenger seat, and Ti-Ben Desrosiers, whom they'd picked up drunk in Old Montreal before leaving, was snoring like a pig on the back seat.

"At his age," said Jean-Paul, raising a hand to shield his eyes from the sun, "you don't think about anything but fucking, eating, and sleeping."

"You forgot one important thing: shitting," said Justin Francœur, with a hearty smile.

The slight smile he drew from Jean-Paul in return was a small but important victory. He hadn't been lucky enough to have had a worker for a father, as his passenger had. His father had been from Outremont and was a top-level civil servant in Pierre Trudeau's government. Francœur was Lancelot's brother-in-law and a newcomer to the group, in genuine revolt against his father. Although he lived

327

and slept revolution, for the moment had to content himself with being a chauffeur for the elder Lafleur. A Lafleur, moreover, who was more distant than ever, preoccupied as he was by the raid in Saint-Colomban, and then the discovery of the farmhouse in Milan by the police two days later. His whole political organization was on the verge of collapse.

They dropped Ben off in Gaspé, went in for a coffee themselves, then drove on through Percé to the top of Aurore, where they pulled over onto the gravelled terrain of a rest stop, marked by a row of wooden guard rails painted white. They parked a short distance from the kiosk. Picnic tables were lined up in the open air. There was no one else around.

Francœur had been at the wheel all night. He shut the motor off and leaned the back of his head against the headrest. Jean-Paul, who'd been dozing, opened his eyes and looked around. He winced, a hand raised above his eyes to ward off the sun, which, although low in the sky above the sea, still shone into the car.

"Wow."

From where they sat they could see only the top of the famous rock emerging from a cloud bank that looked as thick as whipping cream. Farther out, Île Bonaventure was a lump in the fog that lay between the earth and the horizon.

"What time is it?"

"Almost six," Justin replied.

Jean-Paul leaned back against the door for a last short nap.

Justin's eyelids became heavier and heavier. He saw a human form approach his side of the car, and when he lowered the window a travelling salesman leaned in toward him. *It's the Sandman*, Justin thought, and when he looked down at the salesman's hand, it was held out toward him with nothing in it but a handful of golden sand, a small placard stuck in the middle that read MADE IN JAPAN. Then the roar of a Harley broke the silence that had descended around the stationary Chevrolet, and the two men woke with a start.

Shortly after that, *Maître* Brien, perched on his motorcycle, made his entrance onto the panoramic parking spot. No helmet. Long hair kept down by a scarf knotted Apache style around his head, wearing a deerskin vest, fringes flying in the wind, and with a beautiful hippie chick riding behind him.

"Wait for me here," said Jean-Paul, getting out of the car.

Justin watched them discussing something for about fifteen minutes, standing at the edge of the cliff and paying no attention either to the girl beside the guardrail who remained sitting with the Harley's saddle between her long legs, or to him, at the wheel of the parked car. He eyed the girl through the windshield. Brown hair, all legs, braless and buxom under her Indian blouse. She seemed royally unconcerned with his existence, kept her head turned toward the fog-enveloped sea, not moving except occasionally to shake a stray strand of hair from her field of vision. She displayed the patient passivity of an angel. A woman on the fringes of danger, enjoying every minute of it. He wanted to jump her so badly he wanted to cry.

Still talking, the lawyer went over to sit at one of the picnic tables and took out a pocket mirror and a razor blade and had himself a snort. Then he handed Jean-Paul a large brown padded envelope. They broke up shortly after that, Brien returning to sit astride his motorcycle and Jean-Paul getting back into the car with his envelope. The two men watched the lawyer give a gallant slap to the thigh of his passenger, then start the Harley with a kick of his boot heel.

"I thought he'd be pissed with me," Jean-Paul said.

"Oh yeah? What for?"

"For getting him up so early. It's not his style. But I wanted us to meet undisturbed."

"And?"

Justin watched the motorcycle move off in the distance, the girl on the back, her arms wrapped around Mario Brien's body, her long hair streaming out behind her in the wind, like the train of a dress.

"Looks like I worried for nothing," Jean-Paul said after a while. "He wasn't sleeping."

"Ah."

"If you ask me, that's probably what they're going back to do now."

"Ah-ha. And what are we going to do?"

Jean-Paul found himself a comfortable position in the car seat.

"We're going back to Montreal."

Jean-Paul slept until Newport. When he opened his eyes, the car had slowed down to a walking pace, then drew to a complete stop. Lafleur sat up and saw some kids by the side of the road, brandishing little wooden sailboats and running to catch up with the car.

"Kids selling sailboats!" murmured Jean-Paul. "We must be in Newport."

He lowered his window, took one of the boats, gave it a glance, and handed it to Justin. About fifty centimetres long, carved entirely by hand and all in wood. The sails were made of birchbark.

"How much do they want for it?" Francœur asked.

The shouts of the little band rose from the roadside.

"I can't understand a word they're saying . . ."

"They're speaking Paspayan, that's why. It's a local dialect."

Jean-Paul exchanged a few words with the kids.

"Too expensive. Give them a fiver and they'll take it."

"I can't do that."

"Why not?"

"Don't you see how much work's gone into this thing?"

"I know, but they always ask too much, just in case. They think we're American tourists."

"You think they can't see our Quebec plates?"

"You're right. They're a bunch of fucking thieves ... Five bucks is too good for the little bastards."

"Well, at least you know it's not made in Japan. The sum of work in one of these boats. How many hours, do you think?"

"The sum of work? What's that, some kind of Marxist shit?"

Justin had taken two twenty-dollar bills from his wallet and was holding them between his fingers. Jean-Paul took one of them and dangled it out of his window. The gamins pounced on it like a bunch of starved fledgling birds on a piece of bread.

Francœur started the car, the model boat resting on the back seat.

"Did you see how they were dressed? Bare feet on that gravel? It's like we're in the Third World."

"I could show you villages up in the mountains behind here that would give you more than just an impression. It pretty much *is* the Third World. We're in Robin Hood land here. The Kingdom of Cod."

They were quiet for a while, following the curve of Baie-des-Chaleurs, watching flashes of sunlight on the indentations in the cliffs.

"You see, Jean-Paul, you can't denounce the fish-processing plant that steals from them and the forest companies that make them sleep in school buses and the mine that sends them digging deep into the earth, and then refuse to pay child labour its true worth. That's called a contradiction."

"You're beginning to make me sick with all your phrases that are only found in books."

"What's in the envelope? It looks heavy ..."

"None of your business."

"Oh, I get it. I'm stuck driving a nonstop round trip from Montreal to Percé, and I have to keep my mouth shut."

"I don't know you well enough yet."

They retreated to silence and, shortly afterward, Jean-Paul fell asleep. Not much later, Justin almost joined him, but jerked the wheel just in time to bring the nose of the Chevy back between the lines on the bridge spanning the Cascapédia. Suddenly awake, Jean-Paul looked around with a lost air. They stopped at the first hotel they came to and took a room: Chez Guité, in Maria. Jean-Paul paid cash while Justin stretched his legs on the shore.

The tide was out, the sound of waves seemed far off, the air smelled of seaweed. The wet stone pillars of a dismantled wharf poked out of the water to the east like the backbone of a large fossilized dinosaur. Clusters of mussels attached to bunches of sea-wrack and the shells of crabs, turned over and cleaned out by gulls, littered the pebbled beach.

He found Jean-Paul stretched out on one of the beds, fully clothed. The TV was on, tuned to a local program of indescribable boredom. This was followed by Kraft Cinema, showing *A Fistful of Dollars*, sliced up to make room for ads for mayonnaise and some substance that passed for cheese.

Justin took the car along the seafront to buy takeout club sandwiches and fries from a restaurant called the Barli-Coo.

"You know what?" he said when he got back. "The guys at the restaurant say that the biggest salmon in the world come from this area. From the Cascapédia, all along here. Jackie Kennedy fishes here. It belongs to some Americans. It's people like that that we have to get rid of."

Jean-Paul said nothing. His mouth was full. Justin felt encouraged to follow up on his thoughts.

"Our comrades have been caught in Saint-Colomban, and the farm in Milan is known to the police. No more People's Prison. The network is completely busted up. All we have left is the house on rue Collins. It's going to take a lot of money to rebuild a solid organization. You're so desperate that you have to listen to me...Now, imagine holding Jackie Kennedy prisoner in one of these fishing lodges, way up in the mountains, somewhere between New Richmond and

Sainte-Anne-des-Monts. How much do you think Daddy Onassis would pay to get her back? Ten million? Twenty?"

"I don't think they're still together."

"Oh..."

"We'd have to find out first, in any case."

Justin Francœur barely finished the last bite of his club sandwich before falling asleep. When he woke up, Lafleur was snoring in the bed beside his. The sound was rhythmic and also very strong.

Francœur wanted to see the sea again, so he tiptoed to the door. Before getting there, his eyes fell on the brown envelope lying on the end table. He didn't hesitate for a second. He went over to it, picked it up, hefted it in his hands, squeezed it. Then, without making a sound, he undid the metal clip that kept it shut, all the while keeping an eye on the sleeping mound slowly rising and falling with the ample oscillations of deep sleep. He felt the contents of the envelope before pulling them out: a wad of twenty-dollar bills. There were more inside. Several thousands of dollars worth...

Easily enough to finance two or three kidnappings.

OPERATION DELIVERANCE

RENÉ LAFLEUR AND MAURICE CORBO, a.k.a. Le Corbeau were hanging out by a stand of pines on the Nun's Island golf course. At thirty-seven, Le Corbeau was typical of the people being drawn to the ranks of the FLQ. He'd been caught distributing Marxist tracts on the armed forces base in Valcartier, kicked out of the army at the age of eighteen for comportment issues, and earmarked, in the eyes of some, as a "card-carrying Commie." At the moment, Momo was training his field glasses on a foursome driving in their direction on two golf carts.

"Here come the desert commandoes," Corbeau joked.

René, who was sitting cross-legged on the grass, looked up from his notebook.

"Is one of them a big guy?" he asked.

"They're all obese."

"One about half-bald?"

"They're all half-bald. But they're wearing hats."

"And I'll bet they're all in their mid-fifties."

"Bingo."

"The only difference among them is the number of shots it takes them to put the little ball in the little hole."

René had barely finished his sentence when the whistle of a brand-new Spalding split the air and a ball hit the turf literally under his nose before bouncing once and rolling until it came to a stop at the edge of the woods. Le Corbeau instinctively ducked, an old reflex from his army days. Before he and René could exchange a single word, a ring-billed gull that had been cruising over a nearby water hazard flew over and, after making a low-altitude sweep, landed a few feet from the ball, hopped closer to it, considered it from a number of angles, and ended up deciding it was an egg that had fallen from a great height and should be returned to its nest.

He had to make several attempts before he managed to pick the egg up in his beak. But when he had it, he flew off with it and disappeared.

Another ball plopped directly into the water hazard. Then the golf carts showed up. One of them was heading toward the stand of pines at about fifteen miles an hour.

"Let's get out of here!" said Le Corbeau.

"To bring my family origins into the picture like that, it's just reviving the old notion of class structure, and I, for one, warn you that I won't stand for any such Leninist bullshit in my own Renault, no, Madame!"

"Excuse me, our Renault."

Just as Justin was opening his mouth to reply to his wife, they saw a long black car pass them and disappear around a curve. A flat calm fell over them like a crust of greenery on Redpath Crescent, which looped among the rich homes arranged up the side of the mountain.

"Who was that?"

"How would I know? You were talking nonstop..."

"I didn't see what house he came out of. It could have been Hite or it could have been Travers..."

"You were supposed to be keeping an eye on the Travers house, and me on Hite's."

"Yeah, but now what do we do?"

"We fuck off."

Lancelot indicated the Île-des-Sœurs with the end of a broomstick broken in two and used as a magic wand. He was in an apartment in Saint-Henri, empty of furniture and situated across the street from the Auction Hotel. On the wall in front of him was pinned a chart on which a list of names, the abscissa of hours of departure and arrival, indications of place and habits had been written in black felt-tip pen on a piece of white cardboard one metre by two. A battered map of the city measuring sixty by fifty centimetres was pinned beside it.

On the Île-des-Sœurs alone there were forty names. We were planning on sticking up those who played golf, and I can tell you that that would represent quite a packet. Our idea of nabbing four in a single swoop of the golf course and stuffing them into a milk truck at six in the morning was a pretty good one. It would give us lots of time before the alarm was sounded. But since the People's Prison was no longer in the picture, the problem was that we had nowhere to keep them. The question of space limited us to a single hostage, two at the most.

"In any case, we have to take an American," Jean-Paul said quietly. "The other thing is, we have to forget about the Île-des-Sœurs. The access road is too easy to block off. If anything went wrong, we'd be the ones who were trapped."

Lancelot turned toward Pierre Chevrier, who was thinking.

"If it were up to me," Chevrier said, "I'd take an English. You know why?"

He jumped to his feet, took the pointer from Lancelot's hand, and pointed at the chart.

"Look. It's as clear as a page of music. Travers is the real deal. He plays bridge. He's as punctual as an Englishman in a mystery novel. *The commercial attaché John Travers leaves his office at five o'clock sharp.* I'll bet he eats crumpets with his tea. Impossible to mess it up with him."

"Yes, but we're not writing a mystery novel. We're planning a kidnapping."

"A kidnapping that carries a message," Jean-Paul said loudly.

"That Quebec is not a colonial state?"

"Yeah, yeah . . . what do you call economic domination?"

"What do you suggest, J.-P.?"

"We go for both of them. We take an American and an Englishman. That way, we'll cover the whole territory of our alienation."

"Jesus, you sure do talk the talk."

"Larry Hite," Pierre said, tapping the list with his half of the broomstick. "He lives on the same crescent as Travers. Across the street from him."

Richard Godefroid walked east on the north side of rue Ontario. He stopped to examine some hubcaps artfully arranged in the window of Father Scrap, turned his head, and saw his man forty metres behind him. The man had stopped, too, also feigning an interest in a storefront. Now that he knew he'd spotted the man, a childish pride came over him. He thought he'd be better to attribute his success to the stupidity of the other man, to his carelessness and lack of precaution, than to any calculated intelligence on his own part. He turned from the scrap shop and walked quickly on, thinking he would give his tail a ride.

By nightfall, he was still walking. His man had long ago taken off his jacket. During the day, Gode had amused himself by sometimes slowing down or even doing an about-face to vary the distance between himself and his shadow. They both used these occasions to study each other. At certain times, their movements seemed to be choreographed like those of two duellers with pistols in Leone. Gode sized up his adversary. The poor guy was dragging around at least a dozen more years than Gode was. They both smoked, so they were equal in that. It would be a fair fight.

He had just crossed Pie-IX and the sun was low on his back when he stopped at exactly the spot where, six years later, they would build the Olympic Stadium. He walked along the slope, more like a slight incline, that went down to Sherbrooke, glancing over his shoulder like a bicycle racer who had just started a sprint and was watching his most dangerous rivals gathering into a column behind him. With a ridiculous sense of gratification, Gode saw the plainclothes cop try to catch up with him then give up, glued to the spot. He hurried west through the Botanical Gardens and reached the large, wooded Maisonneuve Park, which was almost a forest. Then he started running; he was free.

PEACE

MARIE-FRANCE WAS WAITING for him at the entrance to the cemetery at the corner of Côte-des-Neiges and Decelles. She'd moved into
the area in July, into an apartment between the Café Campus and St.
Joseph's Oratory, on Queen-Mary Road across from the wax museum.

She was beautiful, radiant in her light summer dress. He noted
that she offered him her cheek rather than her lips to kiss, that she
was holding herself back as though she were waiting for an explanation. She'd started her law course in September.

They walked among tombstones and epitaphs with the names
and numbers under which lay Ryans, Gurskys, Burnsides, Handkes,
Thatchers, Tavarones, Yanacopouloses, Szaabos, Mors, Eglis, Apos-
tolskas . . . with here and there among them a few French-Canadian
surnames whose roots had long ago entwined with those of their
neighbours.

"I've got something to tell you," Godefroid announced. "I've quit
the gang."

She'd been paying him so little mind that now she looked at him carefully, standing in the middle of the path.

"Quit?"

"Operation Deliverance. I'm out of it."

"I'm having a hard time believing you."

"Maybe, but it's the truth. The whole truth. Nothing but the truth."

If Marie-France had been cruel, she would have taken the time to savour her lover's humiliation. But fundamentally she was not a cruel person.

"I'm deeply moved, Gode."

"Well..."

"What are you going to do?"

"I thought of . . . maybe going back to the Gaspé. Hitchhike. Camp. But not to Percé! I want to put all that behind me..."

She didn't help him out. She watched him tie himself up in knots with an almost innocent enjoyment. She was honestly interested in what he had to say, but her concern was hidden behind her broad smile, which also held a trace of commiseration.

"What about you?" he finally asked her.

"Me? Florida ... I'm leaving on a forty-eight-footer for Key West next week. For the whole month of August."

"To..."

"A nice couple in their fifties. Someone I don't know. With a friend of theirs. I answered an ad in a travel magazine. We're going to do the Caribbean, take our time. I'll learn my knots."

"Florida," Gode said.

"Yup. Flowerida. I guess if it were you and the others, it would be Texas."

"Why'd you say that?"

"Nicole told me that Jean-Paul Lafleur has spent hours on the phone to Houston lately. He charges his calls to the hospital where she works. She'd do anything for René, poor little thing."

"What do you want me to say?"

"I don't know. But why Texas? It's a terrible place. The sea's full of gasoline."

"Jean-Paul's a big boy. Don't worry. He knows what he's doing."

I didn't ask: what about us? Because the first thing she told me was that she'd figured out that love was never going to be a priority in my life, never the most important thing for me, as it was for her, because I believed I could change my life, whereas for her, if love wasn't the most important thing, if it wasn't what made the difference, the thing that changed life, then she didn't want to have anything to do with it. We could just be friends.

I had about as much desire to be her friend as I had to be slapped in the face with a freshly caught codfish. While I was holding out my cheek so that she could peck it with her lips puckered up like an albatross's asshole, I looked at the tombstone behind her.

In a way, I wanted to give the world a second chance to give me a second chance. But the cemetery was just a station, not the terminus of my illusions. On Côte-des-Neiges, meat retained a certain dignity. Rotting had its place. And I did not go to the Gaspé in the end. I went to the end of everything, in a field near Manseau.

It was billed as the Woodstock of Quebec. Three orgiastic days of sex, drugs, and rock 'n' roll. Jethro Tull and Jimi Hendrix were among the names handed out to journalists by organizers whose professionalism didn't inspire a great deal of confidence. Gode found himself with his thumb out beside Highway 20 one Friday morning, with nothing in the way of baggage but a small cloth backpack and a woollen blanket on which he'd promised himself he'd lay the first beautiful hippie who'd let herself be attracted by his three-day beard and his status as a saviour of humanity. He wore his heart on his sleeve and a huge wind was blowing between his ears.

The site was an entire field behind Napoléon's farm that had been converted into the concert's campground, a drug den, and an experimental fuckfest. The first thing he saw was a man mounted on a horse heading toward the campground with a woman riding behind him on the saddle. The woman was naked.

At the edge of the compound, protesters were demonstrating against the price of tickets for the concert: fifteen dollars. The demonstration was barely underway when one of the protesters fell into the ditch and lay there, completely paralyzed. A bad trip. Some longhairs picked him up and carried him to the gate in the swollen fence. There was a medical unit inside. A guard prevented them from going through.

"Fifteen dollars and you can go in."

The words were punctuated by a flash of lightning followed by heavy, cannonlike rumbling, and the black clouds that had been gathering in the sky above Manseau all morning opened like a faucet, dropping a deluge of rain on the scene. The bucolic site surrounding the stage, over which amplifiers rose like sombre megaliths, was instantly changed into a quagmire of apocalyptic proportions.

Employees whose job had been to fence off the whole sector had taken off the previous night because they hadn't seen the colour of anyone's money, and Gode had no trouble getting into the grounds. He watched four young men wade into the mud, as naked as Adam, to erect a bridge of sorts across the muddy stream.

"Grass, hash, meth, dex," murmured a young woman quietly, brushing against him as she passed.

It continued pouring with rain, and several thousand bodies uniformly covered in mud filled the space. You could ogle as many bare breasts as you wanted, most of them ugly, heavy, pendulant. But even the young, firm breasts, seen in this context, went beyond liberation; they became collectivized, and there was something depressing about it. Shortly after seven o'clock, a brief let-up in the cataract was taken advantage of and the first group took the stage. It was a totally unknown band called the Enterprise, and they looked like they were standing on a sacrificial altar in some blood-crazed religion rising above a sea of mud. The first notes elicited general incredulity, then an immense guffaw engulfed (or rather, drowned out) even the boos. No one had ever heard anything so awful. Gode went off to look for a hole in the fence. He couldn't take any more.

"I love you," a kid said to him, sitting cross-legged on the ground, his eyes raised toward the sky.

Down below, on the stage, the Enterprise had been replaced by the boys from the group Révolution Français, and soon their slightly nasal voices could be heard singing their hit song: "*Québécois / We are québécois ...*"

Back near the stream, Gode watched the same four naked guys still going back and forth with branches and lengths of wood and rotten planks, any debris they could lay their hands on, to shore up their retaining wall, which was now at the head of a sizable lake of dirty water. Gode's lips moved along with the music despite himself ..."*Quebec'll know what to do / If they don't let us through ...*"

Rumour had it that the musicians invited to the festival hadn't yet been paid or even organized, and that some of them were still holed up in their hotel rooms in Montreal, waiting to be given some direction, or even a means of transportation, and also that most of the big names that hadn't actually turned down the invitations had never been contacted.

Sometime between Friday night and Saturday morning, giving up on ever being paid, the security personnel deserted their posts and left the festival site.

When I opened my eyes again, it was daylight, and I was tangled up in my blanket on the edge of the ditch. I seemed to be lying on what little bit of grass there was, and it was as soaked as I was, even through my blanket. A little way off from me I saw one of those small country houses: cedar shake walls, gabled roof. As soon as I saw it, I knew that was where I had wanted to be all my life. What was I doing here, sleeping like a dog on the edge of a churned-up field when I would have given anything to be in the kitchen of that country house with a country woman serving me a plate of country eggs and bacon and beans and a cup of strong coffee.

I took a few steps toward it, my shoulders wrapped in the blanket, and came across a strange procession. There must have been thirty hippies, but mixed in with them were one fat motorcycle cop in helmet and boots, the whole works; a festival organizer with his shiny badge pinned to his chest; and a television crew shooting everything as they went. The four youths walking in front were carrying a body as stiff as a cadaver at minus 40 Celsius, mouth open, eyes rolled back, gripped in convulsions of terror or ecstasy or both, who knew? His hands were in a weird position, fingers spread out and bent, as though he were trying to repel something and grab it at the same time. I knew that scene. The hair on his nude body formed the shape of a cross in the middle of his chest. He had long sideburns, black hair, and a thick, dense beard streaking down from his face. He looked like a religious figure. But it wasn't to the earth that they were consecrating the poor devil. More likely they were taking him to the crazy farm. Where had I seen that guy before?

And then I remembered. The photo of Che Guevara that had been published after his execution in Bolivia. The dead Che. This kid's features had the same expression, a bit ape-like, a bit thunderstruck by grace.

I continued on my way. Farther down, I came upon a guy holding a sign that said: ACID, $1.50.

In the area where the muddy stream had been there was now a muddy swamp. And what was going on in the field around it looked like a wrestling match in Jell-O organized by the Ideal SuperBeach at the campground in Saint-Profond. I felt like I was watching a bunch of pink suckling pigs wallowing in a huge swill of peace and love. Despite the organizers' pleas, the provincial police, which had three hundred officers stationed in the next village, had apparently refused to ensure safety on the site after the defection of the security guards. Drugs openly for sale, public nudity. Maybe somebody upstairs thought that letting all these youths spend their energy on foolishness wasn't such a bad idea; keep an eye on them, sure, but let them work off steam. At least when they're high as kites and fucking like minks, they're not making bombs! And it was pretty much working. In three days, the police had had to investigate only one attempted murder (with a knife), and the rape of a fifteen-year-old girl by a gang of boys of about the same age.

It was also said that the Minister of Health had come to check out the grounds in a helicopter to make a personal assessment of "the drug phenomenon in today's youth culture." And no doubt to take a good look at some naked young flesh without having to risk being seen in a strip bar. Because skin was a big deal. You'd think no one in Quebec had ever seen a tit before, or a pair of thighs, or pubic hair.

Around noon on Saturday, the sun came out. The music improved. I sipped a can of beer and looked around, smiling at everyone and no one. *"Ouiii,"* the band was singing, *"Québec sait faire ..."* At the fence, the complainers had ended up winning their case. The controls were lifted, entry was free, and everyone in the world had crashed the party. Word had got around. Tourists began showing up. The Saturday family outing was there: mom, dad, the kids, and especially the uncles and aunts. In short, everyone came to gawk at the naked hippies ... Some of them even brought ice cream and folding lawn chairs. In a photograph that appeared in *La Presse*, one group was seen setting up beside a kid who was shooting Methedrine into his arm. Around two in the afternoon, when I saw a naked and completely out of it girl take shelter in the swamp, chased by a hundred people who didn't want to miss out on any of the fun, as though she wasn't a poor simple kid caught up in a complex system but more like a gorilla in the Granby Zoo, I decided I'd seen enough.

I left. With my lonesome-cowboy blanket over my shoulder, my thumb out beside Highway 20, "*Québécois, Québécois . . .*" still ringing in my ears, but this time it was giving me a headache.

The driver who picked me up wanted me to tell him all about it, but I didn't want to talk. He'd heard on the radio that the mob had been behind the whole festival thing from the start. I shrugged.

"Nothing is ever going to change in Quebec . . ."

"Why do you say that?"

"Bah. No reason."

I asked him to let me off at the exit to the 95, the end of boulevard de Montarville. Then I called a taxi from a restaurant not far from there.

I sat in the cab for a while, not saying anything. The driver waited, watching me in his rear-view mirror.

"Where to, buddy?"

"Rue Collins."

BABY

EARLY IN 1971, WITH NO fanfare, with a simple order-in-council from the municipality of Saint-Hubert, rue Collins was renamed rue Braffort. The pretext, it seemed, had something to do with the influx of curiosity-seekers who spent their Sunday afternoon drives taking a look at the house in which the vice-premier of Quebec had been assassinated. Apparently Braffort was the name of a farmer in the area. By an absolutely stupefying coincidence, however, a few weeks after the toponymic adjustment, it was also the name of a member of the FLQ who was shot three times in the head with a .22 calibre pistol in a suburb of Paris.

Sam got off the 10 and, leaving the river behind him, turned onto the frightful urban horror called boulevard Taschereau. Then he took the 112 east to La Savane Road, passing the exits to the airport, hangars, and fields, passing rue Nelson, finally turning onto rue Braffort.

The Lavoie Affair, he was thinking, was rooted, like the JFK Affair, in one of those subconscious layers of conspiracy thinking

347

that refused to recognize coincidence, and in which the inevitable, mysterious plot thickened and thickened until the final narrative sucked in facts, links, relationships of cause and effect, partial and total accident, and kneaded the dough into a single, dark but brilliant ball, the yeast for which was provided by an intellectual virtuosity cultivated to the point of paranoid omniscience.

On one level, the name change had had its desired effect: the former rue Collins had definitely ceased to be a tourist attraction. Two parallel and isolated streets surrounded by vacant fields, Nelson and Braffort were the stump ends of a suburban hodgepodge of summer cottages converted into bungalows and low-end split-levels rubbing shoulders with down-at-heel mobile homes. At the field bordering the airport, Braffort ended in a pile of gravel and a pair of concrete blocks, beyond which it was reduced to two muddy ruts heading northwest, which eventually disappeared into a wood-lot of aspens surrounded by ploughed fields.

But if the purpose of the name change was to discourage the curious from coming and sticking their noses into things, as Sam Nihilo and his friend, Fred Falardeau, were doing now, then the city councillors had apparently missed their target.

Samuel was a bit early, but he hadn't been there five minutes before he saw Fred's sedan approaching along la Savane. The next minute, his old drinking buddy from university had joined him on the exact spot where the Chevrolet containing the body of Paul Lavoie had been found nearly thirty years before. They hadn't seen each other in years. They shook hands on the grounds of the former Wander Aviation, in the shadow of Hangar Number 12.

Within minutes, Fred, a thigh hiked on the front fender of his car, began gesticulating, his tone becoming imperial without his being aware of it, his index finger pointing to the scene that they had dredged up from the depths of their memories. A pale October sun shone down on their heads.

"Two things, Sam. In the famous interview in *Temps-Presse*, Richard Godefroid supposedly placed the body in the trunk and got rid of the car at the end of rue Collins. As you can see, that clearly didn't happen: when they got to the end of rue Collins, they turned right and drove a good two hundred metres toward the military base. Why didn't they go in the other direction? At the other end of rue Collins, they would have been in fields and woods and completely out of sight, the perfect spot to abandon an old car with an incriminating package in the trunk. Coming this way, taking the risk of being met by a military patrol, doesn't make any sense."

Fred punctuated his words by slapping the hood of his car with the flat of his hand.

"Second. Godefroid explained their little 'promenade' of two hundred metres with an absurd lie: he said they put the car in drive and let it roll by itself onto base property. The problem with that is that it doesn't explain how it was eventually found inside a fenced-in parking lot. Or why the car keys were gone when the first journalist arrived on the scene... Are you following me?"

"Fred, not only am I following you, but your powers of synthesis are impressing me as much as they ever did!"

Fred patted his stomach.

"I'm a bit hungry. You know what we should do?"

"No, what?"

"Go get us some chicken."

And where else would they go but to Baby Barbecue on boulevard Taschereau, in Longueuil? And order half-thawed fries with some kind of thin brown gravy on them, and the inevitable coleslaw soaked in dressing, all of it washed down with a good Pepsi.

What had Fred been up to? He was writing, of course. How could someone like him not be a writer? But with one mouth to feed already and another Falardeau offspring on the way, he needed to find something to get the pot boiling. A few months earlier, he'd begun looking into the Braffort business for *L'Enquêteux*, the premier TV show on Télé-Québec. The unresolved murder in Paris of Francis Braffort, a few months after the October Crisis, was generally attributed to a settling of accounts within the FLQ. Braffort had been the brains behind the terrorist movement, and often its main mouthpiece. And so, in an unexpected way, Fred's path had once again crossed that of the two Algerians, Zadig and Madwar.

"Do you remember that article in the *Montreal Sun*?"

"I do. It was the Rosetta stone of the Octobeerists."

"Chevalier gave each of us an assignment: he asked you to follow the Chevrier trail while I dug into the business of the two fedayeen."

"Yeah. And we couldn't have known it at the time, but that was the last meeting of the Octos!"

"Did you ever get anywhere with the famous Pierre Chevrier? Tell me something about him ..."

Samuel scrunched his brows and looked at his friend. Physically, Fred was still the almost identical twin of James Joyce, which meant that getting total, undefended openness or even an unguarded smile from him was as remote as integrity and lack of appetite would be in a suburban mayor. Sam hadn't thought their old unacknowledged rivalry would come back so quickly. Fred, good old Fred, was hiding a tiny sliver of a smile behind his chicken thigh that was too innocent for his liking.

Sam returned his smile.

"You go first. Tell me about Zadig and Madwar ..."

Wincing, Fred acknowledged Sam's cautious ruse.

"Ah, the same old Sam. Look at us. You'd think we were a couple of spies in a thriller movie. It's the same old game, isn't it: use the little you know like bait to tease out a bigger piece of the puzzle. Okay, let's go. I'll give you Madwar and Zadig, you give me Pierre. You're getting two for the price of one, though, you dog."

"Agreed that we're a long way from Joyce. We're a long way from Hubert Aquin."

"No, we aren't. We're engaged in an exercise of invention and fabrication, intrigue and history. Even exceptionally creative people launch their little fictions into the world. The difference is that when it works, nobody calls what we do a bestseller. They call it history."

"What are you talking about?"

"About disinformation as a fine art. At a certain level, what you find are not two sides shooting at each other, but a war between two texts. I'm talking about the dispatch that leaves a foreign information service's office, arrives by telex at a press agency, and appears in your morning newspaper the next day, and gradually works its way up to becoming the official version. In the Braffort Affair, the settling of accounts within the FLQ was the cover story. I know as many people who believe that he was eliminated by the secret service as are convinced that an FLQ commando raid was responsible. It's the tied match that sits well with the information community. So much so that the trail is entirely covered up..."

"So, what happened to Francis Braffort?"

LA COURNEUVE, PARIS SUBURB, MARCH 1971

The woman was tall and blonde. Her mouth was dry and her heart was pounding. She stared at the man in front of her, who had just paused in what he was saying to lower his head toward his plate and raise a small forkful of couscous to his mouth. If he noticed the cool, dark figure in the left corner of his field of vision, it was too late for him to do anything about it. Nor did he have time to analyze the brusque movement executed by the figure as it took its right hand from its jacket pocket and raised its arm. He didn't turn his head in the man's direction. The first low-calibre bullet ricocheted off his frontal bone and embedded itself in the ceiling, from which a few bits of plaster fell onto his couscous like fine snowflakes. Blood suddenly covered the eater's face and, as his forehead became adorned with a bright-red split, he leaned forward and vomited onto his plate. The man at the next table moved the .22-calibre pistol, which was equipped with a silencer, closer to the victim's left ear and squeezed the trigger. The man fell heavily to his right, tipping over the chair as he went. Convulsions shook his body and his hands tried to grasp the ungraspable. The other man quickly jumped to his feet and, leaning over the victim, fired a third round point-blank into his forehead.

The woman had stood up, remaining on her side of the table. The killer looked up and saw her.

"They're coming ... Hurry!"

He was already running.

While listening to Fred, Sam remembered being at Chevalier's funeral in la Pérade. If Branlequeue's son hadn't asked him to take charge of the archival chaos in the old professor's office at the university, the story of the chicken deliveries would never have come to the surface and he would not then be sitting here in Baby Barbecue listening to Falardeau, a writer who, like him, had wandered into the secret catacombs of history. For Fred, the road that had brought him back to Chevalier's original assignment had been a television program.

"Hey, Fred! Yoo-hoo! You and me, we've got a master's in literature. We ought to be describing masterpieces translated from twenty-eight languages and the juicy love stories on which readers pounce, most of whom, or so we're told, are women..."

"I know that."

"Good. So who killed Francis Braffort?"

"Madwar, alias Daniel Prince. The RCMP used him to infiltrate the FLQ in 1968, along with his friend Brossard, the future Zadig. Their mission was to create a cell that would act as a Trojan Horse for the secret police. Nothing could have been easier. Anyone could join the FLQ, get involved ... All you had to do was get hold of a few sticks of dynamite. And when thanks to them the group they'd successfully penetrated was blown apart by the police a year later, the Security Service had other projects for our two boys. They got them into Cuba, via New York, and eventually to Algeria. With return trips back and forth to London, Paris, Zurich...eventually they ended up in Jordan. At one point, Zadig even went behind the Iron Curtain, to Hungary..."

"You learned all this from declassified documents?"

"Of course not. But the need to talk is a powerful engine. I developed a few good contacts in the Mounted Police. The old guard, the guys who retired. The ones who missed the good old days like nobody's business. I discovered that those guys, when you give them a chance, are not completely immune to the desire to blow their own horns. Because they won their dirty little war, after all. But we couldn't go on air with off-the-record interviews. My sources refused to be filmed even with their faces distorted and their voices altered. After a certain point, the project was dropped. Except I didn't drop it. I was like a hunting dog on a fresh scent. I continued on my own..."

"Is there a connection between the Braffort business and Lavoie? Was Francis Braffort...?"

"The real assassin of Lavoie? My informants in the Mounties never encouraged me to go in that direction. Of course, they weren't obliged to tell me everything. And I wasn't obliged to swallow everything that came out of their cake holes, either. In my view, Braffort knew a little too much about the counter-FLQ measures and those two maggots in Algeria..."

"Algeria again. Does that surprise me?"

"I certainly hope not."

"Counter-FLQ. That was the Foreign Delegation?"

"Yeah. Nothing less than the brainchild of Western secret services to infiltrate terrorist organizations in the Middle East."

"I think I'm going to need a beer," Samuel said, looking around.

"A cold beer? After eating?"

"What else should a couple of ex-Octobeerists do when they meet?"

"It's against my principles, but you're right. Let's have a cold one."

"In remembrance of all those hectolitres of amber, blond, and red..."

"Those were good times," said Fred after the first mouthful.

"We drank like fish."

"We did."

"Was that all it was, do you think? An excuse to drink, nothing else?"

"You want to know if we were dedicated Octobeerists? We were a circle of friends, drunk most of the time..."

"A conspiracy think-tank, all the same. I didn't see you at Chevalier's funeral..."

"My girlfriend was about to have a baby and ... You know how it was with the Octobeerists and women..."

"But did it never occur to you that Chevalier was way out in left field, right from the start?"

"And that I was wasting my time going out to Saint-Hubert, measuring the distance between the bungalow's garage and the parking lot and Hangar Number 12? That's what my girlfriend thinks."

"Look, Pierre Chevrier, le Chevreuil, he's the key. In the *Sun* article, the anonymous informants talked about a liaison between the fedayeen and the FLQ, remember that?"

"Yes. And I see two possible explanations for that. Either their connection to the October kidnappings is an invention concocted to enhance the legend of Zadig and Madwar and facilitate their infiltration into the Palestine resistance movement, or the link existed and le Chevreuil was in touch with those guys."

"I'm still thirsty... What do you mean by the legend of Zadig and Madwar?"

"I meant it in the sense that the secret service uses it. Legend, from *legere*, to read: a secret agent's cover story is 90 percent words. Sartre said that existentialism is humanism. Myself, I would add that Octobeerism is a hermeneutic. And now, tell me about Pierre."

"I made a list of all the contradictions in the police statements on this subject. The cops appear to have been walking on eggshells with their big boots on whenever the subject of Pierre came up. Like in René Lafleur's kidnapping trial, for instance..."

MONTREAL COURT HOUSE, SEPTEMBER 1972

Officer Rossignol was standing in the witness box. A court clerk handed him a black-and-white negative, which he took between his thumb and index finger, looked at briefly, and said he recognized the grey Chrysler photographed from the roof of a neighbouring house as it exited the garage.

"Do you recognize the man at the wheel?" asked the prosecutor.

"Yeah. It's Maurice Corbo."

"And beside him?"

Rossignol hesitated.

"If you mean Langlais, I don't know him."

An angel passed through the courtroom. The Crown prosecutor and the judge exchanged glances, barely fluttering their eyelids.

"Oh, well, if you don't recognize him . . ." said the prosecutor, scolding him in a friendly way.

The police officer cut him off:

"If that's Langlais, it's news to me. I do not recognize the individual in this photograph."

"Well, at least that's clear." The prosecutor smiled and shrugged.

"Next question," said the judge.

"The police brain is a powerful and little understood organ," remarked Fred.

"I agree. What are you doing?"

Fred's briefcase was in fact a computer case, from which he was extricating his laptop. He shoved aside plates piled with chicken bones, cartilage, bits of yellowed, gelatinous skin floating in coagulating fat and Baby Barbecue sauce, licked his fingers, and opened his machine.

"Let's see what I've got on Pierre Chevrier. It isn't much, as far as I can remember."

Fred tapped a few keys and waited. His search engine sniffed its way through a forest of notes and came up with a single paragraph, like a spaniel sent to fetch a partridge. Fred read the passage, then looked up at Sam.

"He went to North Africa."

For a second, they didn't speak.

"Algeria?" Sam asked.

"Yeah, but that doesn't prove anything."

"No. It could just be a coincidence. One of many. But if I find he was on the RCMP payroll, my friend, that would put the cat among the pigeons, don't you think? What else do you have on le Chevreuil?"

"Luc Goupil met with a Pierre in London," Fred said after awhile.

"Goupil? Wait..."

Fred shut down his laptop. He spoke quickly.

"While researching Braffort, in France, I came across the story of Luc Goupil, the guy who hanged himself in..."

"I know who he was. But what did he have to do with...?"

Fred closed the cover of his computer and finished his beer.

"It would take too long to explain all that now..."

"I'm in no hurry, Fred. You got time for another beer?"

"No thanks, I'm driving. Anyway, the days of getting gloriously pissed in the middle of the afternoon are long gone. That's what 'good old days' means — they were good, but they're gone. When you look ahead, what do you see?"

"At first glance I see myself as the father of a family. Looking closer, I see someone trying to kill time until time kills him."

"I don't have much more on Goupil, Sam. He's just another rabbit I started..."

In the parking lot they tried to arrange a time when they could get together again. It was if they knew that after this meeting they'd once again be swallowed up, Fred by his family and Sam by the great northern forest.

Around them spread a slice of America that provided a good idea of what the human soul looked like once it was paved and cemented from end to end, then lit up with billboards showing images of the female body. They could have been in Blainville or Dallas or Fort Lauderdale, in the airless, winking periphery of any communally administered hell on the continent. What really frightened Nihilo about boulevard Taschereau was the atmosphere of aggressive normality that this architectural and commercial nightmare tended to confer on the devastating sadness of absolute and utter ugliness.

"Fred," he said, "I need you to tell me something. What you have on Zadig and Madwar, you're sure about it?"

"Solid as concrete, Sam. On that point my humans are categorical."

"Your what?"

"My humans. Human sources."

Is that how it begins, Sam wondered. You start to talk like them, and then what? You become like them?

"Until our next cold one, then, Fred."

"You can twist my arm, old buddy. I'll try to untangle myself from the conjugal web . . . And Sam? From now on I'm concentrating on Travers and you're looking into Lavoie. What do you say to that?"

"Done."

They shook hands. Bye-bye, Baby.

On the Champlain Bridge, Sam found himself casting frequent glances at his rear-view mirror. But there was no one on his tail.

On the Champlain Bridge, at a certain point I shot over the crest. Suddenly there was Big Guy Dumont, front man for Éditions _____, watching me from the height of an immense billboard that he'd been paid to appear on, totally naked, stretched out on a queen-sized bed under a velour sheet looking like a sultan and smiling like a cat who'd just swallowed a canary. I felt a pang of sympathy for the poor commuters who had to sit looking at this horrific vision five mornings a week.

"Here's your BLT, honey . . ."

"Thank you, uh, thanks a lot!"

After my meal, I got up and dropped a quarter into the slot of a pay phone on the wall of the Fameux. I'd been trying in vain for two days to call Marie-Québec. It was as though the ghost of Kaganoma had been hanging up on me. After four rings, surprise! A new message.

...I feel compelled to sit at my table, I just want to write and write more. And it's always, always like this, I don't allow myself to get up, I feel like I'm devouring my own life, that for the honey I give to God knows who, you out there in the void, I have to steal it from my most beautiful flowers, I have to tear them up and stomp on their roots. Please leave a message.

I hung up. Trigorin.

When I got back to my table by the bay window, I scribbled a few notes in my book. Since lunch at Baby Barbecue, my brain had been seething. This time I contented myself with one or two reflections on the role played by distance in the jealousy that was consuming me. I suspected it occupied the same place in my love life that time occupied in my research. It separated me from the object of my desire. The goal was the same: a quest for the unattainable, which, coming up against the impossibility of knowing, transformed itself into an unappeasable suffering. The woman I loved was perhaps at that very moment fucking a hockey player in full uniform, or a rock band, six hundred and fifty kilometres from here, as the crow flies, while I, on the corner of Saint-Denis and Mont-Royal, was sitting in a bay window, busily unreeling a string of words on a page, like a trained dog, with a view to writing an essay that I knew I would never write.

And so I did as it says to do in the song. I jumped into my car.

North of La Vérendrye Park I saw a great grey owl perched in a dead tree beside the road. I braked and got out of the car. Peat bogs, hundred-year-old spruces two metres tall, the gentle golden tamaracks. Not another vehicle in sight, the silence seeming to extend for thousands of kilometres. Through flurries of snow that were turning the sky a dull grey, I watched the spectral apparition in my binoculars. What must a day seem like to this bird? Time must seem to wind itself up within the large facial discs through which its yellow eyes registered the dance of snowflakes, this stretch of highway, the observing man and his observant eyes, the heaviness under his wings, the roar of the wind, balancing each image and each sound against their equivalent in silence. Before history, its shouting and its bombs, the raptor's indifference was whole and impenetrable.

Two hundred kilometres farther north, just before Maldoror became visible on the horizon, its smoke plume erased by the blizzard, I turned onto the road to Kaganoma. Snow already covered the ground. Before I even got out of the car I knew the house was empty. Gusting snow was slowly burying it. A single light had been left on, in my study on the second floor, as if the ghost were expecting me. I wasn't sure I was glad to be back. I remained standing in the snow without moving. Wet flakes landed on my eyelashes like kisses. And then I saw them.

The huge, round footprints of a lynx, clearly discernable in the fresh snow. I smiled. They were headed toward the house.

SAINT-HUBERT MILITARY BASE, SUMMER 1966

"CANADA'S CONTRIBUTION TO THE KIND of military operation necessitated by zones of high-intensity conflict," droned the general, tapping out the rhythm of his words on the headquarters' map with his baton, "must be limited to the deployment of the 4th Brigade of Engineers, at the moment stationed in Germany, with sufficient tactical air support. The rest of our Armed Forces are going to need to rapidly reorganize and be given the flexibility necessary to intervene in a vast repertoire of possible conflicts. Which means that our Armed Forces must, among other things, concentrate on the problems of revolutionary agitation, terrorism, and urban guerilla warfare. It must prepare itself to withstand a prolonged anti-insurrectionist war ..."

During the Question Period that followed, a member of Parliament from Quebec who had listened attentively to General Bédard's talk, asked with a perplexed, not to say slightly disconcerted, air: "General, if I understand you rightly, you're proposing that we increase the effectiveness of our military component in areas of low conflict..."

"Exactly," said the general.

"Except that your model, it seems to me, suggests just the opposite: that the importance of the military component must diminish, and that of the civil engineering section be increased, until the intensity of the conflict decreases... isn't that right?"

"Yes. And that's why I'm the first to recognize that the Armed Forces cannot operate to their highest potential in situations of low-intensity conflict. Hear me: the groups best placed to pacifically solve most of these types of conflicts are civil organizations — governments, police, and so on — that may or may not require military assistance. I insist on this point: in the lower half of the spectrum of applied force, the role of our troops is to support organisms implicated in the search for a solution. This seems to me to be absolutely essential. And that's why we need to develop a structure dedicated to being able to coordinate police, civil, and military actions on a large scale. The basis of this structure already exists in Canada: you no doubt understand that I'm talking about our three levels of government. In other words, the law can be modified in such a way that the military can act as agents of peace having as their mission to assist legally constituted authorities. I'm glad you raised this question."

The Honourable J.D. Sheppard, P.C. member for Fort Qu'Appelle, Saskatchewan, had removed his earphone, which had practically disappeared into his ear, and was scraping the inside of his ear cavity with his little finger. He interrupted this operation to raise his hand.

"You mentioned levels of government ... Last week, I read in the paper that the police had nabbed two separatists who were getting ready to steal a cache of arms from a military post in Montreal. Now, am I completely out in left field here, or if, when you speak of social agitation, and recycling the Canadian army into an anti-guerilla organization, you're ..."

The general thrust his square jaw forward.

"Putting Quebec in our sights? That's what you were about to say, is it not?"

"Well, er ..."

The general smiled. Everyone smiled except for Sheppard. What a bumpkin.

"It's three hours later in Regina," sighed the Honourable Jay Vaugirard, District of Joliette, chin in hand. "Appetizer time," he said to himself.

"Mr. Minister," said General Bédard, still smiling, "I'm going to have our documents office send you the last few issues of *The Masses*, a small, clandestine journal that I don't think is distributed in Saskatchewan. In it, I'm sure you'll be surprised to learn that at this very moment, as we speak, there is in Montreal a paramilitary organization whose goal is to replace our democratic government with a socialist state much like the ones they have in Cuba and Moscow."

The general looked at his watch. Almost time for dinner. He cleared his throat.

"To sum up, gentlemen, on the matter of our internal field of operations, we must be sure to apply all available forces to achieve maximum effect. Remember that the enemy operates on the lower part of our level of intensity in conflicts, where its efforts don't habitually meet any but feeble opposition and can take advantage of a disproportionate amount of publicity. And therefore, while the atomic weapons of our allies continue to prevent the outbreak of a total world war between the West and the Soviet powers, we are going to prevent, by the imposition of forces far superior in numbers, equipment and logistics, strikes, demonstrations, disruptions of order, riots, homemade bombs, Molotov cocktails, that can easily degenerate into more serious conflicts. Allow me, in summing up, to leave you with what I call my Mugger Theory. The best way to protect yourself from a mugger isn't to take out your knife and confront him with it on equal terms. It's to corner him at the end of an alley, point a dozen machine guns at him and tell him to drop his knife. And that, gentlemen, is exactly what we intend to do with these young thugs. When the time comes, we'll know how to provoke the right occasion. We'll bring them along to precisely where we want them, and then, after we've surrounded them with our squadrons, we'll provoke them to bring out their knives. And then, and only then, will we engage them..."

The Minister of Defence was one of those who went up to General Bédard during the discussions that followed, armed with transcripts of the Commander of Mobile Forces' talk, and walked with him toward the mess hall.

"A simply remarkable presentation, my dear sir..."

"Bah. Let's just say I'm doing my best to attract the attention of our political men to certain realities."

"Remarkable, simply remarkable," echoed the Honourable Peter Dryden.

"Not for me to say," replied the Commander of Mobile Forces, with a shrug of his shoulders.

Three weeks later, General Jean-B. Bédard received his fourth star. At the same time, he was promoted to Chief of Staff Major General, the first French-Canadian to have risen to the highest rank in the Canadian military. From then on, he had the Armed Forces in the palm of his hand.

RUE COLLINS

THE DISCUSSION TOOK PLACE in the living room, where there was enough Export "A" smoke to muffle the arguments coming from both sides of the room.

The Lafleur brothers were there, and Lancelot, Gode, Élise, Justin, Ben, Le Corbeau, Pierre. And Sylvie, Lancelot's wife, her long legs descending from a miniskirt that covered about as much as a beer-bottle cap. Their two-year-old toddler ran around between everyone's legs with a plastic toy machine gun. Someone had made some spaghetti sauce. There was beer in the fridge, but not enough to cause a flood. Le Corbeau was the only one to make the trip to the kitchen with any regularity.

Since they'd been obliged to abandon the farm in Milan, with its future Prison of the People, they'd holed up in the bungalow on rue Collins, which had become, at the end of the summer of 1970, a sort of headquarters. Tonight, they were discussing the two targets of their operation: Hite, the American, and Travers, the Brit. Taking them both wasn't impossible, but it would seriously complicate the operation. No one considered this plan for action to be premature more than Jean-Paul. His proposal was to continue with the reorganization of the group and to concentrate on long-term preparations: hideouts, vehicles, backup, money, weapons. Élise, whose younger brother had been one of those arrested in Saint-Colomban, tossed the first salvo.

"It's easy to see that you've never had a brother in prison ..."

"But it's going to take more than a hostage to made the government give in. And as of now, we have no place to hide them ... Even this place is getting too hot."

"Yeah, like sometimes you can even smell the heat," laughed le Corbeau. He was in a good position to know, having had to shake off a tail on his way to rue Collins several times.

"We're not dumb enough to bring a hostage to a house already known to the police," Lancelot put in. "We'll have to rent an apartment."

"An apartment? You mean a place with neighbours? What if the hostage cries out, what do you do then?"

"I'd shut him up. It's not complicated."

"We'd need to be in better shape to do something like that. It's going to take more money, better hiding places, more vehicles. The police know about the ones we have. We'll need machine guns. I have a contact in the States that can supply us with guns ..."

Lancelot was pacing nervously back and forth in the room. He stopped in front of Jean-Paul, who'd been watching him from the divan, sitting up on his haunches. Lancelot gave him a malevolent smile.

"Nelson ..." he said.

"Nelson? What Nelson?"

"Robert Nelson, in 1838. He came across the border from Vermont and claimed Lower Canada for the Republic. The Americans had promised him weapons to arm the locals, *les Frères Chasseurs*. The cases of rifles never arrived, and he went back across the border with his tail between his legs. You remind me of him ..."

Lancelot was now talking to everyone in the room, and Jean-Paul, though annoyed, calmly watched him take over the meeting.

"The Tupameros have just succeeded in taking four hostages, and their manifesto has been read in the National Assembly!"

"But they had to kill one of their hostages. And they didn't succeed in getting any political prisoners out of jail."

Lancelot looked Jean-Paul up and down.

"They killed a CIA agent. Four bullets to the chest, that's all he was worth. But look at Brazil. There the authorities negotiated: forty political prisoners for one ambassador. And twelve in Bolivia . . . Why wouldn't it work here?"

The discussion went on all night. With Élise, who tried to slip a word in edgewise into the cockfight, and Justin, who was forced to play the role of mediator with about the same success as a Blue Helmet in the Congo, and René, who always took the side of his brother, and le Corbeau, who kept getting drunker and drunker and only opened his mouth to burp, and Ben, who got hungry and was eating cold spaghetti in the kitchen, and Chevrier, who never said a word and who, behind his thick glasses, looked more than ever like a deer caught in the headlights.

Every once in a while Gode would stand up and take a look out the window. The area was very quiet. The fields. The small houses. Not even a cat could be seen moving about.

Then Lancelot took out the Manifesto. He waved it in the air, like Thomas Jefferson with the Constitution, or as if it was the word of God.

"We worked on this together. We corrected this together. And now the whole world will hear us speak. Who's ready to start Operation Deliverance with me?"

"We'll put it to a vote," Jean-Paul said, unperturbed, as though he hadn't noticed that Lancelot had just pulled the rug out from under his feet.

Lancelot swept the room with his eyes.

"Who's for?"

Élise, his sister, raised her hand resolutely. Her brother-in-law followed suit. Then le Corbeau, after hesitating, making it look like he had no choice. Sylvie and her two-year-old abstained, for humanitarian reasons.

"One, two, three, four . . ." Jean-Paul counted with satisfaction. "Okay, who's against?"

As expected, the former gang from the Fisherman's Hut voted in a bloc: René, Gode, Ben. Finally, Jean-Paul raised his huge paw.

"Two, three, four . . . Someone's missing."

Everyone looked around for Pierre. He'd gone to take a leak.

For Jean-Paul, it was in the bag. He was already breathing easier. Pierre, alias François Langlais, was one of the guys from the South Shore, like the others. A man of few words, which was fine: they only needed one, no more. One single word from him now could prevent this whole thing from slipping downhill. They would then be able to concentrate on long-term preparations, maybe spend two or three years rebuilding the organization, consolidating their secret network, developing connections with regions like the Gaspésie and start up a few others. Create a national structure.

On the other side of the wall they could hear the toilet flushing. Pierre was now standing in the middle of the living room.

"Are you in favour of going ahead with the kidnappings, or are you against? What do you say, *frère chasseur*?"

"I say we should get our asses in gear."

THREE

ZOPILOTE

TWENTY-TWO

THE CESSNA 172 SAT MOTIONLESS at the start of the runway.

Bédard tuned the radio to the required frequency and contacted the control tower.

"Saint-Hubert control, Uniform-Juliette-Oscar waiting on runway six right for clearance to take off."

"Roger, Uniform-Juliette-Oscar, you are cleared for takeoff on runway six right, go up to 1,000 feet and level off."

The general opened the throttle, and the single-prop plane shot ahead 1,500 feet and began its ascent. The horizon expanded beneath him: runways, hangars, roads, fields, woods in full colour, the buildings of the base, the flat, fertile fields extending toward the south and the United States. At 1,000 feet the controller's voice came back on: "Uniform-Juliette-Oscar, do not go higher than 1,600 feet. Make a left turn to leave this sector at Boucherville."

"Uniform-Juliette-Oscar, no higher than 1,600 feet," repeated the general.

The cluster of islands spread out beneath the nose of the plane. He levelled off over Boucherville.

"Uniform-Juliette-Oscar, you have left Saint-Hubert sector. Radar contact terminated."

The former commander-in-chief of the Canadian Armed Forces was a recent retiree at the beginning of October 1970. He could rest on his laurels, he'd had a career that was nothing short of exceptional. His passion for civilian aviation and his "Twenty-Two" (the name painted on the fuselage of his Cessna), based in Saint-Hubert, allowed him to maintain direct contact both with his *alma mater* (the famous Twenty-Second Regiment) and his own baby, the general headquarters of Mobile Forces. Opportunity making the thief, it wasn't unusual for him to drop by the officers' mess for a glass or two after returning from one of his escapades in the Quebec sky. He'd flown as many as three or four times a week that summer and still felt, from the moment he set foot on the base, welcomed as the living legend he in fact was.

He was now crossing the St. Lawrence. Above Charron Island.

"Montreal control," he spoke into his mike, "this is Cessna one-seven-two Golf-Uniform-Juliette-Oscar joining you. Good morning!"

"Golf-Uniform-Juliette-Oscar, please hold . . ."

The controller gave permission to an Air Canada flight to land before getting back to him.

"Uniform-Juliette-Oscar, identify yourself. What are your intentions?"

Bédard flipped on his transponder. On the radar screen in the Montreal control tower, the blip representing "Twenty-Two" showed up clear and precise.

"Uniform-Juliette-Oscar entering Pont-Tunnel sector to circle Ville-Marie at an altitude of 1,500 feet, if available."

"Uniform-Juliette-Oscar, approved for 1,500 feet. How many circuits will you make, sir?"

"Just one. And I'd like to go over to Victoria, destination Lake Champlain..."

"Very well. Contact us when you cross into Victoria," concluded the voice in his headset.

The Botanical Gardens in Rosemont... the huge island seemed to be sleeping under his plane. He liked having this theatrical overview in which the game would be played out. And soon, too, if one could believe the latest reports...

Retired though he was, Bédard, since his departure, had daily conversations with his friend, General Turcotte, who was also a former Twenty-Seconder from the Italian campaign, and his successor as head of Mobile Forces. Turcotte owed much of his irresistible rise in the hierarchy to General Bédard: the present commander of Mobile Forces was, as they say, in his debt. At the beginning of the 1960s, when Bédard ran the Division of Operational Preparedness, Turcotte had even "lent" him his nephew, a private in the Twenty-Second Regiment, whom General Bédard had taken under his wing and initiated into the art of intelligence, and later had him infiltrate into the revolutionaries, putting his personal spy within the FLQ. One of those small guys who push at the edges and heat up meetings and always want to go a little bit farther than the leaders, and manage to get others to follow them... To end up being arrested at the wheel of a van full of dynamite. Since his years of spying (although it wasn't called spying) in Moscow, Bédard had always tried to see trouble coming well in advance, and this time Turcotte was definite: action would begin soon. The thugs were getting ready to take out their knives, Turcotte specified, with a knowing smile. It was already the fourth of October. A week ago, with the approval of his mentor, the head of Mobile Command had placed his troops on alert in Saint-Hubert. CATS was also ready to pounce. All that was left now was to be patient while politics did its job.

Mont-Royal slipped by under his left wing. Outremont. The university. St. Joseph's Oratory.

The scene was set, the net was in place. Thanks to the army reserves, the commanders could count on the loyalty of many civilians who were, in fact, soldiers in disguise. Journalists and police officers, secretly working for the country's armed forces in the heart of the general population. The secretary general of the government, the highest civil servant in the province, was a colonel in the reserve, as was the special counsellor to the premier (although it had to be said that Bob Lapierre was something of an unknown quantity. Who did Uncle Bob work for? A good question...).

Bédard turned to follow the line of boulevard Décarie, putting Westmount on his left, and before long Victoria Bridge came into view. He wanted to make this little tour take him to Plattsburgh. To frolic a bit over the border and take a look, from a distance, in passing, at the base down there. You never knew what you could learn, in Plattsburgh or in Moscow. And though the general did not know what service Uncle Bob was in, one thing was certain, he really loved the Yanks. Even Bédard, whose loyalty to Canada could not be in doubt, felt safer in the knowledge that if things turned really bad north of the border, their neighbour to the south would send troops rolling up the maritime corridor.

"Uniform-Juliette-Oscar crossing Victoria Bridge, request passage toward Lake Champlain."

"Uniform-Juliette-Oscar, passage granted. What altitude, sir?"

"Uniform-Juliette-Oscar, I'd like 3,500 feet."

At 3,500 feet, the headset crackled and he heard:

"Uniform-Juliette-Oscar, this is Montreal control. You are exiting our sector. Radar contact terminated. Would you like a flight plan?"

"No, thank you. That won't be necessary..."

OCTOBER 5, 1970,
8:20 A.M.

THE BLACK TAXI HAD JUST stopped in front of the luxurious home nestled on the side of the mountain among a splash of orange and purple maple crowns and fallen leaves that rustled underfoot like coloured crêpe paper. A blue, blue sky. On the ground floor, Her Majesty's Commissioner of Trade, John Travers, was about to enter history dressed in a singlet, underwear, and socks. He emerged from the bathroom freshly shaven, looking as ridiculous as it was possible for a man to look, but saved from that same ridiculousness by a quarter-century of conjugal intimacy. There he was, trousers in hand, hopping back and forth before the foot of the bed in which his wife is sitting up reading the morning's *Montreal Sun*. The couple's Dalmatian, Fyodor, is curled up in the warm depression where the consular body had lain. What are they talking about? Bridge, of course. But Travers cocks an ear, he's heard a bell: the front door. A long way down, down there. The maid will get it. She's Portuguese.

Travers left the bedroom without his pants on, talking to his wife, and found himself confronted by a young man holding a pair of handcuffs and pointing a .22-calibre Long Rifle pistol at his face, loaded with eight rounds.

"Get down on the floor or you'll be fucking dead!" the young man screamed, words that instantly assumed their place in history.

FOREST PARK, ST. LOUIS, MISSOURI, AFTERNOON OF OCTOBER 5

SITTING CROSS-WISE ON THE BENCH of a picnic table, Gode looked up at the Gateway Arch whose straight, clean lines and full arc soared above the trees in the park that overlooked the banks of the Mississippi.

"What you see there," he said, "is the Gateway to the West. Everything on the other side of that arch was once called Louisiana, and it stretched all the way to the Pacific Ocean. Napoleon — talk about a raw deal — sold them the whole territory for a song. But what they don't tell you in the history books is that a hundred years ago, St. Louis was as French as you and me. It was French Métis who got Lewis and Clark across the Rockies."

Sitting across from him, René Lafleur was trying to coax reception from a small transistor radio. All he could get was gospel, laundry soap, Coca-Cola, fried chicken, and the Bible. A lot more fried chicken. Then the results of a baseball game. The swan song of America.

"How do you know all that?" asked Jean-Paul, peering into the ham sandwich he'd been trying to chew.

"My father had his family tree traced at one point. There were Godefroids who married Chippewa women and went into the fur trade in Wisconsin. I learned about it as a kid. We always called Route 66 the Chippewa Way."

Jean-Paul looked up from his sandwich and watched his mother, the family matriarch, who was walking along the river some distance away with their younger sister. The pair passed an old man who was shredding a cream doughnut and tossing the pieces to some resident mallards. Mother and daughter had accompanied them to Texas. It didn't seem reasonable at first, but when they'd been stopped at a roadblock by the state police in Pennsylvania, the presence of an elderly woman and a young girl in the back seat seemed to have given them a bit of status, and they'd been allowed to pass. If nothing else, family life was a good cover.

Two picnic tables down, a man in a checked jacket was reading a newspaper and smoking a cigarette. Jean-Paul chewed his ham sandwich. He thought about what they had in the cooler. Canned ham. Hard-boiled eggs. Pickles. Mayonnaise. One tomato. Kraft "cheese." Kik Cola. Sliced bread. "Go Weston, young man . . ." A real Québécoise mother, they had, a nourisher through and through.

When their mother and sister rejoined them, René, still hunched over his tinny transistor radio, managed to find a news station. He raised a hand and turned up the volume. Silence surrounded the table.

. . . kidnapped by four gunmen this morning in Montreal. The kidnapping has since been claimed by the Front of Liberation of Québec, a group promoting terrorism and armed struggle in their fight for the creation of an independent French-speaking state in eastern Canada.

"They're still talking about only one kidnapping. The Englishman..."

"They only took Travers."

"That doesn't bode well. . . ." said Jean-Paul, absorbed in his thoughts.

He looked up and saw his mother gathering the plastic utensils and paper plates, putting the lid on the mayonnaise jar, returning the eggs to a jar of vinegar, rewrapping the Kraft slices and the sliced tomato. As if she had already figured out what was what.

"We can't let them go through this on their own," grumbled Jean-Paul. "They'll spill the whole can of beans."

He looked around. Gode and René waited for him to continue.

"Okay, let's go," he said.

When the car with René at the wheel threw up a few grains of gravel as it left the parking lot, the smoker two tables down threw his butt on the grass, folded his newspaper, and walked to a car parked under the trees. He opened the passenger door and got in beside the old man who'd been feeding the ducks, who, sitting behind the wheel, was speaking into a radio transmitter.

SAINT-LAMBERT,
OCTOBER 10, 6:18 P.M.

THE CITY OF TORONTO, in Ontario, is located about five hundred kilometres southwest of Montreal. As far as a Québécois is concerned, the geographical location of the Queen City might as well be somewhere between Kirghizistan and Tajikistan. Paul Lavoie had never set foot in it. The government's deputy premier, a Liberal of the old school, forty-nine years old, was in charge of the state of Quebec when Petit Albert was away selling off our rivers, lands, and forests to Bechtel of San Francisco, or to the money-grabbers on Wall Street. Lavoie was looking forward to going to Toronto in November. He had tickets for the Grey Cup and was taking his nephew.

He had just heard his colleague in Justice addressing John Travers's kidnappers on television, saying the government would not negotiate with criminals. A very loud *no*! Perfect. He'd reserved a table at a restaurant and was waiting for his wife, who was in the bathroom

380

getting ready to go: she was taking longer and longer making herself look less and less young. Paul Lavoie was heading into his unexpected rendezvous with history in this thirty-sixth year, wearing olive green pants with yellow stripes, varnished crocodile-leather shoes, and mismatched socks. But his shirt (sport) and jacket (checkered) didn't look that bad. He wasn't wearing a tie.

He went out onto the porch to get some fresh air and almost immediately was thrown an oval leather ball by his nephew. "Go, Alouettes, go!" the boy shouted. Lavoie had been looking after his nephew since the death of his brother; the boy and his mother lived in the bungalow next door. With a quick movement of his arm, he returned the ball to the youngster and jogged down the stairs and along the path. He made a short curve in his leather crocs to take the pass from his nephew, which spiralled toward him and hit him square in the chest with almost perfect precision. *YES!!!!* He no longer wanted the Justice portfolio, no longer cared if he became premier, he was Peter Dalla, the Alouettes' linebacker and star receiver.

Then, while his fingers felt for the best grip along the seams of the ball and he took a few short steps backward, he became Sam Etcheverry, the former quarterback and current coach, Sam the Rifle, old eagle-eye, looking for an open receiver way up in the end zone. Watch him. Lavoie takes off his jacket like the working-class stiff he never was, he is no longer the politico who prefers to rely on contacts rather than hard work, finagling overtime, handing out surreptitious envelopes and dubious loans that paid good dividends with enough patience to let them mature; look at him — this is not the arm of the former journalist, the Maurrassien in a beret, the man of the pen — no, the man with the football rotates in on himself, turns, puts the ball in the air and on a trajectory that describes a perfect ellipse in the dark blue sky when the sun emerges to spill over Montreal from the other side of Ontario.

"Catch it, Moses!" He means Moses Denson, of course. He means Junior Ah You and the big Sonny Wade, Terry Evanshen and his twenty years of misery, twenty years of Edmonton, of Hamilton, of Winnipeg, twenty years of Russ Jackson — except this year Ottawa will not carry him off to paradise, no, because Lavoie sprints for the long bomb, his nephew pumps for the pass, his arm goes back, his grip is on the last strings of the ball, and Lavoie pivots calmly without losing the count, the missile flies through a sky of perfect, intense blue, he stretches his arms out for it, it's October, he fans out his hands, spreads his fingers, anticipates the slap of leather on skin, but when the ball arrives it comes in like a flopping, leaden-winged duck and slips out of his grasp, lands on the sidewalk, bounces crazily into the street, and rolls away. Straight under the wheels of a Chevrolet that has come swiftly down the street and braked, tires screeching, beside the sidewalk. The doors open like the wing casings of a beetle that has fallen from the sky. And . . .

"I am SSSSSSSSam," Lavoie mutely mouths. "The Rifle."

Then he sees the machine guns, and behind them two men in long raincoats with strange haircuts. He automatically raises his hands. One of the men shouts at him. Something.

Lavoie hesitates, turns his head, and looks toward the house. He sees his wife standing with her handbag in the entrance. Finally ready to go.

TELEPHONE

CAREENING OUT OF A SIDE street, the Chevrolet braked sharply with a loud screeching of tires. When René pressed down on the brake pedal, Gode, sitting in the back seat, was propelled forward, his knee coming into contact with a mass of known but still complex consistency, neither soft nor hard, but which still gave a little, then resisted, emitting a sort of sigh or groan. René could feel it moving under him.

"Shut up!"

"*Let's go!*"

He opened the door, disengaged his knee, and jumped out into the street. Slammed the door as he turned, catching in the corner of his eye the image of a dark spot formed by the raincoat between the seats. Then the door shut heavily. The car had already turned right and was moving south along boulevard Taschereau.

Disoriented for a moment, Gode stood still, getting his bearings. The orange ball of the sun was low on the horizon, and the late afternoon light advanced over the river, the unreal green phosphorescence of the Jacques-Cartier Bridge. Still bothered by the unwelcome intimacy of the contact of his knee with the back of the man stretched out on the floor of the car, he started looking for a taxi.

Marie-France and Nicole watched the news of the abduction of the Minister of Public Works on television. Journalists clustered on the lawns and in the street, before a large, bungalow-style house with a steep roof, in a residential district on the South Shore. There were neighbours, gawkers, camera crews, microphones, cameras, flash bulbs, electric cables, police guarding the entrance, people going in, coming out, escorting family members, political colleagues, close friends, the family doctor with his nerve pills. They saw Paul Lavoie's old mother, wide-eyed and deflated, looking like a shot barn owl, uniformed officers with orders to treat those closest to the victim with respect, inspectors in raincoats coming and going and more of them arriving all the time, Saturday night, madness.

Close-up of the metal plaque screwed to the wall beside the door:

PAUL LAVOIE, BARRISTER

The phone rang. It was Gode. The last they'd heard, he was in the States.

"I'm in the area..."

"You can come over if you want," said Marie-France.

The women were living at 3730 Queen-Mary Road, on the mountain, apartment number 6. Marie-France unlocked the door remotely. His footsteps on the stairs. She was in front of him, watched him pass her without looking up or meeting her eyes and go into the living room. He sat down in front of the television.

"Has anyone claimed responsibility?"

"No. But you must know who it is, right?"

"Me? No ..." he said, nodding his head without taking his eyes off the screen.

Nicole asked him where René was.

"Dunno. If I see him, I'll tell him to give you a call."

Sometime later, Gode left to make a phone call.

"Why not call from here?"

He shrugged.

"I need some fresh air."

Then, after patting his pockets:

"I'm out of cigarettes ... I'll be back in a few minutes."

VEGAS

WHEN THE TELEPHONE RANG, Chevalier Branlequeue was at home, watching *Maître* Brien stoking the crowd at the Paul-Sauvé Arena in the east end of Montreal. The excitement of the masses. Practised rhetoric before three thousand jubilant sympathizers of the independence movement. We will prevail.

It was the fifteenth, five days after the kidnapping. The Chevaliers were living in a small house on a street in Chambly, next to a pet store and across from a butcher's. Éléonore had an important administrative position at the hospital and they were starting to find their feet, financially. The oldest child had his own room, his furniture arranged to accommodate his stamp collection. Branlequeue had organized his Placard in a room that looked like a real office. The colour television had made its appearance in a living room furnished on credit from Bélanger's. The old camp cot was beside the wall in the office, among piles of books and manuscripts associated with Top Flight Editions, and Chevalier Branlequeue was spending his nights on it more and more often, his head filled with words and phrases, his vision blurred, his bronchial passages clogged, his stomach irritated by sleep-inducing whisky.

Within two years, the little family would move to the Domaine des Salicaires, near the river. In four, the eldest, Martial, would pack up his things and move on to make his own life. And a year had passed and the father had been living in this room full time, by virtue of an unwritten pact making his and Éléonore's physical separation official. The new regime gave Chevalier the peaceful and rebarbative impression of seeing his love life dissolve before him, neutralized from now until his death. He'd dispensed with his conjugal duties three years ago, at the age of forty-four, never dared to hit on his students. No dipping of the paintbrush. Vénus, was lanky, twenty, and studious. She hadn't yet found her Sapphic leanings and was taking piano lessons. The youngest, Pacifique left politics to hopeless degenerates over twenty, drank Black Label, and smoked pot and Afghan hash and listened to Led Zep. And La Gros Éléonore, Éléonore, the former marble beauty shaped by some sculptor's hammer, had become a bitter old woman, already cast in rough stone at the tender age of thirty.

But for now, the crisis created by the first abduction, ten days earlier, continued to fester, and *Maître* Brien was making his remarks on the ten o'clock news. "*FLQ! FLQ! FLQ!*" the crowd at the Paul-Sauvé Arena was chanting. And then the telephone rang.

"Chevalier Branlequeue?"

"Speaking."

"This is Bonnard, Raoul."

He'd recognized the voice, a baritone impossible to mistake for any other, with its deep, throaty residue of late nights, scotch whisky, and cigars, and its ineffable, slightly humorous hint of the crooner imprinted at the base end. They had crossed paths from time to time, through their work. Given Chevalier's existence as poet–publisher and his nocturnal life in the bars, the two had several points of intersection. The role of poet laureate he had been obliged to assume after the appearance of *Elucubrations* had ratcheted him into the larger family of artists. But aside from these accidental encounters, during which only a few words had been exchanged, neither of them knew much about the other that wasn't general knowledge.

"What can I do for you, Raoul?"

"Have you been watching the news?"

Chevalier turned so that the TV was in his field of vision. The camera was panning the crowd across the screen, men, women, professors, students, militants, national thinkers, tavern philosophers, versifiers and vilifiers, raised fists, Mackinaw shirts, small, round eyeglasses, long hair. *FLQ. We will prevail.*

"Yes," he said after a moment.

"What do you think of it?"

What Chevalier thought was that *Maître* Brien was playing a dangerous game. Two days earlier, accused of obstructing justice, he'd still been cooling his heels in the Parthenais Prison. The day after the Paul Lavoie kidnapping, after the weak response manifested by the Vézina government, the Rebellion Cell had designated the lawyer, in a communiqué, as their official negotiator with the authorities. The negotiations were now stalled. Little Albert had just issued an ultimatum giving the terrorists six hours to accept safe conduct to the country of their choice, and what was Brien doing? Jumping up to the microphone in an arena full of separatists, taking centre stage with the crowd at his feet crying for blood in a veritable boiling of revolutionary fervour. Chevalier didn't much like what he was seeing.

He opened his mouth to reply, then hesitated.

"I'd be curious to know why my thoughts are of interest to you, Raoul."

"And I'll tell you, Chevalier. I may have only a grade six education, but I haven't done too badly in the school of life. And what I am going to propose to you is that we get together and discuss all this in a quiet spot. A serious conversation, between men. I might even say civilized."

"Just the two of us, Raoul?"

"No."

Both of them allowed a moment to pass in which they each seemed to be listening to the long chain of telephone poles, hearing the silence that cut through their conversation like a beast on the road and that suddenly filled the autumn night between them like a living thing, fugitive, insensate, and obscure.

"I have a friend who would like to meet you, Chevalier…"

"What kind of friend, Raoul?"

"Someone from the nightclubs."

"I'm not sure I'm following you, here, Raoul… What exactly is it you want?"

"What would you say if I dropped by to pick you up in ten minutes?"

"To go where?"

"To Vegas, does that mean anything to you?"

"The Vegas Sports Palace, on boulevard Taschereau?"

"That's the place."

"And you want to take me there to do what after eleven o'clock at night? Play shuffleboard?"

"No. Just have you meet someone. It might give you some ideas for your next book, you never know."

"Tell me one thing, Raoul. Is there a risk of this blowing up in my face?"

"I wouldn't put your safety at risk, Chevalier. You have my word on that."

"Lots of people say that…"

"Yes, but where we're going, my word is sacrosanct."

He'd put on his heavy cardigan and was standing at the front door when Éléonore emerged from the bedroom in her housecoat, her mop of hair piled up on her head, looking ghastly. *Hallowe'en's come early*, thought her husband.

"Would you mind telling me where you're going, for heaven's sake?"

"Urgent business at the Vegas. Nothing serious."

"Where did you say?"

"The Palace, my dear. A little poker to get back what I've lost. The house, you, the kids. Everything will be on the table tonight."

"Good Lord!"

Bonnard picked him up at the door. He was wearing a powder-blue suit, with a Panama hat screwed on his head. His car was a yellow Buick Riviera from a time when its four carburetors alone could justify the installation of one of those solitary donkeys you see nodding their black heads along the highways of Kansas and Oklahoma. They drove north along rue Chambly, turned left at the old shopping plaza onto the former rue Coteau-Rouge, now more respectfully called boulevard Sainte-Foy. Here, where packs of feral dogs and street toughs had at one time pretty much held reign, new laws had created a grid of long streets bordered by comfortable, single-family houses. Gone were the outdoor toilets, the cesspools open to the skies, and the tarpaper shacks! Gone the water-carriers from the better neighbourhoods of yesteryear, who sold water for five cents a bucket. A huge American-style suburb had opened its arms, and the feral dogs had been replaced by police cruisers whose sirens now bayed to the full moon, but less often. Finally, the previous year, Longueuil the bourgeosie had legally achieved social chlorination by voting to annex with its turbulent neighbour, about which no one spoke any longer.

"Are you from around here?" Bonnard asked.

As soon as the yellow Riviera had melted into the night, they'd stopped addressing each other formally, as though the intimacy of the passenger compartment, their nocturnal escapade into the glass and concrete American desert, had brought them more naturally together, made them accomplices.

"No. I landed a post here as a teacher at Saint-Ernest. Rent was a lot cheaper on the South Shore. Then I got mixed up in politics and the good Brothers gave me the holy heave-ho. I'm still out."

Bonnard lit a cigar.

"I grew up here," he said. "My first church was in the henhouse. I remember wearing boots on the bus and carrying our shoes in bags because of the mud. We'd take off our rubber boots and put our shoes on when we got into Montreal. My grade one class was in a pool hall. Which maybe explains a few things. During the war, my father lived in Montreal with my mother and worked in a factory that made airplanes for the Allies. After work, he took the bus from the south end of Montreal and got off in the middle of a field. He and a few others would walk about a mile carrying lumber and other building supplies on his back to work on his house. Around eleven or midnight, he'd walk the mile back the other way, freezing his ass off in winter, snow up to his knees, and get the bus and then the streetcar and get home to bed at two in the morning, if he was lucky, and sleep until five. Then he'd get up and go through the whole thing all over again. You've got to wonder when they found the time to make little Raoul. Whatever you think of me, I am that man's son. And I'm on prime time on Channel 10."

Chevalier coughed.

"Is my cigar bothering you?"

"Yes, but I'll survive."

"What did you think of that epistle they read on television the other day, on the CBC?"

"The FLQ Manifesto? It made me laugh. I was expecting ideology, a political tract. Instead, what we got was pure fiction, Madame in her kitchen and Monsieur in the tavern down at the corner. It was a *joual* document, their Manifesto. Gibberish. The other thing I thought was that ours must be the first modern society in the world in which the prime minister of the country is mocked as a pansy on national television. A fine moment."

"It's because of all the rumours going around . . . Someone who's only slightly in the party, like me, hears all the dirt. Can you tell me why there are so many fags in Quebec?"

The author of *Elucubrations* remained silent.

"Anyway, I wouldn't want to be in Little Albert's shoes," Bonnard added. "By the way, Chevalier, how was the pizza invented?"

"No idea."

"A wop was taking out the garbage and the bottom fell out of the pail."

Luigi Temperio was a short man with a balding head and long, bushy sideburns, deeply sunken eyes, a flattened nose, and a tragic mouth. His mask of the serious clown gave him something of a Louis de Funès look, only much less comic. Temperio was the Scarpinos' man on the South Shore, a faithful lieutenant and manager of the Vegas Sports Palace. Chevalier tried to think of which Molière play he belonged in. Bonnard made the introductions.

"Mr. Temperio, this is Chevalier Branlequeue. That's what he calls himself and there's not much I can do about it. Chevalier, Mr. Luigi Temperio."

"So you're in showbiz, too, eh?" Temperio asked, holding out his hand. "Like, as a writer, I mean . . ."

Chevalier forced a smile and took the outstretched hand.

"Me? No, I keep away from that scene, my dear sir. As much as possible, at any rate. When I began writing, it was all sonnets and alexandrines. Nothing very good. Then I wrote a book . . ."

"He's a great poet," Raoul Bonnard said, in the tone he might have used to announce that it looked like rain.

"Mr. Chevalier, can I offer you something to drink?"

"I wouldn't turn down a scotch," said the Dante of the South Shore, having decided to play the game.

From the outside, the Vegas was indistinguishable from the American, aggressive artificiality and commercial architecture that marked the rest of boulevard Taschereau. The most remarkable thing about it was its huge paved parking lot. Inside: tables, chairs, a bar, a mirror, framed photographs (some of them autographed) of sports and music-hall stars, a stage big enough to hold a full orchestra. Nothing much out of the ordinary. To divine any secrets it might hold would require admission to the area behind the stage.

The previous year, the government had legalized games of chance and conferred the management of its first lottery on an agency of the Crown. It was rumoured in some quarters that organized crime was waiting for its slice of the pie. Vast and well stocked but almost empty, the Vegas seemed to be living in expectation of the snap of the fingers that would transform it into a casino. It stood beside the boulevard like a woman of questionable virtue who was eager to sell her ass to the first customer who came by.

"It ain't right what they done to that man," Temperio said, opening and closing his hand rapidly, as though flapping it.

They were sitting at a table in the corner. The only other figure in the place was at the far end of the bar, a large morose drunk who appeared to be napping, perched on a barstool with his forehead resting on his arm. Chevalier took a cigarette from the silver case that had materialized in Bonnard's thick, sausage-fingered hand.

"A married man," Temperio went on, "a man with a family, with a mother, and sisters, a wife, kids, a dead brother and a sister-in-law who he's taking care of and a little nephew, like they're his own family..."

Chevalier arranged his face as though to say, *Yes, it's not funny, I agree.*

"And what they done ain't good for business, neither. There's cops all over the place. They come in here, they look around. Do you see anyone in here? It's been like this ever since the FLQ took that English guy. And our own MLA, as good a guy as you could wish for. Another family man . . . No, business is bad when something like this happens. Everything falls off. It's like a friggin' morgue in here."

"If it's any consolation, the militants aren't having it very easy, either."

"Yeah, but the organization I work for, they don't get mixed up in politics . . ."

Chevalier raised an eyebrow.

"When you blocked the election of the Parti Québécois in Tailon, that wasn't politics, you think?"

Bonnard was taken with a sudden fit of coughing. He closed his fist over his mouth. Temperio seemed genuinely surprised. Chevalier raised his glass to his lips and didn't back down.

"Which election was that?"

"The last one. The one in which the mob infiltrated the PQ meetings."

"Oh, yeah, maybe, but I ain't the mob, okay? What you said there makes it sound like I control all the muscle on the South Shore. But that ain't the case, the way things has fallen out . . ."

Temperio nodded his head with a tolerant, preoccupied air.

"Is the FLQ looking for trouble?" he asked Chevalier.

"The FLQ?"

Chevalier glanced over at Bonnard, who remained impassive behind his fat Havana cigar. He was beginning to understand why he was here.

"Mr. Temperio, I have absolutely no contact with the men who have done this."

The Italian lightly shrugged his shoulders.

"If you can say that, it's because you know who these people are. You know them..."

"No!"

Temperio turned to Bonnard. Understanding that his assistance was required, Raoul brushed the ash off his cigar, taking his time to think about what he would say.

"Mr. Temperio here," he said in his famous, meat-grinder voice, "only wants things to go back to normal, you understand. He wants to help. You are a publisher, you've published work by separatists, you have contacts in that world."

Between puffs, Bonnard cast Chevalier a shrewd, intense look.

"Mr. Temperio didn't care for the allusion, in one of the texts he heard on television the other night, to 'the Mafia fixing the elections.' And he thinks that, with your help, his message can be conveyed to the right people."

Chevalier reflected.

"I think I'm beginning to understand where you're coming from," he said after a moment. "Because of my name, you've convinced yourselves that I must be behind the fanatical cell called Chevalier. The police think the same thing. They came to my house twice last week to question me and they didn't find Paul Lavoie in my clothes closet. Do you think that if I really was the head of the FLQ, those guys would be stupid enough to use my name on one of their secret cells? I don't know who they are, but I can say that they know their history. Their Chevalier was a lawyer in 1838, the De Lorimier who was hanged in Pied-du-Courant."

Bonnard and Temperio exchanged glances.

"I don't know nothing about that," the Scarpinos' man said after a moment. "Whether you're the head of something or the head of nothing, it don't matter. But maybe you know someone, maybe you know the head of this Chevalier Cell or whoever it is who's got the

Englishman, and maybe you can say something to them, you know, something that they'll pay attention to."

"Don Luigi, you're not listening to me ..."

"Like I said, maybe there's someone who's looking after the hostages, and maybe there's someone else who writes the stuff for the television. And maybe you, mister publisher, maybe you know the people who write the stuff and you can give them the message I just told you."

"I don't know who it was who wrote the Manifesto, Mr. Temperio. But it's true that I would have been glad to have seen it published as a pamphlet."

"Okay, I got a question for mister publisher here. That paper they read on television, what did he think of it?"

"You really want to know?"

"Sure."

"Two hundred years on our knees can be hard on a language."

Temperio seemed to think about it, then spread out his hand upside down.

"Come on, don't shovel me any of that bullshit ..."

"I think you mean *joual*, don't you?"

Bonnard leaned forward and tapped the end of his cigar with the tip of his index finger, dropped the ash into an ashtray shaped like a roulette wheel, then took the bottle of scotch and refilled all three glasses.

"It ain't smart to talk about the Family like that," Temperio said in a level voice. "The FLQ, they should think about that. They should consider that they got a lot of people in prison that we could take an interest in. It would be good if someone could mention that to the right person."

"And what person would that be, Mr. Temperio?"

"The person who's writing things."

As they walked past the bar on their way to the door, the man who'd been sleeping on the counter raised his head. It was Jacques Cardinal, old Coco. The Vegas, an oasis for drifters from the South Shore, was his unofficial political headquarters.

"Well, well," said Chevalier. "If it isn't a bum."

"Well, well," said Coco. "If it ain't a intellectual."

"One do what one can."

Big Coco was almost dead drunk. When he moved his body, the imitation whale-penis skin covering the top of the barstool squeaked under his fat ass.

Chevalier looked behind him. Temperio had not moved from his chair at the corner table.

"You know whatsa diffrence b'tween you 'n' me, Chevalier?"

Coco had taken out his fixings and was laying a line on the bar. Branlequeue watched him, fascinated. Bonnard, standing a bit farther off, had his hands in his pockets.

"No, Coco. Why don't you tell me?"

"The diffrence's that I'm a real patriot, but you, you're a goddamned communist."

He snorted the coke, exhaled, and smiled. A tic developed at the corners of this mouth. His carcass flopped on the counter, shaking as though with inaudible laughter.

Chevalier glanced at Bonnard, who shrugged his shoulders and shoved his hands deeper into his pockets.

"Yes, you're a true patriot," Branlequeue said, taking the ball on the bounce. "A man of the right. Maybe you're right, at that, Coco. Maybe nationalism is nothing but a mask that the left borrowed in order to make a revolution..."

"Ah, don't start with your big words."

Chevalier placed his mouth close to the big man's ear and, separating each syllable, said: "The-id-e-o-lo-gy of de-col-on-i-za-tion!

Does that mean anything to you?"

"Thass enough, I said!"

"In any other country in the world," Chevalier said, "when a man of the right wants to start a workers' revolution, do you know what they call him, Coco? They call him an *agent provocateur*...*"

Cardinal jumped up off his barstool, waving his arms in the air. Chevalier stepped sharply back, his hands raised to his face in an attempt to protect himself.

The Fat Cop charged at him with his head lowered, swinging his fists in front of him as though trying to spread branches out of his way. He was blocked by Bonnard, who only partly managed to intercept him. He stayed on course, pushing back the crooner in his powder-blue suit the way an offensive half-back thrusts himself through to the opposition's zone with a defensive blocker on his back. Chevalier raised himself on tiptoe gracefully, like a toreador. All he lacked was a cape.

Then Cardinal shoved Bonnard off and grabbed a chair, which he threw, spinning around in a circle like a disco ball in the general direction of the place where Branlequeue had been. Then he grabbed another chair and raised it over his head and advanced...

It wasn't a good idea to break up property belonging to Mr. Temperio.

The Riviera slid along slowly without a sound, majestically, as if in a parade, passing the architectural and landscaped nightmares on boulevard Taschereau. Raoul put his hands gently on the wheel as though his palms were caressing the sides of a woman with whom he was dancing the cha-cha-cha.

"Poor Coco..."

"Bah. It wasn't as though he wasn't asking for it."

"Do you know, Raoul, your little friends in there, I'm glad the government hasn't exposed them. Keeping them in the mix is like having a fifth ace up its sleeve."

"What do you mean?"

"As undercover agents to do their dirty work for them, get the radicals all stirred up. Then the police or the army steps in to restore order. In some countries that's the way it works. The extreme right has to be good for something..."

"You've got more imagination than I have."

They remained silent for a moment. Bonnard kept looking in his rear-view mirror.

"They've been there since we left the Palace," he said quietly.

Chevalier turned around. Two large yellow eyes. Raoul slowed down but the distance between them and the car behind them remained the same.

"Do you really think...?"

"When you hang around with the Scarpinos, you get used to it. But he could just as easily be following you. Or keeping an eye on the current affairs of our Sicilian friends. Or it could be politics. *Your guess is as good as mine*, as they say. How would you say that in French, Chevalier?"

"You've caught me off-guard, Raoul."

"So where do you want me to drop you? Your place?"

"You're joking, aren't you? Where else would I be going?"

"And anyway, you've got nothing to tell them, right?"

"Absolutely nothing."

Bonnard remained silent.

When they reached rue Chambly, the phantom car was still behind them. Bonnard passed Chevalier's house and dropped him off at a corner farther down the street. The poet–publisher had turned and was walking down the sidewalk when he heard his name being called. He looked around and saw that Bonnard had rolled down his window.

"Hey, Chevalier! Do you know why wops wear those pointy-toed shoes?"

"Yes, I do. Good night, Raoul."

LUSTUKRU

IN HIS DREAM, THE GREAT Lustukru would disappear with his three children. He was like a figure in the old engravings, with a large pointed hat, a sad, serious face, and a chin as sharp as an ice pick. He burst in through the door and the night came with him, he opened his already-full pack, silenced the cries of the children by telling them a story that was always different, then he shoved them in the sack and threw it over his shoulder before resuming his rounds. In the dream, Chevalier was unable to move, his feet stuck to the floor. His legs weighed a ton as he watched the Great Lustukru go back out through the door, taking all the children who couldn't sleep, *lalala, lalala. Lalalalalalalala, lala.*

"Take me instead of them!" Chevalier Branlequeue shouted out in his dream. The Great Lustukru stopped to listen. "Take me instead!" he heard himself cry. The Great Lustukru turned and began coming toward him. He looked a lot like the literary critic Jean-Étier Blet. Lustukru untied the cord that closed his sack and Chevalier saw

401

its black opening, as black as a cave, at the bottom of which lurked all his fears from his earliest days. The Great Lustukru, pulling the sack down like a butterfly net, shoved it over Chevalier's head and shoulders, down his sides . . . Chevalier was fighting with his bed-sheets when he opened his eyes.

Éléonore, in the deep hollow beside him on the bed, woke up. Someone was trying to break down the front door.

The sound of heavy boots, the window being smashed by rifle butts. The wooden door, split down the middle from top to bottom, sagged on its hinges. Armed men everywhere, police, uniformed and in civilian dress, coming in and going out. There must have been a dozen of them. Chevalier came out of the master bedroom in his flannel pyjamas and made his way half-blind toward where he remembered having left his glasses the night before, beside the irreverent manuscript of a young separatist poet who had stolen Lorca's muse. *Nonosse of Blood*, it was called.

His progress was interrupted by the feel of a cold object pressed against his sternum between two buttons of his pyjama top. He looked down and saw the barrel of a machine gun and, holding the machine gun, a police constable leaning lightly on the gun's stock, pressing the barrel into his rib cage and pushing him back against the wall.

"What are you—?"

"You're under arrest. Hands on your head, please, sir."

Branlequeue half-raised his hands and held them immobilized in the air.

"Do you have a warrant?"

"We don't need one. Not anymore. I told you to put your hands on your head."

He obeyed. Somewhere deep down inside, he felt no surprise as he heard the order, with a mute understanding but filled with defiance: at last the mask has been removed. Éléonore appeared at their bedroom door and was greeted by a machine gun aimed in her direction.

"Holy Mother of God!"

In the kitchen, detectives were using their feet to sift through the contents of the garbage pail they'd overturned. One of them, examining the contents of a container of flour from the cupboard, emptied it on the floor and was immediately enveloped in a white cloud that made him sneeze, then sniff. Then he did the same thing with the container of first-class Colombian cocoa. Another had taken a brick of ice cream from the freezer and was looking at it suspiciously. After a close inspection, he stabbed it several times with a butter knife to make sure there were no sticks of dynamite hidden inside it.

"They're insane," Éléonore decided aloud, in an amazed, almost calm voice.

Held against a wall in their night clothes, an automatic weapon trained on them, Éléonore and her husband saw their three children being herded down the stairs by men carrying machine guns. They were in a line, their eyes still swollen with sleep. Pacifique was holding his Winnie-the-Pooh bear against his chest. The clock on the wall read ten minutes to six a.m.

The children were lined up against the wall beside them. The family together at last. The oldest, Martial, put his fist to his mouth and yawned, prodigiously interested in what was going on around him.

"Dad, what do they want?"

"I don't know, son. I'll ask them."

He turned toward their guard:

"Officer, I'm not asking for myself, you understand, but I do think you owe an explanation to my son, who is right here."

The guard was young, fresh-faced, with a thin moustache that made him look like a twelve-year-old nervously aiming a gun. He was fighting this appearance of weakness by holding himself as rigid as a fence post and systematically avoiding meeting the eyes of his prisoners. When Chevalier questioned him, he blushed like a schoolgirl.

"Officer?" Chevalier tried again with the same ultra-polite tone. "My older boy here would like it if you could answer his question."

The young cop adjusted his cap, his eyes fixed on the wall in front of him. He succeeded in keeping his trap shut.

A considerable noise was coming from the Placard, Chevalier's office. The police were bringing out garbage bags full of material. Everything: typewriter, masses of papers, magazines, books, manuscripts, files, illustrations, pamphlets, address books. One of the detectives stopped in front of the telephone table, took the phone book, and stuffed it in his green bag and kept on going, sack over his shoulder. Chevalier watched him leave.

"Are you being paid by the pound?"

"Shut the fuck up!"

But Chevalier was beginning to have an idea. The idea was strong enough to allow him to stare down the uniformed whippersnapper who was holding his family captive and who, without a word, got out of his way.

Advancing like an automaton, Branlequeue crossed the room, still as blind as a bat without his glasses, and stopped at the door to his office. He could hear what was going on inside clearly: two officers throwing things with a vaguely disgusted air into a pile of papers about a metre high, then shoving it in huge armloads into black plastic bags. One of them was a member of the antiterrorist squad, Detective Lieutenant Gilbert Massicotte, of the Montreal police. He looked up and saw Chevalier.

"What's up?" he asked in a fairly good imitation of the comedian Ti-Zoune Guimond, complete with gestures.

Chevalier swallowed.

"Er . . . that's the manuscript of the second volume of *Elucubra-tions* you're tossing about . . ." He stopped, unable to go on.

Massicotte looked down at the pile of paper. He looked like someone had just stopped him from pulling up a weed in order to give him its scientific name.

"The book is almost finished," Chevalier added in a thin voice.

"I know who you are," Lieutenant Massicotte shot at him. "You've won some kind of prize. I'm a writer, too, did you know that? But I hate Quebec literature. Jean-Étier Blet's right, there's nothing here that comes anywhere close to the *Meditations* of Martine, er, I mean . . ."

"Lamartine, yes," Chevalier nodded, forcing himself to remain calm and telling himself that the police aren't always the animals they appear to be, but they usually are. "And Hugo," he added, "who wrote his *Contemplations*, and Rimbaud with his *Illuminations* . . . and me. All I'm asking, sir, is that you stop this thievery and leave my *Elucubrations* alone, all right?"

"You do your job, and let us do ours," said the detective lieuten-ant philosophically.

An officer came and gently but firmly took the writer by the sleeve of his pyjamas and escorted him back into the hall. There, Chevalier's attention turned to a policeman who, arms full, was coming down the stairs from the second floor and the two children's bedrooms. The author of *Elucubrations* ignored the weapon trained on him and went to the bottom of the stairs.

"What are you carting off this time?"

"Evidence," muttered the officer, looking down at the teetering pile of school notebooks and binders and trying to stabilize them with his chin.

"No, wait a minute," said Chevalier. "That's my son's stamp col-lection."

"We'll let the experts tell us what it is, if you don't mind, sir. This is all going straight to the lab. 'Scuse me, if I can just get past ..."

Chevalier stepped aside, this time truly overwhelmed by what was happening.

A corpulent inspector carrying a raincoat and hat was suddenly standing in front of him.

"You. You're coming with us."

"No, sir, I'm not. Unless you have a warrant, I'm not budging from my house ..."

The policeman gave him his best smile. It was full of well-brushed but nicotine-stained teeth, and his breath stank like a sewer.

"We don't need a warrant. We're done with warrants. There's a special law that was just voted in in Ottawa."

PROVINCE OF QUEBEC (CANADA), OCTOBER 16, 1970

One week earlier, the Canadian Military had been placed on alert. Under cover of routine exercises, troops had been moved to Camp Bouchard, north of Montreal. On October 12, units from the 2nd Combat Division, stationed in Petawawa, Ontario, were sent to Ottawa, ostensibly to guard public buildings in the capital. On the 15th, two Hercules troop transports were readied to fly from the air force base at Namao, near Edmonton. Originally planned for the 14th, then put back twenty-four hours while the Quebec Minister of Justice came up with reasons for the transfer of soldiers and political allies, the invasion was ready to begin.

At noon, the solicitor general of Quebec, who had more or less fallen apart at the seams after the kidnapping of his colleague, signed the famous official letter conferring legal status to the military occupation. General Bédard's successor as the head of Mobile

Forces was warned by a telephone call to his headquarters in Saint-Hubert. The reading of the intervention request was accomplished, as the law required. Then an airplane left Quebec with the missive and flew toward Ottawa. Five minutes later, like clockwork, the new chief of the Armed Forces unleashed Operation Touchdown.

Four Hercules aircraft lifted off in the space of half an hour from the Ancienne-Lorette airport near Quebec City, each carrying three hundred soldiers in full battle fatigues. Others left from Namao, heading toward Montreal. Helicopters left the base at Saint-Hubert to go to Camp Bouchard, where they picked up infantry belonging to the second battalion of the 22nd Regiment, then returned to fly over the city at low altitude.

At the same time, a military convoy of four hundred vehicles left the base at Valcartier, north of the capital, and spread out toward the main cities. In Montreal, soldiers appeared in front of city hall and the courthouse. In sections of the city where the upper crust lived, more soldiers guarded the residences of political figures and other public citizens.

Soon, nearly six hundred soldiers equipped with field materiel had been deployed in the streets of the French-Canadian metropolis. On rue Parthenais, Quebec Provincial Police headquarters were cordoned off by military troops ready for warfare, weapons at the ready. Behind the cordon, in the parking lot converted into a de facto aerodrome, a continuous coming and going of helicopters was kept up.

Seen from the street, the Parthenais Prison, as it was called from then on, formed a vertiginous, coal-black rectangle that seemed poised to crush the surrounding workers' quarter. The Division of Civil Emergency Situations, under the command of the Mobile Forces of the Canadian Army, created the year before, had for the past several days been quartered there to ensure the logistics of Touchdown. Theoretically under orders from the civil authority, the

Canadian Forces, on the morning of the 16th, had the situation well in hand.

Less than two hours before, the Governor General of Canada had affixed his seal to an old law that, foreseeing the immediate suspension of civil liberties and rights, had been quickly resuscitated by the prime minister's clique and voted on in the middle of the night. The Governor General's proclamation said:

> *Be it now known that, on and with the knowledge of our Privy Counsel for Canada, We proclaim and declare by virtue of this Our present proclamation that a state of apprehended insurrection exists and has existed since October 15.*

The ink on the Royal Proclamation hadn't even dried when the three principal police forces in Quebec were thrown into action.

Youths, the elderly, sitting shoulder to shoulder along the wall, passed cigarettes to one another. One of them closed his eyes — he was perched on one of two exposed toilets stuck in the floor, pants rolled down to his knees. He had not chosen the best morning to be nabbed by the police.

"Over here, Chevalier!"

"He knows a lot of people in here."

His political family. Union leaders, doctors, professors, workers, militants, members of popular fronts, poets, journalists, taxi drivers, candidates for municipal office, adolescents, defrocked priests.

Tons of documents had been seized.

"They took my Felix Leclerc albums," said a bemused Doctor Charron, warmly shaking Chevalier's hand.

"Me, too," another chimed in. "They took a book on Cubist painting! Cubist equals Cuba, I suppose. Something to think about..."[1]

The police list also consisted of the works of Jean-Paul Sartre and Fanon, several books whose titles included the word "China," posters of Che Guevara, Quebec flags, decorative swords, and hunting rifles.

They moved aside to make room for Chevalier. They wanted him to tell them his story. During the preceding hours, most of these men had gone through an ordeal identical to his: escorted by two agents through the garage of the Parthenais building, brought before a long table where four civilians were seated. Next they were taken to the seventh floor, forced to empty their pockets, the contents of which were then slipped into an envelope with their name written on the front, searched from head to toe, brought into a large room secured by bars and containing six prisoners and no chairs, two toilets, one sink. Then they were taken to be weighed, measured, made to press their fingers on an ink pad and have their fingerprints taken on four different-coloured sheets of paper, photographed face-on and in profile, escorted down a corridor and then through an air-lock consisting of two grilled doors, activated by an officious guard protected behind a glass wall. They were guided down an aisle bordered by two ranges of cells; those on the left were pierced by only one window while those on the right were grilled. Conducted to a door marked S26 at the end of a corridor, on the right, ordered to cross the threshold of this door by the police officer accompanying them, locked in a large room in which there were already some forty people, lying on the floor or sitting with their backs to the wall, eyes raised to the newcomer.

---

1   This anecdote was told so often, and by so many different people, all of them owners, if they can be believed, of the specialized work in question, that we must consider it apocryphal.

No one had had any breakfast. One of the men, a young actor, suddenly produced a McIntosh apple that had somehow made it through the search without being taken away, and regarded it for a moment as if he were going to talk to it, like Hamlet holding Yorick's skull, before biting into it. No one said a word. No sound but the grumbling of a few stomachs here and there. They could hear the actor's teeth cutting through the apple's peel and crushing the pulp, making the acidic juice of October run down his chin. Just as he was about to take a second bite, he raised his head and, without a word, passed the apple to the man sitting beside him. This man bit into the apple and passed it to his neighbour. By the time it got to Chevalier, there was a little more than half of it left. Chevalier wasn't hungry, but nothing in the world would have kept him from biting into that apple.

In the middle of the afternoon, they were stood up against the wall and each given a baloney sandwich, a cup of some hot liquid that might have been tea or perhaps coffee, and three biscuits.

Called out into the corridor with two or three others. Placed under guard by a police officer. Taken into an elevator with a barred door locked with a key. Caged. Taken to a waiting room, also barred. Then into another waiting room. Called. Reweighed. Remeasured. Searched again. Questioned. Father, mother. Place of birth. Political affiliations.

"Independent."

"You mean separatist . . ."

"No. Independent."

Ordered to undress and deposit his clothes on a table. Forced to wait, standing naked while they examined his underwear and the insides of his shoes. Allowed to dress again. Taken to another room equipped with aluminum benches. Joined there by other detainees. Back into the elevator. Brought down to the second floor. Given plastic utensils and a blanket folded around two sheets, a pillowcase, and a towel. Taken to cell number LAM25. LAM for Left Aisle, Mezzanine.

The loud, clanking door shut behind him. His new lodgings measured six feet by eight feet by seven feet high. Room for three paces. Containing a steel bed frame, a mattress, a metal dresser, a table fixed to the wall, a bench, a second table acting as a kitchen table, a porcelain toilet with no seat, a sink. And a mirror made from some kind of shiny metal, for obvious security reasons.

The detainee cells were situated on the top floors of the Parthenais building. Chevalier, unlike those occupying the lower cells, could see down through three ranges of barred cells. There was a thick layer of pigeon shit on the sill of a window reinforced on the outside by metal plates. His point of view gave him access to a thin slice of the *faubourg à m'lasse*, the former dockworkers' district. The two-storeyed buildings with wooden lintels, de Lorimier Park where Jackie Robinson had once played baseball for the Dodgers and Los Angeles farm teams. A church. A tavern. Small world.

At six in the morning the lights came on abruptly and the canteen came alive with a great clatter of utensils. Chevalier remembered where he was. At each end of the corridor, loudspeakers began emitting a torrent of rubbish from two popular radio stations, a different station playing from each speaker, which rivalled the stupidity of banging your head against the walls. The volume was turned up full blast. Outside it was still dark.

The previous night they'd been allowed the right to dine on more baloney sandwiches washed down with black coffee and the same three biscuits.

Just as the seven o'clock news was about to come on, the speakers went silent. No question of giving them access to the slightest information from the outside, there must be nothing that made sense. Only ordinary prisoners had television.

They communicated with one another by shouting at the tops of their lungs above the radio. That morning, Chevalier Branlequeue, the poet Michel Garneau in the next cell, and a few others were able to hold an improvised meeting that was more or less dominated by the historian Louis Villeneuve.

After having reflected on the situation, Villeneuve had at first hypothetically agreed with the proclamation of the War Measures Act by the federal government. He expressed himself in elegant, learned terms even if he did have to shout to be heard.

"I do not see," he yelled, "what else it could have done. This law has been implemented twice before in the twentieth century, and each time in Quebec, to deal with troubles raised by the Conscription Crisis in 1917, and again in 1944. It must be admitted that the lack of enthusiasm felt by young French-Canadians at the prospect of going overseas to be eviscerated for the King of England represented a source of disappointment, even for those with a good loyalist conscience. It was implemented to deal with the lazy ones who clearly did not understand anything about strategic imperatives in defence of the British Empire. From Victoria, British Columbia, to the Orange bastion of Southern Ontario, and including the walled Rhodesian enclave of Westmount and the Town of Mount Royal, they were nothing but disgusting frogs sleeping on their field of battle....

"This War Measures Act, understand me well, signifies the suspension of civil liberties as recognized in the Constitution. In principle, we could be kept in this place incommunicado, without even the right to know what we're being accused of. And for as long as the authorities deem necessary. No lawyers. No visits. No telephone calls. No mail. No rights. Nothing."

The sound of distant unlocked doors being opened.

The corridor.

The elevator with its guard protected by bars.

An interrogation room the size of a ship's cabin.

Two plainclothes police officers seated behind a table.

Another form to fill out.

First name. Last name. Occupation.

"Poet."

"That's all? Poet?"

"Yes. I used to be a publisher, but you have taken everything that made me one. Poet is something that you can never take from me."

Poet, wrote the policeman.

Father's name. Mother's maiden name. Place of birth.

"Sainte-Anne-de-la-Pérade."

The officer who was taking an inventory of the large envelope containing his personal affects looked up.

"La Pérade? ... That place where they catch the little fish?"

"Where they catch the little fish," Chevalier agreed. "Like here."

"You're a real laugh. Do you know where John Travers is?"

"No."

"Paul Lavoie?"

"No, officer, I don't."

"Tell me about the Chevalier Cell."

"I know nothing about it."

"Why do you think they chose that name?"

"Because of Chevalier de Lorimier, the rebel leader who was hanged in Pied-du-Courant in 1839. Along with Hamelin, Hindelang, and a few others ..."

"Good."

"I had a dream last night," Branlequeue told them. "A classic professor's dream: I was walking down a corridor looking for the room where I was supposed to give my course, but I was lost. The class was about to start, my students were waiting, I was almost running, and in the end I arrived in front of a door. I went into the classroom, and when I looked at the windows they had bars on them..."

The two police officers looked at each other.

"Let's move on and talk about your political affiliations, if that's okay with you."

"Nothing to hide. I've been affiliated with the PSD, the RIN, and the PQ. At the moment, I am affiliated only with poor Chevalier..."

"Do you approve of violence?"

"No. Because you know as well as I do that violence serves only your cause."

"Your comrades on the mezzanine, what do they think about it?"

...

"Are they for terrorism?"

"It's not right, what you're asking of me. At least you have the excuse that you're doing your jobs."

"If you'd like us to proceed some other way, then tell us how."

"You could start by asking me to sign a paper stating that you recognize that you have seized my manuscript. I would like to see the colour of the second part of my *Elucubrations*. And then, my son's stamp collection..."

"Stamp collection?"

"Yes. Someone took my son's stamp collection. If I think about that too much, I'm going to want to break someone's jaw."

"If we return your papers and your stamps, will you tell us who is for the FLQ in your range?"

"No."

"You'd get out of here faster."

"I imagine I would."

"Do you know why you've been arrested?"

"Because I entertain socialist ideas and am in favour of Quebec independence."

"Is that all?"

"Because I have opinions. I sometimes even go so far as to express them ..."

"Ah, so you do understand. And what is your opinion of the FLQ?"

"The government is getting excited for nothing, if you want my opinion."

"Do you know any members of the FLQ?"

"No."

"Are you the leader of the FLQ?"

"No."

"Tell us about the Chevalier Cell."

"Never heard of it. Before October 10, that is."

"According to information we received, you are one of its leaders ..."

"I want to see a lawyer."

"One of the ones who writes pamphlets ..."

"No."

"A form of moral authority."

"No."

"An opinion leader. You've said so yourself."

"No!"

"You are the philosophical leader of the movement. The ideologue ..."

"Not true."

"The Chevalier Cell's spiritual father. The thinker who hides behind ..."

"No. You must have a sycophant somewhere who is leading you up the garden path."

"A what?"

"An informer."

"What was that word you used?"

"Garden."

"No, the other word . . . Sicko-something."

"Fuck off."

"Fine. You can stretch this out as long as you want, we're in no hurry."

Toward the end of the afternoon they were allowed to walk up and down the long corridor that separated the lower cells, which was about thirty metres by four. Picnic tables had been set up. Thirty minutes' recreation. A chance to put faces to all the voices that had been shouting during the afternoon. They were let out in groups of twelve.

The detainees talked about starting a hunger strike the next day. Among them were three Vietnamese and one Greek.

"Why a hunger strike?" asked Chevalier. "You don't like baloney?"

They looked at him uncomprehendingly.

"I was making a joke," he said. "But seriously, I don't quite see the link between Vietnam and Quebec liberation . . ."

The Vietnamese who replied held a Ph.D.

"There may be more rapport than you think, sir. We, too, are patriots, opposed to American intervention in our country."

"I'd like to agree with you, but here it's not the United States . . ."

The Vietnamese contented himself with a smile.

"Feels like home," said the Greek.

Three years previously he'd fled the colonels' regime and embraced the cause of Quebec independence. He worked as a journalist, and somewhere in the three sacks of documents taken from his home were letters from his uprooted father among the olive trees of the Peloponnese. The Cyrillic alphabet had drawn the interest of the searchers; suspecting that the letters were written in code, they'd seized the lot.

Farther down the corridor a small group gathered in front of the cell occupied by none other than *Maître* Brien, the curly-headed D'Artagnan of the Courts. Forty-eight hours earlier he'd still been the official negotiator and flamboyant rouser of crowds before national television cameras. He had been thrown into the brig like a common criminal.

Incapable of not performing before a crowd, he was telling his captive audience that according to information in his possession, information he had received in confidence, the police had discovered and surrounded the two hideouts where the hostages were being held. They were coordinating their efforts for a final assault, and it was now simply a matter of time.

"Are you very certain of that, sir?"

"Absolutely positive, my dear friend. I have it from an honest businessman who has connections in the Cabinet. Well, Chevalier. How's it going?"

The rigours of the bars helped, their raised fists were more celebratory than expected. The others made a semicircle around them.

"*Maître* Brien, explain something to me . . . You know who the kidnappers are, yes, no?"

"My dear sir, my lips are sealed over the bulwark of my teeth, which themselves are barred with double locks."

"Yes, but you couldn't negotiate in the name of someone you have never met. Therefore, you know who the perpetrators are. And the police strongly think the same of me. My question: why aren't they grilling you?"

"Ah, Chevalier. They know me . . . They know perfectly well that I'll never betray a professional confidence like that. No point in their even trying."

"Do you mean to say that they can respect your professional practice and yet still throw you in prison?"

"That's it, yes."

"So your secret is more sacred than our civil rights. This is not necessarily good news."

Mortified, the lawyer shrugged his shoulders then picked up the thread of his story. Watching him sketch the air with his cigarette, one might almost forget that he was behind bars, speaking to co-detainees, and not in a smoky press room, putting on a show for the camera and the same old pack of reporters spiked with microphones, flashbulbs, and notebooks.

"Listen, I don't give a shit about Travers. He's a goddamned Englishman! He'll come out of this with not so much as a hair out of place, wait and see. No, it's Lavoie I'm worried about..."

Branlequeue turned and continued his walk. Farther down, he stopped before the overflowing flesh of Coco Cardinal, enthroned like a pasha on the toilet in his tiny mousetrap of a cell, his pants down around his ankles.

"Well, if it ain't the Tommycod King," muttered Chevalier.

Coco's face, adorned with two eyes like black butter, a lip split down to his chin, three broken or missing teeth, and a goose egg on his left temple, split into a large, nauseating smile. Chevalier shivered with distaste, as though he were looking into the eyes of a shark or the mouth of a stingray. Cold horror rose from deep within him.

He wanted to distance himself as fast as he could, but he heard himself being called.

"Hey, poet!"

Chevalier turned and looked away as the Fat Cop, apparently impervious to any notion of modesty, wiped his huge backside with evil delectation.

"They didn't go out with crowbars, those guys at the Vegas, eh?"

Chevalier said when Coco had finished.

"When I get out of here I'm going back there with a can of gasoline," Cardinal announced, pulling up his pants and walking over to the bars.

Chevalier resisted the urge to run off down the hall.

"Something I still don't understand, Coco, is how you've made a living since you were in the police."

"I fuck. The system."

"Credit cards?"

"Among other things."

"And is that what pays for the sailboat on the Île aux Fesses?"

Coco's eyes, rimmed by huge black circles like those of a raccoon, narrowed and remained fixed on Chevalier, though Coco continued to smile.

"But that isn't why they put you in here, is it, Coco? Credit cards have nothing to do with this business . . ."

"No. I'm here because I'm a patriot, a real one . . . Not like you."

Chevalier then committed the error of turning his head for a fraction of a second. By the time he sensed the danger, it was too late. Coco reached out and grabbed Chevalier by the collar and pulled him against the bars of his cell. He held him there while methodically punching his face with his other hand.

"Oh, nice shiner!" said the canteen man.

He was pushing his little cart between the rows of cells. Chevalier had filled out his order form that afternoon: he wanted a pen, paper, chewing gum, and tobacco.

Chevalier smiled painfully.

"Lucky for me you've also rounded up a couple of doctors," he said. "Meanwhile, I'll take some of your aspirins, if you have any."

The canteen man scrupulously examined the order form.

"The question isn't whether or not I have them. It's whether or not you've ordered them."

"Ah, never mind! Paper, ballpoint, cigarettes. I don't need anything else."

Chevalier was beginning to believe that he'd never see the second part of *Elucubrations* again. He knew only that this iceberg of words, with its death and mammoth metaphors, would one day be considered the mythic tip of his writings. During the years he had worked on his great book, he was ceaselessly caught between the need to earn a living, the reality of having a family to support, and the need to steal more time from his other obligations and ministries. He had known radicals, some of whom had actually advanced to action, who had been arrested and imprisoned. He had sometimes thought of prison as a safe harbour, situated outside of time, an oasis of enforced peace in the midst of the normal harassments of ordinary existence. The privation of liberty seemed a lesser evil, a minimal concession in exchange for the formidable removal of social responsibility, necessary to the work of genius. Why weren't more universal literary masterpieces written in prisons? he wondered. Free bed, board, and laundry, and time stretching ahead as far as the eye could see. To write and avoid going crazy...And above all, above all, to have absolutely nothing else to do. Wasn't that the ideal situation? The recluse any ambitious creator dreamed of?

With the pad of paper in front of him on the metal sheet that served as a table, pen poised between thumb, index, and middle fingers, he stared with feverish intensity and a slightly astonished air into the void of the empty page. It was like staring into his empty life in a prison cell, and he knew it. Nothing came, absolutely nothing.

The next day, LAM255 woke to the sound of funereal music coming from the radio. He knew immediately what it meant.

Through the slow, serene weft of Handel's *Largo*, he could hear the hoarse shouts of two chess players separated by three cells.

"Little Albert on G4 takes Mountie on F3!"

Laughter mingled with one or two pleasantries. The bishops were called Vézinas because, like the premier of Quebec, they moved only on the bias. A Little Albert was a pawn. An Ottawa was a rook. The king and queen were called PET and Beth.

Chevalier Branlequeue sat in a corner of his cell, his back to the bars.

"Garneau..."

"Yes, Chevalier?"

"Lavoie's dead."

"What? Why do you say that?"

"They killed him. Why else would the radio be playing Handel?"

That afternoon, Chevalier tried to write something once more. Still nothing came. It was as though they had won.

GHOSTS

THIS IS THE STORY OF a guy (me) who wakes up in a big house full
of nooks and crannies stuck in the middle of nowhere, in the heart
of a boreal forest, at four o'clock in the morning. Lake Kaganoma.
It's winter, it's 40 below, and Marie-Québec is gone for good. Her
empty space in the cold bed mutilates my side, yanks out my Adam's
rib. And as if that weren't enough, *he* is back. I can hear him thrashing around downstairs, in the kitchen.

Naked as a dew worm, draped in invisible sweat that raised
goosebumps in the cold air of the bedroom, I got up and fetched the
shotgun from the closet in my office. Slid a couple of Imperial shells
into the barrel (buckshot, or Poly-Kor long-range specials). Then,
creeping on lynx paws, I went downstairs.

He was sitting at the table. His hands were badly sliced up and
the marks on his neck where he'd been strangled were clearly visible. Blue in the face, ribbons of dried blood under his nostrils and
in his ears. I recognized the sweater he was wearing as the one Mrs.

Lafleur described at the coroner's inquest, knitted by her own hands for her husband, and which the kidnappers had slipped on their wounded hostage after having taken off the shirt that was soaked in fresh blood. He was breathing noisily. I sighed.

"You know, I've always known it was you who was the ghost of Kaganoma..."

"Take me to a hospital..."

I shook my head.

"It's not in my power. And I can't fix you up, either."

I leaned the shotgun against the wall and pulled a chair up to the table. He seemed as if he wanted to talk. But first, I went over and stoked the embers in the airtight woodstove, then put on my old Mackinaw with the red and black checks that was hanging on a hook by the door.

"I know why you're here, Lavoie," I said to the ghost when I sat down. "You're stuck in purgatory. And history's purgatory isn't like God's. It's names that languish there, not souls. And while you wait to join the heroes and martyrs in the local pantheon, or maybe go back below with the traitors to their country and the dirty rotten souls damned for eternity, you are forced to use the old tried-and-true methods for making us mortals remember you. You send your terrestrial appearance to visit me, I find myself in my kitchen talking to a fake ectoplasm. You could say I'm your last hope..."

He nodded gravely.

I got up and grabbed the bottle of d'Auge Calvados that was sitting on the counter. I poured both of us three fingers in glasses decorated with images of playing cards, and handed him his. Jack of Spades.

"Take it. It'll put some colour in your cheeks..."

With his sliced-up hand, he took the glass I'd offered him and tossed back the alcohol, and I did the same. The Calvados tasted of old orchard, lightning-struck wood, and apples fallen onto yellowed grass and dead leaves pecked at by partridges. October.

I refilled the glasses.

"At the moment, I'm trying to track down the elusive Chevreuil, the famous Pierre. A single certitude about him and I'll be saved. And you can help me, I think, Lavoie..."

A low groan.

"Take me to the hospital..."

I filled the glasses a third time and raised mine in a toast:

"To your health, Mr. Minister."

His only response was a deep sigh, then he tossed back his Calvados like it was a cup of chamomile tea.

"You see, I need to know if Pierre Chevrier, alias Le Chevreuil, went to 140 rue Collins while you were being held there. I know you can't tell me. That I have to discover the truth by my own means. And you, you're here to remind me of my duty to history and to stop me from killing myself. But let me tell you something: those who are moving heaven and earth to erase you from the land of the living, and who have covered their tracks well, aren't exactly the two of spades. You have been sacrificed, Lavoie, but for what? What is certain is that Quebec has abandoned you. That your own political family has let you down, and that Canada has taken a pass on you. And if it's true that you were, as some have said, sacrificed to the strategic interests of the Atlantic Alliance, then the West has also hung you out to dry. And so, rather than raise their little finger and send a bunch of hired killers in to rescue you, your friends in the Scarpino family said: thumb's down. Everyone washed their hands of you."

I needed to pour a lot of Calvados to refill the glasses this time. The neck of the bottle had a tendency to swing back and forth. My voice had become foggy, my tone kind of pasty, full of bitterness. The ghost didn't seem to notice that he was drunk, or feeling better.

Unable to drown the sadness at the bottom of the well of memory, he emptied his glass as quickly as I refilled it, as though his despair was nothing but a kind of politeness.

"You were the perfect scapegoat," I told him. "Drafted into your defence corps, a martyr for made-to-measure Canadian unity..."

I grabbed the still three-quarters-full bottle by its neck and began pacing about the kitchen. The dawn was carving a path through the window.

"The false alarm, Lavoie... Do you remember that?"

He shook his head, eyes half-closed, his expression dead, a milky white infused with galaxies of burst blood vessels. His chin rested on his bloodstained chest.

"Remember... Wednesday, October 14, 1970. They'd been holding you hostage for four days in that room, chained to a bed, handcuffed. At first, you thought the authorities were negotiating, but the positive signs were still far off and nothing was happening. The previous night, one of your captors had been picked up by the police and hadn't come back. And there was a suspicious car that kept passing the house. Each time it passed, it slowed down and the occupants looked intently at the front of the house where you were being kept prisoner. And what happened then, how could you forget?"

While I was speaking to him, Lavoie's breathing had turned into a pitiful groaning that sank into a barely audible moan. But I went on:

"Then the alarm went off, there was the sound of fighting in the bungalow. Your kidnappers decided to save their skins and, in the meantime, to use yours as a shield. They cut off two pieces of an old mop handle and made them look like sticks of dynamite by wrapping them in brown paper and coating them in butter to make them look more realistic. They attached an alarm clock to them for a detonator and enough electric cord to make it look real, then they placed the sticks in a pack and strapped it around your chest. Then they dragged you out to face the door, propped up between the guy holding the detonator and another who held the barrel of his M1 against your head, and you sat there waiting for the first boot or battering ram to hit the door, the rush..."

"*Aaaaaugh*," said the ghost.

"I've thought a lot about you at that moment, the longest moment of your life. You were like the young Dostoyevsky facing his firing squad. Time stretched out interminably, as though each second had become an ellipsoid precipitated by eternity. What did you think about? In one sense, you were privileged. The dead don't always get to have a dress rehearsal..."

Without being aware of it I'd put down the empty bottle and picked up the shotgun while I'd been talking. It was loaded. I pointed it in the approximate direction of the front door.

"Watch out, Mr. Minister! Any second now, the firefight is going to start, the clock is ticking... The dry blast of detonators, bullets whizzing through your guts! Your captors are trembling like hell and they have their fingers on the triggers. Your heart is pounding, you're saying your prayers, your life has become nothing but a simple exchange, like currency. And..."

"*Noooooo!*"

"And nothing. Nothing happens. One of the guys finally gets up and goes to the window, and what does he see? A police raid is, in fact, taking place, but they're raiding the house next door! Who lives there? Kids with long hair, according to Richard Godefroid. For some reason they hadn't been heard from for a while. Five days later, neighbours will tell the police that the house next door had been empty for a month. How do you explain that, eh? Hey!"

The ectoplasm had leapt to his feet and was charging at me, a howl on his lips. Without thinking I pivoted ninety degrees and fired from the hip. Loud, heavy detonation. I thought the house was falling down around my head. The ghost brushed past me in the hallway, I felt his breath on my face, coming from the glacial black-ness of vast amounts of nothingness. I fired again, point blank. I saw him run toward the window, jump, pass through the glass, and run off in long strides into the morning's half-light, like Big Chief at the end of *One Flew Over the Cuckoo's Nest*.

In Kaganoma, hearing a rifle blast was not unusual. During the hunting season, the deep silence was often broken by sudden bursts of 12-gauge shotguns and .30-06s, followed by the return of the deep silence. Powder burns on the four walls was a little harder to explain. But making a living as a writer and being a hermit in the process of losing his mind in the deep woods went a long way to explaining many things, and maybe even would serve as an excuse.

The first blast passed above the kitchen table and carved a hole in the north-facing window about the size of a fist. The second went through the wall below the stairs, making a nice clean round hole in the drywall, but not doing much other damage. After blinking a few times in the rush of cold air coming through the window, and staring stupidly at the empty Calvados bottle, Samuel cut a square of cardboard from a box of books and taped it to the glass. The ther-mometer was registering thirty-eight degrees below zero, Celsius.

"Can I speak to Mr. Guy Dumont, please?"

"What about?"

"About getting an assignment. Any assignment."

"Yes?"

"Hello, Big. It's Sam. You wouldn't by any chance have a story about a young singer who was abused by her father and uncles and manager you wanted me to write, would you?"

"The same old Sam, still hard up. You sound terrible. What's wrong?"

"Nothing I can't handle, don't worry. Come on, Big Guy, for the insignificant sum of five thousand smackers I would do just about anything except shine shoes. Fix the commas in a six-hundred-page history of federal-provincial relations. I need to suffer and be redeemed."

"And I don't like the idea of the business I founded being mistaken for a branch of the Bank of Nova Scotia. But as it happens I do have a manuscript that might interest you. I think it might be just up your alley..."

"I'm on the financial ropes and you're offering me a job that's right up my alley? No kidding, Big, I'm touched. Does it have a title?"

"Wait, let me see...Ah, yes, *The Traverse*."

"That's all?"

"No, it also has a subtitle: *The Story of My Captivity*, by John Travers."

In splendid isolation, in front of my computer in the middle of the forest, I was hyperlinked, my brain had become a nanoplot, lit up under a celestial sphere and sprinkled with infinite numerical permutations. My head was being bombarded with a million frequencies, satellite waves, and information packets. Each hauled a trailer full of fragments of the world it had plunged into, like roots in its patch of earth. I sent out my lines, watched the word tapped into the search engine disappear into the immensity, like a fisherman with his first pre-sonar hunched over the dark sea. Blocks of sound in a saturated void:

François Langlais:

François Langlais, alias Pierre Chevrier. Born 1947. Member of a Quebec terrorist organization named Quebec Liberation Front (FLQ), responsible for many bombing attempts and kidnappings committed during the 1960s and 70s.

Arrested for carrying an illegal weapon in France at the end of the 1960s, sentenced to two years in prison. He became familiar with ways of making bombs and conducting kidnappings that would later serve him well in Quebec.

In the summer of 1970, Langlais travelled with other Quebec terrorists to Jordan, to receive commando training in a camp run by the Democratic Popular Front for the Liberation of Palestine (DPFLP). At the same time, the FLQ announced that they were planning to launch a selective assassination campaign in Quebec.

Langlais was a member of the Rebellion Cell that kidnapped and held hostage the British commercial attaché John Travers the next October, thereby unleashing a political crisis unprecedented in the annals of Quebec history. On October 10, the Chevalier Cell also went into action, kidnapping and later assassinating the number-two man in the provincial government, Paul Lavoie. The hoped-for uprising not taking place, Langlais and other members of the Rebellion Cell negotiated the life of their hostage in exchange for safe conduct to Cuba.

After a twelve-year exile in Cuba and France, François Langlais returned to Quebec and was immediately arrested, subjected to a trial, and sentenced to two years less a day for his participation in the kidnapping of John Travers. He would be out on parole less than a month later.

At first reading, two or three elements in the Wikipedia entry didn't add up. First, the story of his arrest for carrying an illegal weapon was news to me. Did he invent it, and if so, where did it come from?

My request for information addressed to the Prefect of Police at the Prefecture of Paris was, by all evidence, quickly relegated to the bottom of one of those forgotten stacks that make up that hexagonal labyrinth's charm.

The Wikipedia entry for le Chevreuil rehashed the well-known article from the *Sun* from November 25, about a possible link between the FLQ's Pierre and the international terrorists Zadig and Madwar, even suggesting that they had been to the same training camp in Jordan. Otherwise, how else to explain that the first kidnapping plot, which was nipped in the bud in February, had been aimed at the Israeli consul in Montreal?

These questions continued to spin around in my head for days on end. A visitor would have been able to follow my trail by looking at the brown, wet spots on the floor left by my too-full cup of coffee that was always overflowing. I didn't shave for weeks. The mirror reflected the eyes of an idiot staring into the dimly glowing distance somewhere above my head while my unbrushed hair shot flashes of static electricity into the bad light. The telephone never rang. The world shrank from my door. I knew that I was on the right track, but that was all I knew.

I had followed the debate about the fallibility of the online encyclopedia with interest. A fascinating project except for its principal flaw: the autoregulation of the system. One way of dealing with the problem was to remember that there's no smoke without some form of combustion. No effect without its cause. That in our thermodynamic universe, absolute disinterest is an illusion. A causal chain, a root of sense, attaches the most illusory hoax to reality. Conclusion: a pure lie is an impossibility. *Arrested for carrying an illegal weapon in France at the end of the 1960s, sentenced to two years in prison. It was then that he became familiar with ways of making bombs and conducting kidnappings that would later serve him well in Quebec.* A truth hidden in the chaos of stories? Or a simple bit of gossip?

These sentences had been tapped out on a keyboard by some anonymous contributor, someone who must have had a reason for doing so, that was what interested me. Where did the truth end and the legend begin?

When Noune jumped onto my desk to rub against my shoulder or cheek, she sometimes stepped on the keys of my computer keyboard, and what she typed probably made as much sense as anything I typed. When I stuffed another wild cherry log into the stove, the nails in the walls contracted with a sharp snap in the glacial night, and it was as if I were hearing music in my brain.

The night was getting on. I had gone back to sit in my office with a cup of anemic coffin varnish and reread the Wikipedia article for the dozenth time, when suddenly something leapt to my eyes.

The keywords that appeared at the top of the Web page read as follows: *article, discussion, modify, history.* I clicked history.

I discovered that the online encyclopedia gave access to the timeline of corrections, additions, crossings out, rewritings, and various other textual interventions that were normally eliminated by editorial work. It gave access to the history, not only of the subject of the article, but also of the article itself.

Fascinated, I worked backward down the chain of changes, jumping from one version to the next, following in reverse the thread of a series of modifications, mostly minor, but exhibiting a logical and fateful progression. It was as if, before my very eyes, the text opened like a flower to reveal the secret at its core, a sort of semantic buried bone that, exposed little by little to the light of day, eventually became the only thing visible. I then read the following curious notice:

François Langlais learned the art of terrorism in a camp for Palestinian commandos. Then he participated in numerous secret operations in Quebec during the 1970s. The Langlais family eventually moved to Alberta, Canada's oil-producing province, where it continued its struggle for Quebec independence. Today, a new generation of Langlais (including, among others, Dan Langlais and Ray Langlais) has emerged in the west of the country. It actively supports the FLQ and other radical groups linked, according to Canadian and American secret services, to the Islamic terrorist movement (Jihad).

This time the joke seemed obvious: the struggle for Quebec independence taken up in Alberta by a third generation, with Al-Qaida lurking in the background? Whatever!

It was a wink and a nudge, a joke among friends.

I read the entry again and again. It was quite frankly hilarious. The sun would rise another day, I would sleep through another night. Then I jumped.

I grabbed a pen and the first piece of paper that came to hand, and wrote the following words:

Dan Langlais = Daniel
Ray Langlais = Raymond
= Raymond Brossard and Daniel Prince = Zadig and Madwar

The next thing I knew I was standing in the snow, my eyes raised to the sky and its millions of stars. I played with drawing lines between them, making constellations, some familiar, others pure inventions. And in the frozen silence, all combinations were possible. To the east, the band of dark blue swelled behind the contrasting silhouettes of the evergreens. Not a sound could be heard, except for the vibrations from deep space that seemed to emanate from things themselves, from deaf life on a wild winter night at the edge of a northern lake.

They won't catch me firing a 12-gauge shotgun in the house again, no sir. I was no fool, I wasn't going to prove them right. Before throwing myself on the bed, I decided that if anyone in this vast universe wanted to play me for a fool, he would have to pay dearly for it.

RENÉ LAFLEUR VERSUS THE QUEEN

" . . . THE TRUTH, THE WHOLE TRUTH, and nothing but the truth. Say: I swear."

"Yeah."

"Yeah what?"

"I swear."

"Your witness, *Maître* Grosleau."

"Mr. Massicotte . . . If I understand alright, your actual profession is . . ."

"Er, social coordinator."

"And . . ."

"And I deliver chicken in my spare time. I worked two years for Baby Barbecue."

"Good. You are how old?"

"Er . . ."

"What year were you born?"

"Do I have to answer that?"

Sitting at the back of the courtroom, in the last row of seats, Chevalier looked up from his open notebook.

"It's not as if this were your first time in court, Mr. Massicotte," the prosecutor said quietly. "The court already has this information. I'm only asking you to confirm it. Just to break the ice, if that's all right with you."

"I'm thirty-six."

"How old?"

"Thirty-six."

In the section of the courtroom reserved for the press, the reporters remained impassive. But at the back of the spectators' section, his high creased forehead clearly visible at the end of the row, Citizen Branlequeue was scribbling away in his notebook.

In the defendant's box, René Lafleur, his eyes half-closed, was imagining himself balancing his canoe while casting a Mepps fly, a Black Fury No. 3, beyond a bed of water lilies that bordered the channel between the islands in Boucherville. Around him, light and reflections played on the water, pure Monet, and René, a practical man, was happy just feeling the all-embracing warmth of the sun on his skin, the gentle rocking of the wavelets that rippled in the channel like a muted echo of the river through a wall of vegetation. A sudden pressure, the rod bends, the feeling of moving weight at the end of it, the empearled line, taut, vibrating . . . the large-mouth bass must weigh a kilo, it strikes, leads with its nose, and leaps out of the water.

René remembers these things, the crunching of snowshoes on the deep, fine, dry snow of January; the clucking of autumn grouse under cranberry and hawthorn shrubs; the resinous smell borne on the breeze of a June day on a lake full of trout; and the freshness of the atomized, iridescent water suspended above the chaotic rocks in a northern rapids. In prison, such memories had helped him keep himself together.

It was 1973, and things had changed in the two years since his older brother, who had been found guilty of first-degree murder after a hasty trial, had been sent to a maximum security federal prison. Jean-Paul had defended himself, Gode had not. In the end, it hadn't made a bit of difference: the authorities had put the death of Lavoie on their backs and they had accepted it. As for Ben Desrosiers, who had not been directly involved in the assassination, he had been given twenty years for his part in the kidnapping.

In 1973, things worked differently, mostly because the flamboyant *Maître* Brien was out of prison. He had been acquitted on a charge of seditious conspiracy and had returned to the bar and re-established his practice. He had triumphed over the harassment of the judicial authorities, crossed the desert of administrative obstacles inflicted by the bar association, and was once again a force to be reckoned with.

Another difference since 1971: René was being tried in Montreal's municipal courthouse, not in a room in the headquarters of the QPP. The special trial on rue Parthenais was now a curiosity of history.

Maître Brien had explained to his client that the evidence against him was weak. A neighbour who claimed to have seen him at the wheel of a white Chevrolet on rue Collins sometime during the week in question. And experts had found his fingerprints on a box of chicken. "I'll beat that evidence raw," the lawyer had promised him.

Evidence for the Prosecution P-21
Invoice no. 10079
Rotisserie Baby Barbecue
Address: 3056 boulevard Taschereau, Longueuil
Date: 10/10/70

Order: three club sandwiches (3 x $1.60 = $4.80)
+ six Pepsis (6 x $0.15 = $0.90)
+ tax ($0.46)
= $6.16

"Do you recognize this exhibit?" asked the prosecutor.

Rénald looked briefly at the piece of paper held out to him by the bailiff.

"Yes."

"You recognize it as what?"

He hesitated for a moment.

"I don't like your question."

"You ... I beg your pardon?"

"I don't like your question."

As a prodigiously interested spectator, Chevalier made a note of this response in his notebook, then raised his head and met the gaze of *Maître* Brien who, from his seat, met his in return. The lawyer recognized him and allowed himself a faint smile, followed by a wink.

Chevalier turned his attention to the witness, who was rocking back and forth with his hands in his pockets. He saw in the man a certain resemblance to Gaston Lagaffe: the green pullover with its rolled collar, the toupée falling over his eyes. But his was greying. "A salt-and-pepper Lagaffe," he wrote.

"Tell me how the delivery went."

"I parked in front of the house. And then I saw someone come out and come down to the street to get the order."

"Did this someone speak to you?"

"I don't think so, no."

"And what house did this person come out of?"

"From that house — 140 Collins. The address that was written on the bill. I went back there later and there it was: 140 Collins."

"You say you went back to the place ... later?"

"Uh-huh. You don't have a problem with that, do you?"

"But you went back there when, exactly?"

"It's a personal matter."

"Excuse me?"

"It's my private life. It doesn't have anything to do with the trial."

Maître Brien stood up.

"Your Honour, if you'll permit me, very respectfully . . . I believe that what the witness is trying to tell the court is that he went back to see the famous house later, as a simple tourist, like a great many people in Quebec at the time. You know, a short drive-past, on a weekend, a pleasant little outing . . ."

The judge thought for a moment, then turned from the defence counsel and addressed the witness.

"This private life of yours, when was it, exactly? In the days immediately following the delivery?"

"Uh, well. Am I obliged to answer that?"

"You are under oath," rumbled *Maître* Grosleau.

"Yeah, but I don't see where all this is going."

"You say that you returned to the house after delivering the chicken on the tenth of October. When? A week later?"

"No, later than that."

"All right, we'll leave it at that," concluded the Crown prosecutor.

Chevalier continued to scribble in his notebook, then looked up and saw that everyone was peering in the same direction: toward the jury box, specifically at jury member 10, a frizzy-haired youth with an Afro haircut and enough hair poking up between his chest and his Adam's apple to stuff a La-Z-Boy, and an open magenta silk shirt revealing a medallion as big as a Frisbee.

He had raised his hand.

Jury member 10: "Excuse me for interrupting, but . . . isn't someone going to ask him if he would be able to recognize the guy who came out of the house to get the order?"

Finally, sighed Chevalier, someone who's doing his job.

The judge turned to the witness.

"Can you reply to the question?"

"Um..."

"What does that mean, um?"

"It means um. Um, as in um. I could still say something...What I do is between me and my conscience."

"You are under oath."

"Maybe so. But I'm the only one who knows if I'm telling the truth or not. And what my conscience is telling me is that I don't remember the person who came out to take the order."

"Does your conscience tell you anything else?"

"Yes. I'm afraid of the FLQ and I'm afraid of the mob, but I'm not afraid of the police."

"Excuse me, would you repeat what you just said, please?"

"I'm afraid of the FLQ and I'm afraid of the mob, but I'm not afraid of the police."

The Domaine des Salicaires was a modest-looking subdivision, designed for the ambitious working poor, otherwise known as the lower-middle class, the same people who had moved to the South Shore at the end of the Second World War to escape the slums of East Montreal, a human flotilla,the perpetuation of space and their laborious aptitude for happiness sublimated to the production of children.

A corrupt, or simply busy, developer, maybe both, had profited from the elastic nature of his contacts in city hall to wrangle a building permit, then dumped a few loads of gravel into a swamp that had been the home of reeds, bullfrogs, and red-winged blackbirds until then. He sketched out a few roads and divided it into building lots. Even when it didn't rain, the Branlequeues' basement filled with water, and the first time Éléonore saw a rat crossing the tiny rectangle of grass growing on the swamp that was their backyard, Chevalier had turned away and let the crisis pass. Then he had asked the neighbours about it.

"Is it the Norway rat that we have here?"

"No, it's the water rat. You should do what I do: I catch them in a leg-hold trap and by the end of spring I have a fur coat for my wife. And cooked in a stew you'd swear it was rabbit ..."

"It isn't the common sewer rat, Lonore," Chevalier announced triumphantly to his wife, "it's the ondatra!" He used the native word for muskrat. But Lonore was not the kind of person one could win over with a classic fur coat, especially when it was still running around in her backyard.

"You have to place the trap a certain way, so your rat drowns when it's caught," the neighbour had specified. "Otherwise it'll chew its leg off."

"I don't blame it," Chevalier Branlequeue had replied.

In these isolated suburban outposts, where maisonettes, enclosed courtyards, sandlots, swimming pools, and garden sheds edge out woods, fields, and wetlands with impunity, the arrival of a Harley-Davidson on a Saturday morning is the sort of thing that causes no more commotion than an ondatra crossing the end of the yard.

"My Sweet Lord, now it's the Hells Angels ..." whined Éléonore.

"More like a respectable lawyer," replied Chevalier, his nose at the window.

Chevalier Branlequeue was forty years old. His two sons, Martial and Pacifique, abandoned the skeleton of the scooter they were taking apart in the yard to surround the fire-and-chrome charger belonging to *Maître* Brien. They found the chopper's fork, installed by the lawyer shortly after the release of *Easy Rider*, particularly interesting.

Maître Mario, dressed in leather on this brisk spring day — the sun was as hard to catch as a flea, and a cold wind was blowing in off the lake — was greeted at the door by Chevalier.

"You're very lucky, Chevalier: two tall lads to carry on the family name, already practically grown..."

"Oh, I know what you're thinking," replied Chevalier, busying himself with the coffee maker. "For you, I'm nothing but a poor guy worried about barbecuing and the continuation of the race. When you see a child's bicycle in the lane, you allow yourself a brief moment of tenderness, but not enough to make you regret the interchangeable young hippie chicks you hang around with in the Gaspésie on your machine. With the exhaust fumes drowning out the smell of drying cod, it's a perfect life."

"I wouldn't say that, Chevalier. In the world's eye, you're a father second and the immortal author of *Elucubrations* first, the pride of our national literature!"

"Yes, well, the author of a single book who's a little frazzled around the edges and too well known not to be a little suspect..."

Brien shrugged and looked at the Saturday newspapers scattered on the kitchen table. The mistress of the house was raising dust and making noise in the next room.

"I read your diatribe in the letters-to-the-editor column," he said.

"No need to say anything," the poet–publisher said amiably, and smiled. "I was expecting your visit. Let's go into my office."

Maître Brien took a flask from the pocket of his leather jacket and liberally baptized his coffee.

"A drop of brandy, Chevalier? And by the way, is it all right, my calling you Chevalier?"

Branlequeue agreed to both propositions.

The house plan was six rooms; one bedroom for Vénus, another shared by the two boys, even though Martial already had one foot out the door. The father had been spending most of his nights on the mattress in his office for some time. When one looked toward the end of the street, one could see, in the distance, boats passing on the St. Lawrence.

From another pocket of his leather jacket, the lawyer produced a newspaper clipping dated that same day: Chevalier Branlequeue's contribution occupied three-quarters of the page devoted to the *vox populi*. *Maître* Brien had simply torn it out, folded it in eight, and stuck it in his pocket.

"*A comedy meticulously plotted,*" he read. "Holy Crumb, Chevalier, since when have you been a theatre critic? We're on the same team, you and I. And here you are, in the act of scoring in our own net. Because if you say that the trial is fixed, how does that make me look, eh?"

"Like the court jester," Chevalier said, hiding a smile behind his cup of coffee.

At the window, the wind could be heard whistling through the clumps of reeds and shrubs at the edge of the yard. The red-winged blackbirds, perched on their bulrush stems, flashed their bright red wing patches like adolescents on motorbikes. Dissonant and imperious, their strident calls filled the air.

Chevalier folded his arms and leaned back in his chair.

"Massicotte, the chicken delivery man, is a Crown witness, so what rhyme or reason did he have to ham it up like that?"

"He's one of ours, Chevalier. A patriot. Haven't you figured that out yet?"

"Some patriot. Two years ago, at another trial, he gave his age as forty-two. And now he's down to thirty-six. Is it normal for a deliverer of chicken to lie like an actress when asked about his age? Or maybe Baby Barbecue's famous recipe, with thirty-three spices, is the new fountain of youth?"

"He's a strange one, I'll give you that. But his testimony has been the most useful one yet, from my point of view."

"But he was at the point of identifying his client. Did he perjure himself?"

The silence that followed was pierced by the sharp, disagreeable notes of the blackbirds and cowbirds defending their territories, black kamikaze jabberers dive-bombing invading crows.

"Don't you find that bizarre? The guy's a witness for the prosecution, and he clams up? So, who did he see?"

It was Brien's turn to lean back in his chair.

"Sorry, old boy. Professional ethics."

"You mean yours or his?"

"Very funny. But I've just had an idea, Chevalier. If I get René Lafleur acquitted, will you stop treating me publicly like a puppet of the system?"

"You'll never get him acquitted."

"How much do you want to bet?"

"I can't afford to bet. But this is a circus, not a trial."

Maître Brien tipped his head back and drank directly from his flask. Then he poured another drop into his coffee, replaced the cork, sighed with satisfaction, and returned the flask to his pocket.

"You'll see. In the meantime, stop pissing people off with your damned conspiracy theories in the Saturday papers, okay?"

If *Maître* Brien, known as the Maestro to his friends, had been programmed to live for a thousand years, there's no doubt he would still be talking about how the trial of René Lafleur was his finest hour in the year 2942. But he was destined to die peacefully, if that word can be applied to dying in his sleep at the age of sixty-six, to be discovered lifeless in his house on the shore of the Gaspé, on the living-room sofa, where his girlfriend of the moment, an ex-pole dancer and rodeo champion, had sent him to contemplate his sins for the night. He had exiled his practice to this county seat a few years previously and had almost been forgotten. Being away from the public eye had never been his desire, however, and he had resurfaced from time to time as an aging rebel who one fine morning would get back on his 750-cc bike with its extensions to the exhaust system, the better to blast away at political rectitude. In his later years, not having any terrorists to defend, he had made himself the champion of bands of motorcycle cops cheated by their Swiss bankers.

Dying on a sofa was appropriate. He had slept with 1,743 women, snorted four kilograms of cocaine up his nose, poured 430,000 ounces of beer down his throat, as well as 7,200 litres of gin, cognac, and brandy and, for the past several years, a good half a cubic metre of pills. A cerebral embolism took him.

At times, the cross-examinations and sword fights between the rival lawyers took on the aspect of a street brawl. In the end, *Maître* Brien trounced *Maître* Grosleau, gave him a vigorous public thrashing. It wasn't a pretty sight. Years later, when he was watching a sports program and saw Mohammed Ali, in a ring in Kinshasa, allow himself to be taken to the ropes to absorb punches from his adversary, and then grapple with him bodily before suddenly ringing his opponent's bell with a right hook that came out of nowhere, Chevalier thought of the defence lawyer for René Lafleur. Like Ali, *Maître* Brien was a master at the art of trash talk.

As for René's fingerprints on the box of chicken, the Maestro threw them in the face of the experts during cross-examination. He had noticed a slight difference between the chicken box given as evidence in the courtroom and that shown in the official photographs.

"What happened to the flap?" he asked a specialist who'd come to testify.

"I don't know. I must have torn it off. Maybe it was dirty..."

"Good thinking. Except that in the photograph, this one, it isn't dirty at all, and the shadow has disappeared."

"It's because the flap was covered in powder."

"Powder?" murmured the defence counsel, his nostril twitching despite himself.

"Yeah, the powder we used to take fingerprints. The carton was greasy and the powder stuck to it."

"Don't give me any bullshit about fingerprint powder! In the photograph, we see two flaps on the Baby Barbecue box, but one of those flaps is missing on the box in evidence. Why?"

"You're being very technical today," *Maître* Grosleau said, casting a sly glance at his rival's notoriously active member above the American Standard stall in the row of urinals during the break.

"In that regard, I belong to the old school," agreed Mario, reining in his engine. "A photo is not reality. To seem is not to be, that is the question these days, my dear sir."

"But we're talking about one and the same goddamned chicken box, and you know it," fumed *Maître* Grosleau.

"Fine. Then prove it," *Maître* Brien said carelessly, turning his back on the lawyer to pat his curly locks in the mirror above the sinks.

"The defence's only strategy," *Maître* Raymond Grosleau intoned, addressing the jury, "has been to try to cast doubt on the fact that the accused was actually in the premises at 140 rue Collins, in Saint-Hubert, between the tenth and seventeenth of October 1970. My esteemed colleague for the defence has used all of his considerable talents to make you believe that there is a distinct possibility that someone other than the accused (and other than his two accomplices, who have already been found guilty of murder), for example, a member of another cell, was called in as reinforcement at the last minute. Perhaps he did this when the affair had started to take a wrong turn, and the member of the other cell committed the fatal act in his stead. My eminent colleague has pushed this insinuation so far as to actually ask this court to send a commission of enquiry to Cuba, in order to, and I quote, 'shed more light on the interpenetration [sic] of the Rebellion and Chevalier cells during the October Crisis.'

"But if it were someone else who, pardon the expression, did the deed . . . and if this person is now living outside the country, let us say in a totalitarian system, and is now therefore beyond the reach of our laws, not subject to Canadian justice, and without any hope of ever setting foot in this country again, then why not give us his or her name? Why refuse to denounce whoever it is if such an accusation can do no harm, someone to whom such an accusation cannot prevent him or her from continuing to warm themselves on the beaches of Cuba, in their socialist workers' paradise and under the pleasant protection of a Soviet nuclear umbrella, when such an accusation could contribute in a very decisive manner here, today, in whitewashing the man who is before you of any accusation and helping him to avoid a sentence of life imprisonment?"

"Because we're not informers," growled René Lafleur from behind his month-old beard.

The judge called a return to order, and the prosecutor repeated that René Lafleur's fingerprints had been taken from a jar of mustard, a can of Le Sieur number 3 peas, a can of tobacco, and a bag of candies that had been purchased in anticipation of Hallowe'en.

"It's true that these objects may have been in the house before October 10, which was why he insisted to the end on the fact that the prints of the young man in question were also taken from one of the boxes from the Rotisserie Baby Barbecue delivered to the address in question during the fateful week."

Maître Brien's summation lasted two full days, and if the duel between him and *Maître* Grosleau could evoke the Ali–Foreman fight of 1974 in Zaire, this latest piece of the anthology, impossible to reproduce here, was like the famous fifth round, during which the aspirant, after having warded off the worst blows from his opponent, suddenly burst off the ropes to deliver a series of direct hits with both gloves that succeeded in making Foreman's face look like half a battered watermelon floating like a cork on the surface of a tormented sea.

Brien began by spreading open the chicken box on the back of his hand. "The public prosecutor," he said, "tried to prove that this box, produced in evidence in this court, came from rue Collins. The investigators could easily," he postulated, "have procured it from a chicken deliverer sympathetic to the Crown ...

"As for the young man that the neighbour saw at the wheel of the white Chevy, he had medium-long hair. However, a witness came into this court and certified that in October 1970 the younger of the Lafleur brothers was clean-cut. Who was it, in fact, who sported a 'mod' haircut that autumn? Whose hair completely hid his ears in the photos of the Chrysler following behind a moving phalanx of police cars on the day that Travers was freed? François Langlais, that's who. And who signed the ownership papers for the white Chevy under an assumed name? François Langlais. To which FLQ member were the following two connections traced: a link with the white Chevy and a mod haircut? François Langlais. And who, according to what we know, assured the liaison between the Chevalier and Rebellion cells? François Langlais. In each case, the same man!"

Toward the end of his summation, the Maestro insisted at great length on the right of the accused to remain silent. In Canadian law, he reminded the jury, no trial has the authority to exact an oath from an accused person except in the case of a trial for treason. "But René Lafleur is not a traitor. He's a patriot. Ladies and gentlemen of the jury, two days ago my eminent colleague for the prosecution terminated his summation by telling you that the accused has not proven that he didn't kill. The least I can say to that is that is one strange conception of burden of proof! But I'll leave you now to judge for yourselves..."

René took his mother in his arms. Everyone pressed around him. Chevalier saw a young hippie trying to flirt with the judge, whom she said to anyone who would listen that she found attractive in his wig. For one moment, Branlequeue's gaze met that of *Maître* Brien, and in his eyes he still saw the sombre intensity of battle. The lawyer for the FLQ gave him a defiant and satisfied wink, as much as to say:

"You owe me a beer, my friend."

CHEVREUIL

A GLADIATOR ARMED WITH a net and trident, a retriarius, stared out into the silent shadows with lifeless, gleaming eyes. Farther down, skulls lit by indirect lighting grinned immobile. Farther still, past the entrance to the catacombs, beside the first cross planted in the old rock bristling with blue-flag irises from the Gaspé, the man from Saint-Malo was talking to the great Chief Donnacona. In other dark rooms, the colonial pomp of Frontenac's little court, monographs on the Native Peoples of Cataraqui, the Sieur de Maisonneuve, and the good Jeanne Mance were displayed. There had been so many others who had taken possession of this land and repelled the evil Iroquois and the bloody English, lost Quebec, then Montreal, and resisted the advances of Benjamin Franklin and the incursions of New England generals.

Across from the wax museum there were three old-style apartment buildings. The street was variously called the Chemin de la Reine-Maire, Queen Mary Road, or just Chemin Queen Mary by the people of Montreal. In the living room of apartment number six, in the building situated at 3730, François Langlais, Richard Godefroid, Jean-Paul Lafleur, and Benoit Desrosiers were sitting quietly. Dawn had arrived; it was November 4, 1970. They had been talking all night, keeping their voices low for the most part, because the walls have ears. Between them, separating and reuniting them in the brotherhood of blood, was the Minister of Labour, Paul Lavoie, as thin and pale for his date with history as one of the statues in the miserable pantheon created from the ends of candles in the well-appointed museum across the road. The others occupying the apartment were either asleep or pretending to be.

Gode looked at Pierre Chevrier, whom he'd known since childhood as François, the Little Genius of grade seven, and who was now as pale and haggard as the rest of them. For an instant he saw him again in his choir-boy robes, serving mass for Father Gamache, the curate with the Mohawk. More than a few megawatts had flowed under the bridge since those days.

"Amen to that," said Jean-Paul. "Lavoie played his hand and lost. His bluff came back to kick him in the ass. I'm not going to cry over spilt milk. What I'm more concerned about is what's happening now. We're going to need your help, Pierre. We're spinning our wheels, here."

"They're spinning their wheels up in Montreal North, too," replied le Chevreuil.

"Maybe, but up there they've still got their bargaining chip."

"Lancelot doesn't want to know about you guys. He says you've fucked everything up."

"Yeah? And who's dropped the ball, eh, Pierre?"

Pierre lowered his eyes, a boy from the South Shore like them. He remained silent.

"You, they're not searching for you, no one suspects you. You can walk around, you're free to come and go where you want. Ask

Lancelot if he can take us."

"He won't want to."

"Then find us another place to hide. And we need more money. We're broke. We can't stay here."

"I'll see what I can do ..."

Passing in front of Gode, Pierre nodded and, without looking at him, said:

"He played you like a group of school kids ..."

"Who? You mean Lavoie?"

"Not so loud," said Jean-Paul. "We're not going there again. It happened. And we can't do anything about it now. What's important is to get our stories straight, to all say the same thing ... Listen to me, you guys: it's the government who killed him."

They all looked at him.

"That's our story. It was after hearing Vézina nail the last nails in the lid of his coffin, on Friday afternoon on television, that he tried to throw himself out the window and cut himself to shreds like that. It was an act of desperation. Everything that happened after was caused by that one act. That's what we tell them. It's the government who condemned him to death. Does anyone here have a problem with that?"

His gaze made the rounds. No one objected. "So it's settled."

The dawn filtered in through the curtains. The television had been on the whole time. The head of the Great Chief of the End of Emissions was searching for Indians in the snow.

In the subway car, his left hand clutching the metal pole, Pierre idly scrutinized the faces of the people around him. The too-blonde woman with the lined yellowed face, the one with the frizzy brown hair carrying the Adidas bag. Waitress? Security guard? Was she going on shift? Was he going home to sleep? What did all these people do in life? Whose job was written all over their face?

He'd once read a story about a fox who escaped from some dogs by running into the middle of a flock of sheep, jumping onto the back of one of them, and clinging to its wool and thereby evading his pursuers. At seven o'clock in the morning on a weekday, at the Berri-de-Montigny subway station, there were plenty of Saint-Jean-Baptiste sheep about, but the similarity ended there. Because Pierre's problem, as he headed back to the north end of the city, was that some of the dogs sometimes behaved like foxes, English foxes or not, and were wandering into the flock themselves.

The worker in the plaid shirt, green work pants and workboots, who was reading his *Montréal-Matin*. *Too obvious, that newspaper trick.* The accountant with his moustache and double-thick lenses, in his late thirties, greying hair well-combed, attaché case resting on his knees. *Maybe.*

He casually turned his head a quarter turn and became interested in a young man in a purple windbreaker and black serge pants, short-cropped brown hair, face a bit red, hands thrust into the pockets of his jacket. You couldn't find a more ordinary-looking guy. But no bag, no briefcase, nothing in his hands and God knew what was in his pockets. Where was he going, and to do what? Their eyes met briefly and Pierre had the impression that the other man reacted to the visual invasion of his territory, was confronting him without either smiling or looking away. He turned his own eyes and furtively looked at a young woman wearing tight-fitting clothes, an Indian blouse, green velour bell-bottoms, candy-pink high-heeled boots. A hippie, maybe. *Yes, maybe.*

They could be bearded, wearing bracelets, they could have bad breath, big boobs, a lunch pail. They could be old and decrepit, they could have dandruff, long hair, a ponytail, half their face could be disfigured by scars from an accident involving hot grease or acid, the skin as red as raw steak. That's how you can recognize a professional: you can't.

And he, the former aficionado of Sherlock Holmes and Arsène Lupin, was now involved in his own living novel. The genial bloodhound and the master of disguises. The one who hides himself, the one who searches for the hidden. Rarely both at the same time. But this morning, in the subway car full of workers and students, he felt the long, sleepless night in his body, he felt like a man of forty, and this time the roles were reversed. He was the one who was searching, and they were the ones who were hidden.

"Okay," he said to himself, "let's try to spot at least one before Henri-Bourassa…"

The others, Jean-Paul, Gode, Lancelot, all committed the same mistake; they looked for cops who looked like cops. Plainclothes police, inspectors in suits. Not him. Because le Chevreuil *knew*.

On the down escalator in the Henri-Bourassa station, he noticed that the young man in the windbreaker was following closely behind him. Nothing unusual there, everyone was going down. This was the terminus. Casting a glance over his shoulder, he again met the fellow's eye looking up at him. Hands still shoved into his jacket pockets, half a dozen steps back. The man took his time before looking away.

Pierre went to stand in line for the bus and, from the corner of his eye, verified that the young man had done the same thing. Standing there, hands in his pockets, three people behind him. For a moment Pierre's heart beat harder. He advanced toward the bus's open door, then abruptly left the line and walked quickly away and joined the line for the bus headed in the opposite direction. This time the man in the purple windbreaker waited a good five seconds, then calmly walked over and stood behind him.

Now le Chevreuil was certain. His mind worked at lightning speed.

He turned brusquely and met the man's eyes. Without the least attempt at dissembling, the man returned his look and accompanied it with a barely perceptible nod of his head. Then the shadow of a smile appeared on his face.

Finally Pierre understood: an open tail.

He turned on his heels, resisted the impulse to break into a run, and hurried off, taking long strides, and jumped into the first taxi he came to without looking around. He slammed the door.

"1345 rue de la Compagnie-de-Jésus," he told the driver.

FALSE WALL

ON SATURDAY THE SEVENTEENTH, I'd promised Marie-France we'd go dancing at the Café Campus or in Old Montreal. Instead, René and I turned up at suppertime looking like a couple of ghosts who hadn't slept for two days. Jean-Paul had been crashing there since the previous night. René had blood on his pants and he asked Bellechasse, Marie-France's younger brother and roommate, if he could borrow a pair of his. "What for?" asked the brother-in-law (ex-brother-in-law, actually). "Because mine are dirty." The other looked down, saw the dark stains, and asked René, as a joke, if he'd stuck a pig or something, and René said no, he'd been on a hunting trip and could Bellechasse lend him a pair of pants? Because he'd made a mess of his.

As it turned out, it was a waste of time, because when Nicole and René disappeared into the bedroom soon after that, I found some pants that, clean or not, were bunched up in a pile in the corner. It had been at least three weeks since the two lovebirds had seen each other, so it wasn't a surprise, my friends. As far as my situation went, I was still doing penance. Jean-Paul was in the kitchen, editing a communiqué. I went into the living room and lay down on the sofa to watch *Hockey Night in Canada*, as exhausted as an old dead rat. I could hardly keep my eyes open, in there by myself, listening to Nicole moaning over René Lecavalier's play-by-play.

I opened my eyes with a start and there it was: the Chevrolet, Hangar 12, the fence, the police cars, cameras flashing. It was like a nightmare that started up again every time you wake up.

"They found it," said Marie-France. There was no more noise coming from Nicole and René in the back bedroom. Just the voice of the reporter on the black-and-white TV in the living room. Marie-France looked at me oddly and said that responsibility for the murder had been claimed by a new FLQ cell.

I looked surprised. I was surprised. I looked at Jean-Paul.

"It's the Dieppe Royal 22nd Cell," he said, without taking his eyes off the screen.

In Sunday's papers there was a photo of Jean-Paul, wanted in connection with the kidnapping and murder of Paul Lavoie. That night, the television made the same announcement, making him out to be a killer and a danger to the public.

"Not a very good photograph," commented the danger in question. He held the newspaper up at eye level as though it were a pocket mirror. "I'm usually a lot better looking than that, don't you think?"

The Tuesday before, he'd had his face rearranged by the police when they picked him up in a raid, and so his joke didn't go over so well. He told the women that the pigs had brought him to the station to ask him a few questions and had given him a pretty rough going over. All the rest of that day, I could feel Marie-France's

accusatory looks sliding over me like sulphuric acid down the back
of a duck.

On Monday, Marie-France went back to her courses at the University of Montreal. With the imposition of the War Measures Act,
her studies had been suspended. Now her profs had begun teaching
again, and the students stood on campus gaping at the army helicopters.

She came back in the middle of the afternoon, rang the bell the
number of times we'd agreed on, six, and we unlocked the door
from the top of the stairs. She had just run into her brother on the
stairs.

"He told me he was going out to buy wood . . . What's that all
about?"

René was unrolling a rug in the hallway. He looked up.

"We're doing some renovations."

"Hey, where did that old rug come from?"

"It was in Nicole's parents' shed. It'll cut down on the noise, so
we don't disturb the neighbours."

"It's a disgusting colour."

Bellechasse, the ex-brother-in-law. A young prick, thin as a rail, hair
falling down over his eyes. Said he wanted in on the action. Any
action would do. He came from Saint-Profond, in the Bois-Francs
region, and had stopped off at the Fisherman's Hut for the festival
at Manseau, all the best drugs on his resumé. Barely able to put one
foot in front of the other without help, but ready to try anything, so
why not revolution. He was the one who delivered the communiqués that Jean-Paul continued to write, to all the phone booths and
trash bins in Centre-Ville. On the run.

The large closet beside the front door of the apartment suddenly
fascinated René. Especially its depth. He measured it and came up

with his project. That night, the ex-brother-in-law came back to the apartment with six large sheets of plywood and boards cut to the right length, according to instructions given to him by René.

The Renovator got to work the next day. Using the plywood, he built a false wall for the back of the closet, plastered the joints, then covered it with wallpaper. The sheet was removable from the bottom left, and so it was actually a kind of door. With hooks screwed at the four corners, he could pull it closed from the inside. The false bottom was impossible to detect from the hallway, and even from inside the closet. On the other side, René installed two large tables for an office or to serve as beds.

"The wallpaper is a disgusting colour," said Marie-France.

"What did you do with Lavoie's confession?" I asked René.

"Nicole went out and opened a safety deposit box at the bank, and it's in there: as security."

"We aren't going to send it to the papers?"

"Not right away. In any case, they'd never publish it. They'll say it's a fake..."

"But it has to get out. There must be some way."

"It wouldn't do any good. Jean-Paul says we should wait. Let the dust settle for a bit."

According to the papers, the only thing we didn't do to Lavoie was cut off his cock and shove it down his throat. Jean-Paul said to me:

"You should write a communiqué to explain what happened..."

"Why me?"

"Because you were there, with René. And you're also the one who makes the fewest errors. So..."

So I wrote communiqué number seven to explain that we never

tortured Lavoie, and that his wounds had been self-inflicted when he tried to escape.

The next day, we watched the state funeral on television. Saw the security measures, cordons of soldiers surrounding the hearse, helicopters circling the cathedral steeple, and sharpshooters posted on all the roofs. Little Albert climbed out of his limousine, like the star student in a class of penitents.

The following day Nicole's friends came to the apartment and we tried out our hiding place. Not great in the comfort department, but we could stay seated in it, lie down for a bit, drink water, piss in a pot, smoke cigarettes. René had even put in an air vent, which also gave us a bit of light.

No justice. Nicole and René continued to send each other to seventh heaven at least four times a day. It was the only sound we heard. After the hockey game on Saturday night, I slept on the sofa in the living room. Marie-France's brother slept at his girlfriend's most of the time, and Jean-Paul took his room. When I think of how much hay the journalists would make with numerous scenes of the apartment that fall, turning it into a kind of theatre! For me it wasn't complicated, it was my nest.

That morning — about five o'clock — I bumped into Marie-France in the kitchen. She couldn't sleep, either, and was warming some milk. I pulled up a chair. She was naked under a plaid jacket she'd taken from a coat hook in the hall. Her hair tumbled wildly on her forehead and over her eyes, and caressed her cheeks. Under the table, I was as hard as a humpbacked whale.

I knew what she was going to ask me.

"Gode . . . Are you ever going to tell me why you're mixed up in all this?"

"The less you know, the better."

Her eyes went from me to the bedroom, where Jean-Paul was snoring like a fighter jet.

"He scares me…"

"Jean-Paul? Come on."

"I'm telling you, he scares me. Tomorrow, you've got to tell him he has to leave, okay?"

"I can't do that. He's wanted by the police. If he goes, I go with him."

"If you get my brother mixed up in this business, I'll…"

"You'll what, Marie-France?"

We looked at one another. We had come to a certain pass.

"If he keeps his mouth shut," I said, "there won't be a problem. And that goes for you, too."

Down the hall, in the girls' room, the two lovebirds were screwing as if there were no tomorrow, and no doubt they were right. Marie-France came and lay down beside me on the sofa and let me put my arms around her, but that was all. Nothing else to do but listen to the two sex maniacs in the next room groaning and sighing, and the mattress shrieking as if it were being torn apart.

Two hours later, Marie-France woke me up by shaking the morning newspaper in front of my face. My portrait and that of René were there beside Jean-Paul's on the wanted poster. The reward for any information leading to our arrest was fixed at $75,000. The kidnappers of Travers were worth another $75,000.

"Where are you going?" I asked, but I already knew the answer.

"I've rented a room in town…I can't go on living here."

I was completely sure she wouldn't denounce us. But that didn't stop me, when she went through the door, from feeling well and truly fucked.

THE CHESS GAME

THE MORNING PIERRE LEARNED of Ben's arrest, Travers turned his back on him, sitting on a hard, wooden straight-backed chair beside a card table on which was the previous day's copy of the *Montreal Sun* and a chess board. The hostage was wearing a white shirt with the collar unbuttoned and a charcoal-grey woollen vest. His hood had been lifted so that he could read. Its dark material framed his face and encircled his neck and shoulders like a chador. The TV in the far corner was on, but the sound was turned down so that it was nothing but a flickering square of contrasting light and darkness. The single window was boarded up with a sheet of plywood nailed in place. In the middle of the room, a pillow without a slip and a grey woollen blanket had been thrown over a mattress on the floor. A white sheet pinned to one wall and bolts screwed into the floor completed the room's decor. The diplomat was reading an Agatha Christie in French: *Murder on the Orient Express*, a pocket edition. Seated behind him, on the floor, his back propped against the wall

461

beside the television, Pierre was holding his M1 by the barrel. The sawn-off stock trailed down to the floor. His face was uncovered.

"What's so funny this morning?" asked the hostage, in broken French, addressing Pierre without turning to look at him, as he had been instructed to do.

The British accent gave his quite passable French a kind of distinction. He liked to talk.

"The news," Pierre replied. "The police have found the apartment where our friends were hiding out, up on the mountain. But they only succeeded in arresting one of them. The three others were in a closet with a false wall, and they stayed in it until the next night. When the cops guarding the apartment left for dinner, our guys quietly came out of their hidey-hole, slipped out the back door, and grabbed a taxi! Arsène Lupin couldn't have done a better job," le Chevreuil concluded, laughing.

He had lived in England and spoke excellent English, but this was Montreal, and he wanted to mark his territory.

"The police aren't exactly brilliant," observed Travers. "Didn't they ... leave someone behind to keep an eye on the premises?"

Pierre took a moment to think before replying.

"No ... why would they? What are you insinuating?"

"Nothing. I'm just saying it wasn't very *wise* of them, that's all."

"It sounds like you've got something in mind, Travers."

The hostage smiled to himself.

"I think you have something in mind. What happened to your friends?"

"Someone helped them out. They're in a sugar cabin somewhere."

"A ... *Sorry*," Travers said, "I didn't catch that word ... a what?"

"A sugar cabin. You know, sugar, as in 'sugar off.'" He was suddenly annoyed, for some reason. He improved his mood by toying with the back of Travers's cowled neck with the barrel of his M1.

The hostage isn't exactly smiling, but he almost is. A glimmer shines in the back of his deep-set eyes. He's sitting on a case of dynamite, at least that's what it says on it. His torso is sharply silhouetted against the whiteness of the sheet in the background. The box beneath him is empty.

"I feel like I'm in showbiz," he says in his most arch tone.

"You are," Lancelot assures him, clicking the camera's shutter.

Élise absently aims the assault weapon at the aging body visible through the steam running down the shower curtain. The door to the bathroom is open behind her.

Elsewhere in the apartment, Corbeau is watching television, Lancelot is typing a communiqué on the typewriter, Pierre, curled up in the fetid folds of an old sofa chair, is trying to concentrate on the issue of *L'Express* that contains the famous interview in which Jean-Paul talks about the FLQ.

Sometimes Nick Mansell comes and leaves with the latest communiqué. He takes care of distribution, and usually is careful to avoid the crowded apartment.

Suddenly the sound of running water stops, and Élise turns away slowly from the curtain that is briskly pulled aside by the hostage; she sees him dripping, nude. She notes the greying hair, the glistening drops of water caught in his pubic bush. Travers makes no effort to cover himself.

Without looking at him, she tosses him a terry-cloth towel, her eyes staring at her own blushing image in the fogged-over mirror. She is twenty-five. She likes to say she's getting wrinkles. She wants to have children, later, but in the meantime is aiming, almost point blank, the barrel of an M1 assault rifle at a man who is naked, virile, and unarmed.

Travers, the towel wrapped around his shoulders, is still displaying his virility. He has the beginnings of an erection. Now he slowly dries his ribs.

"Would you mind covering your privates?" she asks drily.

"My what? My soldiers?"

"Come on, Travers! Dry your tired, drooping pizzle and get dressed. Let's get out of here."

The hostage vigorously rubs the towel between his legs and upper thighs.

"How do you say . . . in French, to dip one's wick? It's been six weeks now that I haven't dipped my wick. Well, you know, even at my age . . ." He jiggles his penis and calls out like a young moose in rut: "Come on, I'm so horny! I'm hot to trot, baby . . ."

"Stop it!" Élise cries, shaking the machine gun back and forth as though trying to brush the steam aside.

Travers doesn't stop. He's as cool and controlled as a talk-show host.

"You have . . . what, a problem? With me? Or is it your husband who's the problem? Is he still . . . what's the word? Elsewhere?"

"He's out buying newspapers."

"That's what he told you."

"Get dressed, you old pervert! You sleazebag!"

"You want to be like a man, do the same thing men do for your revolution, but if you were a man, Élise, you wouldn't have a problem looking at me, so why . . ."

"Mind your own business and I'll mind mine, okay?"

"And what would your business be, miss? Doing the dishes?"

When Lancelot finally sticks his nose in the bathroom, he sees his sister shoving the barrel of her automatic deep into the diplomat's hirsute belly. Travers is bent double, awkwardly trying to protect himself with the aid of his towel.

"Stop it! Can't you see he's just playing with your head?"

Pierre is walking down Saint-Catherine. He stops in a convenience store, buys cigarettes. Newspapers. He leaves, looking to the left and to the right. Goes into a tavern. He orders a draft, then a second. Over his glass, he surreptitiously watches the other clients. Scrutinizes the regulars, looking for an overlooked detail.

Shoes a little too polished on that one.

He knows they're here, all around him. They're toying with him.

The sales rep eating pork tongue and a pickled egg, washing it down with a Dow.

The man whose moist lips are pursed but no air is coming out of them.

The one who comes up to you and offers to sell you some baseball tickets.

He leaves. No one follows him. He takes the subway. The Orange Line toward Henri-Bourassa. In the car, he relaxes his surveillance, closes his eyes. Almost dozes.

Not even in moments when his lucidity seems to give way to delusions of persecution can he convince himself that each of the nine other people in the car is a policeman in civilian clothing, a member of the Royal Canadian Mounted Police's watch team. That, however, is in fact the case.

Lancelot waved the *Montréal-Matin* practically in his face.

FLQ MEMBER HANGS SELF IN LONDON

If the London *Standard Tribune* is to be believed, a young French-Canadian, Luc Goupil, described as a sympathizer with the Quebec Liberation Front (FLQ), hanged himself last weekend in a prison cell in Reading, England.

According to the article in this London newspaper, the young man of twenty-five hanged himself from the bars of his cell with the aid of his shirt just as the police at Scotland Yard were preparing to interrogate him about recent FLQ activities, in particular those of Jean Lancelot, suspected of being one of the principals responsible for the kidnapping of British diplomat John Travers...

Pierre looked up from the newspaper.

"Oh, shit."

Lancelot pulled up a chair and, sitting across from him, examined him attentively.

"They killed him," Pierre said, slowly shaking his head.

"We don't know that. Listen, it's not as if we're talking about a model of mental stability."

"They killed him," Pierre repeated.

He stood up. Headed for the door in a state of shock.

"Where are you going?"

"For a walk. I need some air. I feel like I'm choking..."

That night, he dreams he is climbing up a scaffold. The gallows have been erected in the middle of Hyde Park. A large but indistinct crowd has gathered around it. The hangman pulling the hood over his head is Karl Marx. While he places the noose around his neck, the maid who helps him grabs the condemned man's sex and yanks it like a lever, as though his penis controls the opening of the trap, and the floor disappears from under his feet and he plunges, crying and gasping, into wakefulness.

He stares up at the ceiling.

The sound of the trap door in his dream exists in reality, but is coming from above rather than from under his feet, as though someone is slowly pushing a piece of heavy furniture across the floor of the upstairs apartment.

At four o'clock in the morning.

Footsteps, the creaking of joists. Then, nothing.

Pierre remembers meeting the tenants of the apartment above theirs on the stairs, a couple, both tiny, is all he recalls of them.

Then he thinks of himself as a child, a good Catholic, a cherubic server at mass in Quebec, kneeling before Cardinal Léger. He does not want to think about Goupil, with his angel's voice, like an androgynous Mick Jagger. Where are his guardian angels now? Protect me. Did he ever believe? Monsters under his bed, the terror of the dark?

The apartment above has again fallen silent. And Pierre is no longer a schoolboy. He tries to figure out what has changed. He knows.

The guardian angels and the devils are working together now.

John Travers, apparently well rested, was waiting for him in front of chessboard, across from the empty chair.

Chevreuil sat down. He was wearing his hood. Travers let him have white. After a moment's thought, he moved a pawn.

"I could ask you what's making you so . . . upset? Is that the right word? Yesterday . . ."

"One of our friends is dead," replied Pierre.

"Oh. Was it . . . an accident?"

"I don't want to talk about it." Chevrier shot a feverish look at the hostage through the slits in his hood.

Travers silently considered his opponent for a moment, then picked up the detective novel he'd left on the table. He'd finished it the night before.

"Have you read this?"

"*Murder on the Orient Express*," Pierre read on the cover. "I've read it, but I forget how it ends."

He shrugged and moved a knight.

"The victim, you will recall, died on a train, killed by twelve stabs of a knife..."

"Now that you mention it..."

"In the end," said Travers, studying the chessboard square by square and then the eyes of his adversary through the holes in the hood, "we learn that the murder victim had been a kidnapper ... a man who had kidnapped a girl and demanded a ransom for her, years ago. But when the ransom was paid, he reneged on his promise to release the girl, you see..."

Pierre nodded without saying a word.

"And so, later, he changed his identity and disappeared, but friends of the girl's parents, you understand ... these friends track him down and organize an act of vengeance. They're all on the train, travelling under false identities, and they have him trapped."

Pierre looked at Travers. It was his turn to play.

"There were twelve of them. They passed the knife one to the other, and each one took his or her turn plunging it into the kidnapper's body. Twelve stabs ... It's a good book," Travers added, and with a determined air he advanced his bishop and left it without protection among the opposing pawns.

"You know what a gambit is, right?" he said.

He's trying to draw me into his territory, Pierre thought. His mouth was dry, he didn't know why.

"In French, Travers. Speak to me in French, okay?"

"You know what a gambit is? What is it?"

Pierre made no reply. He studied Travers's position on the board.

"A sacrifice," Travers explained. "One piece sacrificed to gain a positional advantage..."

"I see that," said Pierre, and under the attentive eye of Her Majesty's commercial attaché, he gobbled the proffered bishop and quickly stood up.

"I have to go to the toilet."

Travers calmly handed him the latest edition of the *Sun* and smiled with a knowing look.

"Need something to read?"

Before the questioning look from his guard, the Englishman added:

"Lots of people here in the apartment. I can understand that … Waiting for the right time, a quiet time, for the big moment."

"I've already got all the reading material I need," Pierre said coldly.

"Here," said John Travers, holding his gaze. "Have a look at the *Sun*."

Pierre took the paper and turned on his heels. He handed his M1 to Corbeau, so the latter could keep an eye on the hostage during his absence.

His pants down around his knees, Pierre quickly scanned the first page. Then, on page three, his eyes fell on the following headline:

KEY PERSON IN CUSTODY

TWO FLQ CELLS MET SECRETLY NOV. 3

He read the entire article, quickly, then read it again. And again. He then focused his attention on the last paragraph.

"While both groups each kidnapped a hostage, one group is definitely against the death penalty — for anyone — for themselves as well as for their hostage," the source added.

And, deep down in his guts, something let go.

FESTIVAL

THE LITTLE CAMP RESEMBLED a battlefield when he opened his eyes. Zero dead, zero wounded. But two bodies found in a strange state. He scratched his pubic hair; there was a fine crust of dried sperm and vaginal mucus. Candles disposed here and there about the room had totally melted down: solid, liquid, solid again, like his penis.

In the grey light of early dawn, Samuel saw a field mouse exploring the remains of their vegetable fried rice. Laundry had been hung up to dry from the ceiling joists. He raised an arm, let his hand slowly descend and settle onto the delicate fold in the curve formed by Marie-Québec's side through the insulating material of the sleeping bag.

In the middle of February, in the subpolar night of the great spruce forest, all it had taken the night before was two or three cherry logs to raise the mercury forty degrees inside the cabin and transform it into a sauna. The stove standing guard on the square of sheet metal screwed to the floor knew only two temperatures: too hot and too cold. They had put out their plates, turned over their wine glasses, and taken off their clothes as though they had suddenly caught fire, but their garments weren't as hot as their skin had been as they searched for and found each other under the blankets. Large animals required large remedies.

"What are you doing?" Marie-Québec asked.

Samuel, in woollen underwear and worn T-shirt, was sipping his first coffee, looking out the window. Through the dirty pane of glass he could make out the tracks of the big cat he'd seen the night before, in the deep snow at the edge of the forest, beside the little lake called Laurendeau on the topo map of the area, and which they had reached by climbing on snowshoes up the stream at the head of the Kaganoma to this minuscule hunt camp. All around them was lynx country. And the camp, according to the ancient laws of forest hospitality, belonged for the moment to whoever heated it up.

Sam shoved another log into the stove and returned to nestle himself against her warm, naked body under the mound of sleeping bags.

How my situation had turned around in a single year. I was living in Marie-Québec's apartment in Maldoror, a small three-and-a-half situated a copper-bearing stone's throw from the foundry from which we could hear the clanking of gigantic gears enveloped in white smoke and arsenic dust, and the bellow of glowing furnaces in the night. It was good to have given up the great work, and even better to have abandoned myself to the arms of my rediscovered love. The insurance company hadn't given me any hassles, the claim had gone through like a letter through the post. The experts, it's safe to say, had seen nothing but the fire!

So I had a few dollars, enough to invite my girl to a restaurant from time to time and to buy her a few Bloody Marys at the White

Wolf, not counting the inevitable rounds of Goldschlager shooters that were *de rigueur* in the wee hours of the Maldororan night. During the day, I read and edited manuscripts when I wasn't writing crap for Big Dumont. Fat padded envelopes arrived regularly by special courier. It was in one of them that, the year before, *The Traverse: The Story of My Captivity,* by John Travers (co-authored with Friedrich Rougeau) had washed up at Lake Kaganoma.

It was the winter of 2000. After Marie-Québec had left, I'd ridden out the Y2K scare in a series of blizzards totalling three metres of snow, two straight weeks of temperatures under minus thirty-five degrees Celsius, including a few days of minus forty, and I still had three solid seasons of my Octobeerist assignment ahead of me before flipping my lid for good.

My enquiries were going nowhere. I'd been able to do nothing with Chevalier's four "P"s, I was running around in circles, spinning my wheels. Pieces of chicken: Rénald Massicotte, the Baby Barbecue guy, had vanished from the face of the earth. Prosecution: I'd spent a week analyzing the trial records in the courthouse archives and had made notes on a good number of irregularities, but nothing more than that. Pierre: whatever his precise role was in this story, it continued to escape me. Police warrant: the trail leading to the neighbouring house had grown cold because I'd failed to identify, even with the aid of the land registry, whoever had owned it at the time. And after thirty years, all the inhabitants of the neighbourhood seemed to have evaporated.

I was therefore in the process of sweating over the manuscript of *The Traverse* when I came across this more or less startling bit of information: good old Travers, with his airs of being the perfect Englishman adept at bridge and the raising of poinsettias, had, in the course of his diplomatic career, been brought in to work (against his wishes, he made it clear) with the British Secret Service. A reluctant spy...

I vaguely knew the book's co-author, Friedrich Rougeau. Just before my Abitibian period, I'd had a few beers with him in a bar in Montreal. I checked in the UNEQ directory, but he wasn't in it, and so I called our publisher. Super Big Dumont's pleasant executive assistant gave me Rougeau's cellphone number and I called him.

"In your conversations, Travers admitted that he'd worked for MI6?" I asked Rougeau. "Just like that?"

"No, not exactly," came my colleague's voice from several hundred kilometres south. "It wasn't MI6, it was MI5 . . ."

He was fly-fishing under the Jacques-Cartier Bridge, but the connection was perfectly clear. As if he were right in front of me, his voice rising after his second pint. He told me he was using an imitation Daredevil, heavy as a cast-iron frypan, and a twenty-pound test line, big enough to haul in a sturgeon. Once, he said, he'd hooked onto a supermarket shopping cart.

While casting and reeling in his big red-and-white in the leaden waters of the St. Lawrence, Rougeau gave me an account of his dealings with Travers, including certain details that, at the time, he'd decided not to put in the book. He'd been in the Public Records Office in London, between two interviews with Travers, consulting a box of archives newly released into the public domain, when a telegram stuck into the mass of papers attracted his attention. Dated November 1970, it had come from the British Embassy in Ottawa and was addressed to the Foreign Office: *In reference to the police inquiry directed to the finding of Travers, we ask to verify information confirming that he has worked for the Secret Service under the name of Frost.*

The response, in the form of a second telegram, was attached to the request by a paperclip: *Impossible to confirm.*

During their next encounter, Friedrich asked him outright why he had hidden this story. And Travers had explained that MI5 had pressed him into service one single time, a simple matter of trapping a Soviet diplomat suspected of trying to recruit double agents. The manœuvre failed, and the James-Bondian career of Travers, it seemed, was equally short-lived. I laughed.

"And the first time a husband is caught in the act, what does he say?"

"He says it's the first time..."

"Yes, the first and only. Even if in reality it's the seventy-ninth time."

"Travers wasn't a spy, Sam."

"Of course he wasn't. You asked him and he said he wasn't."

"They used him for bait. You only have to look at the list of his overseas postings: New Zealand, Malaysia, India, Canada . . . Not exactly hot spots in the Cold War!"

Poor Friedrich, I thought. His naïveté bothered me, you'd think he was doing it on purpose.

"Yeah, you're right, Rougeau: cushy postings in the commercial centres of the Empire. The good old Commonwealth."

"Do you want me to put you in touch with him?"

"Who, Travers?" I thought about it for two seconds. "Yeah."

There was a pause at the other end of the line. Then I heard a sharp, strident sound.

"Sam? I've just snagged something big..."

"What? Hey! Friedrich...?"

"I can't talk to you any... Oh boy! You should see this... bent in two... *kinongé*... I'll send you his...."

"Friedrich?"

"...ail address..."

The connection was cut off.

I e-mailed Travers. I introduced myself as the editor of his book, written in collaboration with Friedrich Rougeau. I needed to clarify one or two points with him. I hoped to reel him in. I played it very softly to avoid frightening him off. I e-mailed him a few harmless questions, then I waited.

Spring arrived. On my land, rabbits became fluffy patchworks of brown and white. At the beginning of May, there were only a few patches of snow under the low-lying boughs of the evergreens. I worked, read, thought, wrote sometimes, looked out the window a lot. Went for walks in the woods. Once or twice a week, I came out of my cave and went looking for a drinking spot worthy of the name. As I was not an aficionado of country music, karaoke, or cocaine snorted through a brown bill helpfully rolled up by a little local mafiotard, I invariably ended up near the foundry, at the White Wolf.

The women of Maldoror knew that I was a bachelor, but they weren't beating a path to my door. One large woman came up to me and opened a bag of Brazilian coffee under my nose and told me she'd bought it especially "for tomorrow morning," smiling in a way that insinuated that the odour of the coffee was a kind of preliminary sampling of much more pheromonal sensations to follow, all the while running her fingers through my hair. Most of the time I jumped like a fox disturbed during his afternoon nap. The chicken house was open, but I remained out in the middle of the field.

Marie-Québec had kept her job as a waitress at the White Wolf, was still carrying out projects at the theatre, was always reading for parts, always had a role to prepare for, a text to memorize, ideas for productions, grants to apply for. And stage scenery, and the placement of ads in the programs, not to mention posters and the actors' diction. She was seeing to everything.

Sometimes we would exchange a few words over the bar. I would see her talking with men who sometimes left with her. One or twice, my nose in my beer, I would feel the tips of her breasts brushing my back through our clothing as she squeezed between the tables with her tray. She was always somewhere under my skin.

The summer sped by in a great flaming of wildflowers. Another October painted itself on the canvas, the forest full of an electric tension generated by the crisscrossing paths of hunters and their prey.

October was the month of the big hunt, and also that of the Festival of Solidarity. Just before Hallowe'en, artists from around Quebec and every other corner of the planet converged here, the Nugget of the Northwest. On the last night, the gala was the occasion for the awarding of the Armand d'Or Prize to the winners in different categories (cinema, song lyrics, religion, municipal politics, sport, literature) at the Loblaw's Happy Times Theatre. The trophy consisted of a raised fist holding a mini-barbell, one of the weights of which was a globe and the other a brave heart. It had been named in honour of sculptor and teacher Armand Vaillancourt, who was in his mid-seventies and had made at least forty of the things. The previous autumn, Sting had been part of the jury and had arrived by private jet accompanied by the great Amazonian chief Raoni. Over the years, Rogoberta Menchú, Paul Piché, Jane Fonda, Desmond Tutu, Jean Béliveau, Jimmy Carter, and the lead singer of the Boomtown Rats had been seen in Maldoror. Another, whose name I won't mention, was rumoured to have exhausted the resources of the town's escort services all by himself. This year, it was announced that Bono and his pink glasses would be in Maldoror. Held in a chalet with seigneurial allures for the nouveau riche that the singer had rented (along with the lake and forty-eight kilometres of shoreline) in Sainte-Bénite, a satellite village connected to Maldoror although separated from it by a distance of some fifty kilometres, the prime minister of Canada had even replied that he would happily attend, wagging his tail like a little puppy dog. The town couldn't have been more abuzz.

In the early darkness of a glacially cold night at the end of October, I stood in front of a wooden barricade surrounding the site on which Maldoror's fourth Tim Hortons (one for every nine thousand citizens) would soon be built, hands in my pockets, reading the following poster:

THINK ABOUT QUEBEC
(POPULAR FRONT CINEMA AND INDEPENDENT JOURNALISM)

A PRESENTATION BY
MR. JEAN-PAUL LAFLEUR

TUESDAY, OCTOBER 3 I, 2000
TIME: 7:00 P.M.
PLACE: CEGEP DE MALDOROR
ROOM A-5630
I 50 BOULEVARD MONSEIGNEUR-HAMELIN

The talk was presented as fringe event of the Festival of Solidarity, and I knew that a handful of leftist militants were going to be in attendance. The weather was calling for snow. A dry cold brought in by a traitorous north wind was pushing the last dead leaves on the sidewalk ahead of me as I made my way to the CEGEP, my coat pulled up around my neck.

Physically, Lafleur, almost sixty, was still an imposing enough figure. Short grey beard, carefully trimmed. Woollen sweater over a white, open-necked shirt. I arrived in the middle of his talk and slipped quietly into the room and sat in the last row of seats. Jean-Paul was talking about the filmmaker Pierre Perrault, then he played a copy of his own documentary, *The Wrong Card*, about depopulation in the resource regions, and urban sprawl, two phenomena he saw as being interdependent. I listened to the heavy, bearish, militant voice coming out from between his whiskers.

There were some forty people in the room. I waited for the beginning of the question period and then raised my hand. Then I lowered it. Then raised it again. He was answering another question. Then he turned his head and saw me.

"Do you know a company in Houston called James Engineering?" I asked him.

Jean-Paul remained silent for exactly five seconds.

"No."

Then he turned his head and saw another raised hand, and nodded encouragingly to the person under it.

I insisted. I interrupted him. He carried on answering the other question without bothering with me. He spoke louder. I spoke louder. The audience got involved.

After being thrown out of room A-5630, naturally, Nihilo turned up at the White Wolf, where Marie-Québec was on duty, as she liked to say. He found her in conversation with the only client in the place and immediately had the impression that he'd seen the guy before somewhere. It was the dead hour, between five and eight, before the stampede arrived for the rest of the night.

Sam ordered a Marteau and heard the guy beside him say:

"You want a little sickle with that?"

"Samuel," said his ex, stiffening a little, "this is Friedrich."

"Right. We've already met."

"How did it go with Travers?" Rougeau asked politely.

He was a remarkable fellow. At the invitation of the festival, he'd come to Maldo to screen his documentary (the festival was showing only documentaries) entitled *Chicken or No Chicken, We're Off!* It was about the raising of poultry and the factory-farmed chicken industry. Friedrich, like a fat cat, announced that Sam's Marteau was on him, and he bought another round of drinks. Nihilo stared into his glass in silence, then said:

"Your friend Travers never gave me a thing..."

"Not true, Sam."

"What? What do you mean, not true?"

"I spoke to him just last week..."

"And?"

"And he told me he remembered your e-mail clearly and that he'd answered all your questions."

"He said that? Really?"

"Yes. Good old John. He goes for his walk with Molly every day, on the cliffs of Galway where he's enjoying a peaceful and, if you ask me, well-earned retirement."

"Who's Molly?"

"His sausage hound."

"Okay, listen: Travers never even answered my e-mail. After a week, I sent it again. Same result..."

"Sam, that's not possible."

"Are you telling me that I live so far out in the boonies that even e-mails get lost on their way to me?"

"I've no doubt that you live a little cut off from the world," Rougeau said with a fluttering of his eyelashes in Marie-Québec's direction.

"Travers lied to you. He's hiding something."

"Yes, Sam, you're right. His kinship with the little green man in Roswell, no doubt. Bring him another Marteau, my love..."

Sam didn't like Rougeau's tone when addressing Marie-Québec. It was hardly subtle. When the glass landed in front of him, he placed both hands flat on the bar, made of B.C. fir, and looked from one to the other.

"You think I'm getting completely hammered, is that it?"

From the glance he cast at Marie-Québec, Sam could see that even she, totally dedicated irrationalist Marie-Québec, was wondering about him. It wasn't a good feeling.

Shortly after nine, Marie-Québec cashed out and came to sit at the bar, where she allowed Friedrich Rougeau to buy her a double Bloody Mary. *Chicken or No Chicken, We're Off!* was in the running for Best Engagé Documentary, and the word was that a fair wind was blowing its way. Samuel thought the wind in question was more like a country breeze blowing over a well-manured field, and characterized the film, which he hadn't seen, as dribblings from some egg incubator. He'd decided to keep to himself and so moved down to the end of the bar to continue drinking on his own.

One by one, people began to arrive and take over the premises, and he soon found himself adrift in the crowd, pressed up against Michel Chartrand beside the pool table, a Chartrand still in his red-and-black checkered shirt and stinking of the straight gin he was quaffing from a beer glass. Chartrand began haranguing him on the subject of water, saying that the water from the eskers in Abitibi was the best drinking water in the universe and that the esker at Kaganoma was the Napa Valley of potable water, but that a huge transnational company, a giant of the agrifood industry that in truth was a goddamned subsidiary of Pepsi-Cola, had its sights on this formidable natural filter and was planning to build an ultramodern bottling megafactory in the woods around here somewhere. Samuel, unable to get a word in edgewise, watched Chartrand's mouth open and close six inches from his nose, all the words coming out of it smelling of straight gin and echoing in his head, and before long he had reduced them to four: *oh such good water, such good water*, and then to two: *good water, good water, bonne eau, Bono.*

The news spread about the room like a trained flea: *Bono? Bono was coming? His bodyguards were securing the place?*

Nihilo, using his elbows to good effect, managed to get to the door in time to see Marie-Québec leaving just ahead of him with Rougeau. He ran up the street after them. An icy wind swept the snow that was now falling across the sky, ululating gusts unfurling from the north through the infernal circumlocutions of the foundry and reducing the halo of the street lamps to fading fireflies.

And it was like in the dream that Sam had had: Marie-Québec moving away from him, not turning, never a glance in his direction, except that there was no white sand in the immediate vicinity, and instead of Branlequeue as the wading bird, it was Rougeau Nihilo ran up against, the marabou, who said to him:

"Fuck off, you little conspiracy-theorist shit!"

I woke up in my own bed. I vaguely remembered an evanescent avalanche blowing against my windshield, stop signs that sprung up out of nowhere in my headlights like haggard, muffled ghosts. Then I became aware of another presence in the room and opened my eyes.

The ghost was sitting at the foot of my bed.

"The house is burning," he said.

And just as he finished speaking, the smoke detector in the stairwell went off.

Sitting up in bed, I tried to think. It felt as though someone was squeezing my head in a vise.

"The old Anishnabe Indians that I meet around here," Lavoie said, "you know what they tell me? That in their language 'Kaganoma' means 'place of words.' Don't you think that's funny? No, well, in your place, I probably wouldn't either..."

"What are you doing?"

The spectre pulled the pillow out from under my back. He showed me his right palm and his wounded and heavily bandaged left wrist.

"I can't take your hand. I hope you understand..."

He turned, raised the pillow, and held it against his chest and face, then threw himself head-first at the window, passing soundlessly through it and disappearing on the other side into the blinding whiteness of fresh snow that covered the countryside. Then I smelled smoke, and heard, finally, the crackling and snapping of flames in the stairway. The smoke detector started drilling into my cranium.

"No ..."

I charged into my office and began hauling out bankers' boxes and chucking them out the window, like ballast thrown overboard so that my house would go up in flames. Folders flew out one after another, the whole history in separate pieces, the puzzle of all these words and all these names that corresponded to lives, some of which had been lived in the vast unknown of the real: General Bédard, Uncle Bob, Madame Corps, Zadig and Madwar, Chevreuil, Gode, Lancelot, la Bellechasse, *Maître* Brien, Corbeau, Machinegun Martinek, the chicken delivery guy, the Fat Cop ...

Even Chevalier Branlequeue. Goodbye and good sailing!

Finally I grabbed my laptop and threw it into the snow, five metres down.

When I left the office, the stairwell was already breathing red flames and pumping them up to the second floor, and the heat was cooking my right shoulder. I went back into the bedroom, threw a housecoat over my shoulders and, seeing the terrified cat, chased it under the bed and went after it into a nest of dust bunnies. I threw it out the window, following after it through the broken glass, to land in a stand of young saplings that settled me gently to the ground on boughs cushioned with fresh snow.

On my road above the house, I met firemen wearing gas masks and fireproof suits that made them look as though they were going off to wage chemical warfare against Saddam Hussein. Three huge, fluorescent-yellow trucks were coming up the road with difficulty between the rows of spruce. Someone tossed a blanket over my shoulders and it slid down onto the ground without my lifting a finger to stop it. A female police officer spoke to me and couldn't seem to make head or tail of my explanations. It wasn't complicated, in any case. I looked for the cat, it was there, somewhere in the snowy whiteness. And Paul Lavoie, have you seen him? The cabinet minister assassinated in 1970? If you did, you weren't even born yet.

To continue along the road as though I had somewhere important to get to but hard to make sense of was probably a mistake. I didn't turn around when she called out something that sounded like: *Freeze!*, which was funny, given the temperature and what I was wearing. I started to tell her that maybe she'd seen too many cop shows on television, and then I just gave up.

That was how I left Kaganoma Lake, strapped to a stretcher, with 50,000 volts in my chest.

Sam plunged the blackened camping kettle into the deep snow, tamped it down with his bare hand, thinking that they'd probably never get used to this strange thing, snow. And with another sweeping gesture, as though scooping a fish into a hand-held net, he returned to the cabin and placed the kettle on the woodstove.

Around the head of the lake, where the spruce and Jack pines had never known a saw, the countryside resembled what the first trappers must have seen as they hacked a portage route with their axes after ascending the Ottawa River, and the Kinojévis met them as they broke out of the woods on their snowshoes: an infinite expanse of intense white, fringed by a dark circle of evergreens weighed down by piles of sculptured snow under a sickly sun. Caw, caw, a coal-black crow passed by in a deep blue sky.

While waiting for the snow to melt, he sat at the old pink Formica table and flipped through the cabin's guest book: a simple notebook with a stiff cover left for the use of visitors on the trail:

It's beautiful, but the trees aren't very big. And no trace of the great moose in these swamps. Frankly, if you're looking for big game, it's much better in the Ngorongoro crater, where at least there were some gnus (www.ngorongoro.com), or even in the Canadian Rockies, with all their wapitis that seem to be posing for photographs.

The bugs were a real pain (we mean the insect kind, obviously, ha ha ha)...

They were probably from France.

When he was being held for observation in the hospital after being tasered (according to the local police report, Officer Kathy Drolet had zapped him with all those volts and secured him to the stretcher to protect him from himself when he put himself at risk of serious exposure) and they asked him if he wanted someone to be notified, Marie-Québec's name was the only one that came to the tip of his tongue. She dropped everything. And instead of bringing flowers, she showed up with *Three Yellow Roses*, the collection of stories by Raymond Carver. It was the kind of thing one doesn't forget.

After his night of observation, Sam went to live with her, in her three-and-a-half beside the foundry, where they spent three days in bed, making love, eating pizza, and watching the ten o'clock news and uncut movies on the Télé-Québec channel.

Remembering all this, he began to feel himself getting hard again. He took off his T-shirt and shorts and got back into bed.

"Mmmmh." She opened her eyes. "Why don't we just stay here?"

"You mean..."

"Tomorrow. Or the day after tomorrow, or the day after that."

"And what would we live on?"

"Porcupines. And beaver stew, essentially. When I was small, I went with my father on his trapline and it was me who had to finish off the ones who were wounded. Say yes, Sam ..."

"But it isn't our cabin ..."

"No, but no one uses it except for two weeks a year, during the hunting season. It's ours for the rest of the time. Fifty weeks a year. And for the two other weeks ..."

"We could go to Mexico."

Marie-Québec looked at him. Wide awake, now.

"Are you serious? About Mexico, I mean?"

"More serious than that. We could spend the winter down there."

"Using what for money?"

"Big Dumont owes me a cheque."

The water in the kettle began whistling gently.

"No automatic coffee maker," Sam declared.

"No. No desk lamp, vacuum cleaner, Jehovah's Witnesses at the door, laser printers, or toasters."

"No neighbours playing music in their kitchen. No telemarketers. No problems with the shower head."

The air in the cabin was redolent of warmth, steam, wet wool, wood smoke, sex, and the Nicaraguan coffee they'd ground the night before.

Marie-Québec was sitting cross-legged on the bed, her eye on Sam's erection, the nipples on her small breasts jutting up into the smoky air like rifle targets.

He took her in his arms, picked her up, and she guided him inside her, they fused their two bodies together, he held her thighs in his hands and she, thus impaled, wrapped her arms around his neck, and he turned around and headed to the door.

"Sam, what are you ... No!"

"That which doesn't kill us makes us stronger."

"Stop!"

When he opened the door, the thick warmth of the cabin met the wall of cold air. A low of minus twenty Celsius, in which their interlaced, tropical bodies began instantly to steam. All this naked whiteness. They disappeared into the field of light and the silent cry of a spruce grouse.

AT THE AIGLE FIN, OR J.C. IN QUEBEC AT LAST

NO KIDDING, I'M ALWAYS MOVED when I see Quebec City springing up on the horizon, the Old Capital perched on its headland, beside the great river, whose actual shores are Autoroutes 20 and 40. Call me sentimental if you like, but to know that the only parliamentary assembly devoted in principle to the defence of the rights of the French-Canadian nation is found in this city gives me goosebumps. Not you?

I can hear you asking me why I don't vote for separatism, or even why didn't I run for the Parti Québécois in the by-election in Vautrin? I can tell you why: I don't like René Lévesque. He's sexually obsessed. And I don't like Bourgault, either. He's a queer. I'm speaking in confidence here, alone with my tape recorder, at the wheel of my car. So, you see, I can speak frankly.

The Parti Québécois could have been an honest offspring of the Liberal Party, if there could ever be such a thing. I mean: part of the family, one that left home after an unfortunate dispute about lineage. But Bourgault's RIN was the Trojan Horse by means of which street disorder and radicalism infiltrated into the heart of democratic structures. The PQ is its dissolute son. The support of the unions and popular groups made it a gangrened left leg of egalitarian ideology. Whereas I, at the heart of the good old Quebec Liberal Party, at least had the possibility of contributing to internal change, even within the Pouvoir-Power machine. Yes, I did.

I won't describe Quebec City to you. I haven't come here as a tourist. Down there is the Legislature, where from now on I have a desk waiting for me in the back benches, on the majority side, last row. Among the purebreds. Under the wheels of my Buick is the Grande-Allée. The Aigle Fin, do you know it? It's the name of the restaurant where we go. But I'm a good half-hour early, so let me suggest I leave my car near the Saint-Louis gate, and you follow me, okay? And I'll tell you a story while my steps lead us along the old route, down rue Sainte-Anne, rue du Fort, rue Saint-Louis, Dufferin Terrace, the wooden steps on the cliff, the cannons aimed to the south and the great brother enemy, out onto the Plains of Abraham, the classic loop, as if I were an old mare carrying a mini-tape recorder instead of a sack of oats. I could even take you for a ride in my *calèche*.

It was three years ago, at the Aigle Fin on Grande-Allée. Paul Lavoie asked me to have lunch with him. I was his political attaché. The justice portfolio had eluded him, and he'd consoled himself with that of labour and immigration. An old-school nationalist, he would willingly have accommodated himself to dictatorship if it meant a chair at the *caudillo*. That day, October 6, 1970, in the absence of our premier, who was down south selling our great northern rivers to the sharks on Wall Street, Lavoie was in command, his tie already loosened, flipping through the newspaper headlines at his usual table in the back when I joined him.

The Aigle Fin is a chic version of those coffee houses and cafés in which the main decorative elements are old fishing nets studded with balsa-wood floats and desiccated starfish. At the Aigle, the whole divider between the room at the back and the corridor leading to the toilets consisted of lobster tanks in excellent condition, with dark green, taxidermied crustaceans holding their tails and claws in menacing poses against an inky blue backdrop. Despite this clear inducement, the upper-level civil servants and parliamentarians who frequented this famous establishment in the capital choose, more often than not, to go with the large T-bone steak, a pound of carefully weighed meat hung on a bone strong enough to knock out an army of Redcoats and served with baked potatoes. It was particularly true of the political generation to which my patron belonged, nurtured as he was on the traditional meat-potato-veg inherited from our pemmican-gumming ancestors. That day, my boss hardly glanced at the open menu in front of him before ordering the famous Moose Jaw beef.

He was a bon vivant, a congenial fellow, as they say, all red-cheeked. At night, at home, he no doubt drank milk and ate those little Vachon cakes, but at lunchtime he washed down his steak with a bottle or two of beer like a true man of the people.

We talked about the specialist doctors' strike. The kidnapping of the British commercial attaché the previous evening was not yet the very big deal it was soon to become. Travers was a diplomat and was therefore the federal government's responsibility. The Québécois were smiling smugly behind their hands. *What's it to do with us? Not much . . .*

When we talked about the kidnapping that day, Lavoie said to me:

"If the FLQ boys allow him to write, he has a chance of getting out of it . . ."

I asked him what he meant by that. He leaned toward me with a sly smile:

"What would you do, if you were in his shoes?"

"The grave," I said without thinking. "I mean, I would remain quiet."

My response disappointed him, I could tell.

"Let's try to put ourselves in his position. He has fallen into the hands of a band of young idiots who have given the government forty-eight hours to accept their conditions, or else they will take care of him. They seem serious. If he thinks about it, he'll realize that the only chance of being rescued quickly is to help the police find him. So, find some way to get a message out to the authorities..."

"Yes, of course, but one of the kidnappers' conditions is that that police stop searching for him."

"Surely Travers isn't stupid enough to believe that the police are going to stop looking for him! He's no fool. He knows full well that the government can't negotiate..."

"Really?"

He leaned back in his chair and lowered his eyes. His fingers instinctively went to the knot in his tie.

"No government of a civilized, democratic country would negotiate with terrorists. Travers's only chance is for the police to find where he's being held as quickly as possible. And so, if I were him and my kidnappers gave me a chance to write a letter, I'd bury a coded message in it somehow. It seems to me to go without saying."

"I don't know. If you're caught, you're as good as dead!"

"Maybe, but a death that, at least, will have occurred on the field of battle, using the only weapons you had at your disposal, namely the words you write on a sheet of paper. Better than waiting to be strangled like a chicken."

"You think they'll..."

He patted his lips with his napkin.

"No, Jean-Claude. They're good little boys from Quebec. They wouldn't hurt a flea..."

That was our conversation, essentially, to the best of my recollection.

The next Saturday, I was in my living room drinking a gin and tonic, sitting in front of the television, half-listening to my wife calling from the kitchen to ask me if I wanted stew for supper — Irish stew, potatoes, carrots, cubes of lamb, onion, and not much else, a good, hearty, autumn meal even better the second day — when the telephone rang. I got up to answer it and learned that my boss had just been nabbed by the FLQ in front of his house. I looked at my watch. It was six-thirty. Then I looked out the window. It was getting dark. It wasn't more than a half-hour since the televised press conference given by the justice minister explaining the government's position (no concessions to terrorists). The news came like a blow to the forehead. I hung up and went to make myself another gin and tonic.

I can't tell you what a horror the next few days were. Nights tossing in my bed like a capon on a spit, days lived in a fog. But this story isn't about me.

The next day (Sunday), after an anonymous phone call to a radio station, a communiqué was found in a trash bin in the centre of the city. A new terrorist cell claimed responsibility for Saturday night's strike. The financial Chevalier Cell was named after François-Marie-Something-or-Other, Chevalier de Lorimier, a patriot who was hanged in Pied-de-Courant in 1839. The cell gave the government until ten o'clock that night to respond to the FLQ's requests — the famous seven conditions, including the release of all political prisoners and the payment of a $500,000 ransom in gold ingots. Failure to meet these demands would result in the hostage, rebaptized the Minister of Unemployment and Assimilation, being executed at the end of the period of grace.

A bit later, a second communiqué was found in a bus shelter. This one had been written by hand. "The least hesitation on the part of the authorities," the kidnappers had written, "will [be] fatal to the minister." And: "We've already made a huge concession by promising to return him safe and sound. Do not ask more of us than that."

Jesus Christ, I thought.

Attached to the communiqué was a letter from Lavoie to his wife, which was made public. He'd dated it October 12, 1970, 7 a.m. (a slight error on his part: it was only the eleventh). "What's important is that the authorities budge," my boss confided to his wife.

That same magnificent Sunday of the Thanksgiving weekend, toward the end of the afternoon, another garbage can, a new communiqué. This one was typewritten. It reiterated the ultimatum and its deadline: ten o'clock that night. "No more paternalism, no more maybes, no more promises," warned the Chevalier Cell. "We know what we want and where we're going and we are determined to get there."

A handwritten letter from Lavoie to the premier, Albert Vézina, accompanied this message, along with a dozen credit cards from the hostage's wallet intended to prove the authenticity of the communication. Honestly, even I was astonished at how many credit cards he carried around with him.

Lavoie's letter to the premier was a bald appeal for negotiations. *"We are,"* he wrote, *"in the presence of a well organized escalation that will only end with the liberation of the political prisoners. After me, there will be a third, then a fourth and a twelfth.*

"My very dear Albert," he went on, *"what follows is very, very important: you must order the immediate cessation of all police searches. Their continuance will be my death sentence. On the other hand, if the liberation and departure of the political prisoners are brought to a good end, I am certain that my personal safety will be guaranteed. We are very close to a solution, I can feel it, since there is no real animosity between my kidnappers and I. My fate*

now collates with theirs. It is up to you to insure my swift return to Parliament Hill in support of you, like the faithful right arm that I promised you I would be. Your decision: my life or my death. I am counting on you, and thank you.

"Warm regards,

"Paul Lavoie."

Described as "pathetic" by the media, this apostrophe to the premier caused high emotion in political circles as well as with the general population. Here was Little Albert's right-hand man, until then a fierce defender of the intransigent position the federal government had taken on terrorism, suddenly becoming a turncoat, apparently cracking after little more than a day in the hands of his kidnappers! It didn't sit well.

From surprise we passed on to fear, and from fear to panic, and from panic to paranoia. Events accelerated:

- October 11, Little Albert makes the bizarre decision to place his entire cabinet under high security in a hotel in downtown Montreal. The provincial government was, de facto, under siege;
- Sunday night, a little before ten o'clock, Vézina reads a solemn declaration on television containing his dramatic response to the kidnappers' demands. Half of his listeners believe he has just opened the door to negotiations with the FLQ, the other half are convinced they heard him categorically refuse to give in to demands from terrorists. As usual, Little Albert has managed to cross the Rubicon without getting his feet wet;
- October 12, in a new communiqué, the Chevalier Cell designates *Maître* Brien as its negotiator. Only one small problem: the lawyer is in prison;
- October 13, *Maître* Brien is released from prison;
- October 13, evening, negotiations break down over the question of preliminary guarantees, all talks broken off, a stalemate, etc.;

- October 14, a group of Paul Lavoie's golfing buddies publicly call for an acceleration in the process of liberating the hostages;
- October 14, evening, rumours of war...;
- October 15, the first troop movements are ordered.

I resolved to do everything in my power to save my friend and boss. I went to find *Maître* Brien in Old Montreal. It was late in the evening, sometime around nine o'clock. The Ministerial Council had just issued a communiqué in which the government rejected every condition of the FLQ except one: it offered the kidnappers an airplane that would take them to a country of their choice, and gave them six hours to decide. Yes, you read right: six hours.

I found *Maître* Brien downstairs at the Brown Hotel, in the old quarter, where he was giving a particularly well attended and fiery press conference. Amid a forest of microphones and bottles of Labatt 50s, he stood above the heads of two dangerous ideologues who had no business being at large: Vallières and Gagnon.

While I listened from the doorway, an anglophone journalist who was being physically thrown out of the hotel practically toppled over me. Then *Maître* Brien swept past and jumped onto his motorcycle. I ran out into the street.

"I'm Jean-Claude Marcel, Lavoie's political attaché. We need to talk..."

He motioned for me to get on. As though it was the most natural thing in the world!

"I don't have a helmet..."

"Neither do I. Hop on!"

I sat astride the machine without thinking, he revved up his metal courser, and we charged off into the night. When we turned east on Notre-Dame, he showed me the street name, Gosford, on the sign.

"If we take the bull by the horns, we'll win the day! Ah ah!" I heard him shout above the roar of the machine.

The cold air of an autumn night hit upon us, *paf*, full in the face. I had the impression of being in flight. We tore down a street at high speed, the river occasionally visible between the buildings of the Old Port on our right, the ancient silos, the water, like tar lit up at night.

He ran every red light. I was frozen as a rat and shaking uncontrollably. We roared under the Jacques-Cartier Bridge, turned onto Pie-IX and headed north. At a certain point we passed a military convoy, a half-dozen canvas-covered trucks moving in a convoy. *Maître* Brien passed them all with his horn honking and giving them the finger, arm raised, full throttle.

He stopped farther on in front of a telephone booth and told me to wait for him. Then I saw him signalling me to join him.

I found him in the process of making a line of white powder disappear up one nostril, as though he had suddenly been transformed into an Electrolux, with the aid of a tightly rolled twenty-dollar bill. I knew such things went on, but it was the first time I'd seen anyone do it. He offered me a line. I shook my head and retreated a step. My back was against the side of the booth. He began whimpering into the telephone. I tried not to think too much about the fact that I was there to help save my boss, Paul Lavoie, who was a hostage of the FLQ.

"I was wondering, my dear, if you would be free for a friend of mine here . . . I see him making huge 'no' signs, but he's a gallant fellow, I'm sure he likes women."

I went out to wait for him beside the Harley. And as happens only in bad police serials, a patrol car chose that minute to pull up beside the sidewalk. I saw the passenger-side window go down and I heard:

"Hey, fuck-head . . . Where's your helmet?"

I couldn't find my voice. Neither could the officer, apparently. Because he'd just seen *Maître* Brien behind me, running out of the phone booth with his fists raised in the air.

"This is Paul Lavoie's assistant! Let him pass!" he yelled, then jumped in the saddle and started the engine without even looking their way. The two officers stared at him round-eyed, jaws hanging open. The FLQ's designated negotiator was a true celebrity, someone they'd seen on television. I had only enough time to jump on behind him and hang on, and we were off.

If I didn't sleep that night, it wasn't because I stayed with *Maître* Brien. No, because when he jumped off his motorbike and ran into the Paul-Sauvé Arena to whip up a pre-revolutionary crowd, I jumped into a taxi and returned to the downtown hotel where the government had been hiding out for three days, and where the Lavoie clan (wife, children, parents, friends, political colleagues, and fellow collaborators) occupied an entire floor. And it was from the bed in my hotel suite, a glass of good scotch in my hand, that I watched El Maestro stir up chaos.

Seeing all the young people gathered at his feet, raising their fists and chanting *FLQ! FLQ!*, I thought of my boss as a prisoner of these zealots, and of the canvas-covered trucks on the boulevard, and could hardly make myself believe in the fearful destiny that was happening before my eyes. It was impossible to fall asleep . . .

I had no idea what time of night it was when, prey to a sudden inspiration, I leapt out of bed and hurried to my photocopy of the first letter from Lavoie to Little Albert. Armed with a pen, I placed the bottle of single malt on the coffee table, so it was close at hand, and reread the text carefully. Then I read it again. And again.

I had just remembered our conversation of the sixth of October, at the Aigle Fin. In the flurry of events, I had hardly had time to think about it. And now it was as though every word written by Paul Lavoie was taking me back to it.

My very dear Albert, what follows is very, very important: you must order the immediate cessation of all police raids. Their continuance will be my death warrant. On the other hand, if the release and departure of the political prisoners are brought to a good end, I am certain that my personal safety will be guaranteed. We are very close to a solution, I can feel it, since there is no real animosity between my kidnappers and I. My fate now collates with theirs. It is up to you to insure my swift return to Parliament Hill in support of you, like the faithful right arm that I promised you I would be. Your decision: my life or my death. I am counting on you, and thank you.

Warm regards,
Paul Lavoie

Of course. Good God Almighty, of course.

"Paul never makes grammatical mistakes," I say. "I want to emphasize the importance of this. His mastery of the rules of language is perfect."

I was in another suite in the hotel, talking to a high-ranking QPP official graced with a fine moustache and a head like that of an electrical repairman. He already seemed to regret having agreed to meet me at such an early hour. While I was wasting his time, his friends, under the provisions of the special law, were busy throwing everyone in prison who leaned even ever so slightly to the left.

I pushed the sheet of paper under his eyes and pointed to the words with the tip of my pen.

The misuse of the word "collates." The use of "insure" instead of "ensure." He was deliberately trying to direct our attention to these two words. He'd already alerted us by doubling the adverb ("very,

very important") at the beginning of the paragraph. I wondered if the two errors were somehow connected? "Collates" could mean a copy centre. "Insure" could mean "insurance." A building housing a copy centre and an insurance company?

The police officer looked at me with boredom written on his face.

But back in my room, I couldn't help feeling I was getting somewhere. So I looked again at the words themselves. The first was the clearest. His use of the word "collates" had to be intentional: the proper word would have been "collides." About the second, "insure," I was less certain. It could have been a simple error, except that Lavoie didn't make simple errors. What if I took the offending syllables from each word and switched them? Then the first word becomes ... Collins.

I took out a map of Greater Montreal and spread it out on my coffee table.

There was a rue Collins in Côte-Saint-Luc. It hadn't been around for very long, since it was named after one of the astronauts of the Apollo 11 mission. I also took into account that there were rumours that Lavoie was being held somewhere on the South Shore, because, it was thought, the kidnappers would never risk crossing a bridge with a hostage in the car. So I looked on the map again ... and found another rue Collins in Saint-Hubert, very close to the military base.

"That's all you can come up with? A street name?" asked the officer this time.

I looked him in the eye.

"No. I did some more research. In his first letter to his wife, Lavoie got the date wrong. He wrote October 12 instead of October 11. And as if by chance, the number twelve shows up again in his letter to Vézina: 'After me, there will be a third, then a fourth, and a twelfth.' Why a twelfth instead of a fifth, or a twentieth? It might just be coincidence, and the mistaken date might just be a case of inattention, but let's suppose it isn't. Is there a 12 rue Collins? Don't you think it's at least worth checking?"

He seemed to think about it. Then he reached out his huge hand and held it poised above my photocopy of the letter like a mechanical goose's beak.

"Can I take this with me?"

I said yes. We shook hands at the door. And I never heard from him again.

Paul Lavoie died the next day. His body was found in the trunk of a car parked near Hangar 12 of the military airport in Saint-Hubert, several hundred feet from rue Collins and the house in which he'd been held hostage and assassinated.

I'd spent Friday and Saturday trying, between two short naps, to speak with the officer I'd shown the letter to. When I realized it was useless, I tried to find Colonel Lapierre. The special adviser was perhaps the only one left with the authority to save my boss. But the War Measures Act was keeping everyone in his world busy. Uncle Bob couldn't be found . . .

Three years later, the time finally arrived.

At the Aigle Fin, on the back wall, there's a large canvas representing a three-master in pursuit of a whale; we see the whale's tail rising above the waves as it dives a cable's length in front of the ship. The whale is white. Beneath the painting is a fireplace in which, from October on, a good maple fire is always burning. And near the fireplace is the table preferred by Uncle Bob, at which he is probably already waiting for me, his eye on the door, his back to the wall (of course), our own Papa Boss, the man who has a horror of surprises, the workhorse, the war wounded. I feel a little as though I am meeting with the Grand Inquisitor in person.

I complete my walk on the plains by coming up George-VI, emerging onto Grande-Allée by way of Wolfe and Montcalm streets. I'm a bit late, and so I step up my pace. Before going into the restaurant I slip my tape recorder into my pocket and leave it on, just in case.

(What follows is a cleaned-up, slightly edited version of our conversation. Background noise has been reduced, the clinking of glasses and utensils, and the inevitable banalities. We hear the Colonel...)

"You see that painting up there?"

"That one?"

"Yes. La Quebrada...Acapulco. Have you ever been there?"

"No, never."

"You should go. Ah, la Quebrada...You know it, it's the cliff from which divers jump into the ocean. They have to wait for the right moment, when a wave comes in...Timing is everything. If they wait too long, the wave is already on its way out when they jump, and when they hit the shallow water they break their necks. Not unlike politics, I find."

(Here the Colonel smiles, and a brief silence ensues and I wonder how long he's going to beat about the bush. It isn't his style, and I don't have to wait long to find out why he's summoned me.)

"My dear Jean-Claude, I'm going to be frank with you ... First, my congratulations. Vautrin was a long way from an easy win at the start of the campaign. In retrospect it's easy to say that a caribou painted red could have shown up and been elected. But the PQ is to be watched up there in the North. A good thing they have those big camps. Without the boys working on construction, I don't know where we'd be. It must be said, my dear J.-C., you were dropped in with one hell of a fine parachute."

"Thank you."

"Not at all. Jean-Claude, recently I've been wondering where all the stories appearing in the Toronto papers could be coming from, the dirt, you know, which suggests, roughly, that the government didn't do all it could have in 1970 to save poor Paul Lavoie."

(This was it.)

"And that even suggest that Lavoie could have been a victim of a settling of accounts within the Liberal Party. That's a bit strong, don't you think?"

(What do I say? What do I do?)

"It would seem," he went on, "that there are those who find it easier to go snivelling to Toronto when they know how their bits of gossip will be greeted by the timorous little mice around here..."

"I really don't see who that could be. But if you ask me what I think..."

"Let's say I'm asking you what you think, Jean-Claude."

"...I think that it might be a kind of reaction to the dirt-diggers who are ruining Paul Lavoie's reputation by dragging his name through the mud in the papers."

"You're speaking of those at the *Devoir* who keep sifting through the garbage heap? You don't think, though, that Vézina and his government have something to do with it?"

"I only say that Lavoie makes an ideal scapegoat, that's all. He was in the government and he had contacts with the Mafia. Lavoie is dead now, so the government has no more contact with the Mafia. It's what is called..."

"A sophism?"

"Yes, exactly. You see, I know what's going on, Colonel. I see you digging your firebreak around the second Lavoie affair. At the worst, now that connections with the Scarpino family have come to the attention of the public, it wouldn't be so bad if people learned that you let him be conveniently killed at the time. That would be a lot less damaging for the Liberal government than if these revelations continue, yes, if the stain keeps getting bigger, like concentric circles in a pond, which never stop expanding. Until . . ."

"You. And me. We're in the same boat, Jean-Claude . . ."

"I don't know about that. Three years ago, he would have been a martyr for national unity. Now, it's a Liberal scapegoat you need. But there are goddamned limits to killing a corpse! How long is it going to go on, Colonel?"

(There is a silence and I can't believe I have just addressed Uncle Bob in such tones . . . But he doesn't react, it's as though nothing living moves in his face, the coldness in his look could come from Resolute Bay or the Andromeda Galaxy. My back is shivering, just thinking about it.)

"Until the next elections."

"Excuse me?"

"It's going to go on until the next elections. And the next elections, my friend, are going to take place no later than this year. Keep that to yourself, by the way. Parliament is going to be dissolved tomorrow. The campaigning will begin . . ."

"But how can that be? It's only been three years . . ."

"It's a good time. The dirt-diggers, as you call them, are busy. There's a wave coming. Everyone is going to be engulfed by it. Might as well ride it out right away. Listen to what I'm saying: the election is going to be held against the goddamned separatists and I'm going to find you a hundred seats, minimum. In six months, no one will be talking about the Mafia."

"And the dissolution . . ."

"Tomorrow. That gives you plenty of time to decide if you're going to run or not."

"If I . . ."

"Deep down, Jean-Claude, you know as well as I do that a caribou painted red can win Vautrin. But we're not going to give ammunition to the PQ. We're not going to dig up any rubbish and serve it to them on a silver platter..."

"Rubbish? What kind of rubbish?"

"Let's say, to take an example, a political attaché meets with the lieutenant of the Montreal Mafia in the Vegas Palace, a joint on the South Shore. And to make things worse, let's say this meeting took place on a Saturday night, at the same moment, or just about, that the boss of said political attaché was liquidated by a gang of separatist piss artists. But maybe it was just a coincidence..."

"You know I met with Temperio... How?"

(Talk about a stupid question. Fucking idiot!)

"I have a tape of the meeting. The walls of the Vegas have more microphones in them than the newsroom at the CBC. Temperio and the Scarpinos couldn't say a four-letter word or fart in the washroom without it ending up in the QPP archives. And then, when the chattering of the good Liberals turns up in the dossiers of organized crime, the boys at the Parthenais are accustomed to warning me about it. Any other questions?"

"I ... discovered a message. In Lavoie's letter. But I got zero collaboration from the QPP. So I took my courage in both hands and went knocking at the Vegas..."

(He had me by the short and curlies. Ouch ...)

"But you have a problem: Scarpino wanted something in exchange. He wanted $300,000, or else fewer cops in the cabarets, or a permit to open a casino. It was give, give, give. And you, you were just a little political attaché who had nothing to offer him, a huge zero. Otherwise, he would have gone and got your Lavoie out for you. He would have sent in three or four of his henchmen and no one would have heard another word about those assholes in the

FLQ. Good, let's be serious: the county of Vautrin, do you want it or not?"

(My reply was a suite of more or less intelligible proposals; then Uncle paid for the cognac, a bottle of Rémy Martin that landed on the table; excuse me, but he was someone, anyway.)

"How are your parents doing, Jean-Claude?"

"They still own a little grocery-convenience store in the east end."

"Yes. They have an alcohol permit, I believe, do they not?"

"Yes, they do . . ."

"Good. I hope they know that it's a great responsibility, and that it could be taken away from them at any time. Selling alcohol to minors, it's a huge problem. We have to make examples sometimes. Say hello to them for me. What about lottery tickets?"

"They don't sell those . . ."

"Perhaps you should tell them to apply for a Loto-Québec licence. It pays very well . . ."

"Yeah, but my father's against gambling."

"But not your mother, I sense. You'll tell them it's the future. And that if it would help, it would give me great pleasure to put in a small word on behalf of the dear old parents of the honourable member from Vautrin. Problems with the application form, with a clerk somewhere . . . In hard times, it's better to talk to the Uncle."

"I'll tell them."

(What would you have said in my place? Yes, Colonel . . . Yes, Colonel . . . Yes, Colonel . . .)

RUE COLLINS, OCTOBER 19, 1970, EARLY MORNING

DETECTIVE-SERGEANT MILES MARTINEK, Gargantua incarnate, hands deep in the pockets of his parka, was conversing with a small group of reporters in front of the house. The living-room window had been blown out by an explosion. A Canadian Army bomb-squad truck was parked a little farther down. The street was closed off. A group of curious neighbours and onlookers were chatting with each other not too far from the house. A few of them were recounting their stories to a couple of policemen, who were taking notes.

Martinek was a popular man among the beat cops. His reputation for ferocity and his total lack of compunction, which he dutifully applied to upholding order and the law of the fittest, made him something of a legend. "According to the first testimonies collected from the neighbours," he was saying, "it seems that the neighbouring

505

house, the one you see there — 150 Collins — was also occupied by a few FLQers known to the police. But they fell off the map about a month ago. However, Saturday night around six, not long after the poor guy's death, the neighbours saw a car with a hitched trailer — others say a van — parked right in front of the house, and then a man filling the trailer with something and driving off."

Sergeant Machinegun Martinek put an immediate end to the questions that the reporters began rattling off.

"That's all we know for now. You'll have to excuse me."

He walked away from the journalists toward a man standing a bit off to one side. He was somewhere in his fifties, with a nose like an eagle's beak. He'd just made his appearance, alone, wearing a trench coat over his shoulders and a tweed cap on his head. Moving away from the crowd, the newcomer walked to the garage door and waited for the sergeant to join him. He stood with his back straight, almost stiff, without wasting any time.

"Colonel Lapierre," Miles murmured.

"Sergeant Martinek ... I'm here under orders of the prime minister."

A nod and nothing more from Martinek, as if to say "Of course." He brought himself almost to attention. The Colonel's eyes went past him to contemplate the raided house behind the sergeant's broad shoulders.

"Who went in there?"

"Just me and the Army guys ..."

The Colonel scanned the sergeant with a solitary, imperious gaze. "You didn't touch anything now, did you?"

"No, not me. But the explosives they set off," he said, pointing in the direction of the bomb squad's truck, "made quite a goddamned mess."

"Good. Find any documents in there?"

"Tons. Drafts of communiqués, from what I could tell, mostly that, actually."

"Okay. Tell Doctor Vale he can pick them up after I've had a chance to go over them."

The sergeant nodded, all casual complicity, as Colonel Lapierre gave a brusque nod toward the house. "You'll show me around?"

Ice in his eyes, and with straight-backed confidence: Martinek was impressed. His own star faded before this man. He settled for a shake of the head.

"Those vultures, I don't want to see them," Uncle Bob grunted, pointing at the journalists milling about in front of the house. "Did anyone take any pictures?"

"Only of the front of the house," the detective calmly replied. "Don't worry, they haven't got permission to go inside yet. I'll give them the tour later on."

"Good. Well, let's go ..."

They walked through the door, stopping in the entrance to the kitchen with a start of surprise. The place was in shambles: chicken takeout boxes here and there, garbage bags left sitting about, cupboards yawning open, and the floor covered with greasy papers, takeout menus, and spilt liquids.

Seemingly, the military bomb squad, expecting to find booby traps, had used small explosive charges to open every single door.

Uncle Bob let his eyes wander to the ceiling. He could see freshly cracked plaster from which a couple of nails poked out, right along a beam. The Colonel thought to himself that the bomb-squad guys sure didn't cut corners.

He walked though the kitchen, stepping over the debris, Martinek at his heels, and stopped before the desk on which the phone sat. A seven-digit number was etched in the gyproc, followed by the letters BB.

"What's that, Martinek?"

"A restaurant, I think. Baby Barbecue."

The Colonel bent down to pick up a telephone lying on the floor in a sorry state. It had been opened up, eviscerated. Wires hung like veins from a carcass. Uncle Bob held it up with an amused look on his face.

"Didn't leave much to chance, did they, Martinek?"

"No . . . Colonel," Machinegun heard himself reply.

MEXCALICO

ROOSTERS HAD BEEN CROWING UP in the village since well before dawn.

Marie-Québec lifted her eyes from her book. This was no doubt the best time of day: freshly squeezed oranges, the joyful whistling of coffee boiling in its Italian contraption on the gas stove. Once out of bed, she accepted the glass of pulpy juice, allowed a smile to flirt with her lips for a moment, and stepped onto the patio to lounge on the sun-warmed stone bench while he put new coffee on the burner, turned on the heat under the pot of *frijoles* left over from the night before, and began cutting the onion, pepper, and tomatoes to prepare Mexican-style eggs. Whenever he bought eggs wholesale at the *tienda*, right at the village's entrance, they were still warm from the chicken sitting on them, and from time to time he would find a downy feather bonded to an egg's surface by a molecule of excrement. Out of the corner of his eye, Sam watched his girlfriend spread out and unfold like one of those Japanese things you drop in a pot of water and watch bloom. That was Marie-Québec in a nutshell: the soul of an iguana in the body of a Huron princess. An hour later, she had gotten her fill of sunlight and came in to eat.

Before Zopilote, she never smiled like that, right out of bed.

On the beach down the hill, the waves stretched out on the sand with dull crashes like the sound of crumbling buildings.

They'd gone almost directly — a week between buying the tickets over the Internet and sitting in one of Air Transat's lumbering beasts as it dragged itself away from one of Mirabel airport's semi-deserted airstrips — from an overheated cabin on tiny Lake Laurendeau to the humid 32 degrees of this tropical sky sullied by the exudations of life forms as diverse as single-celled algae to great flocks of birds. The heat rose like bitumen smoke off the tarmac at the airport in Acapulco.

They'd jumped in a car and driven straight south to Puerto Escondido, where they'd spent the day watching surf bums wait for the perfect wave, before leaving for the Yucatan. In Tulum, they rented a sort of cement *blockhaus,* which, for two days, made them feel like they were living in a garage. The overflow of Cancun tourists ended up dribbling down the eastern coast of the peninsula all the way to Belize in regular waves of rented Jeeps driven by khaki-clad Americans, with their cowboy hats and their T-shirts the size of large jibs. They looked at taco ovens as if they were operated by Doctor Strangelove, about to blow up any minute, and they always seemed to be a moment away from donning latex gloves before picking up the local ham. They saw tankers passing on a dirty, turquoise sea.

They drove right through Chiapas. From the roof of their hotel in San Cristobal, they heard soldiers practising their cannon fire in the mountains. Then off again, on weaving roads, sliding on the side of precipices on every turn. They hurtled down the other side of the sierra to the Gulf of Tehuantepec, their car now rolling between open-air garbage dumps smoking under the sun and tiny anonymous haciendas with crumbling walls covered with political slogans. Spans of shrubs festooned with ragged plastic bags glinted in the grubby light.

Sometimes from this broken landscape a deserted beach would suddenly sparkle into existence: murky foaming waves crashing in, golden mist, the green backdrop of mountains, the naked flesh of sand running off as far as the eye could see.

They'd ended up in Zopilote.

Their rented cabana was located on the hills overlooking the sea, next to the village. A palm-frond ceiling, wooden rooms with bamboo walls. They reached it by climbing a ladder and shared the kitchen and bathroom with Marco, an Italian Zapatista sympathizer perpetually stoned on Mary Jane and cannabis resin, who spoke four languages but hadn't said more than three words since they'd gotten there.

Sam pressed the oranges, made coffee, and sat at the kitchen table with his pocket French-Spanish dictionary, a map of Mexico, and his overripe copy of *La Jornada*. He practised the tongue of Cervantes while following subcommandant Marco's Zapatista caravan through the country. The October Crisis was behind him, far behind him.

Marie-Québec was working on the play she planned to direct in Maldoror the following autumn: *Happy Endings*, the story of the return flight from Acapulco on an Air Transat charter of a gang of boozed-up Quebeckers with their souvenir sombreros. Once the plane lands, all the passengers start applauding. The spectators are supposed to do the same. And the curtain falls.

After breakfast, Marie-Québec would go off with her books and papers, a bottle of water, some fruit. She would take the weaving path that followed the curve of the cliff until she reached an isolated beach, midway between Zopilote and the next village. Mexicans called it Playa del Amor, the beach of love. In the dry, spindly forest, her rustling scared off jays with crests as long as pencils, motmots with their red eyes and thick beaks, and a few green parakeets. Lizards bolted as she came near them on the already scorching ground. In the trees around her hung fruit of which she did not know the name.

An old Indian peasant woman had her shack near the end of the trail. She lived there with her chickens, an enormous turkey, and a boar at the end of a piece of rope. Marie-Québec greeted the old woman as she passed, *hola*, removed her sandals, walked on the sand, and rolled out her mat. Waves exploded against the rocks. Farther off, soaring pelicans in single file skimmed the frothing crests of waves. And high up, far above her head, those long black birds Sam called magnificent frigate birds were letting themselves float on the thermals. Vultures floated down and perched on cacti on the cliff side, and spread their wings in the shimmering heat.

A young Mexican boy walked by, holding an orange. She smiled. He slowly made his way up the beach. Sometimes she'd be the only one there for hours. Later, the old woman walked by above the beach, burdened with an enormous load of wood. Bent forward to keep her balance, she made her way through the sand with the grace of a giant sea turtle filled with eggs.

Marie-Québec thought about getting up to help her. But the fact was, she stayed on her parrot-patterned towel, among her open books.

When he finished his Spanish lesson, or became bored with idling his day away, Sam would walk down to the village and hang out on the beach. On one end of it was the fiefdom of the retired hippies of Shalâlah, where old burnouts-cum-estate agents had meetings with God, or at least one of His subsidiaries. Every morning, as he jogged barefoot in the sand, he could admire a wonderful specimen of the California goodwife, facing the ocean in the lotus position wearing

Eden-like attire and wrinkled by half a century of excessive isolation. She sat there with her eyes closed, breasts low, palms open, invoking in a soft voice the Egyptian princess of a previous incarnation while, in this reality, her merino-wool-sweater-wearing poodle shat in the sand beside her, and a bunch of piglets, a little farther off, were burrowing their snouts in its previous day's offerings.

The Québécois bar was located just before the cliffs that closed off the other side of the beach. It reminded him of the old joke: What do two Quebeckers do when they meet in a foreign country? They open a bar.

The Mono Azul, it was called. The *palapa* that sheltered the bar from the sun opened onto a fine sand beach. The owner knew everything there was to know about Abitibi, Maldoror, Cadillac, Val-d'Or, and the Kaganoma. At one point, he'd worked as a brush cutter in the northwest of the province.

It's a small world. And so he wasn't really surprised when, one night, Marie-Québec told him about her conversation with a former FLQ member called Richard, over at the Mono that afternoon. But he kept silent all the same.

At first she hadn't realized whom she was speaking to. The man was reticent, although he liked to talk, and it was over a few hours that she finally got him to tell his story.

"Richard who?"

All she knew was that he was called Richard.

She saw him again the next day, a chance encounter at the Playa del Amor.

"He's spending the winter here. In a neighbouring village, in fact: Carranza. Zopilote is a bit too touristy for his taste, and he thinks there are too many Quebeckers already in Carranza. He goes deep-sea diving and it costs him almost nothing to live. He fishes his dinner using some sort of harpoon gun. A couple of days ago he saw some dolphins."

"Lucky bastard. And what does he do?"

"Nothing right now, but . . . he's got a film company."

"Ah, it's Richard Godefroid."

"Yes. He told me his name. I forgot to tell you . . ."

"Don't worry about it. You're a much better sniffer-out of FLQ guys than I am."

'He and I might work together."

"You can't do that, Marie. I'm the Octobeerist around here. At least, I used to be . . ."

"He's looking for someone to adapt *The Just* into a movie. In Quebec French. It'd be set in the seventies, with FLQ guys instead of Russian nihilists. He wants it to be a Governor General who gets blown up."

"Sweet. And he offered you the leading role, of course."

"Can you imagine anyone else as Dora, huh? He invited us to supper tomorrow."

"What?"

"He says he'll ask the Indian woman, the one on the beach, to cook some fish for us. He'll supply the fish. *Huachinangos*, or maybe rock lobster, depends on what he catches. I told him about you. What's with your sulking?"

In order to find what I was looking for, I had to stop searching. Gode was reappearing in my life like the corpse of a drowning victim, buried under the ocean's current, spit back out onto hard, dry land.

The minibus to La Cuenca — the major town, a bit inland — was bursting at the seams. Raw leather sandals, sneakers, and finely shined shoes straddled one another like horny toads. Travellers wearing khaki shorts and Oaxacan locals, in communion with each other's sweat, both human and animal — a turkey and three iguanas, legs shackled, destined for the market. Luggage affixed to the roof by straps made for an unstable tower. At one point, a tourist's backpack flew off and fell on the road behind us. Alerted by screams and a generous dose of hand-slapping on the sides of the truck, the driver stopped. With no one behind us, a young boy jumped off the bus and ran to pick up the lost luggage. Running back to the *collectivo* with a smile on his face and the bag in his hands, you'd think he'd just invented a new game. I looked around; everyone was smiling, mothers, workers, farmers, students in their knee socks and uniforms, but also the gringos, as if it were some sort of joke, the best one yet. The tourist got his backpack and patted it in a general good mood. If we'd been in Quebec, we'd all be calling for a board of inquiry to identify the guilty party.

How do you make a man talk? Without ripping his nails out, I mean. I was pondering this question, staring at the bottles of alcohol in a grocery store in La Cuenca, weighing each one, looking at the labels. White wine would usually have been the right choice, but finding ice at Playa del Amor was a risky bet at the best of times. A refrigerator was absolute madness. I turned to the tequilas. Following the slow descent of a reddish larva to the bottom of a bottle of mescal, the sensual dance of the worm to the movement of the liquid inside. Might as well drink formaldehyde. I ended up going for a Cuervo, the large bottle. I felt like I was standing before an armoury's gun rack, comparing calibres. Just before leaving, I changed my mind and got the mescal, as well.

Between La Cuenca and Zopilote, at the point where the road reaches the coast, lay the small fishing port of Puerto Madre. Under a lonely parasol, I sipped a Nescafé and watched fishermen line up their catch on the sides of their boats, then begin their knife work, throwing entrails up in the air to a bunch of squawking birds from which, from time to time, a frigate bird would dive to catch a sliver of intestines.

Life could be simple. I had the proof, right here before my eyes. Life biting into life. Life is life. My copy of *La Jornada* on the table, my French-Spanish dictionary, my notebook filled with new words, definitions, conjugations, declensions, exceptions, my instant coffee, black and sweet, two squeezed oranges in a tall glass next to it, fruit flies, light, the taste of the first beer toward the end of the afternoon, the spiralling of the magnificent frigate birds on the ascending thermals near the coast. Reading Carlos Monsivais's column day after day, following the triumphant advance of subcommandants Marcos and his Zapatour toward the Mexican basin. Daydreaming over the colour illustrations in my bird book.

The last thing I expected was Marie-Québec dredging up what I thought I had escaped when I left Quebec.

I was the only one loafing about on the small beach at Puerto Madre, jammed tight with fishing boats. Letting the sand sift between my toes, I began thinking of my old Professor Branlequeue, to whom even on his deathbed Godefroid had refused to tell the tale of Paul Lavoie's last hours. Chevalier had been anything but a globetrotter. He'd shocked his acquaintances by turning down speaking invitations in Italy and Brazil. He'd never even seen Paris! To those who expressed surprise, he'd reply that he hadn't left the muddy land of his childhood to end up like a cow in a stall, stuck between an airplane window and a "gravimetrically distinct individual." I'd never heard him mention a beach. And suddenly, I couldn't help imagining him with flip-flops, indolently tossing his hat to the wind and running on the wet sand like a madman.

Truly, he hadn't been a happy man. Happy, unhappy . . . so what! But to carry your regrets to the grave . . . After October '70, Chevalier had lived solely to shed light on the ugly tricks played by those who had taken his civil liberties from him and thrown him in a cell, all in the name of some cosmetic democracy that'd been confiscated by the state. One day, he claimed, we'd find out that the entire Province of Quebec had been the target of a true military-police *coup d'état*! And for that reason, he'd never found peace again, not like the one I had found and was basking in right now. A peace that I could attain precisely because I had renounced it all, and he had never given in.

After all, who was Godefroid? One of the last two men who could still tell the true story of what happened on rue Collins the day Lavoie died. He'd been spending his winter in Carranza, on the Pacific Coast, swept into my path by pure coincidence. All these years he'd simply been another name. And today I'd meet the man behind that name, and I knew why I feared being face to face with him. He'd tell the truth, give us a rude awakening, and defuse our bomb. Yes, belief flourished in shadows, and doubt is the basis of our errant faith. What I feared most of all was nothing less than the bright light of naked truth and the ultimate defeat of our old Octobeerist fantasy. In the end, I feared more than anything finding absolutely no hint of controversy at the sharp edge of our beliefs, of all our "elucubrations." No plot, no schemes, no conspiracies.

"The first time I washed up here, in the mid-eighties, Zopilote was nothing more than a pot-smoker's paradise. A colony of penniless tramps strung out between Puerto Madre and Carranza. When someone came up to you, it was to tell you about the healing power of crystals and pyramids, not to show you his home-cooked pharmacy. But today the *narcos* have taken over the country and you can see the difference, even here."

Marie-Québec and Sam got there before Gode and sat around drinking tepid beer, waiting for him. The old Indian woman was bustling about not far off, a century or so away, cooking tortillas and peeling avocados. After a while, they saw their compatriot crossing the cape that closed off one side of the beach from the other and was walkable only at low tide, and begin coming toward them. He walked stiffly, looking about him, like a man being followed. Despite his relaxed outfit, sunglasses, and unbuttoned shirt, there was something ancient and animal in the way he moved, as if he were aware of dragging a shadow behind him.

He'd been holding a sodden plastic bag; inside were two freshly caught *huachinangos* and a rock lobster.

"But this small beach, here," Gode continued, "it hasn't changed at all. You can still hang out here, alone, in the middle of the day, or, if worse comes to worst, share it with a bare-breasted woman," Gode added, with a quick wink in Marie-Québec's direction. "And *senora* Cisneros hasn't changed a bit, either. Seventeen years ago, she was as young as she is today."

"She lives in paradise and doesn't even know it," Marie-Québec said, before licking the salt off the back of her hand and tossing back a shot of tequila, the skin on her face creasing like a sheet of paper as she bit into the lime.

"Imagining that happiness lies in poverty is the pastime of the intellectual," Samuel calmly said. He looked at Gode. "Consider yourself warned, Marie-Québec is the type who's always saving the world..."

"I can respect that," Gode replied, gazing at the young woman. "I passed through that phase as well."

Taking a pinch of salt and a slice of lime off the plastic saucer, he raised his glass in their direction and knocked back his Cuervo.

The turkey was clucking about around their table. Then, planting himself before them, he puffed himself out, tripled in volume, displaying his grotesque, crimson, outraged virility.

"He's dancing at your table," Gode commented, pouring himself another tequila.

Senora Cisneros brought two bowls: a large terracotta one for the guacamole and a smaller, blue, earthenware bowl for the *salsa picante.* She then returned to the table with more lime quarters. She tut-tutted the turkey away, adding a rude hand gesture for good measure.

"You know, I never did help her carry her wood," Marie-Québec said. "And now, instead of helping her out with dinner, I sit here, talking with you two."

"She's been carrying that same pile of wood for a thousand years," Samuel threw in. "And the last thing she needs is to have to soothe our hypocritical gringo consciences."

Salt, tequila, lime.

"With what I'm paying her to cook the fish," Gode added, tilting in Marie-Québec's direction, "she'll be able to live for a month, easy."

They spoke of the Zapatista situation. Gode was somewhat reserved regarding the so-called revolution. He believed they had traded in their guns for cameras once the initial skirmishes had petered out. Then they'd added web sites and the ear of Hollywood intellectuals like Oliver Stone to the mix. Zapatista leaders now travelled surrounded by human shields of Italian pacifists. Their number included journalists, groupies, and sympathizers from civil societies (humanitarian aid workers, union leaders, representatives of popular groups, and outreach officers from a horde of national and international social-progressive parties, not to mention, of course, the usual gaggle of hangers-on) who were all ready to take over the capital by simply stepping off the bus, after having seen the rest of Mexico fall at their feet along their long march, without encountering any opposition, of course. The internationalization of the Chiapas-based movement now seemed inevitable.

"What are you doing on the beach, guys?" Marie-Québec asked, preparing another shot of tequila. "Don't you see that the revolution is passing you by?"

"Sure, the communications revolution," Nihilo approved. He turned to Gode. "Looks like they're succeeding at what you were trying to do, back in the day. If you can't seize power, at least get some good publicity..."

Gode refused to take the bait.

"When Marcos arrived in Cuautla, in the State of Morelos," Gode began, "city officials offered him a painting as a welcoming present. You know what was on it? A portrait of Marcos surrounded by Villa and Zapata. They're all three squatting with something in their hands..."

Gode paused for a moment. Salt on wrist. A small glass of tequila.

"And what did the three of them have in their hands? I'll tell you ... fighting cocks."

"So?" Marie-Québec asked.

"For a fighting cock," Gode continued, leaning in, "there are only two possible outcomes: victory or death. No such thing as a compromise. And Zapata and Villa were real roosters, and they died. In other words, I wouldn't want to be in Marcos's shoes..."

"Beware of those who survive..." Sam said and, lifting his glass, smiled.

Gode looked at him in silence for a moment.

The fish arrived, cooked over a wood fire, and the rock lobster, the choice of the catch reserved by the fisherman for Marie-Québec. Her cheeks were beginning to glow, her voice raised. Gode was already rather drunk. The sun was collapsing over the ocean.

Sam cited, from memory, a passage from Chomsky, which came out dizzied and confused. He spoke of something called the *antineoliberal spearhead* and predicted that Zapatista confusion would spread throughout the world.

"Who gives a fuck about Chomsky," Gode opined, not turning toward him.

"*Gracias, senora,*" Marie-Québec said. "*Muchas gracias ...*"

"At the tip of the point, over there," Gode said, "I saw a killer whale, once. I didn't feel like a big man, with my harpoon gun."

"According to Alain Touraine," Samuel murmured, staring conspiratorially at his fish, "neozapatism is the great paradigm shift that the third millennium needs."

"You can't mess around with those waves." Gode leaned his head with its glassy eyes even further toward Marie-Québec. "I've seen gringos swallowed up under tons of water. Others are just pulled out by the current, and if they're lucky, some small Mexican kid takes his board and brings them back from the open sea."

The sun finally crashed on the other side of the horizon and Gode turned toward Sam, saying:

"I don't give a shit about Touraine, either."

"Okay."

He was thinking of his bottle of mescal hidden over there in the bamboo hut.

"In Carranza," continued Gode, "I walked into the kitchen one morning and it was full of ants. The small red ones. There were about three million of them just going back and forth from the mangos and bananas in the fruit basket. Back home, in the north, we'd have bombarded the kitchen as if it were Baghdad. I contacted the guy who takes care of the huts and all that, some typical peasant from around here, with his moustache and muscles as dry as bicycle tires, and I showed him the invasion in my kitchen. He looked me over and said, with the Pope's own magnanimity: *Se van a ir* . . . they'll leave. I concluded that he simply didn't feel like working that day and said that to get rid of me. But I came back an hour later and there wasn't a goddamn ant left. That's what I think of your Marcos and his conquest of Mexico . . ."

He dipped a corn tortilla in the guacamole and looked around for the bottle. The tequila level was going down faster than you could drink it. To the west, the clouds looked like overripe papayas.

A bit later, Samuel grabbed the bottle, shook it, and examined it. The soldier was all but dead. He poured what was left into Marie-Québec's glass, then Gode's. Salt, fire, lime — no quarter.

A long silence seemed to emanate from the coal box of the burnt sky. Close to the reefs, where brown pelicans feasted on a school of fish, the ocean was boiling. The rock lobster and red mullet were now history. Samuel suggested they have a nightcap — the bottle of mescal.

Samuel had a theory about Godefroid. These past few weeks, at the Mono Azul, Sam had taken time to study the local migratory fauna, the mix of ex-pats, those who were spending the winter, and simple tourists. A small Québécois colony wintered in the place, within a radius of a hundred metres from the Mono. A lot of single men. The first time you spoke to them, they claimed to have never been better. You almost never saw the wound at first glance. But it always surfaced, with a few beers, a promise of love, a small narcotic trans-action, or simply a sympathetic ear. Lost love, professional failure, personal bankruptcy. Divorce. A child who died young. A partner with an incurable disease. A car accident. A cuckolding. Sexual abuse by Uncle Irving. Forgotten at the zoo when they were three years old. And of course, that's without counting all those attempt-ing to hide an acrimonious firing while writing the Novel of the Century.

Gode, Nihilo believed, was one of those broken men; he'd killed, or not, and had paid his debt to society. That wasn't the problem. What was eating him was the demon of the story he wasn't telling. It was the pact of silence and the corpse in the closet of history. The black hole that surrounded Lavoie's death. What's never told has never been lived — the logic of the confessional. And for Gode, this burrowing silence had lasted thirty years now. He'd given a long interview when he left prison and told a story with as many inconsistencies as contradictions, which led to more questions rather than answers. The October Crisis had remained, through the years, the dark side of the moon for Quebeckers. A collective amnesia in the form of a death.

He was spending his winter in a crumbling cinder-block cell, which was covered with a palm frond roof and was just large enough to hold a bed, a hammock, and a chest of drawers. *Mi cabana en México.* And then he saw a beautiful young woman, the kind who understands everything, and he needed to confide in someone like the mortise needed the tenon. Someone who was able to hold her own on the subject of Camus and the Bolsheviks.

And as Sam climbed the ladder, unlocked the lock, and grabbed the bottle in his room, he needed to fight off an image that strayed from darker parts of his mind: she in bed with Gode. Pillow talk.

Sitting in the kitchen, Gode was looking at the *Field Guide to the Birds of Mexico and Central America.*

"I saw a red-headed parrot not too far from here," Nihilo mentioned, brandishing the bottle of mescal.

Gode pointed at the parakeet page.

"I've seen some of these ... as well as those."

"White-fronted amazons! Red-fronted conures! Where?"

"Near Huatulco. I was with a friend, he's absolutely crazy about birds ... He came with his telescope and his list of species he wanted to see. If you want to go over there, we can."

His laborious elocution was interrupted by Marie-Québec, slightly pale, emerging from the white cement cube that sheltered the bathroom.

"If you want ... to ..."

"The conures."

"Yup, that's it."

"In Abitibi," Marie-Québec explained, "Sam would argue with the hunters, since he, Master Sam, could distinguish three species of partridge."

Gode shot a look at Nihilo.

"She told me you'd been to Kaganoma."

"Yeah, that's one of the things you and I have in common. The other is Chevalier Branlequeue..."

Gode closed the bird book.

"That mescal isn't going to drink itself, is it?"

It was almost dark. They walked on the beach, bare feet in the wet sand, the sea glowing from single-cell algae, passing the bottle around. In a leaking, blood-red light, the silhouette of a backlit fisherman holding his net, seemingly frozen like a heron facing the crashing waves. Far above their heads, the marine breeze dragged birds toward earth.

The three of them walked on the beach, almost without a sound, passing the bottle back and forth.

Before reaching the Mono, Sam turned toward the hieratic silhouette of the bait fisherman, water up to his chest, net brandished in both hands. He saw him cast his net as if trying to lasso the waves, then disappear, buried under a mountain of foam. He emerged on the other side of the wave and, fighting against backwash, returned to land, pulling the net tied with a rope to his wrist behind him. When he finally reached ground, he raised the net and it was filled with fish.

Orange tongues and tufts of smoke leapt up from a pyramid of wood some four feet high between the Mono and the sea. The amps spat out the greatest hits from the seventies, and the fire attracted a bunch of people. Lying on the sand, wild dogs with flea-ridden flanks like washboards snarled at the shadows. Someone came to speak with Gode, and the bottle of mescal, passed from hand to hand, disappeared. Sam found the bar and paid for a few rounds of tequila for Gode and Marie-Québec. She occupied the stool between the two men, softly shimmying to the rhythm of the music.

Sam wanted to talk to Gode about *The Just*.

"Don't start with him," Marie-Québec told the former FLQer.

"Why?"

"You won't be able to shut him up."

"S'okay. The night's still young."

She heard them talking. Her body followed the music.

"We've got all night," he repeated. "But I thought you were the expert on *The Just*..."

"I'm an expert in nothing. Except maybe the sun. Or a drop of water on an inch of skin. How many bellybuttons can you fill with the sea? That's my specialty."

Sam jumped to his feet and announced that he was going to go swimming. Gode turned his head a little to look at him, but all he could see was a small print dress suspended on two breasts large as a hand and as firm as mangos that swayed above her stool to the rhythm of the Mamas and the Papas.

Sam barely staggered as he strayed from the bar. He stopped at the fire for a moment, then walked away from the halo and continued to march toward the sea, in the dark.

Gode swallowed his tequila and followed it with a sip of beer, wiping his lips with the back of his hand. He felt incredible. Marie-Québec lifted her glass.

"To our projects."

"Do you know how old I am?"

"Over fifty. I hope you weren't keeping it a secret. You're part of history."

"Exactly. Over fifty. Too old to tell lies, even for a good cause."

"And what is it, your cause?"

"You."

"Okay. And the lie?"

"I'm a director. I should have added a bankrupt movie producer. But to get into the good graces of an actress, it isn't the best line …"

"So your Lynx Productions, it's done?"

"Finished, dead, kaput. Now you can stop talking to me …"

They ordered more tequila. Their pesos were vanishing.

"Your boyfriend, I don't know if you know, but I can see him coming a mile off."

"Really?"

"Really. Writers and scriptwriters, they're a dime a dozen between Carranza and Puerto Madre, and they all come and see me and they all want to know — guess what? They think they can soften me up with their bottles filled with drain cleanser. This place is the asshole of the great plumed serpent."

Over Gode's shoulder, Marie-Québec could see Sam walking back up the beach, his dripping black and green shorts flattened against his thighs. He was drying his face and hair with his T-shirt. Gode followed her gaze.

"Come with me to Guatemala."

"I didn't hear that."

Gode lifted his two large paws to his eyes, as if seeing them for the first time.

"I saw a trapper strangle a lynx with his own hands," he said, parodying the gesture. "Up there, up north … You know what? I think every woman dreams of being caressed by a killer."

"And that's what you are?"

"That's what the judge said I was."

Samuel passed them and leaned against the bar.

"A drink," he demanded.

Soon he was struggling with his small raw leather change purse that he carried on the beach instead of his wallet.

"Um, Sam ... where's the bottle of mescal gone?"

"Into hardened livers, old chum."

"No problem, we'll buy some more ..."

"I'd be surprised if you could buy an entire bottle."

"Not at the Mono, of course. I mean in some local restaurant, where the Indians sell it in old gas cans on the streets of Oaxaca. The local moonshine. In a shack not too far away from here you can buy it straight from the tap. Just be sure you're ready for it, because despite the crystal meth and all the other crap that's in circulation, it's still the strongest drug around here."

Gode steadied himself with both hands on the bar and pushed himself to his feet. He laid what he thought was a light hand on Marie-Québec's shoulder, to avoid staggering too much. Straightening, he removed his hand. He and Sam were now face to face.

"I know you want to knock me down in the sand," Gode managed to say, "but we'll see who falls first."

"You hear that, Marie?"

"Where are you going?"

"To buy some mescal with Gode."

GODE

HE'D GIVE EVERYTHING HE OWNS for her — more than that — the silence of the trees and every bird's song, the cry of the beasts he so wants to catch, the rustle of the wind in the branches of a forest a million square kilometres wide, to be in bed with her. To awake basking in the light of the peace on her face and to feel her warm breath and the heat of her womanly body.

Instead, he's on a couch in the living room, eyes wide open, awaiting dawn.

And so he climbs into his pants and tiptoes out.

The eastern side of Queen-Mary Road, just before the cemetery gates, is still dark. He takes a deep breath of the cold October air, the burnt orange of the leaves half-masked by darkness, turns left on Decelles, walks by Café Campus, climbs Decelles. The words of some idiotic song run through his head.

What's he doing
What's his beef
Tell me who is he?

He's funny looking
That man

He continues walking and reaches the corner of Côte-Sainte-Catherine, turns right, keeps moving, hands in his pockets, slightly bent over, his chin buried in the neck of his sweater. A bit farther on he catches the eastbound bus: a Sunday-morning bus, after the long Thanksgiving weekend. Inside, it's as quiet as a tomb.

The bus descends the flank of the mountain and Gode climbs out at the corner of Mont-Royal, heading east. He meets a few passersby, early birds, others still half-asleep walking on autopilot, a mix of insomniac maniacs and wound-up homosexuals with one destination in mind: the bushes on the mountain.

And while he carries himself through a field of calculating looks, a singular impression begins to come over him — a vertigo, a desire to scream his lungs out. He feels the nervous city begin to quiver around him, the same city as yesterday, but like new, in his own eyes, having become a place for questions: Who? How? Where?

And he *knows*.

And the intoxicating fact that no one else is in his shoes, can see inside his head, propels him out of himself, over himself, and he feels, now, so much more alive.

We won't let ourselves be had
What's he doing
What's his beef

Wait now things are right
Young man
We'll put him behind bars
That guy
If he keeps on with his ways

On the corner of Saint-Denis, he walks into the Fameux, greets the owner with a nod, and sits at a table where he can keep an eye on the still-deserted street. The radio is on, the owner fiddling with the dial.

Even before taking his order, the forty-something rhinestone-clad waitress gives the table a perfunctory wipe and serves him a cup of coffee. Gode thanks her with another nod.

"What's the world coming to?" she says, then: "You gonna eat, hon?"

"Two eggs over easy, with bacon. Did they say who did it?"

"Not yet, but…"

"Those goddamn FLQers," a customer a few tables down throws out, "I'd line 'em all up against a brick wall, and…"

Gode resists the urge to turn around. Must be seven or eight customers sprinkled among the huge pots of marinated red peppers soaking near the windows and on the back tables. Men with the faces of graveyard-shift workers, pitiful solitary partygoers still not in bed, and a few roomers minus a roof. Gode sees a man with a blue plaid shirt leafing through the *Journal de Montréal*'s special edition, devoted to the kidnapping. Once again that strange awareness of himself. His scandalous anonymity at the heart of the event.

He hears on the radio that the abduction hasn't yet been claimed, which means that the previous night's phone call didn't have the desired effect. He devours his eggs and Wonder-bread toast and even swallows the half-dried slice of tomato at the edge of his plate, almost as if this were his final meal. Then he gets up, pays his bill, leaves a tip, nods to the owner once again, and walks out.

The sidewalk. The street. The subway right there. It'll be six in the morning soon.

For the first time since well before dawn, when he opened his eyes, Gode thinks of the man as an existence, like something alive, real. He remembers the feel of his knee against the hostage's back in the car. A living being. It's true. You're going to see him.

LAVOIE

HE'D LIKE TO OPEN HIS EYES, but he can't. He hears the radio, which tells him it's morning. The previous day, in the garage, they covered his eyes with a bunch of layers of Kleenex covered in tape. Then, holding him by the shoulders and pushing him forward, they brought him directly into a house through a hole dug in a wall.

He's in a room, lying in a bed, handcuffed to a metal dog leash whose other side is handcuffed to the bed. He slept by fits and starts, and now can hear his kidnappers in another room. Water boiling in an electric kettle. The hostage strains to listen, hears the kettle's whistle, somewhere behind him. There's a hallway, then the kitchen. He's thinking clearly; a man awake.

He moves, rolls over himself until he reaches the edge of his leash; the mattress creaks under him. He clears his throat once, twice.

Steps. Breathing, right next to him, next to the bed.

The man's voice wants to know if everything is "okay."

"Last night," he says, "when you took me, I was waiting for my wife, we were going to the restaurant..."

"What a shame for you, but that's how it is. Change of plans. Are you hungry?"

"Yes."

"Do you want eggs and toast?"

"Yes. How am I supposed to eat with these on?"

They take his handcuffs off, help him to sit up by pressing his back against the pillows, and Lavoie asks to see what he's eating.

"Take his blindfold off," one of his captors says.

It hurts, as though they were scalping him. He opens his eyes, sees the duct tape with his hair on it; not doing his encroaching baldness any favours.

With the plate on his legs, he eats his breakfast, Wonder bread and scrambled eggs, under the supervision of one of his masked caretakers armed with an assault rifle. And Lavoie can't believe his eyes: they didn't even cover the window! He concentrates on every small detail, trying to avoid looking like a man scouting his surroundings while swallowing his meal. The window lets daylight streak into the room on the left side of the bed. Half a bungalow, a few vacant lots, a stretch of empty street, fields, a few buildings. Maybe half a mile away, a large hangar he immediately recognizes. Lavoie catches his breath. The old political hand, shaking hands and kissing babies; he's in his own county. He knows the place like the back of his hand. During the last electoral campaign, he used the landing strips on the other side of that hangar. The one with the big number 12 painted on the roof. The house where he's being held is right next to the Saint-Hubert airport.

The hostage lowers his eyes to his plate, breaks off a piece of scrambled egg with his fork, and places it on a slice of buttered toast, which he then brings up to his mouth. He chews, swallows, then turns his head toward the young masked man guarding him. Paul Lavoie looks at those dark slits of eyes, and smiles weakly.

"Thanks, the eggs are good."

While he was eating, one of the kidnappers who'd jumped out of the car the night before came back. Lavoie can hear them in the next room, formulating aloud the wording of the communiqué that one of them then types up on a machine.

The Minister will be executed on Sunday, October 11, at ten o'clock at night if the authorities have not responded positively to all the demands expressed following Mr. Travers's kidnapping.

Sunday the eleventh. In other words, today. Lavoie realizes that he must get ready to die.

As his captor moves to handcuff him once again, he says:

"They're writing to the government, in the other room? I thought it had already been done..."

"We wrote a first communiqué, but they didn't find it."

"Could I write a letter to my wife? You know, while my hands are still free..."

12 October, 1970. 7 a.m.
Dearest,

I'm doing well, I spent a good night, almost as if we'd been together, our little family. I constantly think of the three of you. And it helps me cope.

The important thing is that the authorities do something! For
the rest, let's help ourselves, and perhaps Heaven will help us
in return . . .

My love to all of you.
Paul

Avenue Savane is a bit further on. He can never recall the names
of those two tiny isolated lanes that go through the fields. He knows
the area, has already been through it, knocked on doors. He tries to
remember, but fails. Just as he begins to despair, he receives unin-
tended help from his kidnappers: he hears one of them pick up the
phone, in the hallway between the room and the kitchen, and call
a taxi without a care in the world! Motionless on the bed, Lavoie
strains himself to the breaking point to hear what the unknown
voice is saying into the receiver. The telephone table, he thinks, is
just a few steps away from his room's open door, near the bathroom.
    "A car for 140 Collins, please," the voice says.
    Thank you.

Later, he asks one of his captors if he can stretch his legs a little.
After speaking with his comrades, the man comes back, removes
the handcuffs that tie the leash to the bed, lifts the hostage up, and
walks him through the house. A short bathroom break, and it's
back to walking. The smells: frying, burnt bread. The kitchen is
here. With only his ears and his feet to guide him, Lavoie's whole
being becomes an antenna that moves through a darkened space
and brushes up against the walls, attempting to obtain as much
information as possible. He tries to recreate the configuration of
the house in his mind. The television and the typewriter are in the

room next to his own. His eyes are covered and his thoughts turn to death.

A communiqué is read over the radio. *The Minister will be executed on Sunday, October 11 at ten o'clock at night if the . . .* The terrorists congratulate each other in the other room, which must be the living room.

And Lavoie thinks: Collins, rue Collins. Saint-Hubert airport. Hangar number 12.

Around noon, they bring him a peanut butter sandwich.

"Sorry, but that's all there is . . . we've only got bread left."

"It's okay."

"Would you like a nice cup of tea with that?"

"Yes, please."

Shortly before one o'clock, another special bulletin. This time, the communiqué, written by hand, was found in a phone booth, accompanied by Lavoie's letter to his wife.

Again: if before ten o'clock tonight, both governments have not answered favourably to the FLQ's conditions, Minister Lavoie will be executed. If all conditions are fulfilled, Operation Deliverance will be terminated, and Lavoie will be released within twenty-four hours. Any hesitation by the authorities will be FATAL to the Minister. It's a large enough concession for us to be forced to return him alive and well. Do not ask too much.
Quebec Liberation Front
We shall be victorious . . .

A handwriting expert speaks to the authenticity of the letter to the wife. The newsreader speaks in a solemn tone. Now, for a commercial break.

Only nine hours to live, thinks Lavoie.

The other man is back. The one who seems to be the boss comes to the house by taxi once in a while, and it sounds as though he believes they're being incredibly generous to let Lavoie live. He hears them type up another communiqué in the next room.

Lavoie calls to them. A kidnapper comes in.

"Can I write another letter?"

"Again?"

"Yes. I'll write to Vézina. I want to write to my premier. I can convince him. Let me do it, you'll see..."

My dear Albert,

I feel like I'm writing the most important letter of my life. For now, I am being treated well, even politely (...)

We are witnessing a well-organized escalation that will end only with the freeing of the political prisoners. After me, there'll be a third, then a fourth and a twelfth.

My very dear Albert, what follows is very, very important: you must order the immediate cessation of all police raids. Their continuance will be my death warrant. On the other hand, if the release and departure of the political prisoners are brought to a good end, I am certain that my personal safety will be guaranteed. We are very close to a solution, I can feel it, because between my kidnappers and I there is no

real animosity. My fate now collates with theirs. It is up to
you to insure my swift return to Parliament Hill in support
of you, like the faithful right arm that I promised you I would
be. Your decision: my life or my death. I am counting on you,
and thank you.

Warm regards,
Paul Lavoie

The hostage watches one of the masked men slip the letter into an envelope.

"What's in that envelope for it to be so thick?"

"Your credit cards. And you had quite a few, eh, you pig?"

"But why?"

"Identification."

"Why send all of them?"

"We can't use them anyway, they're much too hot..."

"You could've kept them for the next communiqué."

"There's not going to be a next one," the man replies dryly, and walks out.

That night, they serve him Chef Boyardee spaghetti in the can with a slice of bread. Lavoie tells him to take the money in his wallet, something like sixty dollars, and go and buy something to eat.

"You're very kind. But we're not in the habit of holding back."

Are they getting ready to kill him? Do they already know how they're going to go about it?

Lavoie is lying on his back. He's got nothing to read, once again the Kleenex taped to his eyes.

At 9:55 p.m., just before the ultimatum expires, Vézina, also known as Little Albert, Premier of Quebec, reads his answer to the terrorists' demands over national radio and television stations.

The government, he says, *cannot, must, will not remain passive when the well being of the individual is so threatened to its core. Indeed, the values of our people, its exceptional spirit of work and sacrifice, its respect for the Other, its tolerance and sense of liberty, are the best guarantees of justice and peace.* Blah blah blah.

"Just get it over with," Lavoie murmurs under his blindfold.

A few more circumlocutions generously spread with good Canadian cheddar, then Little Albert, seemingly opening a door to concessions, claims that it is because his government so dearly wishes to protect the lives of Mr. Travers and Mr. Lavoie that he wishes to establish, as a preamble to official and direct negotiations with the FLQ, mechanisms that could guarantee that freeing the political prisoners would immediately lead to the safe liberation of both hostages. That this simple concession is a necessary one. "This is why we ask their captors to get in direct contact with us."

"Did he just say what I think he said?" Lavoie asks himself.

Something in the pit of his stomach says yes. He cries out in relief. In the living room, his captors, seemingly as relieved as he is, are slapping each other on the back.

One of them comes and stands next to the bed. Lavoie recognizes his voice. He's the taxi man.

"Saved by the bell, eh?" the man says. "Is Vézina serious? Does he really want to negotiate? You must know him well, you can tell us…"

"Albert is an honest guy. If he says he wants to negotiate, it's because he's going to negotiate."

"Really?"

"I guarantee it."

THE TAIL

AS HE STEPPED OUT OF the Longueuil subway station, Jean-Paul immediately recognized the two guys shadowing him. Two plain-clothes officers with the four-letter word that starts with *f* written on their faces. It was Tuesday, October 30, and it was ten in the morning.

The previous night he'd gone into the city, hidden communiqué number five in the pages of a phone book in a phone booth and went to sleep over at a friend's house.

He led his two new friends around the South Shore for part of the day, taking buses and taxis, before hiding out at the house of a few sovereignist sympathizers he knew. His two tails kept guard in a Volkswagen parked on the street corner.

"Do they actually think I'll lead them to Lavoie?" he thought, incredulous.

He shut himself in the bathroom and stood in front of the mirror with a metal coat hanger, a pair of pliers, and a brick wrapped in a wet towel. Then, after repeatedly smashing the brick into his face and forehead, he did his make-up. Opening the cabinet, he found a bottle of aspirin and swallowed half a dozen with a glass of water.

Then he cut the hanger in half and bent the two pieces, which he slid into his mouth. He examined his newly reconfigured jawline in the mirror. His face was like raw steak and his jaw gave him a crooked smile. Not the subtlest facelift, maybe, but much cheaper than going under the doctor's knife.

An umbrella makes a good cane for an old man. His metamorphosis is complete. Proof of the success of his disguise: his Montrealer girlfriend doesn't recognize him at first. Jean-Paul tells himself it'll do for the cops, as well.

After all that, his guardian angels seem to have flown away.

STRATEGY

"NOT TRAVERS."

"Why not?"

"Because Travers is nothing but a symbol. Goddamn it, it's not as if he's got blood on his hands!"

"So you should've chosen somebody else."

Justin Francoeur nervously twirled the end of his moustache. Having come to the brother cell that afternoon to hear the news, he'd been surprised to meet the elder Lafleur in the apartment that served as a communication point between both cells.

"Our position," Justin announced after a pause, "is that we're going to keep him as long as we have to. But killing him? No, no way."

"Your 'position,' as you call it, hasn't changed since the beginning: retreat until the final victory! Don't you think they've already figured out, when you were reading your communiqués that sounded like a syllabus for Sociology 101, that you aren't prepared to go as far as you need to?"

542

"And yours sound like some low-level Mafia scum's ransom demands."

"Which will be taken seriously, do you think?"

The swelling in Jean-Paul's face was beginning to go down — even though he'd quickly tossed aside the ice pack the hostess had given him — but he still had a truly sinister appearance.

"Now listen up to what we're going to do," he continued. "You can delay Travers's execution until hell freezes over if that's what you want. But at our end, if the authorities sign Lavoie's death warrant, we're not going to fight it . . ."

"What does that mean?"

"It means what it means."

"You're gonna piss away all the sympathy we gained with the Manifesto."

"If you absolutely want to be nice guys, that's your fucking business. But you've got to understand, we're up against the wall. We can't retreat without losing face," Jean-Paul concluded, fingering his destroyed cheekbone.

"I thought they'd negotiate. I was sure they'd negotiate!"

"If Brien can't revive the process, all that's left for us to do is make them pay the price."

"You remember our trip to Percé?"

"Sure."

"I never understood where the money came from."

"The money . . ."

"You know, the envelope Mario Brien passed you, at that place, the truck stop parking lot."

"It came from the holdup at the university."

"I thought it'd been seized at Saint-Colomban!"

"Old Brien took care of it. He got it back for us . . ."

"How'd he do that?"

"I don't know. Maybe we've got friends in the police department.

As sovereignist as you or me."

"Are you telling me the antiterrorist squad bankrolled the kidnappings?"

"Are you crazy? I don't know all the details, but you've got to know that Brien knows what he's doing. He's a smart man ..."

"And how'd it go with the Americans?"

Jean-Paul made a hand gesture that might have meant *comme ci, comme ça.*

"Those are contacts that take time to cultivate," he said in his raspiest voice. "And you didn't leave me much time, eh?"

"Operation Deliverance couldn't wait."

"Operation Deliverance my ass."

POLICE WARRANT

TWICE NOW THE BIG PURPLE Meteor had driven past the house. Inside it, a quartet of guys (trench coats, collars up, sunglasses, a couple of them wearing hats) took the opportunity to scan the front of the bungalow.

"Okay," René said, breathing out, as if he'd suddenly let out all his air. "They've found us..."

He walked away from the window, grabbed the two M1s that lay on the living-room table, made sure the magazines were inserted correctly, threw the second one to Gode, who managed to catch it despite his knees rattling against each other. Ben's hands, already clammy, held the wooden grip of the sawn-off shotgun.

A second car joined the merry-go-round. Black, full of men in leather coats. The two cars followed each other a good distance apart, slowly turning around the hideout on the two tiny lengths of perpendicular road that led them first to Nelson, then Collins — birds of prey.

Gode stood at the entrance, assault weapon pointed straight at the door.

"What do we do now?"

The night before, Jean-Paul had called to tell him he'd been tailed and had managed to get away from his pursuer, but that the most elementary caution required him to stay away from rue Collins for the time being.

René emerged from the closet, his M1 in one hand, the other holding an old mop with a solid wood handle, like some medieval knight. He hit the floor three times with it.

"I think I just had an idea ..."

Back against the wall, gun pointed in front of him, Gode waited for the assault to come. A few metres away, René, nose against the window, surveyed the street. He held a backpack full of newspapers with a couple of sticks of dynamite poking out. Except the dynamite was made from the mop's handle wrapped with construction paper and covered in butter to give them the right finish. An electrical wire poked out of the bag and led to a doorbell, which he held in his other hand.

"They're coming," he said.

The same unmarked cars came streaming toward the house, followed this time by a number of police cars. They all came to a stop in front of the house. Policemen jumped out and spread out up and down Collins.

"Go get Lavoie!"

Ben came back, pushing the miserable hostage in front of him, with the leash still around his hands. The labour minister was shaking uncontrollably. Then he felt the cold barrel against the back of his neck.

"Nothing personal," René said while strapping the backpack to the man's chest. He spoke like a man who was very calmly riding a wave to a nervous collapse. "Nothing personal, but if things don't go well, you'll be the first to go ..."

"No, please, stop it! Have some pity!"

They stood just away from the windows, in case snipers had already been deployed. Gode had his finger taut against the trigger. René kept his own finger on the doorbell masked as a detonator and brandished the M1 with his other hand. Ben stood behind Lavoie, ready to blow his brains out with his shotgun.

Short, nervous gasp came from Lavoie. He sounded like a scared puppy. His fear was physical, pathetic.

Hearts in their stomachs, legs wobbling, they waited. And nothing happened.

After a while, Gode went to the door and looked out.

"No, it can't be ..."

"What?"

He fell back against the wall and slid to his heels.

"It can't be ..."

He was completely, utterly cleaned out. He tried to speak, but his lips moved without sound. He stayed there, mouth hanging open, shaking his head.

René, keeping his finger on the doorbell, tiptoed toward the window to look out.

"They're at the neighbours," he said in a whisper. "Jesus fucking Christ in heaven. They're at the neighbours."

Half-turning, he nuzzled his gun against Lavoie's ear.

"Make a sound, and you're dead."

OPERATION TOUCHDOWN

THE SLOW, PULSATING DRONE OF an army helicopter's rotors shook Gode out of his sleepy trance shortly after noon. It was Thursday. He found Ben at the window, binoculars held up to his eyes, watching the low-altitude flyover of the large bi-rotor chopper that had just lifted off from the nearby airbase. A little later, Hercules airplanes landed on the strip and unloaded columns of armed soldiers, gear and all. René noted that many of them wore green gear covered in darker patches meant to look like greenery. Camo gear . . . He lowered his binoculars to his chest, completely stunned.

That night, they heard the Quebec government's final response to their demands. Vézina, in a communiqué, refused to consider freeing every single political prisoner, but agreed to look at at least five cases. As for the rest, the authorities simply repeated their offer of safe conduct: a plane would await the hostage-takers, ready to take off to a country of their choosing. They had six hours left to make a decision.

"That gives us to three in the morning," René calculated, disgusted.

Gode punched his fist through the gyproc wall in anger.

A bit later, while Ben was keeping an eye on the hostage, Gode and René took the secret passage and ended up sitting in the Chevrolet, René at the wheel and Gode in the passenger's seat. Between the car and the hole dug through the wall, among the distorted, disproportionate shadows heightened by the poor lighting, stood the oil tank, all four hundred gallons of it. In front of the Chevrolet there was a wall, nothing else.

They looked at each other a moment in total silence. Gode felt the road beckoning to him. The great plains of Kansas, with its oil derricks hammered into the ground, tall rusted birds. Very early morning in Oklahoma — a pheasant just standing there on the median strip of the highway.

He lit a cigarette, then gave one to René.

"What did your brother tell you? I mean, what did Jean-Paul really tell you, over the phone?"

"He said to start thinking about the measures we need to put in place to terminate the operation."

"Terminate the operation . . ."

"His words."

"Let's say we let him go. What's to stop us from disappearing, afterward? To just go and make a new life for ourselves in some lost corner of the Gaspésie? To wait to be forgotten?"

"We can't let him go."

"Why not? What do you mean we can't?"

"What, just open the door? Oh, sorry, our mistake . . . It's not possible."

"Okay, but we can't kill him . . ."

"Why not?"

"Because. Not like this. I don't even want to think about it . . ."

"Me neither."

"We can't do something like that. I mean, how would we even do it?"

"I don't know. I really have no idea."

They each lit another cigarette, and then another, and contemplated the wall through the windshield. Gode thought about people who killed themselves just sitting in their car, waiting for the fumes to do their work. It would be so easy, so simple to just open the garage door, back out, and leave.

René was trying to think. He nervously pressed the accelerator with his foot. Or it might have been the brake, he wasn't sure.

Gode tossed the still-lit butt of his cigarette through the window and watched it roll under the oil tank.

"I think I might have an idea."

PAUL LAVOIE'S CONFESSION

"YOUR LITTLE ALBERT, he got us good, eh? He pretends to be willing to negotiate, just to buy himself some time, and now look what's happening..."

Both Gode and René wore masks as they spoke to the hostage, Gode next to the bed and René looking outside with his binoculars. He saw the long column of covered military trucks streaming from the northeast before trundling down avenue Savane, only a few metres from the house. Helicopters continually flying over the neighbourhood. Lavoie was on the bed, eyes covered. Listening to the radio that morning, he'd heard the federal government's declaration of the War Measures Act at the same time his kidnappers had. Seizures and arrests without warrants had been taking place all morning.

"They've abandoned you. They're leaving you to your fate."

"I've got nothing to say to you."

"Maybe not, but I've got unfinished business with you. You've got to see things as they are, Mr. Lavoie. Your party has decided to sacrifice you. As for me, all that's important now is to find a way to get you out of here…"

Lavoie smiled sadly.

"That shouldn't be too hard. Just untie me and let me walk out."

"We can't do that. You're the Minister of Labour, you must know all about bargaining positions. Try to see things from our angle. The only victory we've had since the beginning of this whole story was the reading of our manifesto on the CBC. And even then, they weren't taking us seriously. No, what we need is a text that's really going to hit hard. Something to make this entire government crumble: *The Confessions of Paul Lavoie.*"

René brought the binoculars down. Lavoie said nothing. He was waiting for Gode to continue. The room was as silent as a crypt.

"Since they've decided you're as good as dead," said Gode, "as a bargaining chip, you're worth nothing to us now. But you can still make them pay for giving you up, because you know what's going on, you know their filth. Old-fashioned politics, the old boys' club, dirty elections, and big money. Vézina simply a puppet in the hands of Ottawa, itself a Muppet for big American interests. Brown envelopes, contracts, private clubs, Scarpino, all of it. You yourself, when you were a journalist at the *Devoir*, you saw what was happening, and maybe even blew the whistle on a scandal or two. But all that was before you found yourself on the other side of the fence. Then Vézina arrived. We traded a village accountant for a technocrat, but nothing else changed. The establishment put its man in place and walked away with everyone's money. Listen to me, Lavoie: you know enough to implode his goddamned government! And we're going to help you do it… They think that with their soldiers in the street they're going to turn the people's affection against the FLQ, but we're going to convince them otherwise, one by one, as they're sitting there in front of their TVs. We're going to give them red meat. Names, dates. Special Edition: the Travers-Lavoie Affair, the Bomb."

"They're going to say you forced a confession out of me. That you've invented it all."

"Let us take care of that end, okay?"

"If I do this, they'll never let me walk out of here alive."

René turned from the window and stepped toward the bed.

"Maybe. But if you don't do it, it's the Chevalier Cell that won't let you get out of here alive."

Gode was keeping an eye on the hostage, whose blindfold and handcuffs had now been taken off. He was writing, like Proust and Françoise Sagan before him, sitting at the head of the bed, a notepad on his knees.

Lavoie looked up from his writing and, for just a moment, thought he'd seen movement in the window of the bungalow that he could see from his room, the one on the next street. Without moving, he strained for a few seconds to hear any unfamiliar sounds, but nothing else happened. False alarm. He continued his work without his jailer noticing anything.

"What you're asking of me, in the end, is to renounce my life's work."

"Just say the truth. That'd be a great step forward already."

"A wife and two kids to feed. That's the truth."

"Don't make me weep. Write something in prose and in French — without too many mistakes, of course — that's all we're asking."

"It'd go faster if I could type it up . . ."

Gode looked at him, frowning.

"What I'm writing now is the draft," Lavoie explained. "I'm going to have to make a copy of it in any case. I was a journalist once, you know . . . I could type up a first draft that wouldn't be too bad at all."

"Okay by me. You want me to bring you a typewriter?"

"Not on my knees, like this, here . . . I'd need a table."

"There's a card table in the other room. But there's not much space here, unless I move the bed . . . I could set you up in the other room, maybe."

"If you want."

The old Underwood's heightened, almost joyous clacking could be heard from the communiqué room. In a frenetic parallel to the constantly increasing flow of news of fresh arrests and arbitrary detentions that'd been coming in that morning, the staccato of Lavoie's typing hammered through the house. The arrests made under the purview of the War Measures Act now numbered in the hundreds, and journalists, when they themselves were not in jail, worked to confirm names while rumours began swirling around a few familiar individuals: Godin, Pauline Julien, Chevalier Branlequeue. Lavoie was in the room through which he'd entered the house, the one with the secret passage in the wardrobe. The table was placed against the wall that separated the room from the garage. Under the window, two mattresses lay on the floor, covered in pillows and sleeping bags. Paul Lavoie hit the keys with rhythm and agility, a performance artist. He was enthusiastic, finding his voice, the old fever of the newsroom with a deadline approaching. As long as he kept typing he wasn't a hostage, but a man free to write.

And he was still the same man who, in the fifties, had used such ten-dollar words as "concussion" and "prevarication" when condemning the Duplessis government's scheming; the votes bought with refrigerators and asphalt, the iron and copper and natural gas barons, the salmon-spawning rivers under the control of the

Americans, a banana republic indeed. And what had changed, really? Only this: it was now his own government that Paul Lavoie was denouncing.

But more than anything, he was aware that he was fighting the empire of Colonel Lapierre.

He stopped.

"May I have more tea, please?"

"Certainly."

Gode shouted out to Ben, who made his way to the kitchen.

"What do you do when you're not kidnapping people?" Lavoie asked.

"What do you mean?"

"Do you have a hobby?"

"Snowshoeing in winter. In summer I fish, when I can . . . and a bit of hunting, for small game."

"Have you ever fished salmon?"

"Are you crazy? That's for big shots, like you."

"I've never been a fan of fishing, myself. I'm a golfer, really."

"What a stupid sport. Running after a tiny ball."

After having slipped his hood over his head, Desrosiers brought in a rose-patterned cup of steaming tea.

"I'm hungry," Lavoie said, accepting the cup.

"Too bad, there isn't much left to eat."

"Why don't you go to a grocer's?"

"Because it's not a good time to go out. They're arresting everyone."

"But we have to eat. Why not order something?"

Godefroid and Ben looked at each other.

"I'm hungrier than a rabid dog," Ben said.

"I'd go for some fried chicken," Lavoie added.

"Sure, a nice club sandwich wouldn't hurt . . ."

"There were three twenty-dollar bills in my wallet. Have you spent it all?"

"There's a twenty left," Ben announced, looking at his comrade. "Not as dangerous this way, eh?"

René had joined them. Gode suddenly felt the weight of his weariness. Of accumulated tension, of the too rare hours of restless sleep. The army had practically set up outside their door, and they were all at the end of their ropes.

"Me," René added, "I'd go for a nice chicken breast..."

He was already looking for a notepad to take down everyone's orders.

"A carton of cigarettes, too, don't forget the carton, okay?"

"The last meal," Gode thought to himself. He turned toward Lavoie.

"We're going to pick the order up at the end of the road, just in case you had any ideas."

Lavoie slapped the Underwood's carriage return back into position.

"I'm not done yet."

The small red car from Baby Barbecue's restaurant hadn't even turned its motor off before René ran out of the house and made his way to the street. He paid, leaving a tip for the delivery man, who watched him walk back in with a brown paper bag that contained the chicken boxes.

He came back into the house, bringing with him the warm odour of perfectly roasted chicken, and walked into the kitchen, Gode at his heels. Two entire chickens, three club sandwiches, a carton of Export "A": they'd pinched every penny out of that twenty-dollar bill. Something for everyone. Just as Gode, after taking the boxes out of the bag, was opening the containers to take an inventory of his goodies, Ben walked into the kitchen to take the hostage his meal. Gode threw him a look. He was about to say something, but it slipped his mind. For a moment. Just a moment.

"I don't hear the . . ."

There came the noise of broken glass, right there, in the room, inside the horror show.

BEN

"HE DID *WHAT?*"

Ben turned toward Jean-Paul.

"He jumped through the window. He couldn't jump out the lower half. Two sheets of glass and a screen. So he tried the upper half, holding a pillow in front of him. But he got stuck..."

"Ah, shit..."

"He cut himself. He was bleeding like a pig. Gode ran out of the house and picked up the pillow that had fallen on the other side, in the grass. I tore a sheet and started to wrap his wounds, he had one on his hand, another on the wrist of his other arm. He was bleeding all over the place. His bandages were soaked faster than we could tie them. He asked us to take him to a hospital. I grabbed a piece of rope and made him a tourniquet. And another on the other side. He told me to tighten it, he said it didn't hurt. He was white as a sheet.

"We brought him into the living room. He was bleeding a bit less. I think he must've lost half a pint at least. I washed his wounds with water and soap. Then I made him new bandages. He was still bleeding a little.

"I told Gode and René that we had to either free him or find someone to take him to a hospital. And they told me to come here and tell you what happened. That you would know what to do..."

"You can start by calming down."

"Where are you going?"

"To call my brother."

"Why don't you call from here?"

"Never know, line might be tapped..."

It had been four days now since Jean-Paul had decided to lay low in Lison's apartment, his friend from Montreal, in the South Central neighbourhood of the city, and maybe his nerves were playing tricks on him. But for a while now he'd been noticing unfamiliar movements in the area. So he'd redoubled his vigilance.

"Do you think you were followed here?"

"Do I think...no," Ben replied. "Where are you going?"

"To find a phone booth, I told you."

"You really think Lison's might be tapped?"

"You never know."

"What about the rue Collins telephone, then?"

Jean-Paul stopped in the doorway.

"Cut your bullshit, okay?"

The night was cold and clear in the alley. A cry rang out in the shadows next to him, making him jump. Like a child crying. A shiver.

Come here, he thought, *my little Moses of the alleyways, perhaps you're the one fate has chosen to lead the chosen people of Quebec out of bondage and through the American desert.* Jean-Paul tiptoed toward the sound.

Near an overturned garbage can, two alley cats faced each other. Jean-Paul, fascinated, watched the ritual of intimidation, the psychological confrontation. One of the cats was wearing a collar. Suddenly, it leaped up and tried to flee. The other cat jumped him from behind and the two beasts ended up rolling at Jean-Paul's feet, a whirling mass of flesh and fur torn by claws and whistling spittle. The coward ended up leaping out of the battle, stomach against the ground, and Lafleur watched him clamber up a telephone pole.

"You're done for, now..."

He shouldn't have backed off, he thought, and left to find a phone booth.

ECCE LYNX

GODE MOVES THROUGH THE northern savanna. Before him stretch sparse rows of black spruce, twelve feet high, all the way to the horizon. In this country, when you unleash a dog he becomes a wolf. And it's a lynx Gode sees before him now, walking toward him in the silence and whiteness of the snow, on its large padded paws. *He won't attack me*, he thinks, unable to move, as though paralyzed while the lynx comes so close he brushes up against him like a cat, then climbs a nearby tree and jumps on him, wraps himself around Gode's neck and shoulders like a heavy purring fur collar emitting a warm, suffocating, throbbing heat. "He's eating my brain," Gode has time to think, in his dream.

When he opens his eyes, Gode's head is buried under the sleeping bag and he's breathing with difficulty. He emerges from the bag and takes a deep breath of the cold October night air, flowing into his room through the broken window. And as the lynx's purring is transformed into the staccato growl of a helicopter overhead, it all comes back to him. He isn't in the northern grasslands, but in some bungalow on the South Shore, near a street named Savane, with a hostage who had inflicted serious injuries on himself while trying to escape. That's the truth of it. That's the here and now.

He finds René fighting off sleep on the living-room couch. In front of him, Paul Lavoie sits on a chair, white as a sheet, his eyes closed, his chin against his chest, seemingly unconscious. On his forearms and hands, makeshift bandages crusted with half-coagulated blood. He wears the wool sweater Ben put on him instead of his old shirt, which was drenched in blood.

"How's he doing?"

"As you can see."

"We can't leave him this way..."

"No. We're going to have to make a decision."

The previous night they'd heard Little Albert on television, justifying the imposition of martial law by the necessity of stopping the FLQ advancing to the fourth stage of its plan: selective assassinations.

Selective assassinations! Gode and René had shaken their heads in disbelief.

Then the premier had renewed his single and ultimate concession to the terrorists. Safe conduct to a country of their choice.

"We have to kill him," René said, after a tense silence.

Gode grabbed the shotgun leaning against the wall and held it out to him.

"You wanna blow his head off? Be my guest..."

"Don't get your panties in a twist, for Christ's sake." René rubbed his eyes. "We can't just shoot him here. The neighbours will hear..."

"We don't have neighbours anymore! Don't you remember? They got thrown in jail by the cops!"

"Next door. But what about behind the house...?"

"There's no one there. You haven't noticed?

"We have to end it," René said again, examining the hostage prostrated on the chair. "But not with a gun, it's too risky. We should have cobbled together some sort of silencer..."

"Do you have another idea?"

"Sure. We get him in the car while it's still dark, we go to the end of the road and then keep going, driving right through the field, up to the trees over there. Then we stop, we get him out of the car, we shoot him with the M1 in the heart and leave him there."

"And I've got another idea. We free him. We let him go...Or we leave him here and get the fuck out of here as quickly as possible."

Suddenly, Lavoie moved his head and let out a muted wail, without opening his eyes. Frozen stiff, they stayed there a long moment, without moving, watching his reactions.

"Do you think he heard us?"

"I don't know. Go rest a bit. I'll look after him."

René stopped in the room's doorway and said without turning: "He saw us without our masks on. He'll be able to identify us now."

"Just go and get some rest."

Saturday morning. The military base seems quiet, from a distance. Gode sits before the old Underwood on the card table. A sheet of blank paper in the platen. He's had an idea for a new communiqué, addressed directly to the people. They could attach it to the first pages of Lavoie's confession. But he looks at the keys and nothing comes out. Total block. And it's as if they'd won.

The hostage sits without moving, as still as a wax statue. Gode stands in front of the chair on which he is collapsed. Gode nervously wrings his hands, then lifts them up to his face to look at them. He needs gloves. He thinks back to his dream and turns away to sit back down in front of the typewriter. He tries to remember a poem he'd written in grade seven. The time the teacher (in jail now, from what he'd heard) had read his homework in front of the entire class. He could only remember the two words of the title, now, which he types with two fingers. ECCE LYNX

"How much do you want?"

Gode gives a violent start. Lavoie has opened his eyes, and looks at him.

"Tell me how much you want," the hostage insists.

"I don't know what you mean."

"I'll give you money if you let me go. It can be taken care of easily. I could get the sum together right away, if you let me make a phone call. You don't need to be afraid, I won't give you up. You have my word of honour."

"Your word? Whose honour? The Scarpinos'?"

Godefroid sneers. He doesn't know whether he should find this spectacle revolting or simply sad. A cruel smile comes to his lips. The hostage in front of him has become the enemy once again.

"We know where your money comes from! You should be ashamed. After a week here, you still haven't understood anything. As if we ... we acted for our personal gain!"

"One hundred thousand ... No, I'll give you a hundred and fifty thousand bucks."

"Stop it. Shut up."

"I could find two hundred and fifty. Maybe even five hundred thousand, but it would take a bit longer ..."

"You really are a desperate case. I pity you."

"Pity," Lavoie repeated like an echo, as if the word were a buoy. "Pity. Please, I beg of you, let me go, okay?"

And he begins to cry. Gode gets up, disgusted, his heart upended.

"I'm going to go and make you a nice cup of tea. A strong one . . .
It'll make you feel better."

Lavoie nods his head. He closes his eyes again, his head falls back
to his chest. He seems, once again, to fall into a profound apathy.

Gode leaves him there, crumpled in his chair, and walks to the
kitchen. While the cold water streams from the tap into the kettle
and the burner begins to redden, he hears sirens in the distance.

Talk about a fucking shit show. The kettle began to whistle, but
I could still hear the siren coming closer and closer, as if the two
sounds were becoming one, the whistling steam and the screaming
siren, somewhere along avenue Savane, coming closer and closer,
and I'd forgotten something and left the kettle on and heard the
door to the back room open and the sound of someone running into
the living room, and before I understood what was happening I ran
out of the kitchen in time to see Lavoie running toward the front
door, head down like a running back rushing through enemy lines,
and I jumped like a linebacker and tackled him as he stepped in
front of me, and he fell to the ground and began to yell, spread-
eagled on the floor, and I saw René come into my field of vision
on the right and fall over both Lavoie and me, trying to hold him
down, unable to move but I couldn't either and he was still yelling
and yelling as if he wanted to drown out the goddamned siren that
was now on our street, somewhere above me Ben took him by the
shirt and twisted his collar and I heard Lavoie croaking, fall almost
into silence, a gasp not a roar, René was tightening and tightening
and so was I, "shut up, shut up," René moaned and I held on for a
long time while Lavoie, his body, struggled under me, and there was
a jolt, like an earthquake, that lifted all three of us as if a wave had
screamed through his blood, I'm holding him in my arms and his
life is fleeing but not him, and there's no longer the voice, and then

under my chest it still moved, but like a fish, a last trickle of life that couldn't stop, and the body keeps on, you feel him going, his salt water, his movement, his air is gone, gone nowhere, always waiting, the nerves, the goddamned nerves, *shut up, you'll stop. Shut up I told you, I said did you hear me.*

ZOPILOTE

THE SUN WAS ALREADY WARM by the time he opened his eyes. In the distance he could see the waves mounting into their frilly skirts before crashing on the naked beach. A glass jam jar lay on its side next to him, empty, like a shipwreck dragged to shore by the night's current. He grabbed it, examined it, brought it up to his nose. Mescal.

Looking around, he saw no one. Marie-Québec must've got bored waiting alone at the Mono Azul.

Leaning on an elbow, Nihilo managed to drag himself up. He took off his clothes and lumbered into the sea. Back on shore, he shook the water off himself like a dog. He then began the trek back to the village, following the curve of the beach.

Richard Godefroid was sipping a cup of black coffee under a palm frond roof. Without thinking much about it, Sam had been walking in his direction. However, a few metres from the *palapa*, he hesitated for a moment, until Gode, with a simple hand gesture and without ever turning his head, invited him over. There was no small talk.

After a few moments, Gode said:

"I can't believe I actually told you all that..."

"Right, but there's still something I don't understand. Why did you leave your car in a field, right next to the military base?"

Godefroid lit himself a Montana. His hair hurt, his face was grey. He'd aged ten years. Sam also ordered a *café negro*, as well as a glass of orange juice and, after thinking about it, a bottle of water. Gode thought the orange juice was a good idea.

"Do you really want to know?"

"Of course!"

"We wanted them to find the car easily, as quickly as possible. We thought that maybe it wasn't too late..."

"What?"

"You'd seen a lot of dead bodies when you were twenty years old, eh? Well, neither had we. When we got off him, his nose was bleeding. We couldn't understand what had just happened. We didn't really feel like touching him, you know? He had this wool sweater up around his chin and it was only later we realized that, in the commotion, René had garroted him with the chain he had around his neck. Poor Lavoie. His medal of the baby Jesus didn't seem to have helped him much... When it happened we panicked, and we thought that maybe he'd just fallen into a coma. And that if someone found him quickly enough, there might still be time to save him."

Gode took a sip of water from Sam's bottle, then lit another cigarette.

"But the soldiers didn't move an inch. The car spent an eternity in the field next to the hangar. We'd even left the key in the ignition, but someone took it out at some point. They decided to wait for a journalist to find it, in time for the ten o'clock news... You see, that was the idea of the 22nd Royal Dieppe Cell. The message was supposed to be that the soldiers had left him to die."

"But he was already dead when you left him there!"

"Maybe. But we couldn't know that yet ... It was only when the autopsy report came out publicly that we understood what had actually happened."

Sam pressed his face in his hands. With the thumb and middle finger of his right hand, he poked his eyeball as if he wanted to reach the nerve behind it and follow it up to his brain. They killed him, but didn't even know he was dead.

They'd decided to claim responsibility for his execution as a political gesture. Later they'd understood that they had actually killed him, but it'd been an accident. They'd intended to kill him, then were unable to go through with it, and Lavoie had forced their hand. An accident so stupid that it assuredly could have no meaning in the grand scheme of things. And that's why they'd agreed to claim responsibility for the murder. An absurd story.

Gode decided that the only way to survive the day was to drink a beer, here, right now. He offered to buy one for Sam, who accepted. But only one. Afterward he'd leave the old FLQer alone and would go look for Marie-Québec.

"One last question: Lavoie's confession. What happened to it?"

"No idea. We left Queen-Mary in such a hurry. Later, the whole security box issue came out in the coroner's inquest, and so we never got a chance to get it back. I guess the detectives got their hands on it at some point."

Sam was ready to put this whole story behind him. He had, in a way, found a solution to the puzzle. There was no secret plot. The Octobeerist thesis would finally be put to rest along with the other strange conspiracy theories, buried in the more suspect parts of reality. He thought back, now, to the first meeting, at Lavigueur's on rue Ontario. To Chevalier Branlequeue's not-quite-but-almost-state funeral. And to his haunted, partly burned house on the shore of Lake Kaganoma. An emptiness as great as the Pacific Ocean threatened to engulf his hangover. He felt like an orphan.

They ordered a few sweet rolls with chicken to calm their empty stomachs. Sam watched the two bottles of Dos Equis land on the table. He examined one of the labels. XX.

Grabbing one of the rolls from the basket, he thought: *pollo*.

"*Pan*-pasta-potatoes-pastries," he said out loud.

"What's that?"

"The four Ps."

Gode shrugged. Sam was thinking: *pollo-Pedro-proceso-pesquisa*: pieces of chicken, Pierre, prosecution, police warrant.

He took a swig of lager and slowly brought the bottle down.

"We haven't talked about the second house yet."

"What second house?"

"The neighbours'. The one the cops raided that week. You remember Martinek, the big guy?"

"Do I remember him . . . Of course I remember him! Just the thought of falling into his hands was enough to make me want to piss myself."

"Machinegun Martinek. In his briefing on the morning they discovered your hideout, he told journalists that the house next door had also sheltered FLQ members. But that according to the neighbours it had been empty for a month. Curiously, we never heard anything more about that second house . . ."

"They probably just made a mistake."

"That's what I thought as well. But there's something strange about it. In his briefing, he'd given a detail that fit with the rest of the story: the fact that the owners had left the month before. Around the same time that the Lafleur brothers and you left for

Texas. That's quite a coincidence. The other thing that bothers me is that if the police raided 150 rue Collins during Lavoie's captivity, and they found some young kids, why did they pretend that it'd been abandoned for a month?"

"Must've been another house..."

"Impossible. Two lots down on the other side are empty fields. According to Martinek, the neighbours saw some sort of van parked in front of the next-door house the night Lavoie died, and someone loading materials in the back. Another funny coincidence, wouldn't you say?"

"And where exactly are you going with this?"

"I'm trying to say that there must've been another player on Collins during Paul Lavoie's abduction. Your friend François Langlais, a.k.a Pierre Chevalier..."

"Bullshit. Pierre didn't come to the house once that week."

"Let's say he didn't. He didn't go to 140 Collins. But he was at 150, right next door..."

"No! Pierre was in the other end of Montreal, with Lancelot and the others! We had no relationship whatsoever to whoever was renting next door. What you're saying makes no sense! We didn't even know who lived there! I really don't understand what sort of reason you'd have to falsify the truth like that. And, come to think of it, where did you even get that information? Why are you looking at me like that?"

The cops. The information came from the cops. And suddenly I began to understand. I saw the entire plan unravel before my eyes. It had been right there the whole time. When I'd picked up the phone to talk with Gilbert Massicotte, the retired CATS man, I already had the answer without even knowing it. His cousin, a chicken delivery man, who'd polished the character of the pro-FLQ rebel at the trial, was, of course, a cop and always had been. The small car from Baby's Barbecue had been intercepted somewhere between the rotisserie and rue Collins, and a man from the surveillance team had replaced the delivery boy. That was standard procedure when CATS installed surveillance posts around a suspicious location, that and tapping the phone. Because, of course, the phone had been tapped. That's what they'd done in Saint-Colomban in June. And Saint-Colomban had brought them straight to rue Collins. The early September meeting that had been so crucial had been under surveillance. The antiterrorist squad had the October kidnappers under surveillance all along. I looked at Gode.

"That's where they were," I said.

"Where? Who?"

"The cops. They were next door."

Despite the intense surprise painted on his features, I went on:

"And once they'd started, it would have been foolish not to install a surveillance team in the house behind yours, as well, from which they could look directly into the room in which Lavoie was being held. They probably used your little trip to Texas to do a few renovations to the bungalow. In October, the place must've been absolutely full of microphones. That explains the materials that were loaded into a van or pickup the day of Lavoie's death. CATS had its electronic arsenal to uninstall and lug out of there."

As I spoke, the scenario was taking on a life of its own, questions that had remained mysteries were being answered one after the other, the pieces of the puzzle were falling into place. Details I'd set aside as unimportant now showed the way and began to construct a larger story, finally, a coherent and logical whole.

Quite a story. But the cops' cover story had ultimately led to the secret being exposed, the small story made up to convince journalists and offer them a ready answer to their questions as to the suspicious behaviour neighbours had witnessed that week. The police fabrication had been placed like a seal over their story. And it was so prodigiously secret that as I spoke, my own words startled and shook me to my core, because to speak them, to give the story meaning, I was making it real, giving it body. Describing the truth.

Gode listened to me, saying nothing. He'd forgotten about his beer and his pack of Montanas on the table.

"The house next door was an observation post. Why raid it? To mess around with your nerves. Crank up the pressure. Somewhere up in the ranks the decision was made to sacrifice Lavoie. They aren't idiots. They knew what impact his death would have on public opinion, the anger and disgust of the 'public.' You'd publicly threatened to kill him; there was only one logical conclusion. And they, they simply contented themselves with looking over your shoulder. They pretty much contracted their dirty work to you. The hostage was going to crack, the kidnappers panic, or maybe both . . . It starts Tuesday with the clear and open tail on Jean-Paul. An open tail doesn't try to make itself circumspect, Gode, it's two cops on a street corner making no effort to stay hidden. Or ghost cars filled with zombies driving slowly in front of your door. Do you really think they'd let themselves be seen like that? It was a show, nothing else. And the siren that pushed Lavoie to try to flee the house was probably part of it . . ."

There was a long silence. Gode waited, as if to make sure I'd really finished. Then, slowly, he got up and, without a word, turned his back on me and walked down the beach. Old and grey and wrinkled, as if cracked by the unrelenting Mexican sun, he dragged himself, head hung low, like some large beast hit in the vital organs returning to the deep from which it came. He stopped, facing out over the sea. From where I sat on the terrace, I could follow the rhythm of his deep breathing by the movement of his shoulders.

He began walking into the water, in his shorts and T-shirt, feet bare. The waves ate up the horizon before crashing toward him with their concave, threatening maws. With water almost past his thighs, a wave hit him, throwing him head over heels.

Despite myself I jumped to my feet.

"Gode!"

He'd disappeared, buried under a roaring mountain of crumbled foam. After two or three seconds, I saw a foot pop out. He wouldn't be the first to be pulled out to sea, knocked out or simply made an exhausted prisoner of the current. Before I knew it, I was running full speed to the water. "Hold on! I'm coming!"

I dove in and began to paddle in the muddy foam while stones as large as baseballs were dragged out to sea by the undercurrent, strafing my legs. I reached Gode just as he was getting back to his feet. He saw me and threw a right hook, missing my face by at least ten centimetres. Thrown off balance at the precise moment a three-metre-high wave was rising to crash down on us, he jumped on me, grabbing me by the throat, and we rolled to the ground on the thin sheet of water that was being pulled back by the oncoming wave. I felt the pressure of his nails and thumb on the cartilage of my neck. Then, a green and white noise. We were picked up into the air, flipped and shaken up as if in an amusement park. And during the whole time we tumbled about in the sea, I held on to the only surfboard I could, this fifty-something, hungover man being thrown every which way, who wouldn't let go of my neck even as the waves tossed us around like sticks.

The ten or twelve seconds that followed made me feel like a sock in a washing machine. I woke up after the cycle was done with a broken arm, eyes and throat burned by salt, and at least a kilogram of salt and sand in my shorts. Between me and the sun, Marie-Québec shone down on me.

Farther down, Gode was on his hands and knees, puking up a mixture of salt water, refried beans, and mescal-flavoured bile.

✤ ✤ ✤

A gathering had formed on the beach. Locals, a few tourists, commenting on the nature of the human forms spat out by the savage sea. More gringos who hadn't been careful. A tourist from Saint-George-de-Beauce was explaining to his neighbour, an ageless freak from Limoilou, that the village took its name, Zopilote ("vulture" in Spanish), from the number of bodies that, year after year, were washed up on its beaches.

"We need to get him to a hospital," Marie-Québec was saying to whoever would listen. She then looked down at Sam, sitting very pale in the sand and holding up his left arm. "How do you say hospital? And arm?"

"*Brazo,*" Sam answered, weakly, from the depths of his concussion.

Marie-Québec was pointing to the unmoving arm against Sam's stomach, "*de su esposo, brazo, brazo.*" All the gawkers continued to talk with enthusiasm around her, but no one moved an inch.

"*Hospital,*" Nihilo said.

"*¿Donde esta el hospital?*"

"*Aqui no hay,*" a young and very brown Mexican kid with a large smile informed her.

"*¡Fuego!*" someone yelled behind them.

All eyes looked in the direction of the upraised arm. The village was burning.

The fire had started when a simple *brasero* had been overturned in a kitchen. By the time the flames reached the low-hanging extremities of the palm fronds that made do as a roof, it was already too late. The improvised firemen, throwing shovelful after shovelful of sand on the flames, suddenly saw them increase in intensity and begin to roar above the *palapas*. The wind finished the job.

"*No hay bomberos tampoco*," the young Mexican said, nodding his head, his smile all the larger.

Explosions began ringing out, likely caused by propane tanks.

The villagers began carrying their possessions to the beach: furniture, dishes, children's toys, family mementos, and piles of clothing and blankets, were all thrown on the sand, with their owners running back to their burning homes to try to save what could still be rescued.

Sam dragged himself to an icebox a bit farther off, opened it with his uninjured arm, and grabbed a bag of half-melted ice, which he applied to his broken forearm. He then made himself a cushion out of a rolled hammock and leaned back against it. At the top of the beach, the village was besieged by flames that jumped from one roof to another following the wind's whims, with great belches of heavy black smoke and storms of sparks.

In front of Sam, a human chain had formed. Every old container that could be found — from kitchen sink to chamber pot — circulated hand to hand, arm to arm. At the far end of the chain, he could see Marie-Québec, in the sea up to her stomach with her short dress riding high on her hips, busily filling the containers with water that the excited children brought her. Then, swaying in the undertow, she passed them to the outstretched hands that passed them to their neighbours. It was pathetic. It was magnificent.

Samuel watched her tear an overflowing bucket of water from the sea and toss it to the next man. Sam followed the bucket with his eyes, climbing up the line. A man reached for the handle, grabbed it with two hands, and passed the bucket to the next man with an ample swing of his torso. He turned to watch the next container when he saw him, eyes raised toward him, only fifteen steps away. For one whole second, they stared at each other.

Sam nodded, and Gode turned his eyes away.

MME CORPS AND THE FLOWERS

"CAN I ASK YOU a question, Samuel?"

"Sure, go ahead..."

"If Marcel Duquet's death wasn't an accident, who killed him?"

"That's what I was hoping to learn from you."

"But I thought it was Lavoie's death that interested you..."

"One murder brings about another. It's a link in a chain. While I was investigating the Lavoie Affair, I became interested in the kind of people whose job it is to fake a tractor accident and make it look real. When their work has been done well, you get a few paragraphs underneath the fold. They're anonymous artists, the unknowns of history... For them, killing is only the beginning."

"That has nothing to do with the truth. Your mind was made up long before you came here."

"Maybe. In fact, the only merit in my interpretation is that it's more probable than the official version. More real ... In the end, it's my fiction against theirs."

"I'd like to hear your explanation for Marcel's death, and the next *pastis* is on me."

"If we keep up like this, I'll be round as a button."

"Your mastery of French slang is remarkable."

"Thanks. My friend Fred gave me the *Dictionary of French Bistro Slang*. He wanted to come to Paris, too. Fred is convinced that intelligence agents (or spies, if you prefer) sometimes kill as a means of communication. The body is the message, you see?"

"I understand, but do I believe it? That's a whole other story. Life isn't a spy novel, Samuel."

"Maybe not, but you don't need a romantic imagination to face reality as it is ..."

"Tell me ..."

"The simplest reason for eliminating Marcel Duquet was because he had a big mouth and had begun to open it in front of journalists. He might have been in the know about what we pretty much have to call the American angle ... In my mind, it was Coco who was the principal contact between the Chevalier Cell and the Americans. It's hard to say what Marcel knew for sure. In any case, his strange tractor accident sent a very clear message to those in the big house, still doing their time. Texas was off-limits. Mum's the word. Coco furnished fake IDs for the FLQ, but who helped Coco? We now know that Montreal's CIA satellite office, located on avenue Mont-Royal in 1970, had a resident forger with his own studio. All that's missing is a line between Île aux Fesses and the Plateau. A line of coke, probably. Why are you smiling?"

"Because of l'Île au Fesses. Do you have a girlfriend?"

"Not any more. She left me a year ago."

"You can replace her."

"That's what I thought, too, at first."

"Why did she leave?"

"The month of October must have taken up too much space in my life."

"Go back to her, Samuel . . ."

"What?"

"I see something in your eyes, I hear it in your voice. You love her?"

"You'll have to excuse me. I think I'll have this drink in a train compartment . . ."

Samuel stands up. The beach looks like a marble floor: fine, smooth, white sand. And Mme. Corps couldn't be more French, with her cream-coloured pantsuit and her coquettish pink scarf. He offers her his hand.

"Thank you. You've been quite generous with your time."

She takes the offered hand, tightens her grip. Doesn't let go.

"Forget this foolish investigation and go find her, you hear me?"

"Madame . . ."

"That's all I've got to say."

"Okay. Thanks for everything."

"You'll have to come to the house next time . . ."

"Why not? It could be fun."

"When you're in Paris, you'll come, eh? We'll pick you up at the station, and my husband will prepare his famous rabbit in mustard sauce. You'll like him, Samuel. He's a cultivated man, full of kindness, and politics hold no secrets for him. I let myself be spoiled. I was married too young, but I had a second chance and have never looked back. I don't miss Quebec, I never think about it. My first marriage, with that dearest fattest husband and his gang of cops, *bidasses* and bad men, all that is far, far away now."

Sam looks at Ms. Corps, one foot still on the terrace.

"*Bidasses?*"

"It's slang for 'soldier.' Don't tell me you've never heard it before?"

"Sure I've heard it, but ... What's the link with Coco?"

"Oh, he was friends with a couple of soldiers. Everyone's pretty tight on the South Shore. There was a base in Saint-Hubert, you know, Mobile Command and all that ... I even went to Ottawa with Coco one time. He told me he was going to meet General Jean-B. Bédard to talk about a project they had together, that's all I remember. And tulips, of course, I remember tulips because while he was at his meeting, I took a walk along the Canal, and — okay, so maybe I'm inventing the tulips — but the year was 1968. I remember because of Dalida's *Le Temps des Fleurs*, you know, *Those were the days*, it was always playing on the radio ..."

And Mme. Corps, her cheeks red, closes her eyes and begins to sing.

Those were the days, my friend
We thought they'd never end
We'd sing and dance, forever and a day
We'd live the life we choose
We'd fight and never lose
For we were young and sure to have our way

"Samuel? Are you listening ... Samuel?"

DEER PARK

FRED IS DRIVING HIS SMALL car through the pretty countryside. The tender green of newly unfolded leaves, beech trees, a few oaks, a landscape grown over the alluvial plain by the first few folds of the Canadian Shield. A few kilometres before Sainte-Béatrix, he turns left and drives along Saint-Paul Lane. Horses, three, four of them, powerful legs, muscular haunches and large necks, are galloping in the pasture, a golden light behind them. Past the fields, he slows when he sees the large wooden sign, painted in bright red with a silhouette of a doe drawn on it, just before the turn on the access road whose curve hugs the side of the hill next to the forest.

DEER PARK

He sees a large house built lengthwise, invisible from the road until he passes under a gated arch in the wall and ends in an inner courtyard. A few buildings lie around like discarded children's toys: a garage, shed, cabin. Then a flotilla of vehicles: tractors, ATVs, minibuses, pickups. A bit farther off, a decent-sized pond where ducks play bumper cars at the feet of an old statuesque man scratching at a piece of bread. Benches carved in tree trunks, long chairs, and a windowed kiosk are disposed around the pond. On the benches, more white-haired folk.

Barely out of the car, Fred sees the director come out of the door and walk toward him. He recognizes him by his nose.

"Mr. Falardeau?" asks the director, offering his hand.

"Mr. Langlais?" Fred asks.

He takes the proffered hand and shakes it.

Dominating the enclosure, the observation post is both viewpoint and watchtower. It is accessed by a staircase of pressure-treated wood. Thirty metres up from it, in the middle of a clearing in the undergrowth, the feeding post consists of a pile of apples and carrots, a salt lick, and an automatic corn distributor. The pond's discharge stream sings as it slides between the stones that mark the edge of the clearing, ensuring a supply of water even in winter (the Deer Park director adds).

"Call it zootherapy if you want. I personally have no problem with that. What's for sure is that we've noticed a link between the aesthetic pleasure that our residents take from their observational activities, and the positive results in their cognitive tests. It also has positive effects on memory tests. A stimulating effect, performance-wise, that's for sure."

"Fascinating. And when I think that I wondered whether there'd be a link with Louis XV ..."

"With ..." The director's surprise is obvious. "Louis XV?"

"Yes. The Deer Park. It was the place, at Versailles, where Mme.

Pompadour would store the young women destined to fulfill the king's baser instincts."

"Really? I didn't know...it's a period I don't know so well."

"You should. A fascinating character, Louis XV. To govern, he preferred to trust his spies and secret diplomacy rather than the officers of his own government. The Chevalier d'Éom, you know, the famous transvestite prince of secrets, worked for him. You've heard of him, I'm sure."

The two men face each other in the summer house. Still not a deer in sight.

"Let's go to my office," the director offers.

They're in the office. We won't describe it here or we'll never see the end of this book. But it's a director's office in a long-term care facility for people suffering from Alzheimer's.

"Tell me a bit about your father," François Langlais asks.

"He's a historian ... David Falardeau. Does the name mean anything to you?"

"I'm afraid not."

"His most famous work is on the Battle of Eccles Hill (that's near Frelighsburg) in 1870. Irish Independentists who'd hidden out in the United States tried to invade Canada more than once. That time, they were met with solid resistance, in great part because the man who looked after their supply of ammo, a French doctor called Henri le Caron, was in fact an English spy called Beach. After the Fenians' defeat, he was captured and brought to Ottawa, where those who knew his actual role welcomed him as a hero."

"And ... your father."

"Had a real passion for the Second World War. And was a great admirer of the British Secret Service. Before working on Eccles Hill, he worked on another story having to do with the Fenians: the Victoria Jubilee Plot. Officially, it was an Irish nationalist scheme to attack the monarchy, but it was defeated at the last moment by the authorities. In reality, it was an entire ploy set up by the British secret service to penetrate terrorist groups and compromise the legal independence movement..."

Director Langlais puts his pen down, leans back into his ergonomic chair and, chin cupped in his hand, looks at Frederic attentively.

"Okay. Well you're not here because of your father's Alzheimer's..."

"No. I'm here to talk to you about Pierre."

The Deer Park director begins to lift himself out of his chair.

"I know no one of that name. You're wasting my time."

"Sure, ask me to leave. I knew you would..."

Fred takes a piece of paper from his jacket pocket, folded in eight. He unfolds it slowly and pushes it toward Langlais, who can't stop himself from looking down.

"The Rosetta stone," Fred says, answering the unspoken question.

The director picks up the photocopied page and, adjusting his glasses on his nose with his forefinger, brings it closer to his eyes.

KEY WITNESS DETAINED

SECRET FLQ MEETING HELD ON NIGHT OF NOVEMBER 3–4

He lifts his eyes up from the article for a second or two to stare at Fred. Then he lowers his eyes and reads through the text. His expression betrays nothing as his mouth sketches a dreamy pout halfway through the article.

The two cells of the FLQ that have claimed responsibility for the kidnappings of the British diplomat John Travers and the Minister of Labour Paul Lavoie linked up on the night of November 3rd and held a meeting that lasted until early the next morning, two trusted sources close to the *Sun*'s reporter have indicated.

The accuracy of the information previously given by these two sources, as well as their professional honesty, cannot be called into question.

"The man who led the meeting is still under our control," one of the sources indicated.

"He's already testified, and we didn't learn much, but we're convinced that he still has much to tell us. And he doesn't know that we know.

"We're keeping him isolated for now from a number of other individuals we're currently holding as witnesses.

"He's convinced that we don't have any other questions to ask him. And that's exactly what we want him to believe.

"But, when the time is right, we'll bring him back in front of a judge and he'll have to answer much more direct questions.

"He won't be expecting it. We'll surprise him when his guard is down, and he'll confirm everything we already know.

"Such a corroboration of the facts already in our possession will no doubt be quite a boon to the investigation.

"The only problem is, we still have to wait before bringing him back to testify. But we don't have a choice. Our reasons, when made public, will appear reasonable," one of our sources has claimed.

[...]

"We have no assurances that Mr. Travers is still alive. What we do know, however, is that there have been important disagreements between both cells.

"Of the two groups that have committed a kidnapping, one is radically opposed to the death penalty, applied to whomever: be it themselves, or their hostage," the source added.

He places the sheet of paper back down.

"That's very strange..."

"Mr. Langlais, do you go snowshoeing? Have you seen fox tracks in the snow?"

"I wouldn't recognize them."

"In my case, it was my friend Sam Nihilo who taught me. If the track zigzags, it means the fox is hunting. If it's going straight, you know it's heading back to its den. Sometimes you can follow the tracks all the way back home. When tracking humans, it's always a bit harder. And I know what I'm talking about, since I once spent three months following Goupil in France and England..."

"Are you sure your father doesn't have Alzheimer's?"

"Quite sure. Now, Mr. Langlais, you have good reason to listen to me. You want to know how far I followed the tracks in the snow..."

"I don't know what you're talking about."

"Doesn't matter, it's a fable. It's called *The Fox, the Deer, and the Penguin*. Oh, and there are wolves, also. In the end, the fox is left hanging from a fence, as an example."

Langlais remains silent.

"That *Sun* article you read," Fred says, pointing to the photocopy. "For the longest time, I couldn't understand it. The only thing it seemed to demonstrate was that the antiterrorist police, or the secret service, or both, had been there on the night of November 3 on chemin Queen-Mary. And that they had followed the man they'd seen leaving the apartment, so they knew about the base of operations in the northern part of Montreal, and also knew, a week before his being freed, where John Travers was being held. But the entire business of your role in the story remained rather obscure to my eyes. Why did the anonymous sources insist that the messenger (you!) was in the authorities' hands in November of 1970? I couldn't understand..."

Fred slides his fingers over the photocopy.

"There was an element missing. It was in the previous day's paper, a couple of paragraphs, an unsigned news item that told of a young FLQ kid exiled in London who'd hanged himself in his cell, in Reading, just before being questioned by the police."

Fred stops himself. Through the window behind Langlais, he sees a skunk walking across the parking lot with a grass snake in its mouth.

READING GAOL, GREAT BRITAIN, SUNDAY, NOVEMBER 22, 1970

The prisoner, plunged into a state of lethargy, was already breathing with difficulty when the man knelt over him on the bunk and placed both his gloved hands around his throat. He was serious, had stopped all his sinister jokes (on the high quality of the drug and the colour of the young man's shirt: pink). In one quick movement, he tightened his grip around the boy's throat, breaking his larynx. Then, holding on despite the violent shaking and jerking of the dying man on the bunk, he maintained the pressure until complete asphyxiation.

"Fucking queer," he said when it was all over.

Unsteadily, he moved away from the bunk, let himself fall to his knees in front of the toilet bowl, a bit farther off, and emptied his stomach.

His accomplice, who'd been standing away from the whole scene, came closer and picked up the shirt that had fallen to the floor. Bending over, he slipped one sleeve around the victim's neck, keeping his eyes away from the man's face, and tied a knot. Realizing he hadn't kept a long enough length of sleeve to double the knot, he undid it and began again. Knotting the sleeve with care, he doubled the knot and pulled it tight. The pink shirt looked to have been made out of something like silk. He saw the other man next to the bowl, wiping his mouth.

"Are you okay?"

The man nodded.

Turning back to his work, the other man picked up the body in his arms and, holding it under the armpits, lifted it toward the bars as if he were a bouncer dragging a drunk out of the bar who couldn't stand up on his own two feet. The young androgynous man he was holding between his arms smelled of sperm and shit. He held the body against the wall for a moment to catch his breath, arms straight, before raising it a few inches to allow his partner to thread the other arm of the shirt through a crack over the door. It took a few attempts to make it work. The man who'd tied the knots joked that he felt as if he were slow dancing with the faggot. Closing the door a little, the killer finally managed to wedge the extreme end of the sleeve into the crack while his accomplice, grunting, slowly let go of the hanging man. He dangled at the end of his pink rope. His feet barely grazed the ground.

As they closed the door, careful not to wedge the sleeve out of its perch, the entire body shook in a final death spasm. One of his arms dangled, making it seem as though the corpse were pointing to the toilet bowl in the corner.

"Jesus Christ…"

They looked at each other. They'd forgotten to flush.

"In Europe," Fred continued, "I traced the Goupil family and gained access to the coroner's report. In addition to the unclear circumstances of his arrest and the bizarre way in which his shirt sleeve had been wedged in the door, there was a troubling detail: Goupil was on medication in prison. He took two Phenergan tablets every four hours. Promethazine hydrochloride is a powerful sedative, used, in the past, as a birthing sedative for women. Phenergan acts on the respiratory system, leading, in some cases, to anoxic issues in newborns. What Goupil was taking every four hours was a hundred milligrams of the stuff, the recommended daily dose. In other words, he was completely drugged..."

"Of course they killed him!" Langlais suddenly shouted out, livid. "Scotland Yard's Special Branch...you think I don't know? They're the antiterrorist cops over there. They made it look like suicide, of course. Another day's work for those assholes. You've no idea what they're capable of..."

"I have no idea. But you do ..."

The two men looked at each other for a moment in silence. Fred continued: "During your time in England, you became a creature of the British secret service. There's a fine line between an agent and an informant. What I think is that you were what is now called an agent-informant. In fact, you might have been a French agent when you started working with the British. Or was it the RCMP, through your friends in Algiers? They don't call it the intelligence community for nothing: there's always an overlap of interests in that world, and there are no rules about having more than one master. To what extent you collaborate voluntarily, or are under constraints, or are manipulated, depends on your handler. In any case, the British. You were talking to them, but they didn't have you under absolute control yet..."

Langlais smiled. Fred continued: "A terrorist group preparing a violent action is, for secret services, a bit like a breakaway in a cycling race: the best way to avoid surprises is to place a man in the midst of it. In the Rebellion Cell, you might not have been the only one. Lancelot had his share of questions, and nobody would be surprised if we find out that Mansell was the CIA's man. In any case, there was at least one other agent that autumn in the Jesuit's apartment: the hostage. We now know that Travers was cozy with

MI5. At the time, we took it for granted that Soviet embassies were full of KGB agents, and we went around acting as if we believed democracies behaved differently. Now, suppose that after having foiled a couple of kidnapping plots, the boss of the Combatants in CATS, after having linked up with the RCMP's security service and military intelligence, had said: 'Next time, let's give them a bit of time to threaten the established order. Of course we'll arrest them, but all in good time. Better yet: let's help them. We'll give them the hostage..."

"Yes. A trap, and a good one, from the start. Travers's kidnapping went through without a hitch. Lavoie's kidnapping wasn't predicted at first, but his death was an unhoped for boon, one that multiplied the psychological effect a thousand times over. But it might have also slightly worried your contacts in London. A regular diplomat could have been sacrificed, but Travers was a *buddy* and you know what? *Buddies* are sacred. What if those crazies hurt him in the end? Trudeau might have had his political reasons to let the crisis degenerate, but they probably weren't appreciated by the British. Suddenly their confidence in you and your little friends wasn't as strong. But they had you under close enough watch to know that you read all the papers, and, hey, what a surprise, they were well connected through the media..."

Fred picks up the *Sun* article and waves it at the other man defiantly.

"When I came back from London, I was convinced that Luc Goupil had been brutally assassinated while incarcerated. It's almost by chance that I reread the article about the meeting on the fourth of November, and then everything became clear. It was as if I were reading with another part of my brain. Everything that had been muddled fell into place. I understood the emphasis the article put on the detention and the frankly strange allusions to the death penalty at the end. The article was a coded warning, which pointed toward a man hanged in his cell..."

Frederic stops, out of breath. He notices that his left leg is shaking from thigh to foot. He places his hand on his knee and squeezes it, then looks Langlais in the eye.

"The text was difficult to understand because it was written for a single man. Someone who knew what those people are, as you say, *capable of.* Because he knew all about the killers..."

The sheet of paper is now shaking in Fred's hand. He places it down on the table and slaps his hand on it. If this keeps up, he won't have enough hands to stop himself from shaking. He takes a deep breath and adds:

"If you read this article correctly, you'll find proof that at least one man among Travers's kidnappers was a secret agent, and thus that the entire kidnapping was a hoax. Perhaps one of the most elaborate traps in the history of police provocation..."

Langlais stares at Fred's hand on the photocopy.

"And you invented a father with Alzheimer's," the director of Deer Park finally says, "to tell me this story?"

"Yup," Fred replies.

"And now, what are you going to do about it?"

"My father?"

"No, the story..."

"Ah. Not much. I'm neither a historian nor a journalist. What I do is closer to hermeneutics than anything else: I interpret texts. From a documentary point of view, I'm not sure my story wouldn't crumble under pressure..."

"I understand."

"The best thing would be to write a novel. But, you know, I've got two kids, a girlfriend, a dog, a cat, and all the rest."

"Good luck," Langlais tells him, offering his hand.

They're standing on the balcony-terrace of the residence, flooded in afternoon light and birdsong. On a chaise longue, further off, an old man in a bathrobe is working on a crossword. Frederic shakes the offered hand.

"If everything I said were true, would you tell me?"

"No," the director answers, and smiles.

At the forest edge, at the bottom of the hilly field, where fresh new grass is growing, Frederic finally sees one.

A deer.

He brakes, turns his warning lights on, and backs up, stopping on the shoulder. He looks again, and the animal is there, observing him, against a background of greens and browns, ears alert, aware of every sound, the movement of the breeze. Just as Fred is about to open the door, the animal stomps the ground three times with his hoof as a warning then bounds off, undulating toward the woods. Fugitive elegance, white tail in the wind, deer in flight, regaining the woods, the shadows, the brush. The cover.

THE DEATH OF COCO

THE SMALL FARM IS FALLING apart, the fields around it lying fallow, asters and goldenrod growing up to the windowsills. Fat Coco will never be a farmer, any more than he'll be a global navigator. The writing is on the wall, and in the long line of pure Colombian that he straightens on the table with a Gillette razor blade. Dirty pizza boxes and empty beer bottles jam up the kitchen in the small house bought with a suitcase full of cash. On the table, between the large metal Drum tobacco tin and the bag of Humpty Dumpty chips, is a torn envelope and, next to it, a letter from Commissioner Lavergne, the special investigator assigned by the Parti Québécois government to shed light on the events of October, demanding that he testify. Coco's line of coke starts around eight centimetres from the bottom of the page and drags on toward the edge of the dirty green melamine table, a good ten centimetres long. Cardinal sniffs it all in one go, with a morbid concentration and a touch of the soft quivering of resigned pleasure. He's put on some weight, greying at the temples. His face has less character, a dirty T-shirt covers his belly. His heart pounds, his eyes float in old memories of things that once were but are no more.

If it weren't for the patchy beard, the double chin would not have looked out of place on a Vatican banker's face.

There's a tractor in the yard, an old Massey Ferguson that hasn't seen action for a long time. Next to the tractor, a car has been parked, a real boat. A Lincoln Continental Mark II in mint condition, a true collector's item, looking like it just drove off the assembly line, same as the one of his youth. Except it's black.

BERNARD SAINT-LAURENT

THE MOST FAMOUS GARBAGE COLLECTOR in print media, L.G. Laflèche, was looking at a young man who had introduced himself as Bernard Saint-Laurent. He was intrigued. Officially an activist in the PQ, Saint-Laurent had, before his own eyes, picked up the phone and conversed with Colonel Bob Lapierre, a key player in the Liberal Party. There'd been a question of an assignment, and the Colonel had promised to call him back.

Looking satisfied, Saint-Laurent, who'd been the one to ask for a meeting with Laflèche, had hung up with a smile. The newsroom was buzzing around them. So Saint-Laurent was one of the Colonel's agents? Laflèche was wary, sensing a trap.

The journalist ran a hand through his hair.

"I don't get it, what are you playing at?"

140 RUE COLLINS

THE RCMP GUYS TOOK CARE of the logistics. They were the experts. The others, like Bobby, were there to keep an eye out for trouble and avoid unpleasant surprises. They had placed men on each side of the street, as well as on the neighbouring street, Savane, where it intersected with Collins, and even farther down on both sides of the road. They'd joked about dressing up an agent as a cow and placing him in the field. But the small street was quiet, or as Bobby said: "Dead as a doornail." When he quit yammering for no reason on his walkie-talkie and looked up, he saw, on the other side of the street, through the living-room window, the uninhabited house. In early September, it had been used as a surveillance post by the Combatants, so they could keep an eye out for the scumbags' meetings. And now they were in the house next door, the same sort of people. If the infection kept spreading, it would take over the entire neighbourhood.

He looked up, trying to understand what the man across the street was doing, standing on the kitchen table, head toward the ceiling. Maybe he could learn something instead of standing there doing nothing. He saw the man drill a hole in the ceiling, stick his hand in the opening, and place a microphone. Then, he got off the stepladder, moved it a little, and made another hole, passed the wire though the ceiling into another hole in the hall, and continued on this way to the bathroom. Once there, the RCMP man drilled a hole in the skylight and passed the wire right through it to connect to, Bobby guessed, the transmitter. Then he would probably pass the antenna through the skylight, to ensure a good signal to the house next door, but Bobby couldn't be sure since his line of sight, limited by the bathroom door, only gave him a view of the stepladder, with two feet sticking out. Another man was covering the wires with masking tape before plastering over every hole, leaving no trace of them being there. Bobby had been looking at this work for a while now, thinking the man did his job well. *Anything that needs to be done,* he thought, *needs to be done well.* It was like having his father's voice in his head.

TEXAS

AFTER DROPPING JEAN-PAUL off at the edge of town, near the motel where he was to meet with his contact, and then driving Ms. Lafleur and their youngest daughter to the mall, Gode and René drove to Dealey Plaza, where, it was said, time had stopped on a certain day in November 1963. They parked the car a bit farther off and sat on the grass of the most famous knoll in the universe to smoke a cigarette. Elm Street faced them. The Texas School Book Depository was a bit higher up, the pergola at their back, the fence to their right, the viaduct and train tracks below them.

"He was farther away than I thought," René said, looking up at the sixth floor of the book depository.

"He could have shot him straight on, when the limousine was coming down Houston Street and practically stopped as it turned... Why wait until it drove past him?"

"He was a sharpshooter."

"He was not, not for a goddamn second."

"Maybe there were other shooters. But we'll never know."

"No, but the proof of the conspiracy isn't here, it's at Dealey Plaza. The proof of the conspiracy is Jack Ruby. He's the guy who tries to make the pigeon disappear. The proof is the cover-up, you see?'

"Sounds like you've thought about this before ..."

"Maybe I have. Is there really a single person on the planet who believes that Ruby shot Oswald for the First Lady's pretty eyes?"

"I don't know, but it gets me thinking: remember what Jean-Paul told us about Jackie?"

"No, what?"

"He said that this one summer, Francoeur tried to convince him to kidnap Jackie Kennedy as she was fishing on the Cascapédia, in the Gaspésie."

"Really?"

FREELANCING?

WHEN MILES MARTINEK, reduced by age, knees blown and needing to hold himself up with crutches, showed him his collection of firearms, a couple of pieces in particular impressed Nihilo: the .30-30 Centenary Winchester, with a lever action mechanism and silver incrustations; and the .410 handgun with sawn-off barrels. And, most of all, the walking stick–carbine, that wouldn't have looked out of place in a James Bond flick.

"What calibre?" Samuel asked him.

"Oh, that ... A special calibre. Don't look for another like it, you won't find it. Comes from the States. Back when I used to freelance for the CIA ..."

"When you used to what?"

MAÎTRE MARIO BRIEN
(1942–2008)

SAM EXPECTED TO MEET a bunch of greying FLQers at the lawyer's funeral, but he certainly didn't think he'd end up, once the
ceremonies had ended, nursing a beer with Gilbert Massicotte,
the former member of the antiterrorist squad. What was he doing
there?

"You know, you meet in court. Shoot the shit a bit."

"Are you telling me that Brien was a CATS source?"

Massicotte's smile brought out the wrinkles on his face, which
had been carved all the deeper during his recent battle with cancer.

"Shoot the shit, that's all I said ..."

"Sure. But when you think about it, Brien, may the Devil keep
his soul, clearly knew the shifty role your cousin Rénald played, the
supposed chicken delivery man. In reality, he hid an infiltration
mission. Wasn't for nothing that you told me to call him ..."

"Rénald was an actual chicken delivery man who got caught up in the story by chance."

"Sure. Of course he was."

"I'm telling you."

"Have you ever," Samuel asked, "heard of unemployed people setting forest fires up north?"

"Yes, no, maybe. Why?"

"Because I've been trying for the longest time to understand how the money that was seized at Saint-Colomban, you know, from the holdup at the university, how that money ended up in the pockets of kidnappers in the summer of 1970. As if the cops had placed it back in circulation..."

"And why would we have done that?"

"Because you need criminals. Without them you're nothing. You'd never have the opportunity to show your worth. And when you know about them already, it makes it easier to know exactly who you're supposed to arrest. So, from your point of view, known criminals should be encouraged, no?"

"Well, goddamn, aren't you a clever little monkey..."

ON THE GROUND

ROLAND LANDRY, THIRTY-NINE YEARS OLD, and young Lessard, both active agents of the Royal Canadian Mounted Police, backed up a step as the trunk popped open. The moment before, Landry had taken the key out of the Chevrolet's ignition, and he'd just used it to open the trunk.

They examined its contents in silence.

"Poor guy," Roland murmured.

"Is he ..."

"Without a doubt. Is he your first?"

"Yes ..."

They both heard the sound of the military jeep coming from the base behind them, and turned to meet it.

"What are we going to do with this?" Lessard asked, meaning the trunk.

"Let's not close it just yet, these guys are going to want to see what's inside ..."

Landry slipped the Chevrolet's key in his pocket and reached in for his badge. He was going to show it to the two soldiers before shaking their hands.

A BEAUTIFUL DAY

A BREEZE BLEW THROUGH the mosquito net. Samuel looked up from the Fabio Martinez novel he was reading on the bunk bed, far from the reach of the *cucarachas*, army ants, and scorpions. At the window stood the ghost, like an emanation from the iridescent saline spatter that rose from the unending ocean. Lavoie was wearing a small sky-blue cotton hat and an open Hawaiian shirt. Around his neck, a flower collar had replaced the ichorous furrow the religious chain had left in his flesh. He carried a golf bag over one shoulder.

Sam pushed the mosquito net out of the way.

"Would you please tell me ..."

"I thought I'd stop by to say hello."

"And where are you going, exactly?"

"I heard there's a twenty-seven-hole course that isn't too bad at Barra de Navidad, near Manzanillo in the Colima. I'll start there. After that ... I might try Brazil. I hear that even Amazonia has a few courses now. I met some golfers who'd been bitten by venomous snakes while looking for their ball on the woods. Jaguars are another hazard…"

"You're pulling my leg…"

"How have you been?" Lavoie asked, after a pause, pointing to Sam's arm in a sling.

"Except for the fact that I've got to hold the book and turn the pages with the same hand, not too bad. You? How are your hands?"

"Good as new, more or less," the ghost replied, showing his scars. "I just need to find my putting form."

Steps sounded on the wooden ladder that led to the room, and the ghost was startled.

"Well, then. I'll let you get back to it…You know what we should do? Toss the old pigskin around one of these days. When your arm is better, I mean."

"Around here, people go more for frisbee … But sure, that'd be fun…"

"In any case…thanks," Lavoie said.

Sam opened his mouth, but the cat seemed to have got his tongue.

"No, no…It's me who…"

As the door opened, Lavoie lifted a friendly hand, thumb up, before flying out right over the coconut trees with a light clacking of woods and irons. The golf bag seemed to be as light as a feather.

Marie-Québec, in her short cotton dress of whatever colour, came in with a coffee, black, very sweet, in a small white cup. In her other hand, papaya pieces set on a plate.

"Marie…Am I dreaming?"

"Why are you asking me?"

"You're up and out of bed before me. And you don't even look as if you're in a coma!"

"Must be Mexico. What are you reading?"

"A Colombian . . . Marie?"

"What?"

"Do Dora for me, please."

"Stop it!"

"Dora Dora Dora."

"Okay, okay, fine."

Dora

Perhaps. It's sublime love, solitary and pure, he's the one who burns me clean. Sometimes, for a moment, I ask myself if love is something altogether different, if it can cease to be a monologue, and if there isn't an answer, sometimes. I imagine this, you see: the sun shines, heads bend softly, the heart loses its pride, arms open . . .

Climbing down the path toward the sea, she met a young Mexican, dark brown face, very white teeth, holding an orange. His face turned toward her as if she were an apparition.

"*Hola,*" she says.

He offers her the orange without a word, as if this gesture were the only thing that came to his mind, the only possible thing to do. She took the fruit, thanked him with a nod, and continued on her way.

"This is where I want to live," she told herself. The orange smiled in her hand.

She had just removed her sandals and was beginning to walk toward the sea when, from the corner of her eye, she saw the old Indian woman on the edge of the beach, bent under her daily burden, her lower back crushed under the weight of the enormous pile of wood tied to her forehead.

Marie-Québec walked toward her; she'd been preparing her sentence for a long time.

"*Con permiso, señora ... Déjame ayudarla.*"

The woman turned to her, and god only knows what she saw. Marie-Québec dropped the bag filled with her belongings to the sand at her feet. To lessen the friction of the rope, the old woman tied her own sweat-stained scarf around the young woman's forehead. She then helped her slip under the weight, balancing it on her back. And as Marie-Québec began to rumble forward, the old woman bent down behind her and, one hand on her ruined back, held up the multicoloured cotton bag.

And the weight, on her back, the weight of the wood, the weight, felt good. As Marie-Québec bent forward, sand to her ankles, and walked, it was as if the weight had always been there. Like the heat of the sun, and the cool breeze on her face, coming from the sea to rise against the cliff face and keep rising, keep rising up toward the heavens, where the magnificent frigate birds circled slowly on the thermals, effortlessly, on invisible highways of warm air, where vultures also flew, the carrions eaters, light as air. A beautiful day.

EPILOGUE
ÎLE AUX FESSES,
JUNE 24, 1974

BONNARD AND BRANLEQUEUE, now good friends, got there in the crooner's big Riviera in time to witness the christening. Coco, who'd never been a resentful man, came to greet them near the entrance to the launch site. He was hyperexcited, already high as a kite. He shook Chevalier's hand.

"So? Still writing?"

"Always. And you, from what I hear, you've been deep in Mao's *Little Red Book*, eh? The Great Helmsman?"

"Ah, shut up," Coco answered, smiling.

The *Patriot*'s nose was already in the water. Chevalier was impressed despite himself: it's not every day that you see a schooner sail on its maiden voyage.

And since the ceremony was held among good Quebec pals, a bottle of beer blessed the ship's hull instead of champagne. Coco, in water all the way to his bulging stomach, did the honours. Then he gesticulated wildly to the driver, who slowly began backing up toward the water while the two-master slowly slid into the sea. Applause.

The *Patriot* was afloat. Almost immediately, it began to heel, and...

Coco, in the muddy water up to his neck, was floundering near his schooner, which, masts and all, was itself foundering.

"Noooooo! No!"

AUTHOR'S NOTE

OCTOBER 1970 IS A WORK of fiction. A reconstruction in which imagination took the place of historical investigation. The unofficial history was the novelist's mortar when faced with the patchy official version, which barely stands up to the slightest prodding.

One of the liberties offered by fiction was to drag Wikipedia's invention a few years back in the past. It was easier, and had fewer consequences, than changing the date of the great Zapatista march in the spring of 2001.

It's important to me to honour a few works without which my own would have been impossible. For military inspiration, General Jean-V. Allard's *Memoirs*, as well as Dan Loomis's *Not Much Glory: Quelling the FLQ*, among others, were of great help. As for the October Crisis itself, I'll simply mention a few indispensable books: *F.L.Q.: The Anatomy of an Underground Movement*, was both exceptionally useful and insufficient; and Francis Simard's *Talking It Out: The October Crisis from the Inside*, was also notable for its deafening silences. *The Execution of Pierre Laporte*, the classic by Pierre Vallières, is worth it for the questions it asks, as well as the exceptional photographs at the end. *FLQ 70: offensive d'automne*, a work in French by Jean-Claude Trait, contains all the unedited communiqués by the kidnappers. *A Special Kind of Friendship*, drawn from the epistolary relationship between Jacques Ferron and John Grube, contains, as an appendix, George Langlois's *Octobre en Question*, and was a necessary read. Finally, *Kidnappé par la police* by Dr. Serge Mongeau remains the best available documentary of the arbitrary arrests of October 1970.

However, the most consistent documentation came from the archives: court records, newspaper articles, and so on. In particular, the important media review put together and annotated by John Grube, of Toronto, was given to me by the cinematographer Jean-Daniel Lafond at a time when he was supposedly investigating the "official truth," political plots, and other darker corners of the story.

I'd like to thank the following people for the help they've given me over the years: Francine Bégin, at the Montreal courthouse, Pierre Bastien in the air, Claude-Jean Devirieux, Benoit Perron, Éric Barette (unyielding hunter of Colonels), Carl Leblanc, Paul Hamelin for the land register, Michael Macloughlin, Jean-François Nadeau, Philippe Marquis, Solène Bernier, Denis Cloutier for his Octobrist library, Lorraine Déry, Laurent Hamelin in the field, Bruno Cloutier in Percé, Gilles Prince and the team at Sporobole for their technical support, Luc Gauvreau, Pierre Cantin. As well as Claude and Carmen, and Hélène Girard.

The Quebec Arts Council offered invaluable help more than once throughout the life of this project, which took a few years to flourish. From the bottom of my heart, thank you.

As for the witnesses and actors of the October events, those who agreed to speak with me, please accept my wholehearted gratitude.

L. H.

ABOUT THE AUTHOR

LOUIS HAMELIN is a novelist and academic. His novel *La Rage* won the Governor General's Literary Award for French Fiction in 1989. He is a literary critic for *Le Devoir* and *Ici Montréal*. He lives in Sherbrooke, Quebec.

ABOUT THE TRANSLATOR

WAYNE GRADY is a Governor General's Literary Award–winning translator, and an editor and author. He has published works of nonfiction, short fiction, and a novel, *Emancipation Day*. He lives near Kingston, Ontario, with his wife, novelist Merilyn Simonds.

TELL THE WORLD
THIS BOOK WAS

Good	Bad	So-so
✓		